"You know what these are, don't you?"

He pointed to the two large spheres, each with one side hollowed to form a squarish open booth.

"The Habgates?"

He nodded and pointed to the one with the big "M" scrawled on it. "Habegger's Mouth. Set your bag at the rear corner and step back out."

She did as instructed while he fiddled at the control console. Suddenly a burst of flaring, iridescent color hid the booth's interior. When it cleared, her bag was gone.

"It's working. Come here." He hugged her hard and she hugged him right back as they kissed good-bye. "Now look. I *hope* the timing's right, but it could be off a little. So don't get scared. Just lie still, breathe slowly and wait."

"Yes, daddy. I'll wait for you." She settled in, lying on one side with her back to the rear wall. His hand waved and he started to say something.

Then the colors bloomed and the wall slammed her.

Other AvoNova Books by
F. M. Busby

ISLANDS OF TOMORROW

ARROW FROM EARTH

F.M. BUSBY

AVON BOOKS • NEW YORK

ARROW FROM EARTH is an original publication of Avon Books. This work has never before appeared in book form. This work is a novel. Any similarity to actual persons or events is purely coincidental.

AVON BOOKS
A division of
The Hearst Corporation
1350 Avenue of the Americas
New York, New York 10019

First AvoNova Printing: March 1995

AVONOVA TRADEMARK REG. U.S. PAT. OFF. AND IN OTHER COUNTRIES, MARCA REGISTRADA, HECHO EN U.S.A.

Printed in the U.S.A.

RA   10   9   8   7   6   5   4   3   2   1

To Elinor, who said I could

I

"A *rrow*! Stretching time by a factor of twenty-five, this ship will keep its crew young while it voyages to the farthest stars! Soon now, that crew will enter a Habegger Gate and exist in Limbo for two years before emerging on the ship, traveling at the speed of light. It's hard to imagine—"

Leaving the commentator on the seatback screen to mouth his half-truths to lip-readers, Marnie Allaird silenced her audio; again the muted shuddering rush of the bullet train, half whistle and half roar, vied for her attention. She thought: why couldn't those people do their homework? Seventy-two light-years wasn't exactly the farthest stars. And even a child should know the speed of light was a limit, not something you could actually reach; at the age of almost twelve, Marnie resented being talked down to. But with the screen silenced, she didn't have its babble to keep her mind off her own mess.

She'd tried to like Carl Knapheidt, she really had. Even though it was probably his idea, when he and mama first began dating, that Marnie should always call her Celeste. "It does sound younger, you know," mama had said, brushing her newly brightened blond hair. "So if you would, please, dear . . ."

"All right . . . Celeste." It didn't sound right to Marnie, then or ever. But after a while it was the only way she could think of her mother.

As to Carl, there was more. It wasn't just that he took up so much of Celeste's time; her men always did, even the ones who hung around years ago when daddy was off training or working on some project and Marnie had no idea *why* they

1

did. That was before daddy was assigned to ride *Jovian*, the first Traction Drive spaceship, on its second and more exhaustive mission to its namesake's family of moons. Browsing the asteroid belt en route.

He was gone more than a year, daddy was, and when he came back he really didn't; something terrible happened out there, something no one would explain to Marnie, and Celeste got the divorce. She was so worked up about it that she barely remembered to buy a cake for Marnie's sixth birthday. There wasn't any party, but Celeste wouldn't have let daddy come, anyway.

After that, Marnie knew why the men came around; nobody bothered to pretend they and Celeste slept in different rooms.

Marnie never said anything to daddy about any of this, on the rare brief visits Celeste grudgingly allowed them. She thought about it, but then decided he probably knew already.

Besides, she didn't want to bother him. It wasn't as if he could do anything about anything.

Particularly she'd kept her own counsel during their latest get-together—because it was the very last time they'd ever see each other, and she didn't want to spoil it.

By then, everything was worse. After Celeste and Carl had been dating for about six months and were doping up together nearly every weekend, Celeste quit her job with Newsnet and gave up the apartment and moved herself and Marnie into Carl's big gloomy old house with the creaky floors and loose doorknobs. The place was a mansion, right enough, but for all Carl's money he was too cheap to get anything fixed.

Or else he liked it the way it was, for sentimental reasons.

The move came two weeks before school was out, but Celeste paid cab fare every day so Marnie could finish eighth grade and graduate with her own class, her own friends.

That was about the last break Marnie got. Carl had what daddy called Old Money, and he lived in an Old Money suburb. What kids Marnie had met, one way or another, who were anywhere near her own age—or school class, which wasn't necessarily the same thing—seemed to be snooty types. Adjusting to high school in a strange area, with no friends at all for support, wasn't Marnie's idea of a great future. And even under the Accelerated Study Program it would be three more years before she could use the scholarship from daddy's Spaceman's Benefits to go to Gayle Tech. That was the only way she could see, to get away from home, and it couldn't happen too soon to suit her.

Because the present was no box of chocolates, either. It wasn't long until Celeste's occasional bouts with fun dope got a lot more frequent; Carl's supplies never ran out. Before, usually she'd done nothing worse than sniff a little scat; now, though, she and Carl were popping stuff Marnie didn't even know the names of.

And Carl got bossier—if Marnie didn't do what he said, fast enough to suit him, he'd snap a finger against her cheek or forehead, rap her knuckles with a spoon, stuff like that. And after once or twice, Celeste never said anything; she just let him. Maybe she thought it was all right because right away Carl would come on with a pat or a hug to "make up" with. But if she thought *that* was any kind of reassurance . . .

Marnie didn't say much either; in private she'd asked Celeste for help, and been told, "Carl's going to be your new daddy; you have to mind him and learn to get along with him."

So Celeste was about as much use as fins on a horse. That was one of daddy's sayings, and it sure did fit here. But Marnie couldn't feed it back to him, the last time they met, because pretty soon he'd be gone, so what could he do anyway?

Daddy's feelings were wired for high voltage; at the Greek restaurant where they had dinner, when he wasn't sad he was bubbly and when he wasn't bubbly he was sad. A little sunburned on his lean face, under reddish brown hair shortened to not much more than stubble, suddenly he grinned. "I still can't believe it, Marnie. Clancy Allaird, exec on *Arrow*. And not just for a year's hitch, like on *Starfinder* or *Roamer*. This ship rides time twenty-five to one; the launch crew goes all the way."

She tried not to let her face tell on her, but it must've; he went sober too. "I know, honey, and I wish things could be different. If we were all still together—or even if you and I had the chance to see each other more than a couple of times a year when Celeste decides to feel generous . . ."

Yes, come to that, with any kind of family prospects he

probably *would* have given up his own ambitions. But not the way things were. Marnie said, "I know, daddy; this is it. So—" She brightened. "Tell me what you do next."

It sounded strange. Tonight, take the early train to NASA's starship crewing center, way down south at Glen Springs. First, a few days' briefing. Then, with the rest of *Arrow*'s personnel, enter the Habegger Gate that in two years' time would spit them out inside *Arrow*. At that point the ship would be only ninety days out (". . . a bit over seventy, ship's time") but, after driving uncrewed at five gees, already up to speed: ". . . point-nine-nine-nine-two c, honey, and running time dilation at twenty-five." Which it would do for two–three years, whatever, until time to slow down at the far end.

"But that's more like seventy years here, isn't it, daddy?"

He nodded. After that she couldn't find much to say. They finished dinner, and then he saw her off at the bus station.

When she arrived at the big living room of Carl's house, Celeste and Carl had been smoking something they called spud; it smelled, she thought, like frying cat crap might smell, but at least it put them quiet rather than hectoring.

It was too hot for a fire but they had one going anyway; before the hearth Celeste lay sweating, her robe open. Except for pasty skin and the dark patches under her eyes she didn't look very old; in front she sagged a little but not much, and lying down like this the growing potbelly hardly showed. Her unbleached crotch made a liar out of her blond hairdo; maybe she didn't care about that any more. Or else Carl didn't. Either way, Marnie wished her mother wouldn't sprawl around looking such a slut; it made Marnie ashamed for her.

Coming in from the kitchen hallway with the incongruously catlike walk he had when he was squinked on something, big Carl Knapheidt wore a deceptively serene look. Marnie knew how easily and for no apparent reason that mood could shatter into violent fragments; carefully she said, "I got home okay, and I'm tired. Good-night; see you in the morning."

She tried to leave fast without seeming to hurry, and was around the corner and almost to the stairs when Carl's high, carrying voice reached her. "I'll come say good-night later."

Oh crap!

*   *   *

Marnie wasn't certain how long anxiety kept her awake; she was sleeping solidly when a hand on her shoulder shook her and Carl's giggling voice said, "I'll bet our little girl forgot to have her bath. Come on, get up, let's go."

There was no use yelling. If Celeste wasn't calcified by now she'd pretend to be; after two beatings from Carl, really scary ones, she wouldn't invite a third. Down the hall he took Marnie, to the main bathroom where the loose doorknob rattled when he closed the door.

This was a setup, not mere impulse; in the outsized room the steaming tub was already run half-full. There was no escaping: nightie pulled off, tearing a little in the process, Carl's robe on the floor, ploosh they were both in the tub.

He was too big to fight. And she couldn't think of anything to say to stop him, even if he'd shut up long enough to let her try. "You've seen my cobra, haven't you?" *Stupid giggle!*

Yes, a couple of times, and it looked just about like the pictures in the texts at school. But never this close, before.

If she could have caught up with her breath, maybe she'd have been able to think better. But gasp and gasp, it still wasn't enough. All he did then, though, was soap up a washrag and wash off the parts of him he was making such a fuss about. Then some more soap and he began swiping it all over *her*. The water stopped rising when the tub got full to the mark.

Marnie cringed. Down the arms and back wasn't too bad but across her chest he lingered and she shuddered. Then he dunked the rag again and swabbed it down her belly. Way down.

And pushed it there, and squeezed.

This time it wasn't Carl who shattered, blew up all over everybody. What he did was scream.

She wasn't quite sure what all happened. The Rape Defense lectures at school told you where to grab and hit, so she did. And he was hooting, all doubled over, and she tried to get up and out but he caught her ankle and then slipped flat in the tub so she came down on his head and couldn't get loose right away but when she did he rose up, retching and coughing, lunged out of the tub and she saw she couldn't beat him to the door.

Marnie backed away. Wearing his mean face now, big

podgy Carl stalked her, keeping the angle on her and the door.

Behind her stood the washbasin counter with the cabinets under. The cabinets with all the containers labeled "Caution!"

She whirled and stooped, opened and reached inside, grabbed a spray can and turned back in time to squirt it into Carl's looming face. He gave a grating cry; one big hand knuckled at his streaming, screwed-shut eyes but the other tangled in her hair and twisted.

His mouth squared in a snarl; desperately she thrust the spray can at it and squirted and squirted and . . .

Pain ripped at her scalp; she landed half-rolling on the floor and scrambled up to see Carl's hand, strands of her hair trailing from the fingers, clawing at his throat as if to stop its roaring wheeze.

Now, the door. But she jerked too fast; the loose knob came away in her hand. The one outside hit the hall floor; hers held the little square bar so she stuck it back in the hole and turned it, and took it all with her as she went out past the door and pulled its edge hard, her hand barely clearing its slam.

Now what? Carl's bulk jarred the door twice, then he stopped. No, he wasn't going to break through; it opened the other way. All right, don't leave the knob for Celeste to let him out with; reeling along the hall she held onto it.

She still had the can, too. She looked: tile spray; it killed mildew and fungus. Too bad Carl wasn't a *real* fungus. Well, he sure wouldn't have to worry about Athlete's Throat.

Then she had to fight hard, to stop herself laughing while she still could.

One little part of her mind made perfect sense; she didn't even have to pay much attention. Back in her room, moving faster than anybody should be able to, she dried herself some and put on fresh clothes. Her scalp hurt so bad she thought he'd torn the skin loose, but when she felt it there wasn't any blood.

She switched dirty clothes for clean in the travel bag she hadn't unpacked before, and grabbed stuff out of drawers: her diary, the tiny box with the matched opal earrings and pendant left her by Clancy's mother, her science project medal . . .

A few more items, then she stopped; there wasn't time! Had it been an hour already, or only minutes?

Her small store of reserve cash didn't strain her wallet.

She looked around; on her bed, desk, chairs, dresser, the closet shelf, lay the things that defined her life. Sighing, she closed the bag and walked away from practically all her childhood.

She went out and along the hall, past the bathroom door; from inside came sounds but she couldn't tell what they meant. Was Carl dying? In a rush she carried her bag downstairs, to the big room where Celeste lay spraddled out staring into chemical heaven, one hand beating time to music no one else could hear.

She searched her mother's big pursebag. Marnie's junior grade credit card had limits Celeste's adult version didn't. So switch. And ''. . . good-bye mama; it's not all your fault.'' But this was Celeste, not mama; it was too late for good-byes.

The walk down to the highway and then the transit stop was long enough to make the travel bag heavy. Riding into the city she got almost to sleep but never quite. Carl . . .

Transit went right past a train depot in the nearest suburb, but Marnie didn't get off there. From what daddy said, Glen Springs was a smallish operation, no family quarters; a kid alone, wanting a ticket to there—which would have to include a change of trains at the main depot anyway—could draw questions. So she rode on in to that one. She and Celeste had seen daddy off there more than a few times, back before *Jovian* and the divorce, so she knew where it was.

Transit ran within two–three blocks of it; not a bad walk. And here she knew the ticket sales were automated: credit card in the slot, punch out the destination, ticket pops out. Actually she took passage for the next major city *past* Glen Springs; she'd get off at the smaller place, of course, but no point in leaving a clear computer-recorded trail for Carl and Celeste. And for this transaction, Marnie's own card wouldn't have worked, at all.

Quickstepping to board the bullet train, she came close to grinning. So far, so good.

Settled down in coach, though, a half hour out of town and the refreshments cart already come and gone, nothing but the seatback screen left to provide any distraction, Marnie Allaird was stuck with herself. Fighting tears: as surely as if death had struck, mama was gone. A little at a time, while Marnie

hadn't noticed. And if she had, what could she have done?
She absolutely refused to think about Carl, dead or alive.
But what in the world was she going to tell *daddy*?

Clancy Allaird felt great. Ever since basic training, beginning the Army hitch that got him the GI Bill to help with
college, he could sleep any time they let him hold still; the
train was no exception. And it had reached Glen Springs early
enough that after he caught the minicab to the small NASA
Gating center and checked into quarters, he logged another
couple of hours before breakfast.

Now, full of eggs and toast and juice and coffee, he came
back to his room to get his briefing kit. As he opened the door,
only one thing shadowed his mood: was Marnie going to be
okay?

Then he stopped still. If she were, she certainly didn't look
it.

It wasn't only that the new pudginess, afflicting all his family line for a year or so to announce puberty, put a sulky look
on her normally clear-cut features. Or that her shortish light
brown hair stuck out in all the wrong directions. Riding down
here on the bullet—how else could she have made it so fast?—
could account for the tired look, and if she'd only just arrived,
maybe she hadn't had time to rinse the grime off her face.
The grime that so clearly outlined the tear tracks.

"Marnie!" He moved to hug her; she met him halfway.

Her crying came fierce but ended soon; then, haltingly, she
tried to answer his questions. Clancy shook his head; it wasn't
that he disbelieved her, but what she said didn't make sense.
"You think you may have *killed* Knapheidt?"

"I don't know. There wasn't anything on the news before
I got off the train. But I didn't try to. Just to get away, was
all. He caught me and—" She told it best she could. "I
couldn't *help* it!"

No, she probably couldn't. Dammit, he should go back up
there, and if Knapheidt were still alive which was more likely
than desirable, file charges against him. Except that it would
be Carl's word against Marnie's, and the man's family still
had a lot of clout in that state. Plus, Clancy couldn't possibly
get away from here long enough to do any such a thing.

She was getting heavy on his lap. Still trying to stroke her hair smooth, he said, "Marni Gras, you don't know he's dead. And *if* he is, I'm not sure of the penalty for fungicide."

The attempted light touch wasn't working; for that matter it didn't do much for his own worries. What would feel really good, Clancy decided, would be to go barging into that Addams Family homestead and punch out blubber boy's incisors. Sigh. He said, "We need to learn the score, don't we?" He looked at his watch. "I have to hit a briefing session. You had breakfast?"

She shook her head. "I took the minicab from the station. At the gate there was just the one guard. I said I was here to see you, and she looked at my ID card and told me how to get to this room. But not how to find anything to eat."

"I'll bring a tray from the cafeteria at my first break. And make some phone calls then, too. For now you stay right here, out of sight. Until I can think of some way to explain you to the powers that be."

"But the guard—"

"Took for granted you had authorization or you wouldn't be here. The big brass won't, so stay put."

"All right."

"And get some sleep; you look like you haven't had much."

"No." Meaning she hadn't, not that she wouldn't . . .

One last hug, and he left her. A good thing he already knew this morning's material backward and forward, because trying to listen to the young officer tell it, Clancy had no luck at all.

Celeste didn't know her ass from third base. Coming partly awake and still booged to the follicles, at first she didn't recognize Carl at all. She thought he was a bad spud dream, weaving around with no clothes on, brandishing a big screwdriver like he was going to stab her with it, his eyes swollen nearly shut and the slits showing red, mouth puffed out and splotched with sores, no voice except the rasping grunts.

The second dousing with cold water brought her down; after a while she could even make out some of what he tried to say. "Damn little cunt," she decided, was Marnie—but what she'd done or where she'd gone, Celeste still had no idea. Except that somehow Marnie locked Carl in the bathroom, and until he found the screwdriver in the cabinet under the washbasin, he couldn't get out. At least that's how Celeste understood it.

But where was Marnie? Was she all right? And what had Carl done to cause whatever happened? Something, for damn sure . . .

He made her get dressed and do something about her hair before he put some clothes on, too. Ice cubes applied to his face brought some of the swelling down, but he still looked like the malign alien in a Late Night Movie. And sounded worse.

But he got it across that there was something they had to do, and by now she was less shaky and could drive. Sort of.

She was surprised at where he directed her to go, and what they did when they got there.

Clancy Allaird wasn't *Arrow*'s original executive officer. Coming in now as a last-minute replacement, to a multinational UN crew that had worked and studied together for several months, he felt distinctly under the gun if not behind the eight ball. He hadn't been told the personal reasons for his predecessor's pullout; now he tried not to feel that the others saw him as an interloper.

Maybe they didn't; maybe he simply lacked confidence. It didn't help matters that when the break came at 0945 he couldn't hang around and chin with the group because he had to take Marnie something to eat. Well, he'd try to do better at lunchtime.

Cutting across behind the Habgate building he got to the cafeteria ahead of the rest, loaded a tray quickly and got out with his booty before they arrived. Nothing like avoiding explanations he didn't have on tap . . .

Marnie needed a shower before she lay down. She was glad there was only a stall; she didn't even want to *see* a tub. It seemed no time at all until daddy woke her, but she felt a lot better rested and ate two of the big sandwiches he'd brought, while he made slower work of only one.

There were still several left; he put them away in the room's small countertop fridge. "How come so many?"

"Some for your lunch," daddy said. "I can't get away with ducking out on the crew *all* the time."

He reached for the phone and switched on only its audio function, not the computer screen. At her inquiring look he said, "One of our PR guys I've had a couple drinks with; he has newsroom connections. Maybe even up where you just came from."

She'd never yet made sense of one end of a phone call, so she went to the bathroom for a little while. When she came out, her father was off the phone. He smiled. "You can quit worrying about one thing; there's nobody dead up there named Knapheidt."

It helped some.

He hurried back to the cafeteria, but the gang was already starting to leave their big table. Nicole Pryce, the tall second officer from somewhere in western Canada, gave him a dead-pan stare. "Allaird, eh? Nice of you to find time to join us." And stalked away.

Eh, indeed. Clancy didn't know all the fifteen names yet and could keep straight only about half of those he did. He had no idea which ones were paired off and which weren't (if any). Come to that, he didn't even know if his predecessor had left a shipside "widow"—let alone who she might be.

Besides being introduced, he hadn't traded more than a dozen words with Ellery Dawson, *Arrow*'s captain. Ruddy-faced, bulky like a down lineman on the junior college scale, Dawson was given to occasional bursts of goshwow enthusiasm. Otherwise he went by the book and showed little of his inner feelings. As Allaird nodded to him, muttering "Captain," the man flashed a brief, noncommittal grin. "If your trip gave you the trots, I've got some pills for that."

A fine excuse for ducking out at the break, but one trouble with it: Clarence Engels Allaird had always found lying such hard work that he'd never really learned how. "Thanks, sir, but I'm all right." Resisting the urge to add "and was, all along"; by now he could stop himself from telling *everything* he knew.

He followed the others into the briefing room. The only convenient available seat was on the group's outskirts.

Lunchtime, stuck at table between Second Officer Pryce to his left and a youngish, balding man whose entire attention went to the striking red-haired woman sitting opposite, Clancy ate silently. He'd tried an opening remark on Pryce, to the effect that this voyage was certainly a new approach ". . . and opens up a lot of interesting possibilities."

In dead-level tones the tall brunette said, "Does it?" As she looked away, wavy hair swung forward of her shoulder and hid her expression from him.

Well, up yours, too. Whatever itched her, he couldn't know. Clancy turned to his right, to the man gabbing at the redhead. "Tell me something, Dudley Do-Right. Are you beautiful people always this snooty to everybody, or is it just me?"

The man gaped; all around the table the chatter died. Then from its far end came a raucous laugh. "Jesus H. Coriolis, citizens. The man *is* alive."

"Where are you from, anyway?" said Nicole Pryce.

"Well, I—" Then Clancy could talk. It didn't come easy, in this bunch, but he made a start. The man to his right was Phil Henning, drive specialist; the redhead sitting across, the one who held most of Henning's interest, was chief instrument technician and answered to Sybiljan Baynor. Once she addressed Phil as "Dudley," and they all three laughed.

By the end of the meal Clancy had three more names solidly attached to bodies. The short part-Vietnamese man in navigation was Chauncey Ng. The lanky backup pilot, Edd Jarness, who had laughed at Clancy's needling of Phil Jennings, sat for the most part like a darkly sallow sphinx, saying little. Unlike the slim, very black Kenyan woman, Ptiba Mbente, who would command and pilot the Deployment Vehicle when that unit emerged from *Arrow*'s nose like lead from a pencil, to scout the destination planet before landing personnel and supplies. That one spoke freely.

Her surname sounded familiar; when Clancy asked, she smiled. "Yes. My cousins Btar and Jomo served on *Starfinder*. With the launch crew, cadre A; they've been back nearly three years now."

Some odd rumors circulated about that launch crew: two had been Gated home dead and at least one in irons to face charges. But so far as Clancy knew, Ptiba's cousins weren't implicated. Compulsively his mind checked out the timing: yes, fifteen months for *Starfinder* to hit cruising speed plus two years Habgate plus three since returning—it did add up to right about now. . . .

The captain stood. Time to key into student mode.

Clancy Allaird's space career went back a way, from when *Jovian* returned from its first mission and was retrofitted with Habgate fuel-and-supply facilities to go with its Traction Drive. No crew exchange Gates, though; there wasn't room in the design.

It was the Habegger matter transmission Gates, of course, that made starships possible: crew rotation, continuous replacement of fuel and life support and supplies in general. The two-year transit lag was no problem if you started inGating everything well in advance. Including the first relief cadre.

The next time *Jovie* went out, Clancy was chief pilot. It was a sweet trip, lasting more than a year. He had a little problem with his hormones, maintaining monogamous celibacy against the efforts of Theda Dupree who made an otherwise clean sweep of the ship's male personnel, but he managed. Of course this all occurred before ships' crews entered into group marriage as a matter of policy; Celeste wouldn't have held still for that!

But as it happened, Theda was keyboarding a book: *Sex Slave in Space* or something of the sort, and truth had little part in it. NASA managed to prevent publication, but somehow Celeste got hold of the rumors and blew her top, as yet unbleached. Stuck with the name but lacking the game, Clancy caught the dirtier end of a singularly nasty divorce. He wasn't even sure which neck he'd sooner wring: Theda's, or Celeste's lawyer's. Maurice somebody . . .

His next space-oriented assignment, two years ago, had been first male alternate on *Starfinder*'s relief cadre 1–B under Captain Irina Tetzl—a group which would be outGating on that ship just about the time this bunch here went *into* its Gate. From what he'd heard about "Old Iron Tits" when she'd ridden *Jovian-II* as a UN observer, he felt lucky he hadn't been tagged for that tour. Be that as it may, he'd then been offered the same slot on relief 1–B for the second ship, *Roamer*, due up two years from now. Always a bridesmaid, these days . . .

Except that for some reason no one ever got around to tell him, he'd been hauled in to replace Cal Ledbetter on *Arrow*—

or rather, asked most politely if he'd accept the post. And
under the circumstances, damn right he would!

The drawback was that after all this time and study his
thinking was solidly at home in the *Starfinder*-class ships. But
Arrow was different; most of the numbers he knew so well
and thoroughly were wrong.

Not all, luckily. The circular segment that comprised the
living areas still lay at the ship's outer twenty-five–meter radius, rotated to provide centrifugal equivalent of point-three
gee, and was accessed by means of an unpowered transfer ring
which was braked magnetically, either to rest with respect to
the main structure or to match spin with the rotating section.

Some of the layout, the placement of functions, was also
similar—but different enough that he couldn't take anything
for granted without looking it up. And the smaller auxiliary
rotating segment behind the living quarters, which could be
revved up to provide a one-gee exercise area, was new to him.
The point-three-gee off-duty environment of the earlier ships
had been deemed adequate to maintain crew members' health
for their one-year tours until they Gated home again, but *Arrow*'s people were going the full course. Better safe than
sorry . . .

With a cross-sectional sketch of the ship at hand for reference, Clancy paid heed to what this afternoon's lecturer had
to say.

". . . treated for toxic burns on his face and in his mouth
and throat, Knapheidt was released without hospitalization.
Sought for questioning in the assault is his stepdaughter, Margaret Clarisse Allaird, age twelve, missing since sometime during the night. Authorities are trying to reach the girl's father,
Clarence Allaird, in case he may have knowledge of her
whereabouts."

On the screen, the announcer cleared his throat. "In sports
today . . ."

At the sound of her own name Marnie had pushed the Record button; daddy would need to see this. Now she hit Stop.
Automatically she picked the *Arrow* familiarization brochure
off the floor where she'd dropped it. "Stepdaughter?" She
shook her head; what were Carl and Celeste trying to pull,
here?

She checked her watch. Daddy wouldn't be free for at least another hour; maybe he'd have some good ideas.

Turning the screen off, Marnie went back to studying the brochure, trying to get the feel of this ship that would take him away from her forever. And had herself another sandwich.

The briefing and related social stress had put Marnie's predicament on Clancy's back burner. What she told him in a rush as soon as he came in, plus the replayed news snippet, caught him off guard and stopped his thinking cold. One point stuck out. "Stepdaughter? I didn't know Celeste married the guy."

"Neither did I. I don't see when they *could* have."

"Umm. News should be on again by now. Half over with, in fact." He turned it on, and they sat through over a dozen brief items of no interest to either before "This afternoon the mother of Margaret Allaird, fugitive in the assault on well-known sportsman and shipping heir Carl Knapheidt, made a dramatic plea for her daughter to come home. Here at the aging but still palatial Knapheidt home, Celeste Knapheidt spoke."

Comb and compact, garb and grooming, a good stabilizer for the twitches: Celeste made a fine appearance. Her pitch wasn't bad either, Clancy thought. ". . . see my little girl again. I realize you've been under stress, Marnie dear, and I want you to know there'll be no charges filed. You need help, darling, and that's all I want for you. Then when you're ready, we'll be home again, all of us together."

Between clenched teeth Marnie's answer came out. "Like all *crap* we will." She turned. "Daddy, I can't ever go back there."

"I know. Ssh, listen." Because the announcer was saying that there had been no luck contacting the father as yet, but within the next few hours, government red tape notwithstanding . . .

Clancy turned it off and reached for the phone, shushing Marnie again. "Wait. This needs to come first."

He'd met Senator Bill Flynn, chairman of the space committee, two years ago when Clancy almost but not quite wound up on the relief cadre to *Starfinder*. His pocket computerpad still held two phone numbers that might reach Flynn, and the second one did. "Senator?" Clancy gave his name. "Remember me?" Good. "Well sir I need a big favor. Has it been announced yet that I'm filling in on *Arrow*?"

"Not yet. There's a press conference tonight, so that's—"

"*No!* I mean, please don't. Hold the word another day—two, three, even, if you can. It's . . ."

"Allaird?" Clancy could visualize the friendly, puzzled smile on the senator's freckle-splotched face. "You're not behind on your alimony or anything, are you?" Pause. "I mean, if you are, sure, I'll keep you covered, and authorize advance pay to take care of it. Just so it's nothing worse."

What to say? He couldn't lie, and certainly not to this man. "I'm not in hock to anybody, sir. It's a family problem, a matter of protection, and I need a little time to take the necessary steps without a spotlight on me. Okay?"

After a pause Flynn said, "That's good enough for me. And I hope I can shake loose and come say good-bye to your gang before you hit the Gate."

"Me too. And thanks, senator."

Hanging up, he turned to Marnie. "That gives us time. Now where's a good safe place for you?"

There wasn't any. Daddy had absolutely no blood family of his own—well, a couple of third or fourth cousins he hadn't seen in years and didn't even know where they lived now. And friends? Sure; lots of them, but none to the degree that he could expect them to take her in and fight Carl and Celeste for her—even if any nonrelative stood a chance against a mother's claim.

"If there was *time!*" Daddy gritted his teeth. "Time for a hearing, to have a guardian appointed or something. But that could take weeks—and what I have is two days!"

He frowned. "I'll have to pull out of *Arrow*, is all!"

Marnie moved to hug him hard. "No; you mustn't!"

"I thought you didn't want me to go."

"I don't want to lose you. But I don't want *you* to lose . . ." Everything you've always worked for, always wanted; she couldn't get it all said, but maybe he understood.

Because he stood up. "Ooh-kay. I guess it's time for Plan B." He grinned. "I've always wanted to say that."

Picking up a paper from his briefing kit, he scowled. "It's close, dammit. But I see no other choice. *How*, though . . ."

Once they had all Marnie's stuff together, everything in the bag except what she wore, Clancy added a few items: the remaining sandwiches, a couple of plastic flasks of juice. Now he was ready; it was dinnertime, when all but duty personnel would be in the cafeteria.

He had her make a last-minute visit to the bathroom; then, "All right; let's go." Marnie looked at the three eggs he carried in one hand but asked no questions as they left the quarters and crossed closely mowed turf to the Habgate building. Just outside it he paused and carefully dropped the eggs to splatter on the concrete sidewalk. He paid no heed to Marnie's questioning look; he was concentrating on his lines.

The young woman who sat at the duty desk looked serious, but not especially hard-nosed. Clancy smiled. "My daughter's about ready to leave. I wonder if I could show her the Gates first?"

"Yes, I suppose so."

As she stood, Clancy said, "Oh, by the way, there's kind of a mess on the walk outside. Nothing big, but if you'd like to, while I'm here to watch the store, you might want to clean it up before any brass sees it. I can do the showing around."

"Uh—why yes; that's a good idea. Thank you."

When she came back in, wadding some dripping paper towels into a plastic bag, she said, "If your daughter hasn't left yet, perhaps I could show her some more about the Gates."

"Well, thanks very much. But she did have to go."

When Celeste finally got hold of Clancy, he stuck to his story. "She was here, yes. But right now I have absolutely no idea where she is."

Because when it came to Habgates, nobody did.

The Habegger Gates, developed here at Gayle Institute of Technology by Dr. Alois Habegger, constitute a true transfer of physical mass between two loci in space-time by means of passage through the Aleph Plenum, the greater continuum postulated to be the basic underlying reality of all existence.

"We know, or can deduce, two major characteristics of Aleph. First, that within it exists a point corresponding to each point in our own universe, but in that continuum each is contiguous to every other. Thus all distances in Aleph are identical: precisely one quantum. And second, that the quantum of *time* in Aleph equals approximately two Earth years. Thus, passage through a Habgate is instantaneous to the transmitted person or object, while outside the Gate two years pass. During the developmental period these properties were the source of considerable confusion.

"Gayle Institute may also take pride in the work done here by Haal Arnesson and Anne Portaris, work which resulted in producing the device known as Traction Drive. It is these two developments which have made possible star travel as we know it today."

*—from Gayle Tech Achievements
Review brochure, 48th Edition*

The wall behind hit Marnie like a runaway truck. Gasping, she looked—*up*, it was now—up some kind of shaft to a ceiling so far above her, it didn't seem real.

Fighting for breath she got her wits back, and remembered.

When the woman left, daddy took Marnie down a hall and into a big room where two large spheres stood, each with one side hollowed to form a squarish open booth. "You know what these are, don't you?"

"The Habgates?"

He nodded, and pointed to the one with the big "M" scrawled on it. "Habegger's Mouth. Set your bag at a rear corner and step back out."

"All right." She did, remembering that the "T" on the other was a slang initial that stood for Habegger's Tush, while he fiddled at the control console sitting before and between the two. Suddenly a burst of flaring, iridescent color hid the booth's interior; when it cleared, her bag was gone.

"It's working. Come here." He hugged her hard and she hugged him right back as they kissed good-bye. "Now look. I *hope* the timing's right but it could be off a little. If it is, you'll be nailed in a five-gee field for a while. Not for long, so don't get scared; just lie still, breathe slowly, and wait. The thrust will be toward the back, so lie snug against the rear wall. Got it?"

"Yes, daddy." There wasn't time for questions, even if she could've thought straight just now. "I'll wait for you."

"It could be terribly uncomfortable for a little while; I'm sorry you have to risk it, but this is the only chance we have." He checked his watch. "It shouldn't be long. As soon as you can, leave the Gate. It'll be zero gee then, so keep a hold on something at all times. But don't touch anything that looks like a control switch."

"I won't." She settled in, lying on one side with her back to the rear wall. His hand waved and he started to say something but then the colors bloomed and the wall slammed her.

When Celeste got straight again, with the aid of some high-potency vitamin shots, she began to figure out what was going on. Carl had got them married because "stepfather" sounded better in the news than "mother's resident stud" did. And she found the tile spray in Marnie's room; she just couldn't get Carl to explain why Marnie used it on him.

She had her ideas, though, and now she began to realize how badly, with the dope and all, she'd let things get out of hand. Especially Carl. She'd had no *idea* he was a danger to Marnie. Well, that was a thing of the past. When she got Marnie back, Carl would damn well leave her alone; Celeste would see to that.

When she got her back? Might not be all that easy. . . .

It took Celeste well into the second day to get NASA to tell her Clancy's assignment, longer to find out where he was. Glen Springs Crewing Gate Center: when she did reach Clancy on the phone he barely gave her the time of day. But airplanes would get you there from here, if you could afford the fares nowadays.

Between other calls, while she waited for people to call back, she'd been packing a carry-on; now she phoned for reservations and tickets. It was when she went to give her credit card number that she found she was holding Marnie's.

"Carl! Gimme your card; mine's gone." He didn't want to; in fact he acted like he didn't want her to find Marnie. Too bad for him; married or not, she could always walk out.

Except, by now she couldn't really afford to. . . .

Carl wouldn't know that, though. She got the card.

Then she thought to check on her own missing one. The screen told of a rail ticket purchase, to a city not too farside of Glen Springs. "Be damned!" She hadn't thought Marnie to be quite that devious. . . .

And decided Carl didn't need to know this, either.

Clancy spent the next day figuratively looking back over his shoulder. He couldn't concentrate on the briefings; neither was his social progress anything to write home about.

Late that evening he had trouble getting to sleep; he kept telling himself that tomorrow would see the end of this, but himself reminded him of the situation he'd face on *Arrow*.

He dreamed that Carl Knapheidt had sold him to Irina Tetzl for a bag of broken eggs and now he had to put them back together. Humpty Dumpty was in there someplace.

*   *   *

Breathe slowly. All right; breathing at all was a lot of work, but she managed. The air wasn't stale and that surprised her, until she remembered that only about seventy days had passed here, so the ventilating system would have been left running. Whatever, she appreciated the effect.

No point in trying to roll over; all the view was straight up, which was actually forward in the ship, and the high ceiling was the end of a long corridor.

She couldn't raise her head to any advantage, but hands and arms were something else. To make it easier, first she snaked her right hand over across to grasp her other wrist, then used the strength of both arms to get her watch up where she could see it. Vision was blurred, but finally she made out that she was less than five minutes from Glen Springs. Well, plus the two years' Gate lag.

Two years. Just like that. She had to believe it because she knew it was true, but still . . . And the five minutes was more than two hours passing, back on Earth.

But how much longer, minutes or hours or whatever, before somebody got this five-gee monkey off her chest?

"No. Don't let her in; she has no business here and I don't want to see her." The call, waking Clancy with the news that Celeste Knapheidt was here to see him and demanding entrance, gave him no time to put strategy or tactics together. Five in the morning for Pete'sake! "If she doesn't have a warrant," he overrode the guard's protest, "tell her go get one." Damn!—after he'd sweat it out for nearly two days, why did she have to show up *now*? A few more hours and he'd be safely out of here. . . .

In the background he could hear Celeste working up to screech mode. "Tell her she's verging on disorderly conduct and this is a government facility."

Scheist! Even to himself, he sounded lame.

"Look, Mr. Allaird sir, the director here Mr. Bendixon he doesn't like there to be any fuss, you know, out in public?" Oh jeez it had to be the One Lobe Brain on duty! And "So if you don't mind I'll just let her come inside and you know best how to take care of it I'm sure."

Rot in hell! "Ooh-kay; send her in."

What the hell; for the next two years, Marnie did not in the strictest sense *exist*.

With no warning at all the pressure ceased; Marnie floated free. Fear pulled at her—but after a moment, realizing she felt no sickness from zero gee, she drew a full breath and released it in almost a laugh. Her pulse still raced from the strain of high acceleration, but her breathing was catching up. And now all that heavy weight was gone for keeps. Good enough!

Her relief didn't last long. The slightly concave surface "below" her began a deep hum and vibration, and the entire area made a series of tiny jerks back and forth along the direction of curvature. Meaning, the ship was jiggling in rotation mode with respect to its long axis. This went on for some time before the jerks stopped and the hum sank to a subliminal level—she knew it was still there, but she couldn't exactly hear it.

Time to get herself in gear. Her watch indicated she'd withstood the five gees for more than ten minutes. Well, she had some aches to prove it! And let's see—at the Earth end, daddy had sent her off only four hours early, four and a bit. Well, here she was. . . .

The Gate booth provided no handholds. With one hand she reached to secure her bag; with the other she pushed at the rear wall; the reaction turned her feet toward it, so in a kind of wonderment she touched them to that surface and straightened her knees, propelling herself with alarming speed along the corridor.

When her course angle brought her near one side of it she caught at the far edge of a door frame, jerked to a halt, and paused to see where she was and what she might do about her situation.

Quite a lot, perhaps, if she put her mind to it.

Looking around the small room, Celeste said, "You starship officers don't exactly live at the Ritz, do you?"

Clancy stared at her, stony-faced. The burr haircut made his ears stick out too much. "It's temporary."

She thought he wasn't going to say any more, but suddenly he blurted, "Marnie isn't here; you're wasting your time."

"Where is she?"

"I don't know."

"Where did she say she was going?"

"She didn't."

"You mean you just let her . . . ?"

"More or less. You could say that."

"When did she leave?"

"Day before yesterday. A little after eighteen hundred."

"Dammit, you know I don't keep time that way!"

"Six pee-em. Dinner time."

"Had she eaten?"

"Uh—she took something with her."

"To where?"

"I told you, I don't know where she is."

"Just like that. Oh, you lying bastard!" His mouth compressed; she knew she'd hurt him but couldn't think how to follow up her advantage. After being delayed, getting bumped, missing a connection, here she was but her mind hadn't quite caught up yet. The sonofabitch wasn't going to talk, and here on his own home grounds she had no way to force him to.

All right. Eyes narrowed, she pointed her finger and shook it in emphasis. "I'm getting a court order. You'll tell where she is and you'll turn her over to me. Is that clear?"

"To you and your child-groping ex-jock? You'd better change your drug of choice, Celeste. This one's giving you delusions."

"He didn't!" *Oh God I hope not.* "And anyway I'm her mother. It's my place to take care of her."

She made a firm, decisive nod. "A court order, that's what." And turned to walk out.

When her hand was on the doorknob Clancy said, "Get two. Maybe they'll give you a discount."

Talk about cheap construction! The stupid door was too flimsy to even slam right.

Thinking back to the brochure she'd studied, Marnie had a pretty good idea where she was on the ship, and even which way to go, to get where she'd rather be. Which was the living area, the rotating belt that centrifuged a radial acceleration three-tenths that of Earth's gravity.

And now that she thought about it, she guessed she knew what the hum and wiggle had been all about. The belt wouldn't have been rotating, putting the strain of five gees on its magnetic bearings, during the ten ship's-weeks or so of acceleration. No, it would be programmed to rev up as soon as accel ceased, and the process had produced the noise and motion that had alarmed her. Because action produces reaction, so tangential Traction Drive trim thrustors would operate to keep the ship itself from rotating the opposite way. And they'd have to do it in increments, which was why she'd felt the intermittent jiggles.

If she had it right, the belt should be working now. The trick was to get there.

It wasn't all that far from here; the Habgates were located on the deck level that lay about twenty meters out from the ship's axis, just inside the belt at twenty-five. The transfer ring, normal means of access between the two, sat at the very front of *Arrow*'s cylindrical segment, just behind the conical forward section. About forty meters farther along this corridor.

The decks formed concentric cylinders; this corridor was a longitudinal segment of one. The deck itself, the wider, concave surface, was carpeted with something like Velcro. Including the Gate booth. If she had the matching footwear she could walk it. Or if someone hadn't omitted the handlines the brochure had mentioned, she could hand-over-hand her way, here in zero gee.

But ifs weren't getting her anywhere. All right; that first jump had been a little scary. Let's try it a bit easier. . . . She paused to seat the bag under her right arm, its strap looping across over the other shoulder, and pushed off gently. Aiming this time for a shorter jump, to the next doorframe on the other side, she fell short and met the bulkhead a few feet early.

The doors were paired; she shoved laterally and collided gently with the one opposite.

Which opened. To stop herself she grabbed the handle.

One look told her she shouldn't be in here. This was *Arrow*'s control room.

Too wired to get back to sleep, Allaird washed and dressed. By then it was oh-six-hundred; if he dawdled a little on the way there'd be at least coffee in the cafeteria, and he could work on that while the first batch of eggs was scrambling.

After a moment he had a better idea; some things needed doing, right now. Well, not the doing, so much; there were twenty-one months for that. But the initiating was his baby and here he had only a few hours left.

He punched up his phone's data connection to the Supplies office and began ordering out a few items. As additional needs came to mind, the list grew; she wasn't going to stay the same size forever. Finally he decided not to push it any further, and put End to his onscreen listing.

Being unpaired he'd probably be assigned a room to himself: for Destination he typed Arrow, Quarters, Allaird, C. But specified the cartons to be labeled Allaird, M.

As he let out a deep, relieved breath, another idea came: something that *did* have to happen now if at all. Changing to a blank cassette he switched the phone onto Record and dictated for several minutes before changing the tapes back. Now using the unit's computer screen he punched for Legal, selected a standard form, and filled it out. Then on Local he typed an explanatory note, ending with an apology for the possible imposition, and printed out both items.

The form needed notarization, with witnesses. Moran in Legal would be up by now; he'd helped advise Clancy after *Jovian* and he could keep his mouth shut. Allaird walked to the digs the man shared with two colleagues. Wholly uninterested, the two signed to witness Moran's official stamp.

The mailroom wasn't open yet, but his wait was short. A Number Two standard container held the cassette and papers handily; he addressed it, sent it off Secure Priority, and went out into morning sun.

By the time he did get to the cafeteria the eggs were not only ready; they were cold. Clancy waited for a fresh batch.

Marnie was drifting slowly enough to keep hold of the door handle; her legs and body swung past but their inertia didn't pull her free. Zero gee needed some getting used to; it took a few moments before she realized she could hang there all day and nothing would pull her "down" to the Velcro'd deck.

By now, though, none of this was scary. Just interesting. For one thing, she wasn't going to have to worry about zero-gee sickness; her stomach liked the situation just fine. Looking around at various control positions, the consoles and visual displays accented by indicator lights that glowed or flashed or didn't, she realized why daddy had gone heavy on Don't Touch. There were in this pale green room so many buttons and switches and keys and knobs sticking out all over the place that catching onto a couple by mistake might screw things *all* up.

Briefly she wondered why there'd be a matched pair of Habgate terminals set into the big room's rear wall. Spares or something? Clancy would know, when he got here. . . .

Ooh-kay; she levered her way out of there but the door got away and hung ajar, unlatched. She could have maneuvered to recover it, but by now she felt urgent about reaching the corridor's far end where maybe—just maybe—she could gain access to the rotating living areas.

Because for one thing she hadn't peed in two years. All right, less than half an hour, really—but five gees do have an effect. And even if she could find the zero-gee facilities that had to be somewhere in this part of the ship, she hadn't looked carefully at the part of the brochure that told how to use them.

Daddy would have enough explaining to do already, without her making any kind of mess on here.

So let's move it. The short jump idea hadn't worked too well; how about a long slow flight all the way? At the far end there should be *some* way to stay put.

Optimistically, Marnie pushed off, as near to straight forward as she could manage. Twice she had to fend away from side bulkheads with handstrokes that helped pole her along, before she came to the end. Then, although the transfer ring doors were right in front of her, there was absolutely nothing to grab. Talk about thoughtless design . . . !

Land soft! As her hands touched, she let her arms buckle to absorb impact. Partly it worked; Marnie bounced back away considerably slower than she'd approached, and she put enough English on the rebound to send her safely leftward into the cross corridor that circled the ship, up forward here.

That was where she caught one hand onto the wall-mounted coil of handline that somebody should have strung down the corridor in the first place, and swung herself to rest against the transverse bulkhead.

Marnie grinned. Suddenly it was a whole new ball game.

*   *   *

Why, thought Clancy, did his final day on Earth have to be such a hectic mess? Just as he finished with the paperwork and was checking in a last-minute batch of personal gear for outGating, he was called to the station commander's office. There he found a disgruntled group: the rest of the crew did not appreciate having to run through the mandatory group marriage ceremony all over again, just because Clarence Allaird hadn't been around for the first one.

As far as Clancy was concerned they could have skipped the whole thing. But he went through it along with everyone else, though nobody seemed to want to kiss any brides at all.

Now the entire crew assembled formally for the last time before entering the Gate. This final briefing looked to be a long one; all the bigwigs seemed determined to mark their places in the sun with fulsome oratory.

Senator Bill Flynn, who had coptered in at close to the last minute, made a welcome exception. Before the gathering was seated he'd come around to greet the crew members individually; to Clancy he said, low-voiced, "Everything straightened out all right?"

"Pretty much, sir. And thanks again."

"Good. Any time I can help . . ."

Considering what Clancy had put in the mail that morning, he hoped the senator meant it.

At the podium Flynn set a good example; his speech ran short and to the point, ending with ". . . know you'll do a fine job. And remember: stretching time you'll outlive many of *us*, perhaps all. But the agency's commitment to full support will still be there, no matter whose tails are warming the chairs."

Director Bendixon could have taken lessons; so could the governor, two generals, and a major contractor's rep. But eventually the ceremony wound down and the chiefs left, leaving the Indians to the actualities of doing their jobs.

Gate Coordinator Pollard took the stand. Pollard was a competent, amiable woman who bore an unfortunate resemblance to onetime president Herbert Hoover, including a somewhat similar haircut. Also she cleared her throat a lot. "Uh-umm." She looked at her watch. "At 1720, less than half an hour from now, uh-umm, we will proceed to the Habgate building, where you will uh-umm inGate to *Arrow* in order of roster listing."

Right, thought Clancy. Dawson, himself, Pryce, Amalyn Tabard the Drive chief, Jarness the chief backup pilot/navigator and Mbente the DV commander or maybe the other way around; after that he forgot. And didn't care; he had enough to worry about.

"Uh-umm. We are certain that acceleration will have ended nearly two ship's hours before your arrival, so you will have no difficulty getting clear of the uh-umm, Tush. However, please do so as soon as possible. Departures will be on the half hour, allowing slightly over one minute between arrivals. This should be sufficient to uh-umm avoid any possibility of accident."

She paused. "Uh-umm. Are there any questions?"

There weren't. "Uh-umm. In that case let us adjourn this gathering to the Gates. If you haven't changed to the Velcro shoes, please do so now." Clancy already had. "And may I recommend that prior to Gating you each make, uh-umm, a pit stop? Arriving in zero gee, the precaution may stand you in good stead."

Clancy was glad he'd had Marnie do the same.

Marnie took a deep breath; this was going to be tricky. She'd uncoiled enough line to reach across the transverse corridor and well past the wide elevator-type double doors covering entry to the transfer ring. The first coated StikTite pad already had its clamp lever thrown, to fix it solidly near the line's knotted end. She slid the others back along the line, grouped together next to the remaining coil. One was all she needed right now; the rest would just get in the way.

The trouble was, she had to get across the corridor *and* along it past the big doors, because the control button was on their right-hand side.

What she was looking at was roughly a forty-foot jump and no second chance. Well, not to get it all the way *right*. Because once you laid a StikTite pad on, it was there for keeps. Or near enough . . .

Too bad it wasn't weighted to throw, let alone stable enough to land right side on. As she peeled the plastic coating from the pad's sticky side and spread her grip across the ridged back where the line passed through, she gulped more air.

Then she made her jump.

It was too fast and a little wide; she was still out from the far wall when she floated across past the doors. But she twisted, spun so her legs were out from the wall, and *kicked*.

With barely inches of reach to spare she slapped the bared StikTite pad to the bulkhead, several feet past the doors.

And hung on to come to a halt and swing back.

Bingo.

Pausing before he stepped into Habegger's Mouth, Ellery Dawson seemed to be searching for an exit line. Finally he shrugged. "So long, folks. We'll do our best; wish us luck." As he moved inside the Gate's volume he grinned and waved a half salute. Then the flare of iridescence hid his vanishment.

Clancy sat sweating. One last half hour to go, and he'd be away from Celeste's threats free and clear. Already the wait seemed endless. He tried not to fidget, to let a foot tap or fingers drum. And fought to ignore fierce causeless itchings.

Finally Pollard spoke to him. "Allaird, Clarence E., uh-umm executive officer. Proceed to inGate."

Clancy made no farewell speech at all; he stepped into position, wiggled his feet to make sure his shoes gripped firmly, waved a hand, and saw the colors take over.

Draping loose in zero gee, the line gave Marnie no leverage to reach the single control button beside the transfer ring's doors. If she loosened the clamp and pulled it taut, its path wouldn't be close enough. Even slack, though, it afforded her hand-over-hand return to the bracket holding the remaining coil, where she freed more line, enough to let her tag the forward bulkhead on *this* side of the doors. Grasping the next loose-sliding StikTite she peeled away its plastic coating, took her grip, made her best guess, and jumped.

She spanged her second pad close to the door and pulled in the slack from the first one, then set the clamp. Now she had a taut line across the doors. People wouldn't want it that way later—but for now, all *right*.

Hand by hand she moved within reach of the control button; what it did was call the transfer car and open the door. But of course the car would have been left here at the stationary end, because this was the exit. So if the ring was activated to work at all, by now there shouldn't be any wait.

And there wasn't; smoothly the two door halves parted and moved along their arc to expose the transfer ring's conveyor car: roughly five meters wide, four deep, and three high, it could handle just about anything anyone would want to move to the rotating residential deck. At the middle of the opening the two floor levels matched, but the car's curved slightly less, lowering it not quite two centimeters at each end.

Marnie swung herself into the plain beige interior. Overhead lighting was adequate but not glaring. On the strip of front wall to either side of the doors was placed just one button. She'd expected there'd be one to speed up and match the belt, another to brake to rest with the ship's mass, but each of these was simply marked "Operate." The control circuitry, she decided, would assess its situation and act accordingly.

So she pushed the control before her and released the line to let its own tension spring it clear. The doors slid shut; she began to drift toward one end and to the deck as both angular and centrifugal acceleration grew. None of this was strong or abrupt; well, the brochure said the rotational accel ran to about one-twentieth gee and took less than twenty seconds to get up to belt speed in half a revolution. The belt itself would do a full rev in the same span, which made timing simple: going either way the car could disengage *only* when its terminal on the belt was directly opposite the stationary one on the ship proper.

A brief surge increased her apparent weight until she stood solidly in what she'd been told was three-tenths gee; it probably was. Car and ring clicked into solid rendezvous with the belt; the doors reopened. Where she stood, at one side, this outside floor lay about a half inch lower than the car's—though again the levels matched at the middle. Okay, so the car's curvature was a compromise: intermediate between those of the two decks. Coming back the other way, though, you could trip yourself. . . .

Now she moved outside; after a few seconds the doors closed. Straight ahead Marnie looked along a wide passageway; to either side stretched a ship-circling cross corridor, like the one she'd seen at the twenty-meter level.

Out here, though, someone had a little more fun with colors. Mixes of greens, blues, yellows, reds, shades of orange, all bright and vivid, high in whatever the word was for lots of *light* in the pigment, in patterns that were mostly abstract but surprisingly evocative. The impact might get fatiguing after a while, Marnie thought; the way she felt right now, though, she appreciated it, and would like to meet whoever went wild here.

But this was no time for appreciating decor. What she had to do right now was find daddy's quarters and stay there until he came for her. But how . . . ?

Frustrated, she turned back to the doors behind her; then she saw the somewhat confusing Deck Plan sheet taped to the wall alongside them. Confusing, because when you draw a cylindrical surface on paper, how do you show that the ends meet?

After a few moments the scale of the drawing sank in; this curled-up living area was *big*. But on second thought, maybe not too outsized, at that. A great lot of room, you'd think, for only twenty people, but much of it was taken up with storage, machinery, and probably things Marnie hadn't even thought of.

Such as—now she remembered—a number of rooms with barracks-type sleeping arrangements for the first reinforcements to the ship's crew, the explorers at destination. Because the first planetside Habgate couldn't be operational for well over two years after *Arrow* reached its intended orbit. (Or could it? Was the ship-to-ground shuttle—the Deployment Vehicle—large enough to carry an assembled powered Gate, or pair of them?)

Looking at the deck map she saw a few other things: a conference room, lounge, rec room, dining area . . .

Quarters, though. Logically they and the other places most used by the crew would be grouped along corridors nearest the ring access.

Not, though, the passageway directly before her: this, she noted, was devoted to the common rooms. Well, she didn't need to check those out just yet. The first corridor to her right seemed to be what she was looking for. It held six units, three to each side, and the forwardmost pair, numbered 1 and 2, had "Capt" and "Exec" scribbled on them.

Walking tangentially along the curved deck surface she felt uncertain of her equilibrium; any time she changed direction a little, inertia or something gave her a sneaky shove slaunchwise. Was the belt running unevenly, or what? She stopped.

No, everything was smooth. But when she stepped off at an angle, her foot didn't come down exactly where she expected.

Now *wait* a minute. Marnie thought, then it came to her: Coriolis force, the stuff that made people walk in circles when they couldn't see where they were going, and caused water to make a circular swirl when it went down a drain. Vector product of two forces, memory told her, but wouldn't supply the equation.

She entered the next fore-and-aft corridor and stood before door 2. Would it open, or did daddy have the key?

It opened. In she went, into a largish room. Soft lights came on automatically; Marnie looked around to see furniture of a slim design in pale woods and teal or gray-green cushioning in contrast to cream-yellow walls. All fastened down safely to endure the acceleration period, but easy enough to free.

Lined up along the rear wall, also placed with accel in mind, sat a row of miscellaneous cartons. Daddy was going to have a lot of unpacking to do.

What about the rest of the place? The same rear wall was bisected by the entrance to a short hallway; Marnie walked back and into it. To the right a door opened into a bedroom. No boxes here, but two good-sized chests of drawers—built in, of course. Also, she discovered, locked. Or rather latched with simple turnbolts: more accel protection.

She opened one; it was packed full of daddy's clothing.

Across the way, two doors. One was a kitchenette and dining nook; again the drawers sat latched, and inside one she found utensils packed so they wouldn't clash around under accel. Whoever set this up, thought things out pretty well.

The other door had to be what she was looking for, and it was. She had to peel restraining tape off the toilet and also from the regulating devices in the tank above it, then open the valve to admit water. Finally, two years and ten light-weeks from Earth, she baptized the facility.

The washbasin worked immediately; no reason its faucets would have other valves as backstop. Unbolting drawers she found the hand towels, used one and laid out a second.

Now she went back to the living room; curiously she looked at one of the larger boxes.

And saw it was marked "M. Allaird." Daddy must have . . . But those wrappings needed tools, and suddenly Marnie felt the onrush of fatigue. Christmas, even out of season, would have to wait.

In the bedroom she pulled off her shoes, lay down, and was asleep before she had time to relax.

Clancy hadn't had the chance to visit *Arrow* in orbit; there simply wasn't time for it. But he'd been aboard *Roamer* before Earth's second starship lifted out, and was familiar with the area near its control room. This corridor he saw extending forward of the Tush seemed little different.

Moving away in that direction, gingerly planting one Velcro sole and then another, Ellery Dawson had progressed only a few meters ahead. He showed no intention of looking back, so Allaird said, "Hoy! Wait up?"

Dawson looked around. His face carried no expression, but his posture indicated uncertainty. Surely he'd been in zero gee before; what was eating on him? In the economical way he'd learned on *Jovian*, barely lifting his feet clear of the deck as he slid them alternately forward, Clancy came up beside the captain. "Two aboard, fourteen to go, skipper. Should we have a look into control?"

"I guess so. I mean, yes, sure." Visibly Dawson pulled up his image. "Let's find out where we stand on vee and distance, how accurate the accel program was. Time ratio . . ." Standing at the control room door, he frowned. "The door. Should be shut and latched. Sloppy work. Must have banged hell out of the wall in there when the five gccs hit."

But when they looked inside they found no mark at all. Clancy gazed around the room, its consoles and screens and indicator banks, to note at the rear the pair of back-to-back Habgates that would allow *Arrow*'s crew, at destination, to pass the five-gee decel period safely in Habegger transit. As Nicole Pryce, the latest arrival aboard, peered in to see what they were doing.

The unmarked wall, though. In Clancy's head a sign flashed: *Marnie was here.* "Tell you what, captain. While you folks confirm our navigation data, why don't I go forward and make sure the transfer ring's working? Visit the belt, maybe start to unbutton the galley and put the facilities into operation? Another twenty minutes, we'll have a whole bunch of people wanting to feel at home here."

Dawson didn't exactly say yes; Clancy didn't give him time to say no. "Right, skipper. I'll give it the once-over and report by intercom."

As he came out he saw Tabard the bushy-haired drive chief still standing back near the Tush, talking with Ptiba Mbente. So the DV commander did rate ahead of pilot/navigator Jarness. . . .

Vaguely wondering why no one had set any kind of boarding agenda, Clancy Allaird plodded on forward. He was near the end bulkhead when he noticed the line strung between two StikTites, crossing the transfer ring doors, and then its origin at the coil on this side of the cross corridor. The line should have been laid out along the corridor back to the Tush; someone had screwed up, there. But *this* deployment . . .

It had to be Marnie, but where was she? Mulling on the problem he pulled at one of the StikTites. It had set firmly; until someone injected the proper solvent into its central pocket, the thing was here for the duration.

Then Clancy saw the unlighted car call button, and pushed it. The wait, not quite twenty seconds before the doors opened, confirmed his guess. Knowing his daughter had good sense, he went where she should be and found her there.

III

Senators get more crank letters than they'd like you to think, but Bill Flynn's staff knew that anything from one of NASA's space-going employees went to their boss's desk unopened. The day after Bill got back from the *Arrow* crew's send-off down at Glen Springs, he shuffled through the accumulated stack and paused at the small package return-addressed Clarence E. Allaird, Exec Ofcr *Arrow*, c/o etc., etc. "What in the . . . ?"

The cassette's label read "Please see advisory instructions," so Flynn unfolded the sheets of paper. The first gave him an open-ended power of attorney for Allaird's legal affairs, no limits specified. "Now why in the . . . ?"

The other sheet was a letter. The body of the text read:

I hope you never have to use this tape but that you will do so if necessary. Its purpose is evident in its content, which need not concern you unless somebody tries to take legal steps to invade my privacy on the starship Arrow. *If anything of that nature occurs you will recognize it, and I believe the tape will take care of the problem.*

I realize I have no right to saddle you with this mess but I hope you will back me up anyway.

Most sincerely,

The scribbled signature read Clancy Allaird, not Clarence. "Now *who* in the . . . ?" Indecisive, Flynn scowled. Then prudence and the pressure of backlogged obligation overcame his aroused curiosity. He punched a note into his suspense file, Open Date: Redtab, my att'n, any legal action attempted versus *Arrow* Exec Officer C. E. Allaird.

Putting tape and papers back into the container he tagged it Personal Attention Required, for the files.

Then he proceeded on down the stack, to consider matters more vital to the agency, if perhaps less intriguing to himself.

It was some days later that Director Bendixon's call for help caused him to listen to Allaird's tape.

"Daddy!" His touch on her shoulder brought her fully awake. Marnie sat up to hug him. Never mind that by her recalls they had parted only—how long?—three hours ago?— and that she'd slept through most of those; somehow she *felt* the two years they'd both bypassed. "Did I do it right, coming down here?"

"Here is fine. Tell me how you managed." She did, he interrupting now and then with comments. "I should have thought; my spare Velcros would have been too big, but better than nothing,'' and ''That line was *supposed* to be run from the Gate booth to the transfer ring doors.'' But ''supposed to'' never remedied a mistake, his grimace said. ''All right; you did very well. Now then: I've been aboard only a short time; just a few of us had arrived when I left the control deck. So nobody else knows you're here yet. And frankly I've lain awake some, the past two nights, trying to figure a good way to tell them.''

Out in the other room, the intercom peeped. Clancy went to it and Marnie followed. ''Allaird here.''

''Clancy? Dawson. We've got an intruder aboard. Red Alert, I guess you'd call it, if we went in for that kind of thing. But get up here; this could be serious.''

''Captain—uh, I know what's happened. Believe me, there's no threat to *Arrow*. Or to the mission.''

''You'd better be right. Mister—get your ass in gear!''

''To the conference room, if you please, sir. I'll bring the supernumerary myself.''

Well, it did sound better than intruder.

''What in the name of Christ were you *thinking* of?'' For seven solid minutes now, after barely giving Clancy time to introduce Marnie by name, Ellery Dawson had been straining his vocal cords with questions he didn't wait long enough for Clancy to answer. ''You can't just add someone to the roster like that. Daughter or no daughter. And *why*?''

Nicole Pryce, it seemed, had the lowest boiling point. ''Oh for God's sake, Ellery! Why don't you shut up and let him tell you?'' After a few moments' silence, Dawson closed his mouth.

Gathering his thoughts, Clancy started from the beginning. Marnie looked apprehensive, but she needn't; he had no intention of detailing her indignities. The drug use, the neglect, the petty little physical punishments, yes. But his narrative never approached the bathtub. ''. . . increasingly suggestive advances; the pattern was clear. And we know the irresponsibility of that kind of addict. Finally he scared Marnie so badly that she squirted him a faceful of tile spray . . .'' That much was safe enough. ''. . . and ran away.''

Clancy spread his hands. ''The fact was that in the time

available I had no chance at all of securing her safety after I was gone. I can give you chapter and verse if you insist, but we'll save time if you take my word for it.''

He stood. ''I don't see any short fuse on the situation here; I think a decision could well wait until we get the galley into operation. Personally I'm hungry as all hell.''

Whether Dawson agreed or not, everyone else's feet voted with Allaird.

The tall dark-haired woman, the one who'd blown up at Captain Dawson, came up beside Marnie as she followed her dad. ''Hi. I'm Nicole Pryce. Second officer. Welcome aboard.'' And shook hands.

''Marnie Allaird. Well, I guess you heard. Thanks. I wish the captain felt the same way.''

The woman smiled. ''Ellery's a book soldier. Maybe we can bring him around, maybe not. I'll help try, though.''

Clancy turned in midstride to look at her. He seemed surprised. ''I want to thank you, too. I didn't expect . . .''

''I know; I'm sorry. Personal problem. Tell you about it sometime, maybe.''

''Sure, if you want to. I give great listen.''

She laughed, and they went on into the galley area. The problem was that everything there was so well secured against the ten weeks (ship's time) of five gee that unbuttoning the place took quite some time, even with seventeen people working at the chore.

Or maybe *because* it was seventeen. Five or six, Marnie decided, wouldn't get in each other's way so much.

But after a little while there was enough material, food and utensils both, made available for use that three people could begin putting a meal together. Marnie didn't have any more names down straight yet, but the little Asian guy seemed to know his stuff.

When they finally got around to eating, she decided there was no ''seemed to'' about it.

Wanting to stall because he still felt unprepared to back his case, Clancy got Marnie in tow to join him in volunteering for cleanup duty. Whether or not she did any of this at home, or how she may have felt about it there, here she dug in quietly and with competence. Which, now that Clancy thought about it, might make her some points with Captain Ellery Dawson.

If it did, the man gave no sign. No sooner was the last of the clutter put away than he called meeting. "All right, by now we've had time to consider the situation and come to our individual conclusions. My inclination is that unauthorized personnel cannot be allowed to remain on this ship, and that the young lady, charming and amiable though she may be, should be conducted to the Gate and returned to Earth."

He paused. Or, thought Clancy, posed. "But I'm no kind of dictator here. I command, yes. But in cases such as this, not covered in regulations or mission instructions, I'm willing to go with the majority opinion. So unless Mr. Allaird cares to plead his case further, I am prepared to abide by your vote on the matter."

The hell with this; Clancy stood. "Don't bother. I'm done with pleading; I'll give you a choice. Either Marnie stays with me or I resign, here and now, and proceed to the Gate. So that I can stay with *her.*"

He sat again. They could take it or leave it.

I can't let this happen! The thrust of her legs as she stood took Marnie off the deck; she'd forgotten the weak gravity and had to flap her arms to maintain balance. Feeling foolish, she fought embarrassment to blurt out, "Captain sir I know you're in charge and what you say goes, but please listen a minute. First place, nobody on Earth knows I'm here and hasn't asked you if I am. If they do, whenever, you didn't know because I was hid out." He didn't have his protest together yet, so running figures through her head she went on. "I was twelve" (well, almost) "when I got in the Gate. By Earth time I'm fourteen now, sixteen back there if I went into the Gate this minute. Eighteen's legally adult; all I need is two more years, Earth time. That's"—divide by twenty-five—"less than a month on here, and then if I do have to go back . . ."

Dawson's mouth moved but no audible sound came out. Marnie said, "I don't know for sure if a court would grant me adult status or stick to how much time I really lived. But it's a *chance.* So . . ."

She was out of steam before she'd really made her point.

But, "Captain." Nicole Pryce raised her voice. "I move we accept the girl's suggestion, including the part where *we don't know she's aboard* until we have to. And then stall so she can stay here at least this next ship's-month."

The tall brunette looked around the room. "All in favor?"

Dawson could see when he was beaten; he nodded. "Well, if all our *personal* affairs are in order now, I'd like Pryce, Henning, and Jarness to take the watch until 1600, with Benjamin and Velez on call. I'll have the full schedule posted shortly."

As Dawson droned on, reestablishing his mind-set of authority, Clancy Allaird's hug tightened so hard it hurt.

Marnie didn't let on.

"I've asked you people here," said Senator Flynn, "to avoid difficulties all around." He looked at the beefy ex-athlete and the hollow-cheeked blond beauty. "You've heard the taped deposition by Executive Officer Clarence Allaird, concerning his daughter's report of events during the night she left your home. Of itself it doesn't constitute sufficient cause to convene a grand jury, a process which would gratify my colleague, your own senator Delia Stern. A woman who detests sexual exploitation of minors."

Flynn paused to let the idea sink in. Then he said, "The tape won't support prosecution in the absence of Allaird's daughter Margaret. Now I have no idea why you suppose she's somehow spirited herself away through a Habegger Gate onto the starship her father's serving on. But if you were right, and if you succeeded in having her returned here—a process which would take at minimum the four years in Gate lag, over and above the notorious delays in our legal system—I believe you would find yourselves in serious shit."

Seeing their reaction to his abrupt and deliberate descent into vulgarity, Flynn suppressed a smile. The Knapheidts argued a little longer, to save face, but then they left.

The senator's words fell on Celeste Knapheidt like so many whipstrokes; she felt her shoulders hunch against them and tried without success to fight the reaction. It wasn't fair; she hadn't known what Carl was up to. Of course she hadn't *wanted* to know; maybe she'd been too careful not to see. But still . . .

Beside her she saw Carl's face shrink to a wooden mask. Well, he never was any good at standing up to anyone his own size. Biting her lip, Celeste kept silence and tried to hold her own face expressionless. Carl had to say the good-byes; she would only nod, nothing more.

Outside, getting into the car on the driver's side whether Carl liked it or not, Celeste put the key in the slot and paused before turning it. *I'm not through yet. You may think so, you Irish bastard, but I'm not.*

"Terrific, honey. You really were." Back in quarters and serving up hot cocoa in celebration, Clancy tried to reorient himself. Geez; everything happening so *fast*. Well, he'd always been a quick study, so prove it. "Now a few things we have to get straight."

"Such as?" Marnie wasn't being flip; she really wanted to know.

Allaird sorted out priorities. "You don't have any assigned status yet. Like cadet, anything of that sort. So for the time being, just consider that everybody's your boss and go heavy on the polites."

"Christmas at grandma's."

And she was right; Allaird remembered the big dinner at Celeste's mother's, the one time he or Marnie ever met the woman. Whether or not the "aunts" and "uncles" were any such thing, they all assumed parental-type control over the only youngster in the crowd. "Pretty much, Marni Gras. Except that with these folks, at least they know you have a mind on you."

"I hope so, daddy."

Maybe she needed another compliment, but he couldn't seem to sidetrack long enough to find one. Instead, "That's another thing. Here on the ship we're the only two related; we don't want to rub it in. The way it works is, on duty we use job titles or terms of respect. But the rest of the time, except for the captain or anybody else with a tender sense of rank, we get by with first names. So how about, when I'm on watch I'm Mr. Allaird to you the same as I am to everybody else. And bumming around off duty, I'm Clancy."

He saw how it bothered her, and said, "Well hey! In here and just between *us*, I'm still daddy."

Marnie nodded. "Sure, I see how it goes. I can do it."

Clancy began to think this deal might work out after all. If Ellery Dawson could hold still for it without having a litter.

Modifying the quarters for double occupancy was easy; the unit was designed to allow several conformations. For this one the left end of the front room, after two of its bulkheads' first layers were rather laboriously moved out to form partitions, provided a fold-down bed, pullout drawer space, and a closet. An option in the unit's breaker box put the new room's lighting on its own switches.

Some of the unpacked boxes had to be left in the main area for now, crowding its furniture a bit, but Clancy saw Marnie to bed in her own room.

Next day arose a simple utilitarian problem: shoes, the Velcro kind, for zero gee. These were stocked in the proper size for each crew member—but none, not even the so-called "one size fits all" spares on hand in case of underequipped visitors, were small enough for Marnie to wear comfortably.

Finally Clancy trimmed down the soles from a pair of his own shoes and cemented them onto two of Marnie's. The result was a bit nonstandard: all issue models, Velcro or not, had light fabric tops and folded flat to be stuffed into pockets or belt pouches, but Marnie was stuck with noncollapsible footwear.

Still, they worked for now. . . .

Maybe daddy—uh, Clancy—could figure out Captain Dawson's posted watch sked, but to Marnie it made no sense at all. She knew Dawson and Clancy and Nicole Pryce each commanded a watch, that Third Officer Gretel Aaberg was relief watch chief, and that everybody on the ship worked a shift three days out of four. Plus being always more or less on call if needed. But everyone except the four chiefs rotated between watch shifts by some system of Dawson's own devising, and trying to fit it together from the chart he posted was beyond her. He mixed abbreviations with symbols, and used multi-colored styli to draw arrows here and there between them; the

result looked like a playbook sketch on Monday Morning
Football Review.

She herself had now been assigned various part-time duties—which was all right, except that since everything about
her presence here was unofficial, she wasn't listed on the
schedule and was supposed to be kept informed by word of
mouth.

Sometimes it worked, sometimes not. The first day was fine,
helping Supplies Chief Pilar Velez, who doubled as galley
supervisor for her shift, in making an initial inventory checkup
of ship's stores. Velez, a cheerful handsome woman in her
early thirties, climbed and searched and located and identified
the various items. Then she called off code numbers and quantities for Marnie who scrolled to the proper line on the man-
ifest and entered okays or corrections as indicated. Not the
kind of chore Marnie would have thought to be fun, but the
way Pilar whooped when she finally ran down some elusive
line item, it really was. And working in zero gee, learning
how to use the Velcro soles for solid footing, kept Marnie's
interest all through the shift.

Next came Pilar's day off, and Marnie wound up working
with Galley Chief Pierre Larue. "Pete" claimed to be twenty-
five, but looked younger: a dark compact blend of several
Caribbean breeds and hailing from Haiti. An okay guy—but
Clancy was on watch when Marnie woke, and nobody told
her where she was supposed to be until she was an hour late
to be there, so Pete wasn't too happy with her when she did
show up. And while a little kitchen duty was all well and good,
she didn't want to get pigeonholed into that line of work.

"That won't happen," Clancy reassured her, and also promised to ascertain her schedule and keep her posted. "For one
thing, starting tomorrow it's back to school. Part-time, anyway."

"How—?" But after a moment she knew: the ship's computer, how else? She'd taken a few extension courses that way,
back when she and Celeste still lived in the apartment, and
had also kept up with her regular courses the month in the
sixth grade when she was laid up with the persistent virus that
swept the area that fall. In Carl's house, though, nobody got
around to subscribe to the service. "Oh sure," she said now.

"But do you suppose they'll have all that stuff in the data banks?"

"More than any one person could ever use. After all, we're supposed to have all the knowledge the *colony's* going to need. I mean, start with the Library of Congress and take it from there."

But until Clancy assured her that he and others would supply the necessary human input to her studies, she wasn't entirely reassured.

Clancy Allaird's problem was that coming in as an emergency replacement he had too much slack to take up on his own account. When Dawson said he'd assign work for Marnie, Clancy took it for granted that the offer included seeing the girl was informed. Not so, it seemed. Ooh-kay, Allaird could handle it.

And the school thing, too. He could help, coach her on math up to a certain point, and cover most engineering studies. The areas where he was weak—chemistry, for instance, and most of the social sciences except for history—well, out of fifteen other adults there had to be somebody who could chip in on any one of them, if and when the computer data wasn't adequate to Marnie's particular needs.

What he needed to do was get those people feeling friendly enough to *want* to help.

Right now he was doing some boning up on his own account. This ship, he was finding out, held major surprises—differences he hadn't been briefed on. Not just the greater length, the longer flatter-angled forward cone, or the corresponding taper from the central cylindrical section, back to a twenty-meter tail diameter. For example, these things did change the *shape* of the "pencil lead," the Deployment Vehicle that rode front and center, but not its general layout or overall functions.

It was the new stuff that gave him problems. He knew this ship had a narrow lightweight auxiliary belt set behind the residence area and that it could be magnetically speeded up to give a limited one-gee environment, then slowed to match speed with the main one. He hadn't known, for instance, that it carried only one "car," tangential extent about ten meters, or that directly opposite rode a weight which moved in or out according to the car's loading, to keep the rotating mass in dynamic balance. And particularly he hadn't known that by braking to rest with respect to the ship itself, this aux belt could serve as a backup transfer ring, by way of a large slide-away hatch in the car's "ceiling."

Hell, he was still getting used to the regular transfer ring being two levels high and its passenger/freight compartment acting as an automatic elevator between the two. Because on his familiarization tours of *Starfinder* and *Roamer* in high orbit, he'd been used to the ring being all at the outer level and reached by sloping ramps from the control deck, to getting in a car from one side and out the other, to having three stations on each side, not just one as was the case here. He knew this setup had to be an improvement or it wouldn't have been adopted, but sometimes he wondered. Still, now that he thought back, those ramps had been awkward sometimes, moving heavy loads.

Anyway, it was near time he relieved the captain, on watch.

Ellery Dawson had worked long and hard for this job; now at the age of thirty-six, sometimes he almost wished he hadn't. By nature, he knew and accepted, he was an easy-going sort of man. But there's nothing easy-going about command; you have to make decisions yes or no and they'd better be right because they could affect the entire ship. All too often Dawson wasn't sure what the right answer was, and to cope with that recurring situation he'd developed a standard reaction that even he knew was far short of optimum. When in doubt, he got arbitrary: rushed himself into decisions and then stuck to them in spite of hell. Well, not always. But too frequently for his own comfort, let alone best performance.

Dawson knew he was neither stupid nor ill-trained; his records showed him to be above average in every essential respect. But maybe not *enough* above average.

At the moment he waited, along with drive tech Gina Todisco and navigator Chauncey Ng who doubled as a superb cook, to be relieved by Allaird the exec and whichever two of his watch were scheduled for this shift. Allaird worried Dawson: this business of spiriting the child aboard illegally. Well, certainly without any official sanction; laws might have been broken or might not, but regulations had been purely bent to hell.

Dawson had no children of his own, but he could sympathize. Somehow, though, he really didn't. His emotional reaction was on the order of "I feel for you, but I can't quite reach you." Because while Allaird's concern and even his actions were more or less understandable, still they put a conscientious captain in one hell of a bind, and Dawson didn't appreciate it a bit.

Ah. Here came the miscreant now—several minutes early, which Dawson reluctantly had to add in his favor. "Reporting, captain. Anything on the log?"

"Not to speak of. Time and position correlation well within limits." Which meant that the chronometers reading ship's time and the computer-corrected star sightings indicated that *Arrow* was about where the schedule said it should be. And once he'd logged everyone's safe arrival—well, not the child's—and the putting of *Arrow*'s various systems into operation as prescribed, then what else, except such readings, was there to enter?

"That's the best kind." Turning to the others, Allaird seemed to have trouble finding words. "Uh—Todisco, isn't it? And Chauncey. Chauncey Ng, yes—I'll get everybody straight eventually. Anyway, if you want to cut out early, I'll hold the fort until my people show up."

Dawson felt his face go stiff. "Not regulation, Mr. Allaird. You don't dismiss my watch; I do."

Allaird grinned one-sided. "You do, huh? All right, folks, you heard the captain; you're relieved."

Heat and probably redness joined the stiff feeling in Dawson's cheeks. Todisco and Ng were staring; no matter what he said now, he'd look foolish.

He forced a laugh. "That's a good one. Go ahead, you two." As they left, Ellery Dawson fought to relax his fixed smile and stifle the urge to belt Clarence Allaird right in the chops.

Now why, thought Clancy, had he pulled that foolish stunt? Because he'd tried to make a friendly move and Dawson stepped on it? Childish, Allaird, childish! He said, "Hey, I was only kidding, sir. No offense, I hope."

"Of course not." And rabbits lay painted eggs; sure.

But you take what you can get. "Well, good. I'll just log on then, captain." And you can stay or go or do cartwheels.

Sybiljan Baynor came in while Clancy was checking the previous watch's position increment against the average run. Not that there was much of a stretch to compare as yet, but as time passed it would build a fair baseline. He dropped the numbers off the screen, leaving it free for any current data worth noting, and looked up to greet the woman. "Hi, Baynor."

"*Mister* Allaird." Nothing upstage here; she was just being pert. Red-haired Sybiljan was miscast for pert: along with wide-set green eyes her longish face featured high cheekbones flanking a broad, no-nonsense mouth. Striking yes, pert no. But she pulled it off pretty well—or maybe it only seemed that way to Clancy because he liked her. Physical attraction was no part of it, which was just as well; Phil Henning the number two drive ace was spreading figurative pollen all over her, even though she had maybe five years on him.

Clancy looked around to see his other watchmate come in. Coyote Benjamin the native American tribesman, or so he claimed; the name was official on the roster, so Clancy figured it was real. He said "Hi" and guessed Benjamin's mumble to mean about the same.

Dawson stood. In off-duty mode he said, "Hello, Ky. Well, you're all here. See you later." He left, still less surefooted on the Velcros than Allaird would have expected. Short training program?

Baynor and Benjamin sat and belted in at their duty stations, she observing readings from the outside sensors while he ran checks on the drive monitor console. After a time the man rose and went over to the snack cabinet. Removing a Sta-hot plastic bulb of coffee he said, "Anybody else?"

Sybiljan shook her head, but Clancy said, "Light but not sweet, if there's one of those left in there."

"Two more," and he brought one to Allaird before sitting again. "If they could see me now, back on the reservation."

Interested, Clancy said, "Where was that?"

Benjamin laughed. "It's a joke; my people haven't had such a thing for decades. Hell, records got screwed up so bad, back when the privatizing presidents had the Bureau giving everything away, dumping whole tribes onto the nearest Skid Road, that my own family's not quite certain which subtribe we belong to.''

Allaird was shocked, but Coyote looked cheerful enough. ''I get some mileage out of that. Interviewers always ask, and I say Potowatamie. How do you spell it, they want to know. Why, just like it sounds. And there's two different spellings, so no matter what they put down, I can say they're wrong.''

''Jerk *their* strings for a change, huh?''

''Therapeutic, you might say, sir.''

Clancy decided he was going to like this man.

When her father left for watch, Marnie sat at the room's computer terminal and called up listings for the courses she'd planned to take next fall. Though of course that time was actually two years in the past—two and a fair bit over, but she wasn't figuring that closely. Finding the information, she sampled onscreen a few of the recommended texts and decided they looked about right for her. Lab courses were something else; she doubted the ship stocked the necessities for many. And there went the field trips she'd looked forward to. . . .

She moved to shut the terminal down, then paused; there was something she wanted to look up. After a bit of shuffling through directories she found the section she was hunting: *Gates*, and then a subheading *Local Bypass*, which had to be the pair in control. It began:

''So that *Arrow* might decelerate at five Gs without subjecting the crew to such stresses, it was first planned that all personnel simply Gate to Earth and back. However, this method would leave the ship uncrewed for nearly all the last four light-years of its voyage, allowing small timing errors to add up to excessive risk. Provision of back-to-back shipboard Gates cuts such risk to a minimum. Installation has been made at the rear of the control room, giving emerging crew members immediate access to the controls.''

There was more, but Marnie had what she needed so she abandoned the file. A bit of quick calculation showed her that entering the Local about twenty-five ship's days prior to start of decel would allow the crew, on emerging, to clear the five-gee period nicely. And of course a skeleton team could hold off Gating until just before decel began, so there'd be someone to keep tabs on everything right up until that final tenth of a light-year. Satisfied, she turned the terminal to Standby.

And punched up a time check; if she left now she could have an unhurried snack before reporting to Amalyn Tabard the drive chief, a woman she'd barely spoken with.

What her duties for Tabard might be, she had no idea; she changed into a light jumpsuit that fit in with nearly any line of work, and left. In the galley she saw her temporary boss sitting alone, so picked out a varied lunch and brought her tray over.

"Join you, chief?"

Tabard looked up, a thin woman nearing thirty, medium height, most easily identified by the way her frizzy hair bulked to her shoulders. It was the grade of black, Marnie thought, that would show coppery glints in sunlight. Not here, though.

In repose the woman's long narrow jaw bore a fierce look, but her smile dispelled it. "Yes. Sit down, Allaird."

Nothing more, though; for a time, Marnie ate in silence. Then, sipping the last of her herb tea, she said, "What will I be helping with, this shift?" Regarding Traction Drive she knew near to zilch, and said so: she did know that it worked without expelling reaction mass, by pushing against an inertial framework intrinsic to space-time—whatever that meant.

"Nothing to do with the drive, I'm afraid. Not today. One of my other hats covers setting up exercise gear in the full-gee ring. So you can help me tote a bale or two." Tabard was a Britisher, Marnie knew, but except for a slight clipped accent she didn't talk like one.

Well. A full gee, huh? "Are you going to rev it up?"

Tabard's grin was minimal, but at the corners of her eyes came slight crinkles. "Would you like that?"

"Sure." Why not? "Its first test; right?"

"Since launch, yes. Of course they put it through its paces after assembly, while the ship still hung in orbit. But brought it back to rest then, secured to the belt, to save strain on the supporting bearings during acceleration."

As Marnie had guessed regarding the point-three belt itself. "Sure. That makes sense."

The woman stood, so Marnie did also, and followed her.

Once they had their utensils cleaned and put away properly, they went out into the corridor.

The doors at its rear end, where another circumferential passage crossed, looked just like those of the transfer ring forward, and a similar button opened them. Beyond, though, lay a larger space: this compartment ran only a little over three meters front to back, but its lateral, tangential extent was roughly ten. Enough that the curvature made a real difference.

Inside, Tabard punched the doors closed. Unlike the transfer ring's car, this one had a full-fledged control panel. "First," the woman said, "let's slow this thing down. A tenth of a gee is enough to keep our feet on the deck, and moving the gear around will be a lot easier."

Yes; crates placed side by side along the rear bulkhead, with an expansion jack at one end to prevent lateral movement when rotation had been started up. Opening these containers in lightweight was tricky, but Tabard showed Marnie how to brace herself for best leverage. Then, as they were lifting or sliding the various machines out, the superlightness was a great aid.

Although as Amalyn Tabard pointed out, gravity and inertia aren't the same thing at all. A massive object takes as much force to stop it as was applied to get it moving; caution was the watchword, always caution.

But apparatus legs fitted into deck recesses and clamp levers secured them. First along the ends of the place, then as empty crates could be moved, along the rear bulkhead. Sooner than Marnie expected, all the gear was in place; what the few unopened containers held, she had no idea. "We'll let the next watch knock the crates down," Tabard said, "and take them to our Earthgate for disposal." Then, "Or the watch after. No hurry." That was fine by Marnie Allaird. Tenth gee or no, she had a respectable sweat up.

"Thirsty?" Surprisingly, a flattish bag hanging at Tabard's hip turned out to be a canteen.

Marnie took three small swallows, pausing between them. "Thanks, chief." But Amalyn Tabard was at the control panel again, and now the ring accelerated, building ersatz weight. "How do you know when you hit one gee?"

"I don't. But the control circuits do."

After only the few days she'd been aboard, the equivalent

of Earth's gravity settled on Marnie like a load of coal. She flexed and straightened her knees, not far, and felt the strain. "It won't pay to go too long between sessions here, will it?"

"No. There'll be a schedule posted."

"Another one?" Oh, well. Taking it easy at first but then working up to normal exercise level, Marnie had herself a run on one of the stationary bikes and then a spell on a stretch rig, while the drive chief did some workouts of her own. By the time the woman called it quits, Marnie felt up to scratch again.

Moving to the control panel, Tabard said, "Next time we'll get the games equipment out. Or I will, if you're assigned elsewhere."

"Games?"

"Yes. That's why we have all the open space." She smiled. "You haven't lived until you've tried your skills at anisotropic ballistics."

"Wha—" No; think a minute. Anisotropic meant having different properties along different directions. "The spin, you mean. And the curvature."

Tabard blinked. "That's right. Coriolis force and all that, the cross product of two vectors. I can never remember how the equation reads—but if a top's spinning clockwise and you tilt it away from you, it also tilts to the right." The ring was slowing. Not abruptly; Marnie felt no sidewise push at all. But she could feel herself gradually getting lighter.

"Okay," she said, mind on the ballistics topic. "But take bowling, say. If your alley runs straight along the curve . . ."

"Ah, but you have to *hook* your shot." Granted; Marnie nodded. "And imagine billiards on a properly curved 'level' table, like the one in the main belt rec room. Aside from Coriolis deflection the cue ball *weighs* more, going with our rotation, than against it. You'd be surprised how much effective mass can be added or lost, and what it does to momentum exchange on an angle shot. The corrections can't really be calculated; people either find the knack or they don't."

After a moment, Marnie got it: higher velocity at same radius, more centripetal accel, more "weight." And vice versa.

With a minute jar the ring coupled to the belt; in a moment the doors opened. "All right, you're off duty, Allaird. Thank you for helping."

For doing her assigned job? Appreciating the courtesy, Marnie said, ''Any time; I enjoyed it.''

As Tabard went forward toward the common areas Marnie turned aside. The rear transverse passage was a shorter cut home, and a shower was going to be very welcome.

Clancy wished he knew more about the social dynamic aboard ship. He knew that here, as on *Starfinder* and then on *Roamer*, the required group marriage was intended not as a license for promiscuity but a permissive framework in which pairings could be formed or dissolved without need for further legal action.

From what had happened with *Starfinder*'s launch crew—two of them being returned in body bags and a third in restraints—he also knew the setup could be destructively explosive.

So when it came to putting out signals he kept a very low profile, at the same time trying to guess who was with whom and who wasn't. Without actually asking, of course.

Some were obvious but a number weren't, and part of his trouble was that several appeared to be still going through the human equivalent of avian mating dances. Phil Henning and Sybiljan Baynor were one such example, as Clancy had spotted shortly after Marnie arrived at Glen Springs.

It wasn't that he was in a hurry to hook up with anybody, but he was on this ship for keeps, and sooner or later a man could get lonesome. So it made sense to have some idea of who was already committed. Everyone else presumably had a pretty fair grasp of what was what, but coming in late, Clancy didn't. And couldn't ask, really, without looking pushy. Or feeling that way, at least.

The quarters listing was no help. Regardless of who might be sharing rooms *de facto*, officially each crew member had an assigned space. And that's what showed on the room listings.

No getting around it: in this uncharted wilderness of relationships, what Clancy needed was a friendly native guide. Preferably, in his view, a woman already solidly attached, who could give objective, disinterested advice. Someone like Sybiljan, herself still figuratively bobbing and weaving as Henning displayed his feathers, might take a query the wrong way.

And Allaird did *not* want to air his uncertainties to another man.

Third Officer Gretel Aaberg, he knew, roomed with Edd Jarness, the backup pilot/navigator. And just on casual contact she seemed both friendly and discreet. Aaberg worked an odd sked: relieving each of her seniors in turn, she held down a different watch each day. What this routine did to her diurnal rhythms Clancy hated to guess, but from his standpoint the problem was never knowing when he'd be apt to find her in the lounge, say, so he could strike up a talk.

Daydreaming, he nearly missed something on the sensor records he was scanning, covering a period of the ship's un-crewed five-gee acceleration. Late in *Arrow*'s fourteenth day of accel, Clancy noticed. He stopped the tape, backed it up a way, then started forward again at a slower speed: roughly one hour of real time per minute. If ship's time could be called real . . .

And there it was. Off to starboard, glowering with low albedo in the dim light umpteen billion miles from Sol, a huge dirty iceball of a planet.

A *planet*, of all things; who'd have thought it? He rechecked the record's timing and estimated the distances. A long long way past Pluto; well, to go undetected until now, it had to be. And big? Bigger than Jupiter, certainly, but all light elements, way out here. And no magnetic field, or else a very weak one.

All right; he logged the data, priority-tagging the entries to go into the next report for Habgating back to Earth. Just for the hell of it he named his discovery Niflheim; maybe the name would stick, maybe not.

Only when these things were done did he think to call his watchmates over and show them what he'd found. Sybiljan, at least, was suitably impressed. You could never tell about Coyote.

The end of the watch caught Clancy by surprise; the planet had taken all his attention, cost him his sense of time. No matter; he turned to greet Nicole Pryce, but his relief was Gretel Aaberg in Pryce's stead.

Before caution or shyness or inertia could stop him, Clancy stood and said, "Gretel, I'd like to talk with you. When would be a good time? I mean, do you sleep right after a watch, or later?'' *I'm babbling.* "If it's all right, that is." Firmly he made himself shut up, and waited.

Aaberg nodded. "After duty I will eat something, then I could be in the lounge for a time. If this is convenient?''

"Sure. Fine." He waited for the other members of the relief group to report before dismissing his own, then said, "Your watch, Third," and left, picking his way along the corridor and feeling fine.

The transfer ring car was at the belt, so it took the usual twenty seconds to do its half revolution and come to rest. Inside it, as the ring came up to belt speed, Clancy took a deep breath. *Not one of the worst watches I ever stood.*

IV

When Celeste got home from the pleasant lunch she'd had with a few of her old Newsnet chums, Carl was already smooshed out. Looking at him as he lay back in the big, broken-down recliner with his pants not quite buttoned at the waist and his gaze fixed on no part of the real world, Celeste began to get truly pissed.

Living with a rich stud had seemed like a good idea; being married to him, after he sprang that ceremony on her so unexpectedly, even better. Although the why of it still burned; losing Marnie hadn't stopped hurting and maybe never would. Carl would pay for that; just see if he didn't. It was his fault if she'd neglected her daughter. *If* she had; she wasn't admitting anything. For all Celeste knew, maybe Carl had kept her doped on purpose, so she couldn't interfere with his moves. And she'd get Marnie back, some way she'd do that. But meanwhile . . .

Meanwhile the stud spent most of his time petrified, and all too often right when she really wanted him up and alive. Especially up. And rich didn't mean all that much when damned little of it ever came her way.

Not for the first time, Ada Celeste Malcolm Allaird Knapheidt began rethinking her options.

It was entirely possible, she thought, that Carl could just plain go piss up a rope. With a little help . . .

Refreshed, Marnie put on smooth-soled loafers and took a stroll to the galley. It wasn't her regular mealtime yet, but the work and other exercise had her faunching for a snack anyway.

One trouble with this ship was always needing two kinds of footwear, which meant returning to quarters to change shoes every time she left or entered the low-gee belt. Well, she didn't exactly *have* to, coming in, but Velcro soles didn't feel right on a smooth deck, and wearing them here wasn't recommended if you wanted them to last.

Not for the first time Marnie wished the ship had some of the light foldup shoes, of both types, in anything near her size. What she could use, she decided, was some kind of small totebag to keep her spares in. Her travel kit was much too big to lug around all the time. Maybe Supplies had something that would work; she'd have to ask Pilar.

Velez wasn't running the galley this shift; Chauncey Ng had that duty. In his usual cheerful way he returned her greeting, and gave her a glass of milk to go with the small bowl of spicy stew he dished up. "Keeps the fire down," he said, and grinned.

As Marnie looked around, wondering where to sit, Ptiba Mbente beckoned to her. Marnie knew the black woman hardly at all, but so far the DV commander/pilot seemed pleasant enough.

Uh-oh; how should she be addressed? Walking over, in her mind Marnie tried one version after another; nothing seemed to fit. Arriving, she said, "Shall I join you—uh, commander?"

Mbente laughed. "Commander's only a function; the official job title is DV *specialist*. But I like to keep things simple: last names on duty and first names in our free time. Even though both of mine are a little hard for Euros and Yanks to pronounce. Yes, do sit down, Marnie. I want to talk with you."

"Fine." Marnie did, and began eating. The stew was hot, all right, but hardly a throat-scorcher. "What about?"

"Sleep. You've just done a stint with Amalyn Tabard so you're off duty for a while. I'd like you with me tomorrow, but not on this same shift. The one before it, about ten hours from now. Can you fit your sleep in all right?"

"Sure." The small bowl was finished; Marnie did the same for the milk. "I mean, that's my assignment, I expect?"

"Yes. And with an adult I'd take it for granted. But—"

"Sure." Her answers were getting in a rut. "As long as I know ahead of time. It's just that I'm not on the roster, and sometimes nobody tells me soon enough."

"No." Mbente smiled. "So I'm glad you came in just now. I left word on your terminal, but people don't always check."

To the raised eyebrows Marnie had to admit she hadn't. Then her curiosity took over. "Ptiba? Will we be going into the Deployment Vehicle? I'd like to see it."

"That's the idea. What with getting everything else in order, this will be my own first chance to have a look. Well, since the final in-orbit lecture tour—and that was nearly two years before liftaway; quite a lot of the equipment wasn't installed yet."

"According to Chief Tabard, the full-gee belt was working then. Was the DV behind schedule?"

"Not exactly. On hold, more like, for some late-blooming design changes. First it was waiting for the complete new specifications; then it took time to round up what wasn't included on the original specs' lists of materials."

Mbente shrugged. "There was no hurry. All it meant was that I haven't seen the finished product yet."

"But we will tomorrow; right?"

"Indeed." The woman looked up; her expression showed pleasure. "Hello, Ky. Watch over?"

Coyote Benjamin smiled at them both. "Yes. And Mr. Allaird—your father himself, young woman—running through the accel-time sensor tapes, found us a brand new planet."

Fascinated, Marnie stayed to hear the details. Of course she'd get them straight from Clancy later, too, but still . . .

She didn't fail to notice that the two held hands.

*   *   *

Coming off watch, Clancy Allaird took his first exercise stint on the full-gee belt. Sybiljan went with him, and at the doors they found Pete Larue just entering; all three put in a strenuous half hour before calling it quits. When Clancy returned to quarters, Marnie wasn't in.

He checked for messages: Mbente wanted the girl to accompany her—and probably an adult assistant—on a DV checkout, a couple of watch shifts from now. Gretel Aaberg begged off from their meeting in the lounge, specifying no reasons and requesting a rain check. "Name a time or two that would be convenient for you, and I'll leave word. If we don't meet sooner." All right.

And Captain Dawson wanted to talk with his first officer; the words indicated no hurry but the voice tones sounded anxious.

No matter; Allaird munched some cheese and crackers to tide him over, then showered. When he came out of the bath booth, Marnie was home. "Hi, dad. Tell me about the new planet."

So she'd already heard about it; he filled her in anyway. "Niflheim, you named it?" she asked. "Frost giants, right? Loki was one, on his mother's side."

Not for the first time, Marnie's store of miscellaneous knowledge impressed her father. He chuckled. "He'd freeze his keister on this one." Then he sobered. "Dawson wants to see me. Cross your fingers."

"It doesn't have to be—I mean, it could be *anything*."

"Let's hope so."

As he left the rooms, Allaird thought *I still have an ace nobody's mentioned yet*. Or knew of one, at any rate . . .

"Get me there, get me there, come on goddamn you Carl, *get me there*!" Too doped for good coordination, still Knapheidt wasn't holding her back from orgasm so much as Celeste herself was. Her goal now was strategic advantage, not physical satisfaction; savaging him with words she kept both Carl and herself off-balance.

Until she outlasted his waning stamina and he lay panting, wilted, unable to continue. Then she pushed; he slumped off to one side and she wriggled free. Giving him no time to get any breath back, she leaned close and spat her words. "You're no good, Carl. No good fucking and no fucking good. About as useful as tits on a frog. Why I put up with you . . .''

He reared up; she was getting to him. ''Whatsamatter, lard-ass? Maybe you're on the wrong end of the prong. Why don't you find yourself a good stud to shoot some *man* into you?''

And that did it. Mouth gaped in a snarl he came at her, swung, missed, swung again, fell over.

Hell, she'd need him to do better than that. Bare-toed, she kicked, catching him under the ribs where it hurt. He let out a strangled roar and scrambled to his feet again. One hand caught her hair, the other smashed at her face: clubbing blows to the cheek, eye, jaw, nose; then, as she tried frantically to pull free, a solid punch full in the mouth.

She felt a tooth splinter free; pain almost blinded her.

Too much! She had to get loose; he'd kill her. Desperately Celeste jabbed fingers at his eyes; when he squinched them shut and turned his head away she braced herself to kick a double field goal but lost balance and brought them both down.

One arm was pinned under her; with the other she reached for his crotch. Even now she knew she mustn't injure him badly; it could wreck her case. One hard squeeze, one jerk; when she heard his blubbery roar she tore loose, stood up and staggered back.

Panting, she looked at her rich husband and wiped blood from torn lips. This should do it. She walked away.

Sitting in Carl's study, facing the door just in case, on the phone she said, ''Maurice? I'll be in your office in an hour. Have a notary there. And a camcorder; I need pics *now*.'' The missing tooth gave her sibilants an unnerving hiss.

When the lawyer quit asking irrelevant questions long enough to agree, Celeste said, mumbling through rapidly swelling lips, ''This divorce is going to *skin* Carl Knapheidt. Handle it right, Maurice, and you can afford one of your own.''

''Captain. I got your message.''

Holding the door open, Dawson smiled; it didn't cover his obvious tension as he said, ''Ellery; all right? We're off duty now, Clancy. Come in, come in. Drink?''

Captain's digs weren't as flossy as Allaird expected. Bigger, yes, but much the same decor and furnishings as his own. "Uh, sure. A beer would be nice." And what's on your mind?

Surprising him, Dawson offered the cold beer in a zero-gee plastic squeeze bulb. Clancy laughed. "I didn't know they had beer in this packaging."

"How did you do on *Jovian*, then? The first one, wasn't it?"

"Without." Dawson's brows raised. "We didn't have any."

"Oh." The man's lips pursed; sure enough, he was working to get down to it. Whatever it was. "Our first Gatings to the other ships. *Starfinder* and *Roamer*. What do you think, Clancy? Should we send just our bare log: roster, sensor observations to date, all that? Or do up some vidcap greetings, something more personal? I don't know what's customary, you see, and . . ."

This was all? Sipping the cold, tangy brew, Allaird stifled a smile. "Well now, Ellery . . ." Ellery; it had a nice ring to it. ". . . seems to me there's no hurry either way. *Starfinder*, for instance, wasn't originally equipped with extra, intership Gates; that idea came later. So they may have theirs up and ready pretty soon or they may not. And so far as I know, ours won't send until theirs are operationally prepared to receive."

"Yes, I know that. We have test samples in place and our Transmit switches on; when the samples go, we're in business."

"Well, then," said Clancy. "There you are. And I still doubt there's any rush—not with us at twenty-five to one, compared to their ten."

He sipped again; as he'd noticed in his own supplies, the agency was definitely stocking tasty stuff. "As to what you decide to include, yes I think the personal touch would be appropriate. You in particular onscreen with greetings, for instance. And if you like, others may want to contribute."

Clancy gestured. "I'd say decide at leisure, figure out the kind of presentations you really want to make. Ellery."

After a moment, Dawson nodded. "I think you're right. Thanks, Clancy." He leaned forward. "Now tell me about this planet you spotted on the recordings. I want to look through that part myself soon, but I haven't had time yet."

So while he nursed his beer to its inevitable end, Allaird filled his captain in on the newest addition to the solar system.

Back in quarters when he told Marnie about the visit, they both laughed. More, perhaps, than the incident really warranted.

Unlike *Arrow* itself, where all decks were the inner surfaces of cylinders, the Deployment Vehicle's single control deck was a flat circular cross section, ten meters in diameter, sitting at the halfway point of the spacecraft's thirty-meter nose cone. It made sense, Marnie knew; in operation all effective gee forces would push rearward, thus *down*, here. Now, in zero gee, she appreciated the Velcro surfacing.

She had remembered to ask Pilar Velez about a totebag, and sure enough, Pilar found her one. The strap fastener was a little loose, but mostly worked well enough. So now, going back and forth between zero gee and the belt, she always had her spare shoes with her and was ready for either kind of footing.

After a quick breakfast Mbente led Marnie, along with Eli Mainz, the DV backup pilot, by the "quick'n'dirty" route. Not bothering with spiral ramps or even the fancy swingdown model in the clear space just behind the DV in the ship's central cylinder, by means of handlines and trapdoor ceiling panels she'd brought them directly inship past the decks of control equipment and crew supplies, into the central cylinder itself. Twenty meters was considerable inside diameter—yet somehow the tighter curvature, compared to outship, made it claustrophobic.

Only a thin forward slice—five meters, maybe—was clear of structural members. Behind lay the central holds filled with destination cargo, the primary fuel tanks, and the Traction Drive itself. Near the hatchway where they emerged, a sort of tunnel led back toward the drive rooms. It wouldn't be the only one.

Enough looking. Using handholds on the forward bulkhead, Ptiba Mbente led the way toward its center; there she opened a small inset hatch, leaving the larger cargo doors closed. Once through, the three found themselves in a dimly lit space facing the DV's rear. Its own personnel entrance lay centered within the triangle of landing legs folded against the hull's stern, and opposite each leg protruded a drive node.

Here no line extended. Mbente pushed off across the gap,

caught handholds on the DV, and opened its own outer door before motioning anyone to join her. Inside that door was another; the two formed an airlock. Beyond the second lay a long tunnel, wider than Marnie considered really necessary but well equipped with handholds, all the way forward to the DV control deck.

Near the safety-railed tunnel mouth sat fully instrumented acceleration couches for two pilots and a communicator, facing across the opening to the large forward viewing screen mounted directly opposite. Smaller, nearer peripheral screens covered side and rear views. "Rear's important," Mbente said, "because at destination, tail down is how we land. It'll pay to be able to see what's there to land on. So at that point, we switch the big screen to rear coverage."

She pointed out food facilities along the curving wall beyond the large screen and also, directly behind the operating positions, a pair of latrine cubicles with a small shower enclosure between them. "As far apart as possible, eating and elimination. For psychological reasons, no doubt." She gestured toward the bare, segmented wall arcs between. "Along there, each side, five double-deck fold-down accel couches for passengers. Plus one double each side of the johns. This little beast can crank up to three gees in a pinch. Just one's our normal preferred push, though."

Eli Mainz cleared his throat. A short, chunky young man whose darkly whiskered chin and cheeks never looked cleanshaven even when they were, this morning he hadn't said much. "Are those johns zero-gee or regular?"

"Convertible. And the shower only operates under thrust, a half gee or more." Having answered, Mbente said, "Let's strap in and run tests." As Marnie looked a question the woman added, "Just follow instructions; it won't be difficult. You sit copilot this time; Eli, you take Comm."

Mainz nodded. As all three buckled down snugly to their couches, Ptiba said, "To test our drive circuits safely, we go to Virtual Thrust mode. That's on your console, Allaird: the green knob, upper right. Turn it clockwise 'til it locks. The button in its center unlocks it, so don't until I say so."

"Locked," said Marnie. And then, "What's Virtual Thrust, anyway?"

Pausing in the middle of what seemed to be an activation

sequence, Mbente said, "We change the phase relationship between component fields. So that power can be applied and adjustments made without producing any actual push, and still demonstrate that everything works."

"I see. Thanks."

In a few minutes Mbente was done. "Shutting down." And when the power drain meters read zero, "Unlock Virtual."

Marnie did, and reported it done.

Next Mbente said, "Forward screen on," and Eli Mainz did things at his own console. The big screen lit. Mbente asked for various degrees of magnification, for the limited shift of view Mainz could obtain by swinging to add more sensor inputs at one side of the main array and dropping some at the other, for spectrum shifts in the displayed signal. . . .

"Now we're seeing by long infrared; notice how some of the dim stars light up?" And apparently as an afterthought, "We don't have radio astronomy capability, like the rig in ship's control; an in-system Vehicle has no real use for it." Then, "Okay, back to normal," and she called up side and rear views.

Nothing much showed, of course; those sensors were looking at the surrounding cylinder of *Arrow*'s own structure. But there were, facing each sensor, patterns outlined in small lights. "Just so we can make sure they're all working."

And that they were. Then and throughout the testing, Marnie Allaird became more and more impressed. Especially when Ptiba mentioned that although the DV lacked Habgates, its tanks held enough fuel to go from well past Pluto's orbit to Earth, land, take off, and return to its starting point. A little bucket like *this*? Well, relatively small . . .

"Do you suppose—could I learn to pilot the Vehicle?"

Mbente considered, then nodded. "On Simulations, yes. There'll be plenty of time for that. But no chance to put those skills into actual practice, as Eli and I did on the training vessel. Including actual landings and liftoffs."

It was better than nothing. "Thanks. I'm looking forward to it. Then maybe at destination . . ."

"Maybe."

They didn't eat aboard the Vehicle. By the time they reported in to the captain, who had the watch, and then got back to the low-gee belt, Marnie's appetite verged on actual hunger.

*   *   *

Carl couldn't believe it. First, still so zookered he wasn't sure any of it was real, he'd been hauled out of his own house in handcuffs and locked in a grungy cell. Then, when he'd come down enough for withdrawal pangs to hit, he was rousted out to sit at a table facing Celeste, Maurice Fitzhugh—the lawyer she'd used to axe Clarence Allaird—and a female judge.

"What *is* this?"

"Shut up and listen," said the swollen-faced gargoyle Celeste. "When it's your turn to talk, we'll tell you."

Carl wanted to get out of jail and stay out, so when that time came he said mostly "Yes." Yes she could have the divorce uncontested. Yes she could have the chalet. Yes she could have the beach compound. Yes she could have—god-*damn*it, Celeste!—forty percent of his net assets, down from fifty which was her first demand, and not over and above the previous stuff but including it; well that's all right then. And, but still part of the forty, the Rolls and the this and the that and the other.

And yes he promised never to go near Margaret Clarisse Allaird ever again in his entire life, so help him eight to twelve in the slammer because he'd got mixed up and signed what Celeste handed him to sign, which turned out to be a "confession" she wrote herself, in his name. Or maybe Maurice wrote it.

Carl kept trying to say he was supposed to have a lawyer of his own here, but when they were finished with him there'd been no criminal charges filed, just civil actions agreed to under threat of criminal prosecution. And it was his word against theirs, so he'd never prove anything even if he had the nerve.

Celeste's marred grin displayed perhaps the most expensive dental gap of modern times.

Quite inadvertently Clancy put together a little more of the ship's social jigsaw. Having occasion to ask Amalyn Tabard about a fluctuation in Number Three drive node's exciter stage, after watch he stopped by her quarters and found Ellery Dawson there also. Clancy thought nothing of it until he noticed Dawson's obvious embarrassment, and that after a few moments his unease was rubbing off on Tabard. "Well look,

Amalyn,'' Allaird said, ''it's nothing serious. I just wanted to let you know, so you can take a reading, next chance you get.''

He turned to leave. ''See you later, folks.'' Tabard said something reasonable; the captain only mumbled. Outside, Clancy wondered why the skipper acted so high school; certainly he and the drive chief had every right to pair up if they wanted to.

Gretel Aaberg set him straight. In the lounge, lower-ceilinged than most of the belt, they finally sat to talk; haltingly, between sips of an after-watch cooler, Clancy spelled out his problem, what little he knew and how much he didn't. Then he told her what he'd just run into at Tabard's quarters. ''Why, d'you suppose, the tight collars?''

Aaberg shook her head; sleek blond hair, tied back at the nape, shone in the dim lighting. ''Breakups and realignments, always awkward. Even difficult. Couples mutating into new ones. What you walked into, Allaird, was the consolation round.''

Oh boy. ''You mean, they both got dropped?''

''Yes. Pete and Gina are the star-crossed ones.''

Time for a headshake of his own. ''Hard to figure.''

''People often are; have you not noticed? And really, Gina's too young for our commanding officer; she's barely twenty.''

''You've got a point.'' Though Edd Jarness had to be around fifteen years older than Gretel Aaberg. In his head he ran the list of what else he knew. Henning-Baynor, Benjamin-Mbente on the impression Marnie reported. And now, Dawson-Tabard and Larue-Todisco. Leaving . . .

''Okay, who else?''

''It is hard to know. I *think*, Chauncey Ng with Pilar Velez and Eli Mainz with Estella Holms. But sometimes I feel it may finalize the other way around.''

''Leaving Nicole Pryce,'' said Clancy, not waiting for her to run through the rest of the list. So Cal Ledbetter had been *her* guy. Which might explain her initial surliness toward Ledbetter's replacement. Or might not; he didn't want to ask.

Aaberg said, ''That is correct, Allaird. Nicole is the only woman yet unattached. Whether she remains so is up to you.''

''Not entirely.'' Clancy stood. ''Thanks, Gretel. Coming in

at the middle hasn't been too comfortable; I appreciate your help.''

Smiling, she nodded acknowledgment as he left.

All her life, nothing ever came easy for Ada Celeste. Ada she was first called, before her father left and then while her mother Lenora lived with a succession of men, some few of whom she married without regard to preexisting legal ties.

There were nearly as many cities as men; thinking back, Celeste was sure of eight by name but knew there'd been more, spread from one coast to the other with stops between. The one she left all by herself, at fifteen, was Indianapolis. The man was Durward Blaine who talked with his fists more than not, and the bigger stepbrother was Alvin who knocked her down and made his best try to hold her there and screw her, like it or not, but was lucky if he ever screwed *anybody* from then on.

After what she did to Alvin she didn't dare stay around and face Durward. The other stepbrother, Boodie, was pretty much her size, Ada Celeste being skinny and all. So with Alvin shoved into a closet and the door jammed shut she put on some of Boodie's clothes and in about ten minutes gave herself near enough to a boy haircut, and from Alvin's pants which he'd taken off she swiped his ID card which the picture looked like anybody with any face at all, and with it the wad of Alvin's money from dealing scat down at the park, nights.

She looked for her mother's cashstash but hadn't found it when she heard somebody coming in and went out the back fire escape toting just the one shopping bag stuffed with some of her own clothes. Needing away in a hurry she cut through an alley and then over to the Avenue where she got lucky and caught transit downtown.

An hour later she was on board Greyhound to the Coast and no real trail behind. A month after that she was working afternoon cocktail waitress at the Irreverent Oyster, with bright red curly hair and the best ID money could buy, under the name of Celeste Malcolm. Malcolm was risky, but Lenora hadn't used it for years and might have even forgotten.

Besides: what the hell? Indianapolis was a long way from here.

Always a quick learn, Celeste picked up fast on how to talk, how to act, what to stay clear of. Floria on swing shift wanted to recruit her for a hooking partner but she knew bad odds when she saw them and declined without prejudice. Three years and two jobs later, when she met Clancy Allaird, Celeste's experience with men consisted mostly of about a year lived with Stavros who pumped iron and kept canaries. Sweet guy, Stavros, even if his blood had to be at least half garlic.

She'd dated other guys, of course, before and after Stavros—even during, sometimes. But Clancy was different. A *spaceman*. And, Celeste realized quickly, her ticket out of the hustle. She married him and lived with him and maybe even loved him for a while, such as when she let herself stay pregnant and birthed Margaret Clarisse. Overall, probably the most content period of her life. She even found a respectable and rewarding line of work to fill out the slow spots; at Newsnet she was considered a comer. And liked it.

She had a bad scare one time when she went to do a background interview and the woman with the hot tip (which didn't pay off, after all) turned out to be her mother. Fifteen years or so hadn't treated Lenora too badly; she was married now to a construction boss named Parker, got along well with his rather large family, and didn't seem to be holding any grudges. Maybe she'd had enough trouble with the Blaines, herself, to figure that Alvin deserved what he got.

With misgivings, Celeste accepted her mother's invitation for the Allairds to join her and her new family for Christmas dinner. Except for the tendency of all the Parkers to take the role of surrogate parents when it came to bossing Marnie around, it went fairly well. Still, Celeste was relieved when Parker's next job was overseas. A few months later she received a plaintive note from the man; Lenora had left him, and he was wondering if Celeste knew where she was.

Celeste didn't; further, she didn't want to. Thankfully, she settled back into her comfortable routines.

But the trouble with spacemen is, they get sent places without their families. Living with Clancy taught Celeste to like sex. She hadn't, much, before; maybe it was the garlic. So when he was gone she drifted into the habit of straying just a little; actually, when she thought straight about it, the term was slutting up a storm.

For the first time in her life Celeste felt guilty about something. Alone at nights she had imaginary arguments with Clancy, defending herself on grounds she knew wouldn't hold up.

This went on a long time, while Marnie grew from infancy into childhood. It got especially bad when Clancy went on *Jovian*. She dreaded his return; surely someone would betray her to him.

When he did come back, and the tabloids printed the stuff about this woman writing a book telling how Clancy and the other men had her as a sex slave, Celeste went apeshit and struck first. She went to this lawyer Maurice Fitzhugh and he took it from there. Maurice looked like a vulture and it fit.

She hadn't planned to take Clancy for most of what he had, just keep him on defensive and herself safe from accusations. But it got out of hand. And there she was alone with Marnie and the child support payments she didn't really need, plus a job that suddenly wasn't so much fun any more.

For some years, then, her life experience was on the marginal side; she'd tie up with someone for a while but it never took. When she fell for a guy ten years younger and he threw her over, she sort of came apart for a while there.

That was when Carl showed up: a big rich ex-jock who could show you a good time out of any baggie in his briefcase. He was a distraction from her malaise and she accepted gratefully. She knew she was overdoing but somehow her brakes were shot.

Now it had all gone to hell. Carl was history, Marnie had vanished. What Celeste did have was a lot of money and the freedom to act without asking anybody.

It had taken a long time for her and Maurice to penetrate the obstacle course of the government's legal maze and get what she needed, but now she was primed and ready.

So when Senator Flynn insisted on seeing her about the court order she'd obtained, entitling her and her lawyer and a U.S. Marshal to board the starship *Arrow* and bring back one Margaret Clarisse Allaird, a minor, Celeste wasn't worried one damn bit.

She let him have his say, then answered, "Carl Knapheidt is no concern of mine; I don't care if you hang him. And I have his deposition on file, stating that any offenses he committed were done without my knowledge. So if that's all, I'll be on my way to Glen Springs. For starters."

He waved her away; as she left she heard him saying on his intercom, "Get me the Gate Center. I need to put a message through. I'll dictate a letter to follow."

And a fat lot of good it'll do you.

The changed design of *Arrow*, tapering to a twenty-meter width of stern rather than maintaining a fifty-meter diameter all the way back, eliminated the annular cargo space which held the earlier ships' macroGate components,

The large ring-shaped macroGates, placed in orbit at each destination to pair with their near-Earth counterparts, were built to Gate *ships* between stars. Thus, second and third stage explorations could be mounted, losing the crews no subjective time in reaching the latest jumpoff point.

Arrow carried the makings; they were deployed differently, was all. Externally, in the form of twelve longitudinal fins, rounded slightly at the outer corners and faired smoothly to the hull's contours. Beginning near the forward rim of *Arrow* proper where it joined the DV's conical nose, these fins curved back sixty-eight meters, past the cone-cylinder interface to roughly midway of the cylindrical section. At destination, first the forward ends would be levered free of the ship and swung to hinge together in pairs. Then, in precise sequence, adjacent pairs would be freed at the rear and joined to form what would unfold into a circular construct, each fin providing thirty degrees of arc, and large enough for even an ill-aimed ship to pass safely.

The finer points of assembly puzzled Clancy, but he had faith that it would all work as intended. Meanwhile the fins, piercing the interstellar gas at the speed *Arrow*'s drive maintained against that gas's friction, helped to stabilize the ship's flight.

Why all this especially mattered to Allaird right now was that Captain Dawson assigned him to accompany two of *Arrow*'s Gate specialists on an inspection of one such fin. "We'll need to check them all eventually," Dawson said, "but one at a time is enough work between regular watches."

So when Nicole Pryce had breakfast following her post-watch sleep, Clancy and Eli Mainz joined her for coffee. Then they proceeded to a hatch marked "Hull Access," one of three on the control deck level. Each opened into a radial passageway, skirting the tapered forward water storage tank, before emerging into a short circumferential corridor just inside the hull, serving its own group of four adjacent fins.

Pryce and Mainz, Allaird saw, each wore belt-slung tool kits. Was he supposed to have one? Apparently not; "I guess we're ready to go" and Nicole punched buttons to open the hatch.

Once through it, Clancy was relieved to find that the designers hadn't skimped on handholds; with all the inevitable changes of orientation, this was no job for Velcro.

Pryce led; Clancy held back, granting Mainz second place in line as they emerged into a structure roughly ten meters square in overall cross-section, curving nearly twenty-three meters sternward and at least twice that forward. A meter or so in from the segment's outer bulkhead lay the completed main deck; aided by handlines, the three went to it.

The overall layout wasn't apparent immediately; the lighting, when Pryce found the switches, left much to be desired, and a skeleton of structural members crisscrossed the interior. All in all, Clancy's first impressions were more confused than not.

Eli Mainz laughed. "You give some people a Bild-it set, they go crazy."

"The compartment dividers go in later," said Pryce. "Now let's see where this segment's Gate generator units are. That's mainly what we're here to check."

If you say so. Thankful that here at least there was Velcro, Clancy followed her in dutiful fashion to a wall-mounted equipment console, then watched the two run a checklist he understood not at all. They seemed satisfied, though, and he figured they knew their business. Next the second officer directed Mainz to go in turn to the various equipment positions spaced along the fin's arc, and from each to transmit test signals and verify receipt of those she sent in return.

That routine and variations on it continued for several hours. Standing around with little or nothing to do bored hell out of Clancy, but he did his best to look both interested and cheerful. When Mainz wrapped up his final checkpoint, Nicole said, "That's all we need here, for this time. I have a few more notes to take, but you can go on inship if you like, Eli.''

"I think I will; thanks."

As the man monkeyed his way back along the line to the open hatch, Allaird fought his own version of stage fright. Sooner or later he had to talk with Nicole Pryce. But was now the right time? And what, and how much, should he try to say?

It didn't happen. By the time he worked up his nerve to try an opening, they were on their way back inship and she was nearly due to go on watch.

While no one was paying attention, the intership Gates came active. *Roamer*'s first, according to the indicators, but *Starfinder*'s not much later. In each case a packet appeared in the respective Tush; both ships sent capsuled logs plus some miscellaneous material: greetings, commentary, and so forth.

So one day, following Clancy into the lounge, Marnie was in time to see and hear Ellery Dawson recording his own greetings. ". . . old lines to you people by now, I suppose, but still new to us. Sometimes, looking out there, I'm too thrilled for words. Why, just seeing that new planet . . ."

Anyone too thrilled for words, Marnie thought, always had the option of shutting up and maybe should. As though she'd spoken aloud, Dawson looked at her and Clancy, then cut off recording. "That's my fifth try, Allaird; I still can't get it right." Self-consciously he said, "Want to see my latest?"

Clancy nodded. "Sure. Take it from the top."

So the captain punched up the screen and there he stood, stiff smile and all. "Greetings to you who have gone before us." It began creaky and took a time to ease off, but after a few minutes Ellery Dawson was well into showing his goshwowboyoboy side, culminating in his confession of excess thrill and the abrupt cutoff. "What do you think? So far, I mean."

Soberly Clancy nodded. "Reads fine by me. Why don't you tell 'em a little about Niflheim, wish 'em well, and wrap it up?"

"But they'd know, wouldn't they? I mean . . ."

"Both those ships' courses are at wide angles from ours; neither of them went any closer to that big rock than Earth does. Not a chance they could have spotted it."

"Oh well, then . . ." Seemingly heartened, Dawson began to turn on his rig, then paused. "Look, Clancy; why don't you do the description? You noted it all down, and I haven't really familiarized myself thoroughly."

"Okay. I'll get my notes from control. You go ahead and do your windup; we can dub my part in where it fits."

With nothing better to do, Marnie followed her dad down to zero gee. As they neared the control room, a woman emerged from the cross corridor at the rear and came walking toward them.

A stranger.

V

"**W**hat the—?" Startled, Clancy came to a halt. The woman approaching him, towing a bulky carryall bag, was a little under medium height, slender, with short curly red-brown hair. As she came closer he saw she was older than he'd first thought, somewhere in her late forties. And smiling.

He stepped forward again, to reach the door to control before she did. "Excuse me? I don't—"

Only a few paces away, she paused. The smile vanished. "Weren't you expecting me? I put word in the initial message bundle. On *Roamer*. Didn't anybody read it?"

Damn Ellery! "I thought the captain had. Look—I'm Clancy Allaird. First officer. Welcome aboard."

He held out his hand; she reached to shake it, and the sight of hers, missing the forefinger, stirred his memory before she said, "Anne Portaris. Sorry to be the bad penny, but . . ."

Finger or not, her grip was solid. "Not your fault. Here, let me take that bag for you. Come on into control; I'll get on intercom and twist the skipper's tail for you. He's been . . ."

Preoccupied? Stewing over making a good impression with his greeting capsule? ". . . busy."

She laughed, a light sound showing more good humor than real amusement. "Aren't they always? Lead on . . . Clancy."

Anne Portaris. Three-fingered Annie—only don't ever call her that where she can hear you. This woman, along with her husband Haal Arnesson, had invented the Traction Drive! Face-to-face with one of her heroes, a real legend, Marnie ran more than a little short in the breath department. "Ms. Portaris? I'm Marnie Allaird." And she too shook the maimed hand. "It's a pleasure—I never thought I'd *meet* you . . ."

"Nor I you. But I share the pleasure." The tone was dry, yet somehow Marnie didn't feel she was being made fun of. Portaris raised an eyebrow. "Aren't you a bit young for ship's crew duty? Or perhaps I've been out longer than I thought."

Out? To space, yes. At a loss, Marnie sought for words. Clancy saved her. "My daughter, Ms. Portaris; no official status as yet." As yet? That sounded good. . . . But, "Long story, I'm afraid. And now you'll be wanting to meet the captain."

After a few brief words at the control intercom, Allaird led the way to the transfer ring doors.

Ellery Dawson, Anne decided after less than five minutes, was earnest, self-conscious, insecure, and a bit stuffy; all in all, though, she liked him more than not. ". . . frightfully pleased you're aboard . . . terribly sorry . . . been meaning to read through that lot; you know how it is . . . utmost admiration . . . your contribution to star travel . . ."

And how long did you spend on *Roamer*? And how far out are they by now—or, rather, when you left? She had to say hardly anything at all, really, and after the hubbub of her going-away party on *Roamer*, less than a subjective hour ago, she found the drone of Dawson's voice quite relaxing.

Then came a mealtime. Being out of sync for this ship, Anne wasn't very hungry. What she did welcome was having the rest of her luggage brought downship via the belt and then being escorted along with it to her assigned billet. The VIP suite, she was told, and certainly it fit the label. *Roamer* boasted nothing like this!

At any rate, sleep was exactly what she could use.

The little Allaird girl had wanted to talk, Anne could see that. But there'd be plenty of time. . . .

Back in quarters, Marnie had an hour or so to spare before reporting for a spell of galley duty. Clancy was studying something in hard copy, so the computer was free; she sat down to catch up on the math she'd been scanting lately.

Differential calculus made sense: y-plus-delta-y equaled a function of x-plus-delta-x; what you wanted, the derivative or rate of change, was the value of their quotient as delta-x approached zero. You could set it up onscreen and work it out—the simpler cases at least—and seeing how your answers fit what the text said gave you confidence in the parts that were too complicated to derive the hard way.

But integral calc? It was all there in the Table of Integrals, except sometimes you had to fudge some fancy substitutions to make it work—but how did anybody ever derive those tables in the first place? Just differentiate everything under the sun until you came up with what you wanted?

Letting out a breath of exasperation, she put her mind on hold and searched through the tables for an example that applied.

The hour passed quickly; she closed out, stood, and stretched. "Gotta go, daddy; I'm due in the galley."

"Mmm." He waved a hand but didn't look up. Concentration.

Going into the galley she met Eli Mainz and Estella Holms coming out. Eli said hello but Estella only nodded. She was a shy one. Tall, built straight up and down all the way, with her brown hair cut too short to comb. She and Mainz seemed really taken up with each other, so Marnie guessed the young woman must have more to her than showed on the surface.

No one else was inside at table, only Pete and Gina on the job. Which was okay—Marnie liked both of them—except that when they shared duty they clowned around lovey-dovey and didn't get much work done. And Gina was *twenty*, for heaven's sake; you'd think she could act a little more grown-up.

Right now they were huddled over the dishcleaner and it

looked like Pete was teasing her, or maybe the other way around. Marnie could play that game too. Neither had seen her come in; she said rather loudly, ''I expect that's right, captain!'' When they jumped apart and whirled to look at her, she only grinned.

Maybe her prank had been a good idea; during the rest of her stint, until Gina left early to catch a nap before standing watch in control, the pair stuck to business more than usual.

When she came back to quarters, Clancy was sleeping; after a quick shower Marnie went to bed too. Currently they were quite a bit off-sync; when he arose to go on watch she half woke, enough to mumble a greeting before dozing again.

When she did have her sleep out, Marnie got up feeling energetic; rather than taking time to hit the galley she made do with fruit and cereal and juice. No coffee; Clancy let her have some on special occasions, but right now she felt no need of it.

With a vague sense of getting into a rut she put on one of the standard jumpsuits she was maybe wearing too often lately. At least they came in different colors; this one a light tan with pale blue trim, not matching her dark khaki totebag worth beans.

Outside she walked forward to the cross corridor and turned right just in time to see the transfer ring doors close behind someone. Oh well . . . In no hurry now she strolled over to the call button and waited a reasonable interval for someone to vacate the ring and someone else, perhaps, to enter it. Then she pushed, and twenty seconds later the doors opened.

Once inside she punched the button for transfer. Standing first on one foot and then the other as deceleration gave its slight sidewise nudge and weight dropped to zilch, she changed shoes, stuffing the smooth-soled ones into her dangling totebag.

Gently the ring thunked to a stop; the doors opened and Marnie bounded out. Or started to—for only the second or third time since she'd come aboard she forgot and stumbled over the slight ledge at the doors' side. One hand saved her from sprawling in air; the totebag jounced but she pulled it back safely and this time stepped out without mishap.

Embarrassed, she looked straight ahead and went to control.

Behind her came the sound of a faint bump as the doors closed.

So far, Anne thought, this ship seemed fairly congenial. True, two of the current watch weren't what she'd call loquacious. The pilot Jarness, probably the oldest crew member at something past forty, put in a good line now and then, but for the most part appeared content to listen. The tall flat-figured young woman with the brush haircut largely made do with smiles or nods as she worked on the intercom; it had developed an annoying squeal, so to save everyone's ears she had it turned down while she tinkered.

But Allaird, the watch officer, made up for both of them. Over the two hours or so since she came into control, the first officer had shown her not only the current outside sensor indications but interpreted them, throwing expanded views of computer-corrected starfields on the main screen and rotating them to display the ship's position with regard to known reference stars. No doubt about it, *Arrow*'s equipment had more than a few sophisticated improvements over what she'd seen on *Roamer*.

Switching the screen back to normal view, Allaird said, "Would you like to see Niflheim?"

Her puzzlement must have shown; he said, "I'd have thought the news went out with the first packet to *Roamer*, but maybe not. Well, it's a new planet we found—our sensors did, anyway, while the ship was still doing five gees and no one aboard—a long way out from Pluto and bigger than Jupiter. Mostly ice, I expect, if you include methane and ammonia."

"All the makings for life," said Edd Jarnell, "just waiting there in the cosmic deep freeze." Hydrogen, oxygen, carbon, nitrogen—except for trace elements, the man was right.

The young one, quiet up to now, licked her lips. "It's frightening. So big—and so dead."

"Oh come on, Holms," the officer said. "It's just a big ice cube, that's all. And not even suitable to put in a drink."

The woman blushed and said nothing more, as Allaird put a slowly moving view onscreen. "We're late in the fourteenth day of accel here," he said, "crowding twenty percent of c.

I'm showing this speeded up a bit, and with brightness enhanced." He pointed. "There it comes."

And so it did: first a dim splotch, then growing and at the same time brightening. After a few minutes he froze the image. "Closest approach, here. Nothing much to see; just a featureless ball, streaked by a few impurities with differing albedos."

She nodded; the object began moving again, inching to and then off the screen's edge. "And how far out is this planet?"

Allaird shrugged. "Something over twenty billion miles; that's as close as I've tried to figure. What you saw is all we know, except that no magnetic field was detected."

"So?"

"So if anyone wanted to mine it for frozen gases, there's no radiation belts to worry about."

Having run out of questions, Portaris was more pleased than not to see Marnie Allaird, a little breathless, come in. "Hi." And directly to Anne, "Is—uh—Mr. Allaird giving you the deluxe tour? How do you like *Arrow* so far?"

"Fine. The viewing controls are quite advanced."

Next the girl asked about *Roamer*, seeming especially interested in the two ships' differences. By the time that vein petered out, Anne was beginning to feel slightly beleaguered; as always at such times, she found herself rubbing her thumb against the missing finger's stub. When she saw Marnie's gaze fixed on the action, she stopped, but the intent expression didn't.

Anne knew the question in the child's mind. Dammit though, she never *had* talked about that incident. A foolish quirk, perhaps. But that idiot reporter making a joke of it— and Annie was a nickname she'd hated all her life. . . .

Estella Holms, intent on fixing the intercom, suddenly turned the volume up; a raised, strained voice came. ". . . going on there? The damned transfer ring won't work; I push the button and nothing happens. It's been nearly an hour now and I'm overdue to relieve you there!"

Nicole Pryce sounded anxious. "I can't even use the backup route. Somebody's in the aux ring—exercising, I guess—and there's no way to reach them when it's revved up."

"You stay here, Edd." Moving fast, Clancy left control. As soon as their reflexes registered, the others followed.

*   *   *

Never since she came on this ship had Marnie felt so small, so ashamed—so *dumb*. There it was, right out there in front of God and everybody, compressed down to less than an inch at the middle but still holding the transfer ring doors from closing: one of her smooth shoes, fallen from her totebag when she stumbled coming out.

Stooping, Clancy pulled at it but it wouldn't come free; he had to punch the doors open first. Then as they closed again he straightened up, turned to meet her, and made a sarcastic bow as he handed it over. "Yours, I think?"

"I'm *sorry*—I didn't know—I tripped but I didn't see it get loose—oh, *daddy*!" And that was worse; she wasn't supposed to call him that, not with other people around. "I—"

"Oh for heaven's sake!" Putting an arm around Marnie's shoulders, Anne Portaris raised her voice in protest. "Didn't anybody else ever drop something and not notice? You'd think . . ."

Clancy snorted out a deep breath. "You're absolutely right. Marnie, I apologize; this could have happened to anyone. We—"

By now the ring's car had visited the belt and returned; the doors opened and Nicole Pryce stepped out, hair and disposition equally ruffled, with Sybiljan and Phil Henning right behind her. "Will somebody explain just what—"

"Something got dropped and blocked the doors open." Clancy's voice came flat, with no hint of explanation or apology. "Estella had the intercom turned down so she could get the feedback squeal out of it without driving us all up the bulkheads. Or else we'd have heard you right away. Okay?"

Smoothing back her rebellious hair, Nicole visibly got her steam pressure down to safety levels. "Yes. All right. It was just not *knowing*, not being able to find out . . ."

"Sure." Allaird patted her shoulder. "Don't blame you a bit. But everything's all right now."

"Then we'll go take the watch. Phil? Sybiljan?" Clancy and Estella trailed the three; after all, Marnie realized, they hadn't been officially relieved yet.

*   *   *

The girl still looked a bit lost; stepping into the transfer car Anne Portaris said, "Let's go down to the lounge and buy ourselves a treat."

"Sure."

The ring did its stunt; changing shoes, the two stepped out and walked to the lounge room, finding it unoccupied. Marnie fixed herself a sundae of some sort, heavy on the syrups. With an inkling of what she was about to do, Anne left her bourbon on rocks at almost its original color. "Let's sit down."

Deliberately holding her glass so the finger stub faced Marnie, Anne cleared her throat. "About my hand. You're curious; that's understandable. Well, it was a long time ago. Haal and I . . ." She took a sip and then continued.

As she spoke, for the first time in years she relived it all. The chilly, poorly lit room hastily commandeered for their impromptu demonstration lab, the breadboard model of Traction Drive laid out on the bench, and Senator Wallin sitting hunched on a folding chair as Haal brought up power to the exciter, the multipliers, finally the vector node.

Here and now she saw Allaird and his two watchmates come in, but she kept talking anyway. "The dish *flared*. Not like the Habgates, but running down the spectrum as it spread."

Anne pointed her missing finger. "It caught my attention; I gasped, I suppose, and gestured, something like this—and it reached out and got me."

"What—?"

"Suddenly that finger was several hundred years old, and it fell off." The girl's eyes went wider. "The plane ride had jiggled adjustments on our demonstration model; its field components were out of phase. So, as it turned out, the drive pushed against time instead of space." Anne shrugged. "Luckily the intensity drops off rapidly with distance; Traction Drive won't do for a death ray!"

Now it was Clancy Allaird giving her a strange look. Anne Portaris grinned at him. "All right; I've sat on that story long enough. Your daughter seemed like the right audience, so now I've told it. *But*—I still don't want to hear the nickname that Tri-V smartass tried to hang on me."

"And you won't," said Clancy Allaird. "Not from me, you won't." Then, "You okay, Marnie?"

"Yes, I'm fine now."

And so, for some reason, was Anne Portaris.

Before bundling up the greetings packet for *Roamer* and *Starfinder*—a bit overdue by now, perhaps, but better late than never—Captain Dawson insisted that his officers critique his own videocap once again for possible last-minute improvements. In this version as in all the earlier ones, Ellery was still too thrilled for words. Clancy had made one try at the phrase, suggesting revision of the passage on other grounds, but the cliché clung like a StikTite.

Clancy himself had done the piece on Niflheim; Amalyn Tabard sent data on how the souped-up drive had performed, bringing *Arrow* up to speed under a thrust of five gees; Sybiljan Baynor reported on instrumentation changes that might be retrofitted, advantageously, to the earlier ships. "I've already sent these recommendations to Earth," she added, and of course all basic information was backed up in digital form. The other officers and specialty chiefs, and then the rest of the crew, made briefer personal appearances on the vidcap portion and drew a certain amount of ribbing at the final showing.

Anne Portaris made separate datacaps and copy bundles for each ship, and did not offer to let anyone else see them. Curious, Clancy couldn't find a tactful way to ask her why. It was Marnie who gave him the answer. After both bundles were duly Gated, he and she—nearly on the same sked for a couple of days—headed for quarters. As they sat down for a bedtime snack, Marnie said, "I like Anne."

"Hey, who doesn't?"

"I'll be sorry when she goes back to Earth. You know what?"

Clancy didn't.

"She wanted to tell just one friend of hers, on *Starfinder*, someone she hasn't seen for a long time, Rance Collier I think his name is, about that thing with my shoe and the ring doors. She said he'd appreciate it, and wouldn't laugh at me. But she *asked* me if she could. If I'd said no, she wouldn't have."

Marnie smiled. "And she told me, I didn't ask, she won't

mention me on Earth until it's official I'm on here, one way
or another.''

"Now I wonder how she picked up on that.''

And there was another thing he didn't feel he could ask.

Portaris spent only a week on *Arrow*. Marnie hated to see
her go; for the first time in her life she'd met an outsider who
felt like family. Nicole Pryce came close in that regard, but
their situation was complicated; it was going to take longer.

The ship had never had occasion for a good-bye party; Anne's
was impromptu. Pete Larue broke out some hoarded frozen lob-
ster and did the galley proud; afterward, in the lounge, the party
straddled a watch change so everyone could attend.

It wasn't anywhere near New Year's, but while Anne stood
in the Earthmouth just before it was activated, the group sang
some rather bad harmony on Auld Lang Syne.

It took a day or two, then, before everyone settled back into
normal routine.

When Sybiljan brought the latest packet of stuff from Earthtush into control, Dawson took a moment to sort through it.
Some routine ship's business, no hurry; the usual scattering of
personal mail, which he put in the pickup basket.

One envelope caught his attention: for First Officer Clarence
Allaird, with the official imprint of Senator William Flynn.
Now what . . . ?

Dawson knew the senator and Allaird were on speaking
terms; at the departure ceremony he'd seen them shaking
hands and talking. Was something going on here he should
know about?

Insecurity battled caution and lost; he left that envelope unopened and put it with the rest. Another thought came. "Sybiljan? This might be important. Would you take it down to
Allaird's quarters for me, please?''

If you're obviously cooperating, you *have* to be one of the
good guys.

Pleasantly full of lunch but not overstuffed, Marnie showered. She heard the door chime but by the time she had a
towel around her and got there, whoever it was had gone. On
the deck, though, lay this envelope.

She picked it up. Senator Flynn, huh? Right; the one her dad had called, from his room at Glen Springs. And the man had done something to help; Marnie wasn't sure quite what. But why was he writing *now* to daddy? It wasn't like they were old school buddies or anything. Maybe . . .

Marnie knew she shouldn't open her father's mail but she did anyway.

What she read dismayed her. She couldn't lay this on daddy; he already had enough to worry about. But she certainly couldn't handle it by herself.

So who was there?

While she was still gathering her things together, because it couldn't hurt to confuse matters as much as possible, Marnie checked the roster to see who had the watch, and made her choice.

Until Nicole read the message flimsy Ky brought in from Earthtush, she had grave doubts that she'd done the right thing. True, the girl—normally as level-headed as they come—had been crowding the edge of panic. And maybe her story did make sense. "Don't tell daddy! Promise!" was hard to swallow, but finally, overcoming her reservations, Nicole agreed.

Now, only minutes later, she read what Coyote Benjamin handed her and decided the child had called it just about right.

Marnie wasn't in quarters when Clancy got there, but that was okay; since the first few days she was getting around a lot more. He showered, put on a robe, debated whether to have a beer or a soda and the beer won. He went to sit at the data terminal but stopped, frowning at the envelope and crumpled sheet of paper lying on the deck, and picked them up.

Senator Flynn? Oh jeez! Quickly he read:

Clancy: Your ex and her lawyer have a court order to go aboard Arrow *accompanied by a Federal badge and take custody of your daughter. If she's there, which begins to strike me as a likely prospect. I thought I had the woman scared off, but she's dumped Knapheidt— stomped him, I understand—and is no longer concerned with protecting him. I can only give you this advance warning and advise Glen Springs to allow these people no shortcuts through procedure; from there it's up to you. Although if any hearings should result from your actions, I'll do my best to see they take place under friendly auspices.*

Good luck. Bill Flynn

Well. Bill had done all *he* could—so now what? Looking around carefully for the first time, Clancy saw no indication that Marnie was currently in residence. Her closet was half-empty and her travel bag was gone. A lot of her extra clothing remained, of course; the bag wouldn't hold a fraction of what he'd had sent aboard for her. But since the whole crew had met her, then no matter where or how she'd gone into hiding, there was no point in trying to deny she *had* been on board.

Had been, or still was? Resisting the urge to go find out, Clancy forced himself to sit. Think first, look later.

The intercom broke in. "Mr. Allaird? Second Officer Pryce here. I think you'd better come up to control. Now."

Her official tone told him a lot; his indrawn breath came with a shudder. As he began to dress he thought, *it starts.*

Steaming, for two days Celeste fussed and argued with NASA flunkies. But for all of it, nobody at Glen Springs would move paper one bit faster. They'd put her in a dusty room with non-functional air-conditioning, while Maurice Fitzhugh roomed with Federal Marshal Edgar Payne in the quarters building farthest from her. "Bunk beds, for God's sake," Maurice fumed, "and one big latrine for each floor." Skinny and gaunt-faced as he was, the lawyer's look of disgust qualified as an art form. "I expect the building began life as a BOQ. And not recently."

Visiting the room, which at least had cooling, Celeste decided she'd been too critical of Clancy's accommodations.

The food was okay. If there'd been any way to feed their group separately, Celeste suspected, it would have been awful.

Her travails here she blamed on Bill Flynn, and found nothing to do about them but hunker down and wait the system out.

On the third day the three were given more shots than Celeste believed truly necessary, their luggage was inspected, and they were taken to the Habegger Gate building where another stack of forms awaited signing. When those were done, the woman who looked like the pictures of onetime president Herbert Hoover told them to walk into the Gate booth and stand still.

A young man began playing Chopsticks on a control panel. As he did so, Celeste heard him say to the woman, "You're sending her aboard in high heels?"

"So I am." Then a burst of colors curtained vision.

Still blinking, trying to see where she was, Celeste felt her stomach lurch. She reached for something to hang onto and found only Maurice's arm; her grab set the two of them turning in different directions. Maurice caught hold of Payne, whose greater bulk stemmed their joint motion; still all three wheeled slowly in midair until a man stepped—*stepped*—forward and brought the bizarre dance nearly to a halt.

She looked up to a brown face—some kind of Indian?—showing no expression. "Thanks."

"Somebody forgot to issue you your Velcros, I guess." The poker face, she decided, hid amusement. He put an arm around her waist. "Let go now," and he had her. Not quite standing but not quite bundled under his arm either, she tried to relax as he began to move with an odd sliding gait along the corridor that stretched ahead.

Looking back she saw that a tall dark-haired woman was towing Maurice and the marshal with even less formality, one hand at each man's collar as legs and bodies trailed ineffectually.

Not exactly an impressive entrance. Her stomach wasn't helping much, either.

Allaird knew he wouldn't like what he'd find in the control room, but thanks to Bill Flynn he was braced for it. His gaze went past Pryce and Benjamin and Gina Todisco to the three who didn't belong here: belted into auxiliary observer seats were Celeste, the skeletal Maurice Fitzhugh, and a large swarthy man, curly black hair greying around the edges and thinning on top, who had to be the badge Flynn had mentioned.

"I called you as soon as we got word they were coming," said Nicole Pryce. "Not five minutes later, here they were."

Feeling not at all pleasant, Clancy made no effort to fake

it. "They would be. Thanks anyway." Ignoring the Federal officer, size and all, he glared at his ex-wife and Fitzhugh. "If you brought a paper, let's see it."

It was the big man who proffered one. Clancy glanced through it; yes, it ordered him to produce one Margaret Clarisse Allaird, a minor, and turn custody over to Ada Celeste Allaird (no Knapheidt? Some kind of ploy here . . .) by authority of Marshal Edgar Payne, accompanying said Ada Celeste and so forth.

As he reread it, searching for loopholes he knew he wouldn't find, Celeste said, "So you've seen it. Now do it."

Clancy wondered: where's Marnie? What could she have done? To his knowledge she couldn't have learned to operate a Gate, but who said he knew everything? She could hardly use the one in control; the watch crew wouldn't let her. But the others—to Earth, or to *Starfinder* or *Roamer*—nobody sat guard over any of those.

More likely, though, she'd gone to ground somewhere on the ship. At this moment it really didn't matter; what did was, "I have no idea where she is."

"Now don't try to give me—"

The marshal cut in. "You're ordered to cooperate."

"And I will. If you want to search the ship, I'll show you around."

"Oh, sure you will! Everywhere except where you hid her." Celeste's sneer hadn't lost its edge as she said, "You probably bundled her off into another of those damn Gates. Which one?"

She pushed against the restraining harness. "Who's running this show? Here, I mean. Here and now."

"I'm watch officer," said Nicole Pryce. "The captain's off duty, probably sleeping." Overriding Celeste's rejoinder, "I'd advise you to wait, rather than disturbing him. I can—"

"You can tell me where my kid is, that's what!"

"To the contrary. I have no information whatsoever."

Thank God! Because sure as Clancy knew anything at all, Nicole was lying through her teeth. He said, "The Gates, you mentioned. Well, we can put queries through the intership units; the four-year round-trip is only about sixty days, ship's time, if you care to wait. Or of course Marnie may have doubled back to Earth." She wouldn't, but . . .

Maurice Fitzhugh spoke. "You're being childish, Allaird. And it could get you a contempt citation. I will—"

Flat-paced, Clancy strode to stand over the lawyer. "You will eat your nose if you keep opening your mouth. Six years ago—actually eight, counting Gatelag—I had more than enough of you. And I still have. You—"

"All right!" Payne's voice called a halt. "Fitzhugh, Miz Allaird, you're out of your territory. Me, when I go into new terrain I study it first. Now then, Clarence . . ." The man had a really nasty smirk. "You forgot to mention your in-and-out Gate setup right here. Maybe you just stashed the child away in that one. Temporarily, for convenience. How about it?"

"What?" Celeste demanded an explanation; Payne gave it, and she said, "Well if that's all! I'll just go in after her."

Clancy choked back a laugh. "I've half a mind to let you. It doesn't work that way, Celeste. Think back; what did you three do together on the way out here?"

"Why . . ." She blinked, then said, "All right, damn you, where is she?"

"I told you, I haven't the faintest idea."

"Then you." She swung to face Nicole Pryce. "You're in charge, you said, so you'd have to know."

Pryce shrugged. "Afraid not."

"Then we'll search this ship from asshole to teakettle. Come on, Maurice—Marshal Payne. Find us some of those trick shoes, and we'll get started."

Clancy did laugh. "Why sure, Celeste; it's a big ship, but go right to it. One thing you might keep in mind, though."

"What's that?"

"Carl Knapheidt." She didn't get it; he said, "You did him a real big dirty, they tell me." Now don't stretch Flynn's words too far! "But you're off Earth now and he'll know it. Four years minimum—plus twenty-five days for each one you stay aboard here. Do you really think that scumcake isn't moving heaven and earth to get even, and you not there to cover your butt?"

It shook her; he could tell. But Celeste, tossing her hair back, raised her chin defiantly and said, "The four years is committed, no matter what I do now. A little extra, here on the ship, won't make that much difference."

Again she turned to Payne. "Are you going to get us those shoes, or not?"

The marshal looked baffled. Nicole Pryce said, "Ky? Bring these people three pairs of all-size Velcros, would you please?"

As the man left, Celeste said, "Who's going to play guide? You don't expect me to trust that conniving ex-husband of mine, do you?"

As she unbuckled the harness, her movements set her floating free. Her face changed; she grabbed at the chair arm. "Oh shit! This is getting me. Take me where there's some *weight*, before I throw up!"

When everything settled down, Clancy and Nicole had control to themselves. She'd assigned two spare rooms to the unwelcome guests. No question of VIP lodgings for this brood; they drew ordinary crew accommodations and well away from major facilities.

Coyote helped the men with the luggage of all three while Gina shepherded Celeste, who wasn't doing too well with the Velcros, toward the transfer ring. Once the new arrivals settled in, Ky and Gina were stuck with chaperoning them on the first stage of their inspection tour.

So in the control room, peace and quiet made a comeback.

"Nearly two hours left on this watch," said Pryce. "I'd better call Edd or Pilar to fill in. Or both, unless you're staying. Regs say it takes three on duty."

As she reached for the intercom, Clancy's hand caught hers. "Don't, just yet. Tell me about Marnie." She started to shake her head; he added, "You bluff fine, but I could tell."

Then he reconsidered. "Not where she is. Because then I'd have to lie and I've never been—I'm no good at it. Just, is she safe?"

"Definitely. And I'm the only one who knows where."

"Good. For now, could we keep it that way? And thanks, Nicole." He tensed, forcing himself to say more. "I—there's things I want to talk about with you. If it's all right."

"Why shouldn't it be?"

"Well . . . it's personal, and we haven't really got to know each other. I don't know where to start."

As she smiled her eyes narrowed, catlike. "How about admitting we're both alone and either we can stay that way or give each other a try or wait around for somebody else to break up? Is that a good place, do you suppose?"

To start, she meant. Well, "I wasn't quite that ready."

Clancy had never thought of himself as a shy guy. No superstud, maybe, like Kevan his best buddy down the block all through high school. But while Kevan was shaggin'n'braggin' as the saying went, Clancy went through more than one sad sweet love affair. When, rarely, the path of romance found its way to bed, that part began with a sort of timid joy and ran its course to an ending filled with tender regret. Later it struck him that all parties might have been overly influenced by holodrama, but at the time the pangs and heartaches felt gratifyingly vital.

College was different; there wasn't the *time* to play those oh-so-sincere games that sometimes led where both wanted to go but neither cared to admit. Young Clarence had two very arid school years before taking the fancy of Luise Altner, a severe-looking physics lab instructor you wouldn't believe how-different-she-was-at-home-just-the-two-of-you. They couldn't move in together; the school's view of such matters was dire to say the least. But one way and another his room got looking dustier and less occupied than a person would ordinarily expect.

When graduation wrenched him from Luise, a platoon of violins couldn't have expressed his anguish. A month after NASA accepted him for space training, he wrote her a final farewell and mailed the fifth rewrite.

His next two years ran from hectic to grueling and romance played very little part. On his first real leave, given in honor of earning his Pilot/Nav First certificate, he wound up staying in this bar all evening and eventually picked up the cocktail waitress, Celeste Malcolm. Or possibly vice versa.

She was different from the drama queens he'd known, and he never quite understood how they two wound up getting married, but he wasn't complaining. While he was off on assignment she waited, when he got home she was there, and then Marnie was, too.

Clancy had it made.

Until *Jovian*, and Theda's stupid book which never hit print after all, and Maurice Fitzhugh who could peel a rock and get juice. From then on, Clancy found himself living mostly lonesome. Not wholly celibate, but close enough to qualify.

Any time the drought did break, it was more or less by serendipity; he'd meet up with a woman he liked and—well, half the time he wasn't even sure who made the first move. And somehow, with all the travel and different assignments, nothing ever lasted long.

But a situation with this kind of sharp, clear-cut edges: his problem wasn't shyness, it was being totally out of practice.

"What do you need? To make your mind up." Her voice and expression, each turned cool and dispassionate, belied the context. Her dark hair, today skinned back to a smooth roll, wasn't adding its usual sensual touch to the overall impression.

But these weren't factors Clancy could cite. He said, "Could we start out by getting *acquainted* some?"

"Haven't we been? Well, maybe not—but it's not *my* fault. You didn't seem interested." She stared at him. "Are you?"

"Uh, I think so." *Idiot!* "I mean yes, sure I am." And that was the understatement of the year; here and now, up close, suddenly he knew how much and how fully he wanted this woman. "Yes," he said again.

"All right then. You're free next watch?"

He had to think. "Yes."

"Then would you like to come to my quarters, half an hour after I'm relieved here? I'll call Edd and Pilar to cover the rest of this shift with me. So you can go get yourself relaxed."

Fat chance. But he went anyway.

VI

"When did this happen? Why wasn't I called?" Firmly atop his high horse, Ellery Dawson glared at his second officer.

Because either way you were going to be a pain in the ass, and why rush it? "We all need our rest, captain," said Nicole Pryce. "And it wasn't any kind of emergency. I knew you'd have no trouble at all, getting on top of things."

"So what's happening? Where are these intruders?"

She told him. Drafting Ptiba Mbente to help, Ky and Gina were conducting the three new arrivals separately, dividing the search to save time. Coyote had made printouts of a simplified version of ship's layout drawings: "At least they'll know where they're going and where they've been. Gives them a sense of accomplishment."

Some of the redness left Dawson's complexion. "And when they find the Allaird girl they'll get off my ship?"

"If they find her."

"And why shouldn't they?"

Assuming her very best innocent expression, Nicole shrugged. After a few more questions the captain gave it up and let her go off watch.

The gripper-slippers were a little too big for Celeste, but an extra pair of socks took care of that; then she could get used to them and had an easier time of it. For the first hour or so, anyway; after that her legs and feet began to ache because of the different way a person had to move, walking with just Velcro to hold you down.

The woman showing her around was nice enough. Gina

Todisco her name was, built slim but strong, with long tawny hair and a complexion no makeup could match. Said she came from northern Italy, which Celeste wouldn't have figured by her coloring.

Anyway, when Celeste got tired and needed to rest, Gina didn't complain about waiting, but showed her on the plansheets where they were and where they'd been. It wasn't encouraging: all that space and not much covered yet. Even with Maurice and the marshal working their own routes to split the job. The thing was, just the three cylinders of decks between the rotating part of the ship and its central tube, they added to something like three or four acres, all in sections you had to go back and forth through a lot, to cover. Up one corridor and down another, checking to see what might be inside each and every door.

And that didn't count the big central tube (mostly sealed cargo, thank God) or the Deployment Vehicle or rotating belts or twelve damned *fins* Gina helpfully showed her on the plans and Celeste would just as soon she hadn't. All this had to be checked, and maybe Marshal Payne knew for sure Marnie couldn't sneak past the micro-vidcams he and Maurice and Celeste were all using, planting them to monitor points of access while specific areas were searched. The devices weren't going to run out of film or tape or whatever the hell they used, he explained, because they were movement-activated. When something *changed* in the field of view, the thing began recording, and then kept going as long as any motion continued. So all you saw when you ran it off was people moving past, not the long stretches of no action.

But Celeste still had her doubts. Even though Payne had marked for her, on the plansheets, the camera sites and the order in which she was supposed to utilize them.

The whole mess was discouraging as all hell.

But after booting herself four years ahead on the calendar by the time she got back to Earth, Celeste Malcolm Allaird (and the hell with Knapheidt) hated to give up. Enduring twinges, she stood. "Okay, hon. I'm ready for another lap if you are."

Seeing the ready bright smile and springy stance, Celeste almost hated young Gina Todisco.

*　　*　　*

Tensed inside, Clancy shoved the bottle of wine at Nicole Pryce as soon as she opened her door. "Here. I thought—"

"Well, thanks; you didn't have to. Come on in." She didn't look so standoffish now: a casual dress, her hair's rebellious waves unbound, even a hint of perfume.

As he moved to step past her she caught his arm. "Let me open this. If it's—oh yes, you've cooled it." They stood facing and close; why? What did she want?

Tentatively he started to put an arm around her but she stepped back, saying, "Sorry, wrong signal. Sit down, won't you? We can sample the wine." As she walked toward her kitchen area she added, "You told me once you give good listen; remember? Well, that's what we need first of all . . . I *think*."

Clancy's brief laugh ended more relaxed than it began. "Whatever you say." He chose a compact armchair facing a small table, and waited while she brought two glasses, filled higher than your average restaurant usually does. She pulled a lighter chair over to face him, and raised her glass.

He responded. "Here's to listening. Talk away."

After their ritual sips, Nicole said, "I had you all wrong, Allaird; I thought it must be your doing, Cal's being pulled off the ship and you taking his place. Because you had previous space experience and were senior, and maybe wanted—"

As he started to speak she cut him off. "Oh, I know better now. I was fighting the idea that Cal Ledbetter would leave me of his own accord." She made a sourmouth face. "I never did find out exactly what happened, just that he ended up on the wrong end of some kind of official inquiry. But I do know that when Cal left this ship it wasn't his idea, or yours either."

She spread her hands. "So."

"So thanks for telling me." Tasting the wine again he felt self-congratulatory about his selection. But now what? "Uh— is there anything more you think I should know?"

Her grin came impish. "I wouldn't touch that line with a decapod from Warsaw."

His mind was tuned in another direction, so for some moments he didn't catch on. When he did, first he chuckled and then he kissed her, and it all went well enough. But not where Clancy partly hoped and halfway expected; they wound up sharing a sort of foldout chaise longue and watching an old

holo of *Bittersweet* starring Janeiro Montego and Elspeth Lud-
winne. That one really took him back. . . .

And Nicole did give great cuddle.

"How do you know? How can you be sure?" Soaking her
aching legs in the pulldown sitting-trough that passed for a
bathtub in her assigned quarters, Celeste glared at Marshal
Payne. "This rabbit warren of a ship! When you search a
section, how do you know my daughter hasn't doubled back
and got past you?"

The way the big man's brows drew down, his patience had
to be worn close to blowout. He said, "If you placed the
microcams as marked, in the order I indicated, leaving them
in place every time we stop to eat or sleep, your coverage
should be complete. Mine and Fitzhugh's certainly are."

More than once they had worked straight through the night;
Celeste had no idea how long since she'd felt caught up on
her sleep. There had been another attack of zero-gee nausea,
but not for long; now she seemed to have it whipped. But not
the main problem. "We must have missed something."

"I assure you, Ms. Allaird, that young Margaret did not
evade our search. She is not, in fact, on this ship."

The residential belt? The high-weight auxiliary? The exter-
nal fins? All three operating-tube decks? The central tube with
all that cargo space and the drive rooms? The Deployment
Vehicle? "You haven't missed a possibility, Ms. Allaird. And
neither have I. She's not aboard. I've busted my butt for you
on here, lady, and I'm happy to tell you my work is done."

"Like hell it is! There's still Clancy."

Payne sighed. "All right; what is it you expect now?"

Talking with Nicole Pryce, Clancy decided, was habit-
forming. On this second meeting in her digs, she wearing more
casual clothing, they were practically exchanging life stories.
A bit at a time, actually, as one of his experiences would
remind her of one of hers, or the other way around. He was
into an area she couldn't match, though—his tour on *Jovian*—
when the chime interrupted.

She reached to the intercom. "Yes?"

"Is Allaird with you?" Dawson. "I've checked the galley,

rec room, his quarters—and he's not here in the lounge. He—"

Now how had the captain picked up, so soon, on this barely budding attachment? Oh well; Clancy moved over. "Allaird speaking. What's up?"

"More trouble. Your interloping friends demand your presence. Given a choice I'd have them tossed into the Earthgate bag and baggage, but I doubt that regulations give me the authority. So you'd better report."

Allaird sighed. "Yes, sir. Right away." He turned to Nicole. "I'm sorry. Maybe this won't take long, but just in case . . ." He'd been looking forward to kissing her again; now he did, and certainly she was putting more into it this time.

As he disengaged, she kept hold of one arm. "Wait a mo, while I change. I'm coming along."

Shucking her garb to don a jumpsuit, she showed no qualms at being seen in only bra and briefs. And trim as she was, why should she?

Whatever this was all about, Nicole Pryce figured it was becoming her business so she'd better pay attention. Preceding Clancy Allaird into the main lounge she looked around to see who all was in the game.

The blond harpy, of course, and the outsized badge-toter and skinny lawyer. Fitzhugh had to be a fairly young man, but between lowering brow ridges and prominent cheekbones his eyes were sunk so deeply as to give him a cadaverous look. Well, it matched his attitude. And all three had their things packed, luggage sitting next to the seats they occupied.

Ellery Dawson held the watch, backed by Edd Jarness and Estella Holms. So with Allaird and herself, the only ones not sitting and belted in, control was as full of people as Nicole had ever seen it.

"Reporting as ordered, sir," said Clancy, and Dawson acknowledged. When no one else spoke, Allaird said, "Whatever it is you want, Celeste, get to it. Or whichever stooge is next up to bat."

The marshal cleared his throat. "Since you've failed to comply with the court order, Ms. Allaird demands that I cite you for contempt and extradite you to Earth to face charges. How long will you need to get your belongings together?"

Seeing Clancy's grin form, Nicole braced herself. But he spoke mildly. "None. Because I'm not going anywhere. If you are, then bon voyage."

Maurice Fitzhugh raised his voice. "You're defying not only the courts but the authority of a United States Marshal?"

"You're out of your jurisdiction," said Allaird.

"On a NASA ship?" Fitzhugh shook his head. "Distance doesn't change anything. You're in contempt and you'll answer for it."

Ellery Dawson's expression brightened; here, it said, was his chance to get an oar in. "NASA built this ship, yes, but funding was provided by way of the United Nations Space Consortium. And beginning with the precedent set by *Starfinder*, all ships are crewed and administered under UN auspices. I'm sorry, Marshal Payne"—obviously he wasn't—"but you have no more authority here than you'd have at the UN Building on Earth. You might say that aboard this ship Mr. Allaird holds diplomatic immunity."

Clancy stared; obviously he'd had no more idea than Nicole that Ellery had it in him!

Payne glared. "That's not what I was told when they sent me out here. And I'm not going to poop off four years' Gate lag, going to Earth for confirmation and coming back." He turned on Clancy. "All right mister, your smartass tactics just cost you a few more points. Your friends can send your effects along after you. Right now you're coming with me."

"You and what army?" Unbuckling, Edd Jarnell approached the marshal; Dawson and Allaird weren't far behind him. "Just how do you figure to kidnap our man?"

Payne stood also. "The word is arrest and the means are right here." From inside his bulky jacket he drew a large, awkward-looking machine pistol. "Any more questions?"

Nicole felt her face draw tight. Her voice came out shrill. "One you should have asked before you came here! You stupid fool, do you know the penalty for bringing that thing aboard a ship?"

She'd rattled him! Overcoming a sudden stammer the marshal blurted, "I'll worry about that when we get back. Come on, you," to Clancy, and to Nicole, "You too. You're an officer; should be able to work the Gate for me."

Damn him. "I'll come, all right, and I'll be right behind

you at Glen Springs. You won't so much as get off the base before you're in custody. Whatever you expect the courts to do to Clancy won't be a patch on what *you* get.''

For moments she thought he was going to shoot—whether her or Clancy, or both, she wasn't at all sure. But even while her gut clenched in fear she glared, trying to stare the man down.

Finally he lowered the gun. To Celeste he said, ''My fault; I didn't do enough homework after all.'' Then to Clancy or Nicole or maybe both, ''I could still take the round trip and come back with a warrant that *would* hold up. But it's not worth it; a man has to take a loss once in a while.''

He exhaled an explosive snort. ''All right, Fitzhugh, Ms. Allaird. Let's get our tired ass in gear and go home.'' He turned to match Nicole's glare. ''You figure you can work that Gate now? And think again about charging me with anything; since I won't be taking Allaird, I doubt anybody's going to more than slap my wrist about the piece.'' The gun, he meant. . . .

''Forget the piece,'' said Clancy Allaird. ''Just keep it under your coat, or maybe stow it in your bag. As long as you're leaving peacefully—and I trust you'll keep things that way at the far end?''

Payne nodded. ''Seems best, Mr. Allaird.''

''Then I see no reason we should even mention the weapon in our own reports.''

Now Nicole saw why Clancy had stayed quiet through so much of this hassle. If others wanted to carry the ball, and could, he let them. But when his turn came around he spoke up, all right.

She found it in her to smile at Edgar Payne. ''That sounds reasonable to me.'' She gestured. ''This way to the Gate, folks.''

Walking to the rear end of the control deck, then halfway around its circumference to Earthmouth, Clancy carried Celeste's bags. Moving beside him, still incongruously awkward on the Velcros, his ex-wife held silence. When they were nearly there, Nicole up ahead already bringing the Gate's circuitry to operational mode, he said, ''If Marnie's back on Earth, Celeste, I'm asking Senator Flynn to set up a guardianship for her.'' The request hadn't gone in yet, but let this woman think what she would. ''Don't fight it, okay?''

''Why shouldn't I?'' Her tone made it a question of reason, not spite. Then, abruptly, her eyes widened. ''You mean you *really* don't know? Where Marnie is, I mean?''

''That's right.''

He saw her chewing over his answer. But then, ''How can you ask me never to see my own child?''

''I'm not. Just don't try to make her live with you, is all.'' His mouth twitched; play-acting or not, his anger was real. ''What she told me, that bastard Knapheidt . . .''

Celeste stopped in her tracks. ''All right, what *did* she say? She didn't stay around long enough to tell *me* anything, and I never did get any answers out of Carl.''

The old rage clogged his throat; finally he said, ''He had them both naked in the bathtub and got grabby. Is that enough?''

In a rasping whisper she said, ''I'll kill him.''

''If he's using half as much dope as Marnie seems to think, by now the stuff may have done the job for you. For *us*. And speaking of dope . . .''

She shook her head. ''All right, I let it get out of hand. That's over.'' She paused. ''Anything else you want to say?''

He thought about it. ''Just—Celeste, you knew me pretty well; for one thing, you knew I can't lie worth owlpoop. So why wouldn't you believe me when I told you I'd had no truck with Theda on *Jovie*?''

Shockingly her face went white. ''Don't *ever* ask me that!''

And then Nicole had the Gate ready. Without another word Celeste joined her two companions in the booth, and after a few seconds while the Habegger fields built, Clancy saw the colors burst to hide the group's departure.

Whatever reasons Celeste had, he'd never know them now.

Closing down the Gate's transmit mode, Nicole came over and grasped his arm. ''Come on, sailor. I'll buy you a drink.''

It was the best offer he'd had all night, but passing control on their way to the transfer ring, Clancy and Nicole caught a hail from Ellery Dawson. ''Now I need you to fill me in on our legal position here. We have to be careful . . .''

''Oh sweet heaven!'' Nicole looked every bit as steamed as

she sounded. "Ellery, you heard everything; it's in the can."

Frown. "I'm not certain we're legally clear . . ."

Clancy had to laugh. "Now look, cap'n sir. You talked 'em out of jurisdiction, Nicole nailed the big teddy bear on what amounted to a heavy weapons violation. He bluffed, we bluffed, ours worked and his didn't. End of litigation, before it starts." He took a deep breath. "Okay, captain?"

"I suppose so." Dawson looked plaintive. "But how do I write this up in my report for Earth?"

Nicole sighed. "Who says Earth has to know everything? Tell you what; let me do the log for this past hour or so. If you like it, put your name to it."

After a moment's frown, Dawson nodded. And about time, too. Suddenly Allaird was in a hurry; it was all too long since he'd shown Nicole Pryce how much he really needed her.

"You were great . . . so were you . . . all I could do to keep from laughing . . . scared for a minute there . . . me too . . . wondered why you didn't speak up sooner, but then . . . really nailed him . . . almost felt sorry . . . all over now . . . let's hope so . . . here, let *me* unfasten that . . . sure; oh, I see how . . . yes, there, yes *now*. . . ."

For a time then, in Nicole's quarters, no talking except brief and urgent words, very much to the point. Until after a spell of quiet, "My God, did I do that? I didn't mean to."

"It's all right; look at yourself, right there. I'm sorry."

"Same here. Or better, let's don't be. I guess it's been a while for you, too."

"Yes. I don't usually . . ."

"Me either. It just . . ."

The wounds of love proved minor, with only a few real scratches. Ice helped the swellings but induced a side effect: giggling. "Not *there*, you beast."

"Can't seem to keep my hands off you."

"Don't try—but *hey* . . . !"

"Well then, let's . . ."

This time was slower, more gentle—and on Clancy's part at least, ended with all tension gone. As he lay, feeling his pulse slow to something near normal range, suddenly he realized what it was he had unaccountably, unforgivably forgotten.

"Nicki?"

"Yes?"

"Where the hell *is* Marnie?"

Nicole stared him eye-to-eye. "I have to tell how it was." He nodded. "She came into control panicked, keeping herself on tight rein but not by much; she was terrified all to hell and it showed. On a hunch I made up errands for Ky and Gina, so she could talk freely. Well, you know the story. And here came mama to drag her back to *that*. So"—spreading her hands—"I went out on a limb all the way. The loop Gate was what she wanted; she insisted it was the only really safe answer. Finally I agreed and in she went."

For a moment he hugged her so tight something creaked, then eased back. "That's the *best*. I'd hoped, but there didn't seem any way it could have worked. And no one suspected at the time? Asked any questions?"

She shook her head. "No; it was the errands, you see. Ky's was to get some treats from the galley, and I sent Gina for an item I knew wasn't there. They weren't thinking about Marnie."

Already his mind moved ahead. "How long . . . ? Let's see, it's been—what?"

"Another two weeks, I think. Give or take a day." He stood; she said, "What are you doing?"

Turning up the computer, Clancy said, "Composing a message, for Ellery to send to Earth two weeks from now."

He got so involved with his wording that for the first time since boarding *Arrow* he was late relieving the watch.

To Clancy the next days dragged; waiting for Marnie's reappearance was one of the hardest things he'd ever had to do in his whole life. She was all right, of course—he *knew* that— but still and all . . .

To distract himself he began checking the general news from Earth. On each of the two earlier ships, he knew, there had been an initial period of isolation from home developments: from the time the Gates were energized to transmit the first relief cadres until approximately the end of acceleration. Then news would begin arriving—but two years old and compressed ten to one.

Here on *Arrow* there'd been no news-dry period, but the

time lag existed and compression was even worse. A year's events in two weeks, for heaven's sake! Even with severely selective culling at the far end, the glut had a paralyzing effect on Clancy's interest; unless someone else told him about some Earthside event it passed him by completely.

Now he began skimming the incoming reports—and found he still wasn't much interested. Scandals of all kinds: political, financial, and general celebrity-type hanky-panky. Sports? He'd lost track of the changing headliners. Disasters, crises: at this apparent rate of occurrence they all blended together in an almost-uniform stream of alarm and concern.

Yet he was fairly certain things in general were no worse than when he'd been there to experience them in real time.

The hell with it. Allaird's attention reverted to his own concerns.

More and more his excitement built. If he had the timing right, his daughter's return would happen on one of Nicole's watches. To be on the safe side, he showed up nearly an hour before his best guess.

Once the tall second officer sent the other two out of the control room, Marnie talked fast: why she couldn't let Celeste take her back, why daddy mustn't be left in a position to be blamed, why the back-to-back Gate pair was the only solution that wouldn't put her in the power of strangers, why something had to be done *fast*. Pryce frowned and shook her head a lot but finally agreed, so Marnie stepped into the local Mouth.

She'd brought her travel bag so they'd think she'd left the ship; now, having no idea how a Gate transit would affect her balance in zero gee, she squatted on the lumpy thing, her Velcros holding her in place, and leaned against the booth's rear wall. From last-second urgency she called out, "Don't tell daddy. Promise! Because—" But the flare of colors cut off the last word, and

she found herself saying, "—he can't lie!" from the different perspective of the Tush and to Clancy himself, seated next to Nicole Pryce and holding her hand. As Marnie stood, the two came forward, smiling, and both hugged her. Wow; just turn your back a second, and what happens?

"Did Celeste come? Is she gone now? What . . ." Still

wound up in the anxiety that brought her here only a few minutes earlier, Marnie couldn't stop talking. Even though now she had time to notice several others in the room, watching with evident curiosity.

Finally Clancy shushed her. "Came and went, Marni Gras. A bit of a hectic time but it's done now." He told it so fast he had to be skipping a lot, but she thought she got the gist.

A Federal marshal no less, besides that vulture-faced Maurice Fitzhugh; Celeste hadn't spared the horses. "But you got rid of them. And they won't be back?"

"What use?" Clancy shrugged. "By Earth time it's well past your sixteenth birthday. Before you could reach there, your eighteenth will have passed. In fact we're sending a message to that effect, to be filed with the court of record. Want to see it?"

"Sure." He handed her the single sheet; after a long official-looking address and salutation the text part read:

> INASMUCH AS THE PRESENCE OF MARGARET CLARISSE ALLAIRD HAS BEEN DISCOVERED ABOARD THIS SHIP, AND
>
> INASMUCH AS HER DATE OF BIRTH IS MORE THAN SIXTEEN YEARS PAST AS OF THIS WRITING, AND
>
> INASMUCH AS, DUE TO THE TRANSIT TIME INHERENT IN ANY HABEGGER GATE, SHE WOULD BE CHRONOLOGICALLY ADULT BEFORE SHE COULD REACH EARTH,
>
> THEREFORE THE QUESTION OF CUSTODY IS NO LONGER GERMANE ON EARTH, AND IT IS REQUESTED THAT THE COURT DISSOLVE ANY ORDER PERTAINING TO SUCH CUSTODY.

Signed by none other than Captain Ellery Dawson, now sitting with a self-conscious grin on his face.

"Thanks, captain!"

"Thank your father; he wrote it. I only signed it."

What could you say to that? "Well, thanks anyway."

"Okay, what else has been going on?" Back in quarters, Marnie seemed pretty well recovered from her scare; what Clancy saw in her face now was pure curiosity.

"Such as?" She only waited, so he said, "Well, the ship

keeps moving along. Nothing of special interest spotted in space lately, but we still scan the sensor records just in case.'' Marnie was frowning so Clancy eased up a bit. ''You have to realize I was worried sick, not knowing where you were. But of course Nicole couldn't give me any specific information until Celeste and Company were gone; I understood that and I'm glad you thought to tell her.''

He paused. ''And what else? Well, your mother looked pretty well; she says she's off the dope and I believe her. Zero gee gave her a couple of sick spells early on, but then she got used to it. Well enough to give me as much trouble as she could manage, but there's nothing new about that. Especially with that carrion crow Fitzhugh here to jog her elbow . . .''

Clancy shrugged. ''I guess that's about it.''

Marnie looked skeptical. ''Nothing else important happened?''

''Can't think of anything.'' *That I want to talk about . . .*

''No? What about Nicole Pryce? You two looked pretty chummy, I thought.'' Her level stare held him. ''Decide to pair yet, or just working up to it?''

His hand brushed air, warding off the words. ''I don't know. Maybe. I think . . . it's early on; we . . .''

''Ooh-kay.'' She looked around. ''Hasn't moved in yet, I can see that much. So I don't need to hustle my own quarters for a while, anyway.''

''Quarters? Why? Don't you like Nicole?''

''Sure I do. She's been nice, and it sounds like she jumped right in when the marshal pulled his showdown. It's just that—'' Marnie shrugged. ''I'm the wrong age to live underfoot of a couple of newlyweds. Wouldn't you say?''

Now that Clancy thought about it, she was absolutely right. He told her so. And, ''You're growing up too damn fast; you know that?''

Judging by her grin, she listened not to what he said but what he meant.

Partly by design and partly by luck, none of *Arrow*'s crew had arrived on board carrying any cold or flu viruses to pass around. That no visitor, welcome or unwelcome, had done so was the purest of gravy. Be that as it may, the result was that in over seven weeks of shipboard life, nobody had come down with anything of the sort. Or for that matter, any ailment worth mentioning.

So when Estella Holms reported to Clancy's next watch looking and moving like twenty years at hard labor, naturally he asked her what was wrong.

"I don't know; I just feel horrible. Can't eat, Mr. Allaird, and I'm not sleeping well at all. And then I get these awful pains." One hand to her right side. *Here.*" It looked a little high for appendicitis, but you never know.

"Estella, maybe you should go lie down. I can call someone to fill in. And then if you're not feeling better . . .''

No, she insisted; she'd be all right. But about twenty minutes later she grabbed her side and bent forward, groaning.

What the hell! Allaird considered: *Arrow* had no real medical facilities; none of the starships did. In case of urgent need the Gates gave immediate access to the best NASA had to offer, so why bother?

But Chauncey Ng in his younger days had been a navy medic at the petty officer level, and for this assignment he'd had a crash update on that training. So Clancy got on the horn for him, and soon the stocky man, looking worried, reported. His examination, eyeballing then palpating for soreness, took less than a minute.

"This is a guess, mind you, but I have to say gall bladder. I'm not that pat with the symptoms; notice how yellow the whites of her eyes are, though. That smells like jaundice."

Estella was quieter now, but her face showed pain. Allaird said, "Can you do anything?"

"Yes. Send her back. Right away. Put in a message first to alert them at base, while we gather what she'll be needing immediately; the rest of her things can go later. But Mr. Allaird, I say send her *now.*"

So they did. She was barely conscious enough to realize what was going on, and to say good-bye.

Eli Mainz, Nicole thought, looked like a kid who's just been told Santa Claus is a child molester. Carrying the last of Estella's things to Earthmouth for transmission, he stood disconsolate as Pryce brought the Gate up operational.

"Don't look so sad, Eli."

"How can I help it? If they'd left her stuff here, I could think she's coming back. But this way . . ."

"Regulations, that's all. Maybe she'll be back, maybe they'll send a replacement. Either way it's two months before we find out." This was what? Day fifty-three since boarding? Something like that. Less than four years on Earth.

Eli sighed despair. "Somebody else, it wouldn't be the same. Estella and I . . ."

"Yes, I know," Nicole said. She thought of Cal Ledbetter and of Clancy Allaird. "It never is."

Sometimes it's a lot better.

Nearly five years! Celeste found it hard to believe. But besides the doubled Gate lag she'd been on *Arrow* about two weeks; times twenty-five, that made almost a year in itself. Clancy hadn't been kidding.

On arrival at Glen Springs she first proved to her own satisfaction that Marnie hadn't returned here. These people logged *everything*; she could see no way they might have doctored the records—nor, to be fair, any reason why they should. A lot of these weren't the same folks she'd seen before; mostly they didn't know her or Clancy from a can of spaghetti.

She had a bad day while she swallowed the bitter fact that Marnie was gone, gone, *gone*. Her daughter wasn't here, supposedly wasn't on the ship and she guessed Marshal Payne did know his business well enough that she could take his word for it. Which left one of those goddamned Gates—and anything that takes two or four years to check out each possibility, you can't do a helluva lot about. So she faced her loss and ate it.

Taking a last look around the place, she wondered what had become of the Hoover look-alike; Celeste had some words to say to that one. Send her off to zero gee in heels . . . !

At first bite Maurice wanted retainer for the full period and by Earth reckoning. She dickered him down from that, but still he took a whopping slice of her assets. Even though they had grown considerably, she having made some pretty good term investments before she left. And if Carl had tried to do her any damage behind her back, as Clancy had warned he might, it didn't show in her overall accounts.

She still wanted to recoup a bit, though. And she had some ideas about that. Such as combining profit with paying off someone she figured she owed a good swift kick in the jewels.

There was no way to get at Senator Flynn and Celeste knew it. Oh, she could mount a nuisance lawsuit for interfering with the execution of a court order, sending Clancy warning of her arrival on the ship. But that would take years to prove, if she could at all; more likely, only Maurice would gain.

Carl, though. Carl, by God! She considered and discarded several plans before settling on one. When she rented an apartment across town from him, using the name Ada Malcolm, she wore a darkish skin toner to complement her hair—now shortish, curly, and dyed black. High heels gave way to flats, and sleek bright dresses to sober tweeds. Maybe her precautions were overly elaborate—but the way Celeste saw it, if nobody recognized her, nobody could nail her.

Then she had to check out a few matters. Things hadn't changed all that much: Carl still lived at his home, of course, and there various young women came and went quite often. By frequenting some really seedy streets and taking chances she probably shouldn't have, Celeste learned the current whereabouts and phone numbers of two of his major suppliers that she knew of. A third had vanished. That was the dope business for you. . . .

Then one evening she spent a brief but busy time at the telephone. If the orders she placed with Slide-action Cartiere and with Jambones Tully, "calling for Carl—*you* know, the ol' Knapper," were delivered as promised, the combined Fed-and-city drug bust her tipoffs had initiated might well establish what Celeste had reported on the phone: that Carl was a really, really big man in the operation. He had done some dealing in the past, she knew that much for sure—but mostly as middleman, to insulate his rich colleagues from the likes of Slide and Jambo.

She didn't stay around to see all the shit fly, only long enough to collect her reward: a percentage of the rather modestly estimated value of the drugs seized at Carl's house and then—when the wringer began to squeeze on Carl—at Slide's base and Jambo's. An hour after she cashed the checks (depositing the proceeds quickly into another bank under her legal name), she was in the United Delta boarding line. And, with the temporary aid of the new blond wig, looking pretty much her normal self again.

Which wasn't all bad. One thing about this whole mess: here she was, not only appearing but *being* five years younger than her calender age. Over the long haul, it couldn't hurt.

During the next couple of weeks Celeste caught the Carl Knapheidt story in bits and pieces on the late news, from her high-rise suite overlooking Golden Gate.

It was nice to be back on the coast.

VII

Everywhere Marnie went, now, people reacted differently to her. It took her a while to figure why: to herself, her spell in the "deep freeze" had been no time at all, but to everyone else she'd been gone a month and that's the way they greeted her.

Once she knew, it didn't bother her; from then on, getting back into ship's routine was easy.

First chance she had, when Nicole Pryce came off watch and Clancy relieved her, Marnie tailed the second officer to the galley and managed to join her over a snack. The problem then was, what did Marnie want to say? Well, to start: "I haven't thanked you for saving my hide, there."

The woman's grin was wide. "Frankly I wasn't sure I was acting properly, by ship's regs. But there didn't seem to be a choice. Anyway, Marnie, I'm glad it all worked out so well."

So am I. Marnie chewed and swallowed. "Clancy says you were a big help later, too."

"I was?" Did Pryce look a little on the wary side?

"Sure. When that marshal pulled his gun, and all."

"Oh, that. Well," vehemently, "it needed doing."

"And you're the one, did it. I like that." Marnie paused, finishing the last of her sandwich. "So does Clancy."

One eyebrow tilted, Pryce said, "Are you trying to pump me?"

"Not very subtle, huh?"

The woman laughed. "Not too." She leaned forward. "I'll tell you anyway. Yes, I think your dad and I just might be working up to something important together, and yes, I hope it happens that way. Would it bother you if we do?"

Marnie thought she'd made up her mind on that question; now she found herself hesitating. Then she saw the unspoken plea in Nicole's expression and her barriers melted. "Well, it's like I told Clancy; I don't want to be underfoot. Give me a little warning, okay? So I can get myself a quarters assignment."

For a moment Nicole Pryce stared, but she didn't ask any personal questions. "You get right to it, don't you? That's a good way to be. Well, don't worry about quarters; if I were to move into yours, say, mine are permanently in my name. Would they suit you?"

Would they? Officer's quarters all to herself? But, "You sure the others, the captain, would go for that?"

Pryce smiled. "Why not? Anyway it's my say-so, not anyone else's. Except yours, of course. So?"

"You've got yourself a deal, Nicole. If it all works out." Finished eating, Marnie stood. "I hope it does; he's been—well, never mind." Alone, she meant. "And thanks again. See you."

Back in her own and Clancy's digs she thought on how to tell her father about this talk. After a while she decided it could wait; until something actually happened, why bother him with it?

It was Phil Jennings the drive specialist, not Sybiljan the chief instrument technician, who first detected the dust cloud and reported it to Clancy Allaird who had the watch. The thing was too tenuous to show on *Arrow*'s sensors; it evinced its presence only by the increased fuel consumption needed to hold velocity against the friction of greater particle density. "Not very much so far," Phil said, "but it could get worse."

Alarmed, Clancy asked for exact figures. *Starfinder*, he

knew, had run into trouble this way. Its fuel was fed at a fixed rate, any excess being automatically jettisoned. But slowed by friction, the ship experienced a lesser time ratio; input came slower by ship's time, and fuel tank levels fell.

Worse yet: accelerating from that disadvantage, trying to regain normal time ratio and fuel supply, for a time the ship used more fuel than was gained in the process; *Starfinder* came near to running dry, to killing its Traction Drive. And restarting that device in space—from scratch, exciters and all—with two years of Gate lag added to each and every passage of information or materials between ship and home base, could have delayed the mission by decades, Earth time.

Some very creative juggling of parameters saved *Starfinder*'s bacon. Clancy didn't know the details and was fairly certain his own training wasn't up to reinventing them. The realization didn't panic him; it did impel him to call for a think-tank conference, effective one hour after his watch trick ended.

Marnie wasn't certain what it was all about, but if Clancy was worried, so was she. Half-perched on an end table in the lounge, Amalyn Tabard sought to reassure everyone. "It's not the same system, Allaird. After *Starfinder*'s problem the entire approach was changed. They operated from a constant feed, and when the tanks overflowed the excess was vented offship. So it wasn't there when they needed it, later."

"What's different?" Clancy looked stubborn. "And how?"

"In those days," Nicole Pryce said, "nobody had noticed the feedback effect—that a Gate won't accept anything there's not room for at the far end. Just as it won't transmit unless a Tush will be on line to receive when the lag time is up."

"So how does that help?" Clancy wasn't convinced yet.

"Simply," Tabard put in, "that the feed is always at high pressure. If usage is up at this end, the flow increases at the origin. And vice versa."

"So there's no danger . . ." Clancy began.

Excited, Marnie jumped up. "You mean, on Earth they can detect what's happening here two years later? I mean, more than just whether a Tush is ready to receive?"

"Well, in a sense," said Ellery Dawson. "But there's no practical use for the phenomenon; that would mean faster-than-light communication, which is impossible by definition."

In Allaird's expression, realization followed amazement. "Or just maybe *not*!" And then, "How come nobody's ever followed up on this before?"

Patience clearly strained, Tabard said, "If anyone tried, I'm sure they found it a blind alley. Because we're talking about an irrelevant effect, like phase velocity or atmospheric potential. How could anyone possibly make use of it?"

Not quite able to hide her excitement, Nicole Pryce stood. "Why don't we take a stab at finding out? Clancy?"

"Yo. I'm with you on that." And, "Amalyn, even if you think we're loose in the lobes on this, how about sitting in? You're the one, knows fuel feed *equipment*. And so far that's all we have, that we can tinker at." Her disapproval showed; he added, "On paper, I mean. We won't really mess with anything."

Yet. He didn't say it, but Marnie could tell.

Even without the two inexplicable deliveries he hadn't ordered, Carl's normal stock of drugs ran well above the level set by law as the outside limit for "personal use" and a misdemeanor plea. The bundles of packets that came in from Slide and Jambones, less than an hour apart on the evening of the midnight bust, put Knapheidt far past any chance for an exception under the court's unofficial and discretionary tolerance policy. He was up for major dealing and that was that.

And paying for those commodities had cleaned him totally out of cash on hand. He knew better than to stall; arguing with the delivery people employed by his suppliers was guaranteed hazardous to your health. Luckily the family's mossback law firm persuaded the somewhat notorious defense lawyer of Carl's choice that the Knapheidt credit line was solid.

His trial happened soon and fast. Going less on the tagged evidence, apparently, than the relative behavior of Knapheidt toward his two co-defendants and theirs toward him, the judge more or less pegged Carl as small potatoes; her instructions to the jury resulted in letting him off with four-to-seven.

Tully and Cartiere caught twenty-five each, and in high-security at that.

In a way the judge's leniency did Carl a bad turn. Among the inmates in his cell block an alarming number had a great yen for fat bunkies. For the time being, his wary alertness kept him a jump ahead of their attentions. But in a light-security environment there were all too many chances.

Carl dreaded the prospect with a fear that owed nothing to ignorance; he'd had more than enough of that sort of thing one summer when he was still prepubertal and his two older cousins weren't. In recall, the humiliation still ate at him.

His fourth day in the block he received a postcard; it read, "Now you'll get what's coming to you!" No signature, but he recognized Celeste's printing, and knew that somehow she'd done this to him.

It wasn't fair! Friggin' hell, he hadn't intended to *hurt* the kid—just initiate her a little. She was big enough, the signs starting to show and all. After a time or two she'd have got to like it; a lot of reluctant ones did, he'd heard, once you got them going.

For now, though, Carl sweat and shivered. He had a right to; he was still partly in withdrawal.

In practice the science of hydraulics is somewhat less than exact, and if smooth laminar flow is disturbed enough to give way to turbulence, all normal rules fly out the window. With obviously labored patience, nursing a beer in Nicole Pryce's quarters, Amalyn Tabard explained these matters.

Frowning, Clancy nodded. "So any flow rate detector has to be physically unobtrusive. Are there any like that?"

Well, yes—but nothing sensitive enough to detect the minute variations any feasible maneuvering of *Arrow*'s drives might produce. "Those are big pipes, Allaird; the rate is no gallop."

Silent for a moment, then he snapped his fingers. "Venturi!"

"*Gesundheit!*" said Nicole.

She was, he thought, still on her first beer. "No, no—I mean the Venturi *tube*. You know; pinch down the size of the pipe for a short stretch, and through that part the flow has to move a lot faster."

So? So any variations would be magnified too. Well yes. So you hang this souped-up flowmeter, this *little* thingie, out in the middle of the pipe on skinny streamlined fins so as not to disturb the flow and risk turbulence, and then you . . .

"And then you *what*?"

Allaird blinked. "Well, how much dipsydoodle would it take with the drive, and for how long, to give a reading back home that would say we did it on purpose?"

Amalyn Tabard cleared her throat. "And supposing we did, and some kind of rudimentary code could be agreed on, God only knows how we manage *that*—then how long would it take to say anything worth saying? With Earth, don't forget, reading it slowed down by twenty-five to one."

"Who knows?" Nicole said. "Until we try?"

It wasn't that easy. Everything looked good on paper; there was no need, Clancy saw, to get into fiddling with the ship's velocity to affect time ratio, since a simple increase or decrease in thrust could probably vary the flow rate detectably. In fact, to *avoid* messing up velocity and scheduled distance over any given period, signal elements should produce no overall change. Sine wave cycles seemed like a good choice; longer and shorter cycles, differing in both length and amplitude, could make a fair approximation of Morse code. So far, so good.

Not good at all was what communications people call keying speed and computer folk refer to as byte rate. Traction Drive did not rev up and idle down like a sports car engine. Due to limitations built into the drive control circuitry for safety reasons, increased thrust built slowly, and easing off gave an equally slow decrease. Either way, the change in fuel consumption would be gradual.

"The best we could do," said Tabard, seeming every bit as disappointed as if she'd favored the investigation all along, "is something like a ten-minute rise time. To make a clearly detectable difference, I mean. And that's only a quarter of the cycle; forty minutes all told. That's your dot; the dash should be at least fifty percent longer. So the letter 'a' in Morse takes us a hundred minutes to send."

And on Earth, Allaird thought glumly, nearly forty-two hours to receive. Which still didn't count the necessary pauses between letters.

He stood. "It was a good try, anyway. And at least we can be satisfied we're not overlooking something simple."

Tabard blinked. "But we are." To a bevy of uniformly blank expressions she said, "There's a limited use here, maybe more. Just supposing someone back on Earth wants to know . . ." And she went on to explain.

Her idea, Clancy thought, had possibilities. And anyway, the dust cloud was now behind them, having caused no real trouble after all.

It had been too long. What with Marnie's return—and thank God for that!—and then all the to-do about possible FTL communication, Clancy hadn't been to Nicole's quarters in some days. When she let him in they kissed briefly but hugged a lot longer. Until she said, "We got chairs, too, mister, but they come extra," and he laughed with her.

They didn't talk much beforehand. Sat and smiled and sipped chilled wine from small glasses until one said "Now?" and the other nodded.

In bed things got a little loud. Afterward Clancy was glad he hadn't thought about the quality of bulkhead soundproofing until later; it might have inhibited him.

Nobody got scratched, though; it hadn't been *that* long.

Not exactly dressed, afterward, but covered well enough to answer the door in case of need, Nicole and Clancy sat very close together on the big sofa, each with only one arm free to deal with their refilled glasses. She said, "Clancy? Have you given any thought to where we go from here?"

"A lot." But saying how he really felt had never come easy to him. "Now and then, anyway, between all that's happening."

"Good enough. Decide anything?"

"Yes. I want us to—well, you know. Marnie, though." At such close range he found it hard to look at Nicole directly and keep her in focus. "She said, did I tell you?—she said she'd go take other quarters, if we—but oh jeez I don't know . . ."

She smiled at him. "You don't have to. We talked, she and I. If I move in with you, she gets these quarters."

Clancy stared. "She talked you into that?"

"No. I made the offer and she likes the idea."

He finished his wine without giving it due respect. "You

know something? I thought I was ready to go home in a little while. But I'm not.''

She laughed. ''Here's to fringe benefits.''

A few days short of her twelfth birthday by biological time, Marnie found blood on the sheet when she got up. She wasn't surprised; at school they'd learned all that stuff the year before, and for some months Celeste had fretted about its taking Marnie so long. As if starting later than average was some kind of deficiency.

Well, Clancy wouldn't worry either way. He might be embarrassed; some men seemed to be, about these things. In any case he wasn't here right now. Marnie showered and then began to search for what she needed. Rummaging in some of the boxes Clancy had provided, that she'd had no occasion to open yet.

And found nothing of the sort. Clancy had thought of all kinds of possible needs, but on this one he'd drawn a blank.

Oh well. Nobody's perfect. Improvising a pad was no problem; fastening it into her underbriefs was iffier. How long it would stay put was anybody's guess.

What Marnie wanted was the kind of thing Celeste used. Inside. There'd be some in Supplies, so Marnie went looking for Pilar Velez, and found her in the rec room playing pool on the anisotropic table.

Waiting until the game was over—Pilar beat Chauncey Ng by only a few points—Marnie made her request. ''Well, sure.'' Velez gave her an appraising look. ''I think there's some Juniors back there someplace. Everything else is.''

There were, and a good thing, too. The pad didn't hold position all that well; Marnie was glad to be rid of it.

She didn't actually tell Clancy at all; the day she didn't need the device any longer she left the container out on the bathroom counter. After seeing it, all he said was, ''You've started, I guess. Everything okay?''

''Seems to be. No cramps or anything.''

''Great.'' He yawned; just off watch, he was nearing his bedtime. ''Give us a hug?''

Sure thing.

*   *   *

When Carl found blood on his shorts it had nothing to do with any natural function, periodic or otherwise. Nor did it betoken the loss of his virginity.

Bolton Graef was just too damned mean to grease up first. In retrospect, cousins Rodney and Orville, who had never hurt him more than their aims required, began to look better all the time.

As Marnie entered the rec lounge, Pilar waved her to come over. "I think I found something for you." More tampons? Hardly a big thrill. But "Come on, I'll show you," sounded better, so she followed Velez to Crew Supplies. In the clothing area, the older woman opened a small carton. "Shoes, ship issue. Velcro and smooth, both. And could be your size. Or close."

"How . . . ?" Squatting down, Marnie began sorting through the variety at hand. Sure enough, these were smaller than average; of the three sizes represented, one fit snugly and another a bit looser. Selecting two pairs each of inship and outship models in the snug version, she said, "When did these come in?" There was no point in asking if Pilar had any idea *why*.

Looking at the attached shipping list, Velez said, "It arrived right after those people—that woman—well, you know . . ."

"My mother, you mean."

Velez shrugged. "You don't resemble her—except maybe the small feet." Then, "Your *mother*, though; I shouldn't say . . ."

"It's okay, Pilar. I've said a few things myself. Why do you think I hid out from her, anyway?" Belatedly, Marnie felt a pang. So many years, she and mama had loved each other. Until—how had it all gone so rotten?

As Pilar answered, "Hey, I don't know."

"Well . . ." No. Nothing against Pilar Velez, but this wasn't anyone else's business. "We had some differences."

"Sure. Happens in any family." So that was all right.

Standing, Marnie shifted her stance from one foot to the other, enjoying the new feel of lightweight footwear. "Thanks, Pilar; I'm sure glad you spotted these on the invoice."

Velez waved a hand. "Me too. Glad to help out."

*   *   *

"You got me, Marni Gras; I have no idea." Clancy shrugged; how the shoes could have been ordered out was a total mystery. Just in case, he switched his terminal on and called up the outGate listings from Earth on the ship's day marked by the advent of Celeste and Company. The one immediately following was all hardware and mostly spare parts, but the next: "Bingo!"

"You find something?" Marnie definitely looked interested.

"Sure did. For one thing, this popped in less than an hour after your sainted mother my not-so-recent wife and her pet vulture the legal extortionist, not to mention Whatsisbadge."

"Wow!"

Marnie seemed to like the patter but Clancy had run fresh out; he said, "Second item: I think this was supposed to be a marginal note but somebody got literal-minded and copied it onto the official invoice."

"Copied what?"

"What it says is: expedite, no delays, authority W.K.F."

Marnie cocked an eyebrow. Or tried to; the way it came out, Clancy thought, couldn't be what she intended. She said, "Does that mean something I should understand?"

"Bill Flynn," Allaird said. "His middle name's Kenneth."

And just on a guess, he'd done that? What a guy.

Suddenly the Time Thing hit Clancy. By his own reckoning, only sixty days ago he'd shaken hands with Flynn. Maybe less; he put his watch log onscreen, to check. All right, call it fifty-nine. On Earth that was—what? Four years and two weeks, give or take a long lunch break. Plus the two years Gating. Right now, Flynn was more than six years older than he'd been, only two of Allaird's months ago. And if Clancy sent Bill a note today, thanking him for the shoes, he'd get it—let's see now—only about three months short of six years after he'd had them sent. And likely wouldn't even remember doing it.

Clancy shook his head. Maybe the only way to make sense was to think in ship's time and forget the rest of it.

The trouble was, ships' officers didn't have that option.

Allaird's mood was rapidly becoming a total loss and no insurance, when a new thought yanked him out of it.

*   *   *

Why, Marnie wondered, did Bill Flynn's middle name make Clancy look so woebegone? As he sighed and shook his head she tried to think of something to snap him out of it. Then, looking up again, he grinned. "You know something? I just figured it out. The days on here, minus what you spent in Habegger's Icebox—happy birthday, honey! Those shoes from Bill Flynn are your first present."

Recovering from the hug Clancy gave her, Marnie realized he meant days actually lived, adding up to her twelve years. Or close enough, anyway. And how long by Earth time, since her birth? About a month short of eighteen was her best guess.

As Clancy put it, no point reminding the captain of her time-experienced age. So instead of any "public" celebration, she and Clancy had Nicole over for a private party in quarters. Nicole brought a silk scarf Marnie liked a lot, and Clancy issued her a regulation-model technician's chronometric calculator.

As Nicole Pryce saw it, she and Clancy had definitely agreed to cohabit. But day followed day and nothing happened; he hadn't mentioned the subject again and she felt hesitant about bringing it up, in case—well, she didn't want to look pushy.

On the other hand, maybe Allaird was waiting for her to make the next move. As she showered and dressed, she wondered what it should be. How about the formality of notifying Ellery Dawson of the switch in quarters, so he'd know where to call her in future? Especially when it came to leaving messages.

Yes, that should do it. Nicole checked schedules. Dawson was off watch and so was Amalyn Tabard; they might be together and likely were. But Tabard was up for duty within the hour, and Ellery the Correct would never send her off still warmed by the flames of passion (the phrase, from a holo-drama Clancy and Nicole had viewed recently, provoked a chuckle).

So it was safe to call now. Amalyn's rooms, of course. Nicole did. "Like to talk with you, captain . . . in person, yes . . . no, nothing serious . . . all right, see you in a few minutes."

About four, actually, and perhaps Nicole had misjudged Ellery Dawson; Amalyn did show residual signs of arousal. Or maybe not—for one thing, brushed or mussed her hair looked much the same.

After hellos Nicole said, "I just wanted to let you know I'll be sharing quarters with First Officer Allaird. Marnie says she doesn't want to be underfoot, so I'm giving her mine."

Dawson nodded, but Tabard said, "Now just a minute. We've got sixteen adults aboard—officers, section heads, the lot. Some doubling up and some not. And this *child*, who's not even on the roster, gets one of the four best spaces on the ship?"

She was overlooking the VIP suite but Nicole didn't quibble. Frowning: "You don't like Marnie?"

"Of course I do. What does that . . . ?"

Nicole wasn't done yet. "You're drive chief; the difference between your place and mine isn't all that much." She didn't let Tabard interrupt. "If you want to upgrade quarters, what's stopping you and the captain from sharing *his*?"

Ellery couldn't get a word in edgewise, not that he was trying. "We don't choose to," Amalyn snapped out.

"But you'd take mine?"

"Not me; I only—"

"Then who did you have in mind? What's your—"

"Shut! Up!" Red-faced, Ellery Dawson shouted. "Pryce, I think I see Amalyn's point. Let's hear yours."

"Why . . . only that doubled or not, all crew members still keep title—so to speak—to their own assigned quarters. Which means, or should, they can use them however they want. What I want is for Marnie Allaird to feel good about her dad and me living together. And . . ." She nodded. "That's my point. All of it."

"This is your own idea?" Dawson sounded wary.

"Yes." She told how it had come about. "Marnie did wonder if it would be all right. I told her it would; I hope you won't make a liar out of me."

Rising, Amalyn made a show of checking her wrist chrono. "I'd better hurry; I'll be late. Look, Nicole. I don't know why this hit me wrong, but it did. I'm sorry. All right?"

"Well, sure. And—"

"No," said Dawson. His voice was tight; he looked like a man facing punishment. "It's my fault. Amalyn, we'll move your things into captain's digs as soon as you come off watch. Or after you've rested, whichever you want.''

Tabard stared. "You're certain about this?"

"Yes. We're overdue for it."

"I'm glad you agree." She stepped over and kissed him. "And now I do have to go."

Whatever Ellery Dawson had on his mind, and there looked to be plenty, Nicole wanted no part of it. Not just now, and preferably never. "Me too. Thanks, captain. Once I'm moved, I'll change the entry on the intercom screen."

Quickly she followed Tabard out; the door closed.

Side by side and keeping step; hup-hoo-hee-ho! but not out loud. "Is this a monkey wrench I see before me, its handle toward my hand? Didst I toss it into none of my business, Amalyn?"

Laughter, quickly repressed to a strangled snort. "With Macbeth it was a dagger. But no, you tossed it just right. Thanks, in fact."

Uh-huh is usually safe; turning from the cross corridor toward Nicole's own quarters and the transfer ring doors, Pryce put all her trust in it.

But Tabard said, "Ellery's always seemed to need his own place all to himself. We never met there; everything's kept just so and I might mess it up. And here you go, turning a *kid* loose in yours."

She tugged at Nicole's elbow. "You see what I mean? Why it began to curdle on me?"

Sometimes uh-huh isn't enough. A hug can help.

All at once it seemed *everybody* was changing quarters. After she and Clancy helped move Nicole's things and Pryce returned the favor, Marnie wanted to get fully unpacked for the first time, in this the largest space she'd ever had to herself.

But then, at Nicole's suggestion for which she gave no reason, the three of them pitched in to get all of Amalyn Tabard's possessions into captain's quarters. Just as well, thought Marnie, for Dawson wasn't much help. He did carry things, but mostly he seemed to stand around telling people where *not* to put them. Until Clancy and Nicole and Marnie took to setting their loads in the middle of the main living room and letting it go at that, scuttling back out before Dawson could organize his thinking enough to tell them any different.

Eventually that job, too, was done. Clancy had already left, to relieve Gretel Aaberg from watch; Dawson and Tabard were politely not-quite-bickering over what should go where. Marnie was glad to follow Nicole out and to the galley for some lunch.

Finally, then, she was free to delve through cartons she'd barely glanced at, and spread things out a little in her new home. Free for the next four hours, anyway, until she was due to report to Supplies and help Pilar for half a shift. All right . . .

This was really interesting. Clancy had sent clothing not just for now but for some years to come. Holding up one of the older-size dresses she was pleased to see he was betting she'd slim out again in a year or two.

Marnie purely hoped her dad was right. ―

Clancy took to sharing digs like a seal to herring. Living full time with Nicole he realized how much he'd missed the closeness of marriage. He almost asked her to take that step with him before remembering that by way of the mandatory group wedding ceremony, they already had!

So instead, one evening when Marnie joined them for a dinner they fixed together, then took her leave to catch up on some studying, Clancy pulled in a deep breath and said, "Nicole? When we reach destination and set up a normal society more or less, how about you and I just marry each other and nobody else?"

Below her level gaze, the corners of her mouth worked at holding back a smile. "*De jure*, the man wants. We'll see. Right now, what do you say to a little *de facto*?"

A few days later, half an hour before he was due to relieve Aaberg on watch, Clancy found himself at loose ends. So he called control, thinking to ask if she'd like to get off early.

No answer. That was strange. Maybe a new batch of visitors had blown in, and everyone was down the corridor at Earthtush. Or possibly, this time, a different Gate. Ooh-kay; in no hurry he assembled what he needed for the shift and rode the transfer ring. But in the control room he found Gretel, along with Ptiba Mbente and Eli Mainz, sprawled in their duty seats and out like so many snuffed candles.

"What the *hell* . . . ?" One and then another, he shook them; no responses. More checking: they were warm and had pulses, slow but steady. Their breathing carried no smell of booze or dope. None that he could recognize, anyway.

This was one for Chauncey. Summoned, the man arrived quickly and had a look. He shrugged. "Sedated, Clancy, that's all I can determine. What or how, I don't know. Nothing lying around, that I can see; no pill bottles, whatever."

Ptiba began to stir; muttering, she scratched at the side of her neck. Moving her hand away, Clancy saw a small red dot, like a puncture wound or insect bite. He turned to Ng. "You think . . . ?"

"Let's check." Aaberg and Mainz were still out flat; carefully the two men looked, disarranging clothing as little as possible.

Gretel had a mark on her upper arm, just below the shoulder. Eli was too hairy; thorough inspection simply wasn't feasible.

Two out of three was close enough. "I'd better call the captain," said Clancy.

Then Pete Larue rushed in. "Hey, come quick! I was just down by the back corridor. Gina's lying right around the corner there, and she's out cold."

Todisco was no worse off than the others. The tiny red mark just below her right cheekbone made it three out of four. But finding her in that specific location, between control and the offship Habgates, put a new slant on the enigma.

Dawson arrived only a few minutes before Amalyn Tabard and Coyote Benjamin reported to Clancy's watch; what with the captain being past his first questions and the other two just beginning, Allaird got irritated. "Let's get in phase here; all right?"

Ptiba came awake now—not exactly chipper, but cognizant; Gina seemed to be pretty well aboard again, though not saying much as yet. Gretel and Eli still looked groggy; Chauncey fussed over them as Dawson questioned Ptiba Mbente. "How long after I called you, about your DV maintenance log, did this happen?"

"You called me? I don't remember that."

When it turned out that Mainz and Aaberg also lacked memory of the incident, a matter of perhaps thirty–forty minutes past, the mystery developed a deeper grade of murk. Dawson wanted a total search of the ship, for saboteurs. Unfortunately Marshal Payne had taken his tiny microcams back to Earth; point-to-point checkup would require more people and new tactics.

Frustrated, the captain settled for conferring, low-voiced, with his drive chief and roomie. Amalyn didn't say much.

Clancy's call had found Dawson in the lounge; the man's abrupt departure roused curiosity. It wasn't long before everyone awake on *Arrow* converged on control. Marnie, Allaird noted, wasn't one of them. Knowing how she hated to miss anything, he resigned himself to telling her the entire story when she did show up.

Nicole Pryce was one of the last to arrive. Unlike most, she asked short questions and listened to the answers. After a few minutes she pulled at Clancy's arm. "Did anyone check for intruder traces before this herd trampled the place up?"

Baffled, he shrugged. "There wasn't—it all just got away from us, Nicole."

"Sure; I can see how it would. Well, let's *think*, then."

But their joint thinking, and then that of the overall group, came down to a very few unsatisfactory conclusions:

1. Somebody we don't know got on this ship.
2. They may still be here or may not.
3. We don't know where they came from or where they went.
4. Or what the hell they were after, and still might be.

"If they're aboard this ship, their ass belongs to me!" said Captain Ellery Dawson, but wasn't alone in wanting a slice or two. And now the search, which had been so difficult when performed by Celeste and her party, became much simpler; each member of *Arrow*'s crew had a personal stake in the matter.

First, lock all Habegger's Mouths out of Transmit mode. Then seal each level from the next except for one guarded access. Not all at once: start from the residential belt and work inward; the only interface that needs guarding is the one between secured and unsecured country.

"What do you mean, overdue?" The call from Glen Springs caught Senator Flynn dozing at the midafternoon rest his doctor recommended; waking up wasn't as sudden as it used to be.

"I know they don't return all at once," the director said, "because we don't send the relief cadres that way. But it's nearly two weeks past the normal four years, since Hayes Morton and cadre 2–A Gated off to *Starfinder*, and not a single member of 1–A has shown up yet. Frankly, senator—"

"I'm getting worried," Flynn mouthed silently.

"—I'm getting worried."

"Let's see." Flynn called up directory, subdirectory, and file. "1–A: that's Jimmy Hanchett, Fleurine Schadel, Rance Collier, Su Teng, Dink Hennessey, and Benita Torres. No personal problems reported out of that gang. Nothing like the launch crew." Two dead, one imprisoned for the killings . . .

"Don't remind me. Anyway, my question is, what do I do about it?"

At four years round-trip answer time? "You know as well as I do. Send a message—or an investigator—and wait."

"Come on now, Bill. You know what I mean. What do I tell the bloody *press*?"

In Bill Flynn's reactions, exasperation slowly gave way to mischievous satisfaction. "It pleases me a whole lot, Jerry, to remind you *you're* the one who gets paid to decide that."

But savoring the barb didn't keep *him* from worrying. Sometimes it seemed that *Starfinder* had a jinx on it: the killings, then hitting some kind of immaterial obstacle in space and barely regaining drive power . . . Now this!

The senator didn't have all that long to fret; Torres and Hennessey arrived, belatedly, at Glen Springs, along with a report from Hayes Morton who had gone out with 2–A as executive officer but now seemed to be captain. The lump sum of data read: Rance Collier and Su Teng had fled the ship via the *Roamer* Gate. *Why?* The following were missing with no explanation: from 1–A, Schadel and Hanchett; from 1–B, only halfway through its tour of duty when this message originated, Captain Irina Tetzl and her pairmate Cleve Rozanski. And from 2–A which would have been beginning its year aboard, a young couple Flynn must have met before they left but couldn't really remember.

Frustrated, the senator muttered a few choice obscenities. *Damn* Habegger and his time-consuming Gates!

Leaving Coyote on watch alone with the door locked from the inside and an improvised code knock required for admission, Clancy and Amalyn each headed up a search team. First order of business was securing the residential belt, with a perfunctory check of the exercise compartment, just in case.

Approaching his own digs, Allaird's group met Marnie coming out. "Anybody else in there?"

"Course not. Why would there be?"

"Come with us; I'll fill you in as we go."

It wasn't that easy; Clancy hadn't really expected it would. But with the belt secured and the transfer ring immobilized though not by a shoe this time, he called a chow break. Maybe eating would slow her down a little.

". . . unconscious? . . . nobody saw anything . . . still on the ship, maybe . . . have to search *all* of it again? . . . can't imagine who . . . what they'd *want* . . ." And then the jackpot question: "What if they're armed?" Watching her father, Marnie waited for answers.

Looking worried, Clancy shook his head. "I don't know, Marnie; we don't know anything, really, except what I've told you. One thing, though." He explained the concept and mechanics of secured *vs* unsecured areas. "So until this is settled, I'd rather you don't go into unsecured country alone. Just with me, or someone I okay to look after you. All right?"

It made sense. "Sure. *I* don't want to get laid out."

Securing the belt had been a breeze; now the hard part began. Hard and long; when it was finally done, Clancy had lost track of time. But they knew, the officers and the few others gathered in control, that no unknown person was at large on the ship. "So are they on Earth?" Tabard said, ". . . or on one of the other ships?"

"They're not on *Roamer*," said Nicole. "I checked the Transmit counters on all three Gates, and that one's unchanged from my last log entries yesterday. Unfortunately . . .''

She glared at the group in general and the captain in particular. "Unfortunately some people can't be bothered to log their transmissions. There's at least one to *Starfinder* and two to Earth that weren't documented." Her brows raised. "Anyone?"

Nicole got her confessions. The only problem was that on one the timing was wrong, and the others were too indefinite. *Starfinder* was unlikely but Earth was distinctly possible. "They log outGatings there," said the captain. "Why don't we ask for a transcript? Without saying why we want it? Might learn something."

"Two months from now we might. Four years Earth time." Clancy's frustration and disgust showed in his voice.

Dawson tilted his head back and stared coldly. "In that case there will be no word of the incident from this ship to anyone else whatsoever. It is entirely our problem. And that's an order!"

Oh shit. Allaird felt chagrin. Ellery hadn't pulled one of his dumb adamant decisions for some time now—and Clancy had to be the one to trigger it. Some days you can't win for losing. . . .

Another thought came. He looked to the back-to-back Gates at the rear bulkhead and said, half to himself, "Y'know, about twenty-nine days from the time this flap started, it might not be a bad idea for somebody to be on hand here."

Clancy's grin felt tight on him. "With a baseball bat."

VIII

The fuss wound down; after another two days the incident might as well not have happened. At least as far as casual talk indicated. How people really felt, Marnie thought, might be different. She knew *she* still had a mild case of the creeps.

It wasn't as if the Invisible Zappers could still be on *Arrow*; no one, especially any who didn't know the ship by heart, could have evaded the organized search. No, they'd Gated off some way: to Earth or *Starfinder* or *Roamer*. Or maybe just doubled back as Marnie herself had done, to hit control again after twenty-nine days of effective nonexistence.

In that case, Clancy said, *Arrow* would be ready for them. He didn't go into detail about the plan he and Chauncey Ng had worked out "with more help from the captain than we really needed," but it involved a tactical contact squad holding the fort in control, that room to be locked from outside, and vidcams relaying events therein from four different angles.

It all sounded pretty good to Marnie.

Immediately after Dawson put his security lid on the whole mess, Clancy had moped for a while; later that evening, visiting with him and Nicole after dinner, Marnie was glad to see him brighten up, then busy himself at the keyboard and print out some message flimsies. "Here, Marnie, Nicole—take a look. And tell me: do these in any way violate Dawson's order to report nothing of the intruder incident, off ship?"

On all three, separately addressed to Glen Springs and *Roamer* and *Starfinder*, the texts were similar. To both ships:

This is to confirm that no authorized personnel departures have been made through this Gate.

Earth's copy, of course, specified that no one had Gated home since the return of Celeste's party.

On her first reading, Marnie wasn't sure what Nicole was breaking up about. By the time she finished a second, she couldn't talk for laughing. Finally, "It's great. Unless something weird *has* happened at their end, they'll think it's just more dumb official stuff. No reason to answer, even."

"You hit it, Marni Gras. That's exactly what I'm hoping. But if someone did show, any of those places, the alert's out."

Clancy took the messages down to the Gates himself. Nicole said, "Don't you love it when he goes out in left field and hits pay dirt?"

Marnie hadn't thought of it that way before, but the tall woman was right. "Yes. Yes, I sure do."

Pryce smiled. "That's just one of the things I like about Clancy. You're lucky to have him for a father."

Well. If Nicole had no idea how things had been for Marnie the previous six years on Earth, leave it that way. But for the time now, on *Arrow*, she was absolutely right. So, "I know."

When Clancy came back from his errand, just as Marnie was leaving, he may have got a bigger hug than he expected.

Returning to his Glen Springs office from a weekend down on the Gulf, Director Kennerly found his In basket backlogged. As usual, though, Helene had sorted out the Now stuff for him.

The top item was definitely Now: medical emergency on *Arrow*, with a crew member offGated; she had arrived here Sunday morning and was in surgery by noon. Well, it beat the last time a ship sent crew members back unscheduled—the three, ten–eleven years ago when Kennerly was basicaly a glorified clerk, that *Starfinder* had returned: this one was neither dead nor in restraints.

Kennerly looked past the authorizations and so forth to the important part. Okay, Estella Holms was going to be all right. But not ready for duty just now, if at all.

So, a replacement. That assignment, subject to his approval, was on page five. Kennerly looked, then got on his intercom.

"Helene? Who in hell picked this guy for *Arrow*?" Then, "No, it doesn't matter; just kill it, is all. And screen me up a list of qualified candidates."

Because whoever had been holding down the desk had ignored the principle of balanced crews and chosen a male to replace Estella Holms. Not good thinking. "On second thought, Helene, I do want to know. Anyone capable of that grade of mistake is in the wrong job." But not for long . . .

The screen showed him more people, more data, than he really had time to study at any length; he began skipping. Then one entry caught his attention: Trish Pembrook, specializing in instrument installation and maintenance. He checked those qualifications against the Holms file: close enough.

But what struck him about this one was that although she was barely of legal age, Pembrook had lived in high orbit, the last two years working with an installation crew wiring the sensors and electronic nervous system into the uncompleted structure which would eventually become macroGate One. She'd gone out with her parents some time back, in dependent status, but later applied for an apprentice slot and then made the most of it.

Onscreen he highlighted the listing. "Helene? Send this one a query. If you get an affirmative, start the paperwork."

The fat envelope, Bill Flynn saw, was from Allaird. To the best of his knowledge the man was out of the woods now; what *else* could happen? Opening the packet, Flynn's first alarm gave way to relief. Here was no personal problem; rather, some of *Arrow*'s people had an idea they wanted to try out. Flynn read further:

> "*. . . vary thrust according to a sine curve, beginning positive for yes, negative for no, amplitude plus and minus ten percent of normal, the cycle requiring about forty minutes here or slightly over sixteen hours at your terminal, ending with all conditions back to normal. The initial change predicts the result, but only the completed cycle can confirm a purposeful answer rather than fortuitous maneuvering. See attached suggestion for a Venturi modification at your metering point, which might shorten the necessary signal length to some extent.*

Well. Drive Chief Tabard appended some thoughts on optimum detection methods. And maybe, thought Flynn, some of his NASA specialists might have even better ones.

He skimmed through the last paper: Ellery Dawson signing off as official sponsor of the suggestion, and "we shall be prepared to try the experiment on receipt of notice to that effect."

Good on you, *El Capitan*. . . .

Flynn switched on his intercom. "Eloise? Would you see if you can get me Dr. Alois Habegger, up at Gayle Tech?"

"Like a basset hound, you know? Those big sad eyes." Sitting across the small table in a corner of the lounge, Pilar Velez gestured. "Well, and you remember, Nicole, how he and Estella and Chauncey and I first made a foursome all together. But then we separated into couples like everybody else, and that was fine too. Less complicated. You understand?"

Nicole hoped so; she wasn't entirely certain. "And?"

"And with Estella sent home sick to Earth, Eli wants to go back together as before. Except, now there's only three of us."

When it came to expressive shrugs, Velez was tops. "I wouldn't mind. Eli's a nice boy. Could lose a little weight off the middle but he's young yet, plenty of time if he doesn't let himself go like some do. *But*—" Her widened eyes rolled to rake far horizons. "Chauncey says we decided: he came with me, Eli went with Estella, the deal's made and no fair asking for new cards if you lose one."

"Umm, yes, I can see his point . . ."

"But poor Eli; he has nobody." Pilar leaned forward. "Not even friends, really. As four together we were something different; everybody gave us extra distance, you see what I mean." And with a resigned shrug, "I don't think we ever closed it up very well."

Nicole began to simmer. This was getting out of hand; whatever she said, Velez shifted and took the other side. All right: "Well, maybe Clancy and I could help with that. I'll check; next time the duty skeds fit together right, we can invite him to have dinner with us. Sit around and talk, make him feel at home. You think that might do his problems any good?"

"Some, I guess." Pilar looked dubious. "Not with the horny part, though."

Nicole Pryce put on her officer face. "I don't consider that aspect any of my business." *So there.*

Still, as she left to meet Clancy after his watch, Nicole wondered how it would all work out. Because in a small closed society, aloneness could be a very destructive condition.

"No, senator. The Gate fields don't notice what goes through; some kind of standard flow sensor, you want." He paused. "Ummm—this Venturi tube squinch, you get some extra out of that, I think. Heats the liquid where it skootches through the narrow part, going to expand it some, right there. Give you a little more push. So you measure just coming out from the throat part, you understand me?"

"Right. Thanks, doctor." A few more exchanges and the call was done. Next Flynn called the fuel supply depot that fed all three starships and was gearing up for the next one. "Charlie? Bill here. Look, I'm imaging over to you some stuff that came in from *Arrow.* I don't want go into detail on a public circuit, but so you're on board, here's the gist: detecting minor changes of flow rate in the feedpipe. How easy is it?"

"Dunno, Bill; we've never tried. All we measure is volume provided over a month's time, for payment purposes." After a moment, "That's always been good enough before. What's going on? Somebody trying to pick nits in our procedures?"

"No, no—nothing like that. This is all scientific, not political. Can you get some people on it? I'll send the ship's material right away, with a cover letter to authorize you."

"Okay." Another move begun. The senator shook his head; why did all managers view any new endeavor as a threat?

Meanwhile, just for the hell of it, why not do a tryout *before* all the improvements went in?

As it happened, though, once the project work began the facility was no place for would-be experimenters getting underfoot. Bill Flynn had to cool his heels like anybody else.

"And once you have your first one," Celeste had said more than a few times, "you're not a girl any longer; you're a woman." Then she'd nod a time or two. "Everything's going to be different—the way you act, the way you feel. You'll see.''

Well, Marnie had had her first period and might be considered due for her second. Of course the early ones could be irregular and usually were; fifth grade SexEd had covered all that stuff, so she was prepared for a certain amount of leeway.

What bothered her was the feeling part. Feel like a woman, not like a girl? Well, did she or didn't she? And how was she supposed to know how a woman felt? As near as Marnie could tell, she didn't feel any different at all.

Except for being saddled with this worry about how she was *supposed* to feel . . .

For a couple of weeks and more, when nothing more immediate occupied her mind, Marnie had fretted over the question. Then one morning as defined by her own duty schedule she woke early and for a time half dozed, drifting on a quiet tide between awareness and something cozier. Until she came surfacing with an incompletely formed thought she struggled to hold. Most of it escaped; all she could remember solidly were the words: ''Celeste didn't know.''

Blinking, Marnie sat up. There'd been a dream, partly warm and partly grim; no details remained. Except that like a coin, the phrase had two sides. The grim side—that would be Carl, and it made sense that Celeste hadn't known the dangers of him. But the good side, the warmth—all the subliminal associations were *here*. So here and now, what didn't Celeste know?

That Marnie was still safely aboard? Obvious, but no cause for worry. Certainly nothing to dream about.

Then: of course! Celeste didn't truly know and never had, how Marnie might feel or was supposed to feel. Let alone how she *did* feel.

Getting up now, how Marnie felt was really good.

The complex planning of design and timing needed to introduce experimental procedures into a major pipeline Gate operation was truly impressive. But, Bill Flynn began to realize, hardly a patch on the sheer *mulework* required.

Build your alternate pipe, with the fancy Venturi which by God they better have it right the first time because doing cutover without affecting the flow is going to cost like a small war, and the budget won't hold still to swallow it twice.

Considering everything, the job got done damn fast.

Flynn himself became so involved, and his staff with him, that he came near missing deadline to file candidacy for re-election. But once past that formality he put thought to what answers he really wanted from the starship *Arrow*.

On their side of the Gates, the senator reflected, all the work here had taken only about two days. So he could spend a few more hours getting his message just the way he wanted it.

He wished he knew when, if ever, some of Habegger's ideas for more-advanced techniques would make it to the hardware stage.

"Eli, yes," said Nicole. "Pilar was saying how he goes around like a lost puppy; I thought we could invite him over some evening. Dinner and so forth. Some time when it's more or less the evening for all three of us, I mean. With everything that's been going on, I forgot. But now . . ."

It made sense; Clancy nodded. "All right; ask him, whenever you like. We can spare a little time for morale purposes."

As it turned out, Clancy himself ran into Mainz a few hours later and made the invitation. The younger man hesitated. "Well thanks, Mr. Allaird. I'd like to. But could it be another time? I, I'm, uh, busy after this next watch, and . . ."

"Sure thing. We'll try again." Mildly curious, Allaird didn't pursue the matter. For one thing, he felt the need of some full-gee exercise, and nowadays that facility was scheduled in one-hour periods. Unless the unit happened to be vacant during a given hour, you had no choice but to wait for the next one. And right now that next one began in about three minutes.

The only other person waiting was Chauncey Ng. As the ring revved up, Allaird asked "How's it all going?" and was surprised when the chunky man gave him a flat, inquiring stare.

"Like what?"

Clancy shrugged. "Nothing special. Just, you know . . ."

Rotation steadied, presumably at one gee and Clancy's muscles certainly felt like it. Ng said, "You mean Pilar? All right, I'll tell you. Four of us together worked fine on Earth, but here with all different schedules, the sharing was too hard to even out. Sometimes people got their tail in a knot, so we gave up on the idea and split pairs. *Into* pairs," he added.

"Yes, I know."

"And maybe you know, with Estella gone—"

"I might have heard a little something."

"Well. Nothing against Eli but my life's complicated enough without mixing up *two* other people's schedules in our quarters. So I said no."

Umm-hmm; Allaird nodded.

"Work it out for yourselves, I said. Just don't mess with *my* skeds; they're hard enough to keep track of as it is."

And so? Clancy let his eyebrows do the asking.

"So every now and then, once in a while when I'm on watch anyway and they're not, she goes to see him." The man's scowl was intent. "I don't mind *that*, you see. I like Eli, always did. And how can I cherish Pilar's kind heart and begrudge what it tells her?"

Apparently relieved to have his attitudes spelled out clearly, now the man smiled. "You understand?"

"Yes, I think so."

"All right then. Anybody asks, you can tell them."

The discussion seemed to be over. Time for exercise.

When Clancy reported to Nicole she said, "We'll invite Eli once more, anyway. If he begs off again, we can forget it."

Throughout the all-plenum, in which each point-locus lies contiguous to every other, uniquantal movement of volitional entities or inert masses between point-loci groupings is and must be entirely causal in nature.

Yet in recency have been noted displacements of indeterminate origin. Normally such phenomena would hold only abstract interest. Unanticipatedly, however, movement of this anomalous nature gives rise to vastly irritative stimuli.

Inert mass does not displace of itself, nor without cause. But at and proximately prior to nowtime along the consensual chronal-prime vector, masses unexpectedly change their *dimensionalities* at random only to revert to initial frameworks at equally illogical loci, each momentary obtrusion leaving traces which resonate severe malaise. Communication by spatial admixture confirms that these effects become growingly widespread among certain specific loci groupings.

Additionally, other mass aggregates so displace themselves and remain thusly, admixing with normal configurations in manner both invasive and discomforting. And finally, of most recency, some few impulses have manifested in opposition to normal chronality. These latter have particularly disruptive effect, causing actual pain of seldom precedented magnitude and posing eventual threat to orderly causation.

Origin of such anomalies must be sought, and its activities ended. First need is to identify those specific dimensions, among all existing, which correspond to trans-plena movement traces. Such groupings constitute sub-continua of n dimensions, such that only $n+1$ point-loci can be mutually contiguous. Long known to exist, such sub-plena lie loosely entwined within plenum-major and normally cause no disturbance. Only when, as in currently progressing nowtime, components achieve extension into dimensions non-innate to themselves do their movements aberrate process in contextual reality. Such displacings create anomalous discontinuities in the affected sub-plena, reflecting disorder on the quantum level into the fuller continuum. Causative anomalies result, creating further effects both noticeable and unpleasant.

Still: since pain emphasizes trace impressions, dimensional identifications are simplified. The specific demi-continuum involved proves to be one previously noted for other puzzling phenomena: in particular, a locus wherein part of the sub-plenum itself is destroyed and recreated, that locus possessing an inordinate rate of spatial/chronal progression.

This phenomenon, recently ceasing for no observed cause, had carried no danger, being confined to the sub-plenum itself, and of magnitude easily subject to detection and thus avoidance. But since mass in the newer disruptions repeatedly obtrudes to exploit parasitic congruity, a drastic dissociation from the all-plenum emerges as the least effortful solution. Probable effect on the lesser sub-plenum is a matter wholly unknown and of very little concern.

Of paramount importance is ridding the greater continuum of painful intrusion. Among other possibilities, therefore, dissociative measures are a prime consideration.

Bill Flynn went to Glen Springs in person to put his messages into the Gate for *Arrow*; then he flew to the fuel staging base to see with his own eyes what the newly installed flow sensors would show. After waiting two days with no decisive results, the senator gave up and returned home.

He should have done that sooner, and he knew it. Early in his career he'd lost one wife by simply being away too much; he couldn't let it happen again with Mara, his bride of only a few months. Well, part of the time she'd been off to Tashkent with her university's cultural exchange team—but any sensible man would have made a point of meeting her on homecoming.

The trouble was, he'd been practically glued to the sensors, watching for word from *Arrow*, from the future. And hadn't been able to bring himself to leave. Not until it became a clear case of back to the drawing board.

Had something happened to the ship? No, he wouldn't think that. For the time being he wouldn't think about *any* of it.

Now, entering the Georgetown residence, their in-session domicile, he carried the traditional offerings of the ardent swain or wayward husband: flowers and champagne. They stocked the latter for parties, of course, but getting a bottle out of the case didn't buckle enough swash.

"Mara?" Walking through the spacious, uncluttered living and dining rooms, he repeated his call. As he reached the smallish kitchen and set his booty on the dinette table, she came in by the back door. "Hi!" And they had their home-coming kiss.

He stepped back and looked at her. Well, she'd said she was going to do something about the slight but growing encroachment of grey in her hair; its coloring was a slightly darker brown than he was used to. At least it wasn't shortened noticeably, which was something salons tended to do as a matter of principle or something; the smooth sweep still reached well below her jawline. She smiled. "Home with your shield? Or on it? How did the experiment work out?"

The last phone talk: how many days ago? No matter. "It didn't, I'm afraid. And I have no idea why. Haven't been able to raise Habegger; maybe I'll fly up there tomorrow. Or—"

He stopped; what was he *saying*? "Hey, forget that." He handed her the flowers. "Welcome home. How was Tash-kent?"

For now, the hell with faster-than-light communication; he orchestrated a homecoming evening no prodigal could fault.

* * *

They'd tried to plan for anything that could happen, Clancy reflected, but how do you allow for the way tension builds up? Assuming the intruders really lay doggo between the Gates in control, known timing put their coming emergence at some time near the end of the next watch or early in the one following.

For those shifts, then, normal skeds went up the spout. Clancy himself drew the first, along with Chauncey Ng and Coyote Benjamin. On the second, Ellery Dawson had Edd Jarness and Pete Larue for backup. In Clancy's estimation either Amalyn Tabard or Pilar Velez could beat Edd's reflexes, but the captain didn't believe women should be allowed into possible combat situations. The armed forces, yes; Ellery Dawson, no.

Arguing the matter would have made a good distraction from the suspense of waiting, but the watch team couldn't work up enough disagreement on the issue to keep the discussion alive. Clancy, for one, found it hard to concentrate.

He fiddled with the short *kendo* staff leaning against his chair; it wasn't a ball bat and he was no kind of expert at the martial art it went with, but he figured it might do him some good in a pinch. Coyote had something similar, but longer; Chauncey made do with a pair of heavy leather gloves and didn't say what they were good for.

Sitting with seats turned sidewise, restraining belts snapped closed but left unclamped in the interest of sudden mobility, the three took their routine instrument readings in quick glimpses stolen from strained, staring surveillance of the local Tush. If and when somebody appeared back there, the idea was to act *fast*. And not get pinked with whatever kind of pigstickers had zapped the watch crew a ship's-month earlier.

What he expected, Clancy didn't know; who could be out here with destructive motives? The world was full of protesters and even terrorists, but how the hell could any of that sort get through Glen Springs in the first place? Especially without being noticed, and no word had come. It didn't make sense. . . .

Time crawled; he got up for coffee. It crawled some more; he had a snack. So, at one time and another, did Ng and Benjamin—though of course never any two at once. Coyote did a little dance and lifted his squeeze flask of coffee in a toast for the benefit of the four wide-angle vidcams aimed diagonally downward from each upper corner of the room, relaying the scene to the team monitoring in control's Daily Supplies room two doors forward along the corridor. Either they or the watch crew could report by intercom to the rotating belt, where the transfer ring car was held blocked except for designated movement of personnel going on or off duty.

After the watch shift passed midpoint it seemed to go even slower. Was something going to happen, or wasn't it? Finally the shift ended; the control room door was unlocked from outside and the relief group came in like people in a cop holo, peering in all directions. As if any of the room could pose a threat, other than the Tush itself . . .

Dawson led the way; behind him Edd and Pete moved quietly. "Pretty dull, eh?" the captain said, belying his SWAT team manner, and moved over to sign in.

"We like it that way," Coyote said, straight-faced.

"The monitors work okay?" Allaird asked.

"Total coverage," said Jarness. "The action wasn't much, though. You should fire your writers."

"I'll think about it." In a hurry to use the zero gee toilet across the way, Clancy left. Being locked in control for four hours with no breaks wasn't something he was used to.

Nicole relieved Phil Henning on the monitor team about an hour before the control room watch change. Observing dutifully, she didn't find the surveillance all that interesting. It perked up a little when Dawson and company relieved Clancy's team, but for another two or three minutes after the first group left, that was the high spot.

Then at the Tush the colors flared. Nicole sat bolt upright. The main feature was starting; her pulse sped.

The chromatic display faded to reveal several people but only one woman standing; all the rest lay sprawled together, shifting gently in zero gee as the woman gestured left-handed and said, "Medics! The Gates—something wrong . . ."

But when Dawson and the other two stepped from their seats to help the sturdy woman with the frizzed-out blond hair, she crouched; her right hand came into view holding some kind of handgun. Three rapid aims, three apparent firings though no sound accompanied them: first Ellery Dawson poised between steps on one toetip, then Edd and finally Pete came to weaving halts and swayed against the tug of their Velcro anchors.

Pacing quickly from one to another the woman paused to pick something off each: from Dawson's cheek, her touch dislodging his shoe's grip on the deck, then from Jarness's neck and Larue's jaw. At the room's door she paused for a moment; her body hid whatever her hands did there. Then she moved to tow one of her limp companions from the Tush over to the Mouth.

Unfreezing, Nicole hit the intercom to control. "Stop! You're covered!" and then, just to throw in a little confusion, "Tactical squad! Move!" She waited to see no more; standing, she pushed free of her chair. To her left Ptiba Mbente scowled and muttered something Pryce didn't catch; on the other side Eli Mainz was saying "But she can't ..."

The hell she can't! Damn. Nobody had thought of anything like this, and too late now. Blaming wouldn't help; Nicole Pryce ran to the door and yelled down the corridor, "Clancy! Anybody! Unlock control and get the hell in there. But watch yourselves!"

If Nicole said it, she had a reason. Emerging from the latrine cubicle, Allaird lunged across the corridor. The outside lock disengaged but the door stood firm. Locked from inside; damn and blast! He had a key, everybody did, but nobody carried them because who, forGodsakes, ever *needed* it?

"Nicole? You got your key here?"

Well, she *would*. "Thanks."

Inside control Edd Jarness and Pete Larue more or less stood, both out cold and both breathing. Along with two floating strangers, a man and a woman.

But no Ellery Dawson.

First things first; Clancy called the lounge. "Aaberg! Watch relief: you and Henning and Tabard. On the double." Time enough later to report what had happened, was happening.

As Ptiba began to help Chauncey with their own casualties, Clancy stared at the comatose interlopers. "Ky, get some flex cord; we'll tie these two up, for now."

Even potentially they didn't seem all that dangerous, but what the hell. He gave them a closer scan. The man was youngish, medium-sized, with crewcut dark hair; unconsciousness left his face clear of any definable expression. His companion was a slim young woman, delicately pretty, with fluffy brown hair now totally mussed. Oh well; Clancy secured her wrists behind her back as Coyote did the same for her associate.

"All right, let's take everybody out of here; the watch won't need us underfoot." As Aaberg led the relief team inside, Allaird said, "Gretel, you handle the report to downship. The intruders were here; they must have gone back in the Gate because there wasn't anywhere else they could have. They zapped the watch, took Ellery with them, and left two of their own. When I know more, so will everybody else."

"What do you mean, they took Ellery?" Amalyn Tabard.

Oh bloody hell. "Amalyn, all I know is what I just said. People came out the Tush, coldcocked Edd and Pete, and ducked back into the Mouth. You see who's here and who isn't; Ellery has to be on hold in the Gates. Perfectly safe."

Ignoring her further protest, "Come on, let's clear this place." So the zapped-out quartet was towed out to the corridor.

"Now where?" asked Chauncey. Allaird thought it over.

". . . two unconscious intruders are under restraint; I expect Mr. Allaird plans to interrogate them. Edd Jarness and Pete Larue got knocked out also but they'll probably be all right, the same as all four of us were the last time." Over the intercom Marnie heard Gretel Aaberg clear her throat. "I have to report that Captain Dawson is missing, no doubt abducted by the other intruders. Control was locked tight; the only place they could have taken him is back into the local Gate, so . . ."

The voice stopped; Aaberg could be heard breathing but that was all. Then she spoke again. "Mr. Allaird says, as soon as he knows anything more, you all will, too."

And that was it. In the lounge, sitting with Gina and Sybiljan and Pilar, Marnie stewed in frustration. Everybody else was upship where things were happening, and she was stuck here!

She couldn't sit still any longer; up and pacing she tried to avoid the snack table and couldn't. She'd already made up and eaten two sandwiches; she wasn't hungry at all. Yet here she was putting a third together. Oh no! This one she zipped into a sealbag and tucked away for later.

There had to be something she could do to keep her mind busy. "Hey, Gina; want to shoot some pool?"

Todisco shook her head. "I'm worried about Pete."

"What for? Getting zapped didn't hurt *you* any. Come on."

Distracted or not, Gina had a feel for anisotropic ballistics. Marnie kept it close, but lost by two points.

By that time, though, she felt a lot better. When he could, Clancy would fill her in.

The supply room was as good as any; Allaird directed the moving and disposition of the four sleepers. "Let's make 'em comfortable, folks." When they woke up he might learn something. Meanwhile . . .

To Nicole he said, "Was this monitor setup recording or do we have to depend on what everybody thinks they saw?" Seeing her eyes narrow he said, "Thanks for giving me the holler so quick. And you seem to be the only one smart enough to carry a key."

Nicole smiled; he was in good again. She said, "Oh, we were recording, all right; Ellery was making sure to cover his tail. Do you think viewing it will help us any?"

Impatient, he said, "*Not* seeing it sure as hell won't."

No matter how many times Clancy viewed it, normal speed or slowed, the sequence ran the same and still made no sense. The Tush flared and produced six persons, one awake and aggressive, the rest in drugged sleep. The bushy-haired blond, her features a bit too heavy for prettiness, made her plea for help, then potted the watch team. Suddenly Clancy stopped the playback. "A damn dart gun, it has to be. What she's doing, right there, is retrieving the darts so we wouldn't know. Just like last time; we thought it was a hypo, maybe. Something handheld, anyway."

And why hadn't anyone thought of this alternative? *Just stupid, I guess.*

But wait a minute here . . . "Ptiba. You and Eli. Suit up and get back here.'' As DV specialists they'd have had more suit drill than most.

Mainz stared. ''They can't be *outship*. And at this speed it's suicide . . .''

''Last time there was nearly an hour unaccounted for; there could be more than one group. I'll want you both in control with the watch. A suit just might stop one of those darts.''

''Oh, right.''

With that pair gone, Allaird and Pryce had custody of the four sleeping beauties all to themselves. Clancy unfroze the playback. Now the woman got three of her charges, two men and a woman, into the Mouth area. She started to go for the other two, paused, and grabbed Ellery Dawson instead. Then, quickly and competently she set the Gate for brief delay, jumped in, and seconds later was gone with the usual flare of colors. At the last glimpse of her, she was crouched and facing partway to her left, dart gun poised. Against what?

Clancy shook his head; what was he missing here? All right, take it from the top again. When he reached a point where all six new faces showed on Vidcam Two he stopped the action and ran up magnification, peering intently.

At first nothing clicked. Then, ''I will be dipped in gravy and served on toast!'' Yes; the unconscious woman the other had taken along with her. Put grey hair in a smooth short straight-around cut in place of the pale blond curls sheared close at sides and back, and who did you get? ''Old Iron Tits!''

Nicole's brows raised; Clancy said, ''Colonel Irina Tetzl from the Russian Republic. UN observer on *Jovian-II*, the second Traction Drive ship and the first with Habgates. Cleve Rozanski commanded. Those two were on *Starfinder* later— relief cadre 1–B. Only that time she was captain.''

He looked closer. ''This one guy here could be Cleve; with his eyes closed and mouth open I can't be sure.'' Clancy turned off the playback. ''Let's dip into the computer. Ellery had files on all the starship crews up to when we left. A hobby of his; maybe they include visuals. For *Starfinder*.''

Nicole took the keyboard; as she made a file search, mentally Allaird began figuring back. All right, Tetzl and 1–B hit *Starfinder* two years before this crew arrived here. How long ago? Earth time, *Starfinder* at ten to one and *Arrow* at twenty-five—he lost track and had to start over.

His time on here was roughly seven Earth years so Irina Tetzl started her ten-year hitch nine years ago; she was three years short of having any business here at all, let alone appearing after an onboard Gate lag. *Wait* a minute . . .

To arrive here two years ago, Old Iron Tits had to have been dragged off her ship at the five-year midpoint of her duty tour, when relief cadre 1–A was due for rotation home. Now what . . . ?

"I have something," Nicole said. Onscreen came the ID plates for *Starfinder*'s launch crew, sections A and B both, with full-face pics at the upper right of each.

Allaird vaguely recognized several of these, but they were irrelevant. "These people were all back to Earth long before we inGated." Even Steffi Holm and Red MacDougall, and Ali Saud who had killed them both. "First relief cadres, please, Nicole."

And there they were. Irina Tetzl with the blond curls even that long ago, and yes the one gaping sleeper on the disc really was Cleve Rozanski. But no other intruder came from 1–B.

1–A, though: *gotcha!* The heavy-featured haystack blond with the zap darts was Fleurine Schadel, and the other guy she'd hauled back into the Gate was sure as hell her pairmate Jimmy Hanchett. At one point, Clancy recalled, he'd been in command, but of course Tetzl had since taken over that job. All right; Hanchett and Schadel were due to leave ship for home at about the time they must have Gated here instead. Now why . . . ?

Arrow's two new unscheduled passengers weren't in the files. Allaird could guess why, but no need. Dart-drugged people were beginning to wake; he could ask them directly.

Pete Larue was first to show something near full awareness. "Hey, I'm due for intruder watch; I gotta go." And then, "How did I get up here to zero gee?"

So all they learned from Pete, and from Edd Jarness when he came around only a couple of minutes later, was what they already knew: that the drug, whatever it was, wiped memory for a time *before* the dart hit.

At least now the limits were defined better: something between twenty and twenty-five minutes, likely varying with individual metabolisms and maybe even with where the dart hit.

Which didn't explain why the two unknowns, who must have experienced more real time since being zapped, were still out.

What did was that on inspection the woman turned out to have two puncture marks, and the man three.

It was when they woke up that things got interesting.

IX

The woman stirred first. Her eyes opened; for a moment she seemed calm enough. Then as she sat up and looked from face to face, shoulders jerking as her wrists tugged at the bindings, her expression went through disbelief to fright. "Who are you? What are you doing here? Where's the captain? I . . ." Her voice trailed off; wild-eyed, she shook her head.

Then she saw the man, not yet moving. "Alton!" And, "What have you done to him?"

Nicole went to her. "Easy now; it's all right." She looked over to Clancy and gestured; he nodded. "Here, let me untie you. But you're not on *Starfinder* now; this is *Arrow* and we belong here. What we'd like to know is why you are. Here, I mean." She paused. "What's the last thing you remember?"

Busy flexing her freed hands and wrists, the young woman made no answer. Allaird said, "Let's start with who you are. And who Alton is. We've already deduced you're both from *Starfinder*, relief cadre 2–A. Are we right?"

"Y-yes." Pushing her hair back from her face the woman nodded. "I don't understand, but—I'm Paula Trent and he's Alton Darnell; we're paired. We've only just arrived, a few hours ago. On *Starfinder*. Captain Tetzl called a meeting—not everybody, just a few of us—to decide who stayed aboard and . . ."

She shook her head again. "I didn't understand most of it. We were supposed to relieve 1–A and serve one year aboard, ship's time. But the captain said plans had changed. The main thing was, she wasn't going back when her term ended; she was holding command all the way to destination. And choosing who she'd keep on with her. The ones she didn't want, she said she'd warehouse; I'm not sure what she meant by that, but it had to do with Gate lag someway. Do you think . . . ?"

Clancy certainly did. He said, "How did everybody else react? You, for instance. And Alton."

She didn't answer directly. "There'd been another gathering, earlier. Just some of the men, meeting with Captain Tetzl. Alton was there; he told me everything was going to be all right. And of course she's *captain*."

Allaird thought of old rumors concerning *Jovie-II*. "And the other people? How did they seem to feel?"

"Well, Mr. Rozanski and Mr. Hanchett, the co-execs, backed the idea; most of the other men didn't say much either way. But some of the women were against it. Fleurine Schadel, Mr. Hanchett's pairmate. And two or three others, Benita Torres and the Romanian woman, Zsana something. But not speaking up as much as Schadel did."

Keeping in mind the retroactive amnesia effect, Clancy went back to Nicole's question. "And what's the last you remember?"

Her brow wrinkled. "We were in captain's quarters; that's where she had the meetings. When the argument got a little hot, Captain Tetzl said let's have a bit of food and maybe a drink. That's what we were doing . . . I don't remember any more."

The man was awake now, had been for some time though Clancy wasn't certain just how long. "Alton? If we untie your hands will you behave yourself?"

"Sure. Why wouldn't I?" So Pryce took the cords off.

"Now then—does Paula's report sound accurate to you?"

The man hadn't wakened in time to learn where he was

now; Allaird had to fill him in first. Then, "*Arrow*? That's where Irina was going to pipeline surplus people. So she decided against us after all." He shrugged. "She had me fooled."

Oh yes? "How? For instance, tell us about this earlier meeting Paula mentioned. Just Old Iron Tits and a bunch of the boys, eh?"

At first Alton balked. Clancy could guess why. He said, "Mr. Darnell you're looking at a man who's fresh out of patience. Tell me this: is Paula important to you?"

"Of course she is!"

"Then answer my questions. Because if I don't like your attitude, I can pipeline you until she's twice your age!"

Nicole's horrified look said he had no such authority, but Darnell bit; embarrassed to the stammering point, including a nonstop world's record blush, he related how Irina Tetzl had directed a sexual circus with five men's activities all focused on her person. "Half the time I didn't know what I was supposed to do; she was—uh—busy and couldn't tell me. But Mr. Hanchett or Mr. Rozanski always seemed to know just what she wanted next, so it, well, it all worked, you could say."

The way he looked at Paula she might have been the hangman. Relenting, Clancy said, "If it's any comfort to either of you, this is old tricks for Captain Irina." So the *Jovie* rumors were true, all right. "By now she has to be an expert."

He reached to the playback control. "We can't fill in what took place at the last, on your ship, not for certain. But I'll show you what happened at this end. After you were taken from the *Starfinder* Tush and put through our local Gates once."

"Wait." Paula's gesture sought defense against the words. "You mean, what with coming here from our own ship, we've lost *four* years? Six, before we could get home."

"Let's say, stockpiled them." Play began; the emergence, the deceptive plea, the zapping, Schadel taking three men with her into the Gate. "So I guess," Allaird commented at the end, "our Fleurine took it on herself to change *all* the plans."

Looking apprehensive, Darnell, said, "What happens now?"

"To you two?" Clancy thought. Estella's illness left *Arrow* short one hand. "What are your specialties, shipwise?"

"Instruments," said Paula. "Outside sensor calibration, that kind of thing."

And Alton Darnell, "Inship maintenance. Power systems, drive control circuits. DV emergency backup."

Like Clancy himself, these kids were trained for *Starfinder*-class ships, not for *Arrow*. But if he could adapt, so could they. Except, they'd signed for four years Gate time at half pay plus a shipboard year at ten-to-one: fourteen years off Earth and twelve years' pay. While *Arrow*'s crew was aboard all the way.

Still, "We're shorthanded for a time. I could assign you here, if you like: notify Earth, make it all official. There'll be some hell raised about this mess before it's done, but if you're telling the truth you should come out clean enough."

While the two looked at each other, neither acting first to take the plunge, Allaird said, "I don't know how much you're counting on your scheduled return date. Or on your overall expected pay for the tour." As he spoke he was figuring, and came up with "Three months on here, a bit less, would get you home on sked with eight years' wages. I can't get return word from Earth in less than two of those months, anyway."

"Eight years' pay? Is that all?" Alton sounded plaintive.

"For three months' work you're getting a bargain. And certainly nobody's going to pay you for Schadel's detours. Unless you can sue it out of *her* when we get hold of her."

Paula tugged at the man's sleeve. "Let's take it; at least we can salvage *something*. And these people aren't crazy, like—"

Allaird suppressed a chuckle and turned to assess his own casualties. Edd Jarness sat, resting his chin on one hand and looking glum. "Edd, why don't you go downship and lie down?"

Pete Larue, though, was wide-eyed and taking it all in. "You feeling better now?" And at Pete's nod, "Then escort these two down to the belt. Ask Pilar to outfit them a little, and you assign them the two nearest crewrooms." To the new hands he said, "Did you get any sleep aboard *Starfinder*?"

Paula shook her head. "We'd stowed our duffels in a room

and eaten lunch. Then all the other things . . .''

"So you've had no sleep and one meal in the past six years. Take 'em down, Pete." Jarness followed.

Left alone with Clancy, Nicole watched him sigh. "So much for that. Now, just how do we get things back to normal?"

Surprised, she said, "Well, first you might make it official that you're in command."

"Oh hell; I hadn't thought of *that*."

Leaning forward, Pryce laughed. "Give us a kiss, sailor."

"Well, sure." At some length, he did. "What was that for?"

"For being the kind of guy who *wouldn't* think of command, first shot out of the box. Now then, as captain—acting captain, whatever—it's up to you to get the watch skeds on track again. I expect Ellery had them laid out for the immediate future; from there you can just continue his system."

Groaning, Allaird said, "System? You ever try to decipher one of his roster charts? I've never had any idea how he figures them. Just that everybody shuffles around a lot, working with different people. What the progression is . . ."

Nicole frowned. Not command itself, but the *idea* of it, had Clancy in a spin. "Then set up your own. Better yet, delegate the chore. Ellery was never any good at that, kept everything in his own head which is why we have so many loose ends here."

Now he grinned. "Fine. Have the new sked on my desk by the end of the watch, and—" He stopped. "Uh-oh. We're short a watch officer. Now who . . . ?"

"Why not—" No, this was when to shut up. "Never mind."

Concentrating, he didn't seem to notice. "Ptiba. After all, as DV commander she's sort of an officer already." He checked the time. "From what we know of the timing two months ago, we're past the interval when any other people could be Gating into control, so . . ." On the intercom: "Mbente and Mainz, you're relieved; you can go unsuit. Ptiba, you're now a watch officer. Nicole will have the new skeds ready. So's you'll have time for a snooze, you won't be taking the next trick."

Who would, Nicole wondered. Aaberg was on now, and neither Clancy nor herself was especially well rested. Oh well . . .

Another thought came. Whatever had happened to last names on duty, first names off? It had been that way not too long ago; when had things changed? Gradually, maybe. Or perhaps the sudden absence of Ellery Dawson and his by-the-book attitudes, plus the disruption of routine, had tipped the balance.

She felt no need to comment. What she did say was, "Clancy, there's no sense in all of *us* getting pooped, either. You're going to want to take over the next watch, I expect. Why don't you go doss down until then, while I do those skeds? I'll pick up the current roster sheets in control, to give me an idea who's had the most time off lately and should be due."

"Yeah. Okay." Allaird sighed. They shared a hug and kiss, stood, and went separate ways.

Adjourned to the galley, Pilar and Sybiljan and Gina and Marnie were finishing off the thick stew Pilar had put together, when Marnie looked up to see Pete Larue come in, followed by two total strangers and Edd Jarness.

Marnie jumped up first but not alone. "What—?" "Who—?" "How—?" Everybody tried to ask at the same time; Pete yelled, "Hold it!"

When he had quiet, he said, "These aren't intruders like we mean the word; they're from *Starfinder* and brought here out cold. Matter of fact, the captain's signed them on for duty, temporarily at least. What with Estella gone, and all. So . . ."

"Captain?" Confused, Marnie went on. "I thought he—"

"Mr. Allaird, I meant," said Pete. "He doesn't seem to realize it yet, but if he's not captain we don't have one. Until Captain Dawson pops out again, that is."

He turned to the newcomers. "You want anything here, before I show you your rooms?" Headshakes. "Okay; Pilar, these folks don't have anything with them but what they're wearing. Could you issue a few things, what they'll need right away?"

Velez said, "How about names?" She stated her own; in a few moments everyone was introduced. Then she said, "Personal kits, sure, and I expect we have some spare clothes to fit.'' With Alton and Paula following and Pete bringing up the rear, she led the way out.

At the door Pete turned. "Marnie, I know you're full of questions, but save 'em; when your dad comes down here he needs to rest. He's stretched tight and doesn't even know it, is my guess. So be easy on him."

"Why sure, Pete." Startled, Marnie felt rebuked, then realized that wasn't Larue's intent; he meant it for everybody, but cautioning her alone would seem less bossy. *All right.*

So she went to her quarters and took her unsatisfied curiosity out on the computer until she felt relaxed enough to sleep.

Coming onto the belt and walking to the galley, Allaird braced himself to tell the whole damn story and probably more times than one. But only Sybiljan Baynor and Gina Todisco were there, standing now and apparently ready to leave. "Hi," said Gina. "I guess everything's under control now? When you have time you'll have to tell us all about it."

But for now, surprising the hell out of him, both women merely smiled and went out.

And Marnie wasn't even waiting in his quarters! Perplexed but grateful, Clancy kicked his shoes off and took a nap.

As long as she was stuck in control anyway, Nicole took watch duty as well, relieving Gretel Aaberg. "As new watch officer, Mbente's the junior, so you can have a regular shift now if you'd rather."

"Actually I'm used to this. Can I talk with Ptiba and let you know later?"

Damn; that's what you get for giving people options. This scheduling was bad enough without waiting for other people to make up their minds. "I'd rather know now, if you don't mind." If she sounded officious, too bad. Still, though: "Tell you what; I'll leave things as is for a time. If you want to change in a few days, when I have a better handle on how this works, we'll see about it."

Looking mollified, Gretel left. As Pryce got back to shuffling duty assignments, Phil Henning brought in a packet from

Earthtush. "One piece from the brass for Captain Dawson, marked urgent. Should I call Mr. Allaird?"

"He's sleeping, or should be. He's relieving me in—" She checked the time. "About two hours. Here; I'll give it a look and see if he needs waking just yet."

Sheest; *everybody* was giving her these "Who do you think you are?" looks. Shrugging it off, Nicole opened the folder, then closed it quickly. "Oops; captain only, it says. Could have put that on the outside, I'd think."

"Then I'd better . . ."

"It's been two years getting here. What's two more hours?" And if Phil translated that to Earth time, she was going to say something she probably shouldn't!

Her face must have said it anyway; Henning shut up.

Curiosity had Nicole obviously edgy. When Allaird—somewhat rested, sketchily showered, and minimally fed—showed up for watch, he waited only until Tabard and Henning checked out as Todisco and Benjamin relieved them. Then, opening the folder marked urgent, he summarized its content aloud. "Cadre 1–A hasn't returned from *Starfinder* and there's no word, either. Do we have any news, they want to know?" He grinned. "We surely do. Two here, along with a couple from 1–B, two to *Roamer*. The other pair . . ." He shrugged.

"Are you going to report what we've learned?"

"You mean, Ellery's information blackout? I don't think that applies any longer. But I doubt there's much point; four years after they sent this, they're bound to have newer data."

"But not from here. If Schadel sprayed darts around before she inGated her group there, possibly nobody on that ship has any idea where they all went."

"You're right." Clancy nodded. "I'll get it off right away. Except . . ."

"Hmmm?" She looked a question.

"I'll give the facts, such as we have, about who went where. I see no reason to pass along Darnell's story about Tetzl's stag party. If he wants to write it up himself, all right. But from me it would be purely hearsay—and the woman's not here to defend herself."

She ruffled his hair, grown nearly long enough to comb and getting a little shaggy around the edges. "Good old Clancy.

Is there anyone you wouldn't give the benefit of the doubt?"

"Hah!" He snorted. "You've met Celeste's lawyer." He declined even to speak the name of Carl Knapheidt.

After Nicole left, Allaird scrutinized the logs and data readouts. Outside the ship, at least, all was normal.

Dutifully Marnie's alarm woke her a half hour before midwatch, when she was scheduled to help Gina Todisco with a routine check of drive parameters. While she was dressing, though, the room terminal's message light caught her attention. The readout button brought a revised watch schedule onscreen and Marnie saw that Gina was currently at duty, with Ky, on Clancy's watch. This hadn't been his scheduled shift, but apparently it was now; the reshuffle for intruder guard and the loss of Ellery Dawson must have shaken things up. Sure they had; now she saw Ptiba Mbente listed as a watch officer.

Oh well. Marnie was hungry anyway. Nothing in the room stock appealed to her, and besides she wanted to find out what all was happening; she finished dressing and went to the galley. Chauncey had some customers for scrambled eggs and didn't mind expanding the order.

When her tray was loaded Marnie looked around and saw the new people sitting with Nicole Pryce. She walked over. "Okay if I join you?" Nicole's expression said yes, so Marnie sat. "Hi," to the newcomers. "Getting settled in okay? Must have been a jolt, finding yourselves here all of a sudden."

"To say the least," said Paula Trent. "And if it wasn't for your vidcams, we wouldn't even know who did it."

"Let alone why," Darnell added, staring at Marnie for no perceivable reason. "Which we still don't."

"Mr. Allaird and I have a few ideas," Nicole said.

Mister, huh? All right. Ignoring Alton Darnell, Marnie said, "Officer Pryce, could you give me a quick rundown on what's *happened*?"

"Quick it'll have to be," and briefly Nicole related what she, along with Clancy, had seen and learned. The way the tall woman paused now and then, Marnie had a hunch she was leaving things out. Maybe Clancy's version, when he had the time, would fill in some of the blank spots.

* * *

Near the end of Clancy's watch came another urgent for Captain Ellery Dawson, from Glen Springs. Wondering how anyone could mark urgent on anything that took two years to get here, Allaird opened it. Well, heigh-ho; now they knew, back on Earth, that Collier and Teng had gone to *Roamer*, because Hennessey and Torres had reached home to report that unscheduled detour or desertion or whatever the hell it was. What they didn't know was that Tetzl and Hanchett and Rozanski and the two youngsters were right here on *Arrow*. Well, more or less. But they would know, Real Soon Now such as another two years, because Clancy had sent his report off something like six or seven hours ago. Or, considering the rate of exchange, just about one Earthside week.

When Ptiba Mbente came to take the watch and Marnie cornered Clancy at a brief galley stop, he brought her up to date. Nicole had told her a lot, so all he had to do was answer questions. Of course he left out the juicy parts.

"So this Captain Tetzl tried to hijack *Starfinder*?"

"Well, not in the classic sense. She didn't want to divert it to some other destination. Just to keep command all the way instead of leaving when her hitch was over."

Marnie shook her head. "I don't see how she thought she could get away with it."

"Maybe we'll find out when they all come through again."

Alton Darnell, Marnie felt, wasn't going to be easy to get to know. Not exactly sullen, but he did have a guarded manner, as though he had to protect himself at all times. Yet at the same time his presence seemed to push at her, in a way she neither liked nor understood.

With Paula Trent, though, she hit it off right away. By actual birthdates Paula was five years and two months the elder. But while a person might think her three Gatings would bring their *lived* ages closer, that wasn't how it worked. Two Gatings plus *Arrow*'s time ratio spread the difference to nearly eight, with Paula twenty and Marnie only a little over twelve.

They clicked—or cliqued—anyway. Paula may have been young for her age; Marnie had for years schooled with older children. No fan of shipboard news bulletins, now she pumped her new friend about the three years she'd spent on Earth after Marnie left. Was Rodeo Cesar's music still popular (and never mind that "still" meant six years ago)? "Ro-*day*-oh? He's immense on the west coast, but . . ."

Or, what's been happening with clothes? Only shortly before her graduation had Marnie become interested in fashions; not long after, events cut her off from that phenomenon. Oh, she'd seen how people dressed in the dramas on holovid caps sent out for the crew's entertainment, but she knew enough to realize those getups weren't typical of real life. She wasn't too impressed, now, by what Paula reported, but with any luck the styles might look better than they sounded.

They worked out on the full-gee ring and showered at Marnie's quarters. Paula offered the use of hers, but Alton might have dropped in while she was there and Marnie would have felt funny about that.

Afterward they sat drying their hair. By now the short sculptured fashion haircut Celeste had financed for Marnie's graduation had grown from its initial artfully uneven look to anarchistic raggedness. Brooding into a mirror Marnie noticed Paula watching her and made a face. "Pretty rasty, huh? Nibbled out by mice, looks like."

Holding up a couple of fingers Paula squinted over them. "Bangs, fairly heavy but not long. Blend into short sides at the front, show your earrings, smooth up the ragged ends across the back. I could do it in five minutes so you grow out presentable all the way." Marnie didn't have the proper tools for the job so Paula fetched hers.

A bit later Marnie kept a date for dinner with Clancy and Nicole. Well, dinner for Clancy and breakfast for Nicole; Marnie was two hours past lunch which she'd skipped on purpose. At sight of her refurbished appearance Clancy said, "Looking good, Marni Gras," and Nicole added "Yes, you are."

Marnie could have used something more effusive in the way of compliments, but you make do with what comes.

As the day came when the group's suggestions for attempted FTL communication could bring a return response from Earth, Clancy began waiting for the other shoe to drop. He kept pestering control, calling during his offwatch hours to see if anything had come in through Earthtush. Finally Nicole Pryce, on watch, told him, "Look, Clancy; everybody's seen the notice you posted here: that you're to be called immediately, any time, awake or asleep. Now give the squawk-box a rest.''

So, like it or not and he didn't, Clancy followed Nicole's advice. The unseen powers that control undropped shoes being what they are, the box's chime caught Nicole just beginning climax and Clancy about thirty seconds short of it.

Although they didn't stop—largely wouldn't but partly couldn't—the distraction took some of the bloom off. Most unusually, then, they disengaged without afterplay and Allaird went to answer the call. Gretel Aaberg said, ''We've heard from your senator. And there's a sealed envelope for you personally.''

In the somewhat-crowded control room Allaird addressed his other officers and the tech chiefs. ''They like the idea; the senator co-opted Dr. Habegger himself as a consultant, and the old Gatemeister threw in some new wrinkles. They've implemented my Venturi gimmick and added some advanced measuring methods—not just flowmeters but impulse sensors, to detect the onset of plus or minus changes.'' He paused. ''Not to bog down in all the numbers here—I'll pass this around later, if you'd like to check through for yourselves—what it boils down to is that based on extrapolation from small-scale models, and let's hope it holds good, they suggest we go with two-minute rise times, total cycle eight minutes for a yes or no. Yes beginning with a pressure rise and no just the opposite, remember, and with short pauses between answers. Which brings it down, at their end, to only three hours twenty minutes for a response. Not exactly speed reading, but well up from what we had.'' By five to one, yes.

''Now here's a new one: Habegger turned in a proposal for auxiliary pumping units to be added at both ends and give us *two-way* comm. Using smaller components the signal could be a lot faster; there's something about a trinary code . . .''

Clancy shrugged. ''But then he ran into design problems, trying to fit any such things into our existing Gate interfaces. So plus the fact of two years to send us the gadgets and another two for pipeline lag, he scrapped Cloud Nine in favor of Cloud Eight-and-a-half. Which, it seems—''

''Clancy.'' Amalyn's voice held a cutting edge. ''You're

keeping Senator Flynn waiting at twenty-five to one. Get to the part where we do something *now*."

The first something came out of Allaird's personal envelope from Bill Flynn. Questions he was to answer before proceeding to the general list. Then after all that was done they were to await response, via the Gate, to *their* replies.

Allaird looked again at the Senator's note:

> *Clancy: these questions are confidential between you and me; nobody else. All you say is yes or no.*
>   *1. Is your daughter aboard?*
>   *2. Is she all right?*
>   *3. Do you need any further help concerning her?*
> *If you do, I'll try to devise questions over the next few days to determine what's needed. If not, best of luck to you both and let the festivities proceed.*
>
>   *Bill*

The matter took no thinking. To Amalyn Tabard at the drive controls Clancy said, "Your first three answers are yes, yes, and no." Then, grinning, he quoted the senator's final phrase and added, "Let 'er buck."

Though actually, thanks to the governing safety circuits, the drive's thrust variations were rather sedate.

The main body of questions, following Allaird's trio of private and privileged communications, made up a mixed bag.

"Has the crew suffered any deaths? If so, send one cycle of yes for each death."

No.

"Are all members of the crew in good health? If not, send one cycle of no for each ailing person."

No.

"Are any ailing persons being treated on board?"

No.

"Have any Gated to Earth?"

Yes.

"Have any Gated to another ship?"

No.

Fascinated, Clancy began to appreciate the difficulty of composing a list of questions, none of which could depend on earlier answers. He was glad the job hadn't been his.

The list continued. "Do you require any male replacements? If so, send one cycle of yes for each male requested."

No.

"Do you require any female replacements? If so, proceed as above."

Clancy looked around. "I think not. Either Estella or someone else should be on the way already, plus we still have Trent and Darnell for the time being at least. Does everyone agree?"

No had it.

The line of questioning changed. "Have you had any major personnel difficulties: i.e., any requiring action or advice from this end? If so, additional queries follow later."

No. Although Dawson, Allaird thought, might have quibbled a bit on that one. Smuggling Marnie aboard, for instance.

"Aside from Dr. Anne Portaris, have you received any visitors from other ships?"

They'd already know that, but *Yes.*

"From *Starfinder*?"

Yes.

"If so, how many? Count as before."

Redundant or not, *Yesyesyesyesyesyes.*

For *Roamer* the same sequence followed. Sybiljan Baynor said, "You know, these are odd things to ask. You'd almost think they *knew* something's going on."

"I'd bet on it," said Clancy Allaird.

Succeeding questions became more prosaic. Any problems with Traction Drive? Life-support? Instrumentation?

Any new phenomena encountered in space? Not since the dust cloud, already noted in reports; would those have reached Earth by now? At twenty-five to one, Clancy wasn't sure, but *No.*

Supplies: any shortages? A list of categories followed and the string of noes continued. A few miscellaneous queries, some puzzling and others apparently frivolous, wrapped up the list.

From there it was sit and wait. Flynn and his people were certainly taking a long time, Clancy thought, to firm up their list of follow-ups. A little delay and confab, he could see. But—he checked the clock and did his twenty-fives—two days?

Then Sybiljan, who had drawn Earthtush monitor, brought in a new message. Scanning the paper, Allaird frowned.

"Well?" said Amalyn. "What's it *say*?"

Slowly Clancy read it off. "It is long past time we should have received a response to our queries. I hope nothing has gone wrong. Perhaps our calculations were too optimistic. Please repeat your entire series of answers, increasing change levels to your originally proposed parameters of ten percent."

A postscript followed. "Meanwhile we have been notified of arrival at Glen Springs of your ailing crewmate Estella Holms. She has undergone surgery and is doing well, but pending determination of her fitness to return to duty, a replacement has been selected and Gated to you."

That part was all right. Still, to himself Clancy swore. At the slower speed, repeating everything they'd already said was going to take about half of forever.

Sitting through the process promised to be a bitch.

The day following the communication attempts, Flynn did go up to Gayle Tech, and there he pried Dr. Habegger out of his lab long enough to try for some answers. "Not a thing, doctor," he wrapped his report up. "Only the same slow, small, seemingly random flow variations we'd been getting all along." Looking across Habegger's desk he sipped the coffee an office helper had brought. "I don't understand it; your models worked out fine, and surely the size wouldn't make such a radical difference."

Habegger shook his head. "Size, no. Shouldn't, anyway."

"But everything else was the same, exactly to scale. We . . ."

"Not the same. Not the same at all."

"What was different, then? You saw the plans."

"Aleph Plenum. No way I could put that in a model, senator. But when you test with *Arrow*, there it sits. Right in the middle and who knows what it does there. *We* didn't, looks like."

Bill leaned forward. "But it never does anything to whatever we send. What goes in, comes out. Two years later, sure. But not changed. So why *this*?"

"Comes out, yes. Back, no. Maybe time in Aleph has a one-way valve to it, just like here."

Drawing on the desktop with his finger, Flynn protested. "Look. You put fluid into a line—fuel, in this case—and it comes out the other end just the way it goes in. In, out, no change. Am I right? How can it do anything else?"

The doctor's heavy brows lowered; for a time he said nothing. Then suddenly he looked up, eyes agleam. "Got it! You want to smooth out a flow, mask the variations—actual, you don't, but it's what you're getting—you put in a section, acts like a balloon."

"What—?"

"I could make you a model, you want me to. Have the far end change flow, just like you told *Arrow*. This end, all you see—" Habegger spread his hands. "What you *do* see."

He smiled. "Clear now? In Aleph, maybe extra dimensions act like that balloon. Or maybe some other way; I'd have to run the math to be sure. But one thing I tell you. Forget asking questions for next year to answer. Not going to happen."

What about the advanced proposals, miniGates with specially sensitive fluid-handling signal units? What about . . . ? Flynn asked more questions, but no luck. The curvature of the universe, it turned out, put a lower limit to the size of Habgates, and the existing ones came near it. And no matter how refined the fluid-squirters, most likely Aleph's balloon effect would nullify them.

Finally the senator gave up. "Well, thanks for your time, Dr. Habegger, and all the effort you've put in." He stood. "Too bad the research was useless."

Habegger rose also, and reached to meet the handshake. "No research is useless. We just don't know yet, what's to use in what we learn, once we have time to figure it out better."

"Great. I should ask you down at budget time, so you can tell that to the committee."

He flew back the same day, and from his office sent a message to *Arrow*.

On the way home, then, once again he picked up flowers and champagne. What the hell: a homecoming is a homecoming.

After the five times slower repetition of answers to the entire list of questions, Clancy let everyone but the scheduled watch

gang go off duty. Including himself. Pooped out of all recognition, he made his way to quarters. Nicole had sidetracked
to the galley, but Allaird was beyond hunger.

"What happened? What went on, that was so important?"
Why Marnie was here he didn't know—but avid for information, she wouldn't be denied.

Nor should she be. Through fatigue haze Clancy sought for
meaningful phrasing. "The FTL experiment. Communication
to Earth. Didn't work. They had us do it again, only slower,
for a bigger signal. Then we waited, but they haven't said."

He gestured come here, gave her a hug and good-night kiss,
and pushed her in the general direction of the door. He got all
his clothes off before climbing into bed, but they lay wherever
they happened to drop.

When the chime brought him awake and he sat up, Clancy
could tell he hadn't really had his sleep out, but he felt more
good than not. Reaching over to the intercom, "Yes? Allaird
here."

"Aaberg. Just to let you know, we have word from Earth.
To drop the FTL tests. Dr. Habegger says they won't work."

"Habegger? Why not?" Well, she'd know what he meant.

"I'm not sure, Allaird. Something about balloons."

Tentative dimensional realignments show promise. Offending spatial vicinities once identified, volitionals may act on
preliminary warning signs to avoid inadvertent admixture with
momentary or sustained trans-plenal mass intrusions. Such
measures prove sufficient to circumvent deleterious effects of
both transient and persistent initially-evident phenomena.

The onset of adverse-chronal impulses, however, is of
greater potential concern; even minor uncompensated derange-
ment of accomplished causation imperils not only subcontinua
but all of contextual reality.

Yet intensive study reveals this aberration to be less dangerous than first assumed. The cross-vector products created
by such impulses reinforce or attenuate according to the spatial-chronal curvature of the medium in which they propagate.
In this especial pairing of sub-plena, that parameter lies barely
on the side of conservation of causality, giving the effect of
added dimensions absorbing any disruptive effect. Thus, along
all operational chronal vectors, margins of safety exist.

Against these especial sub-plenal anomalies, therefore, contextual reality stands proof. Anxiety is relieved, and proposed dissociation of the subject sub-plenum appears to become unnecessary. Also wasteful.

Unless further variations of hazardous and distressing obtrusion should develop.

X

Next time Clancy reported on watch he found another envelope from Senator Flynn. Not marked urgent, this one, and apparently no one thought it important enough to tell him earlier. Maybe they were right, he thought, and ran through his routine logging chores before sitting to open it.

Hah! Not urgent, maybe, but certainly welcome. It read:

Clancy: maybe it was cheating a little, but I gave Dr. Wyatt instructions to ask Estella Holms some questions while she was groggy from the anesthetic, and she told him in all innocence that your daughter is doing fine aboard Arrow, performing various tasks assigned to her and learning progressively more as time allows.

All things considered I decided to make it retroactive that she is officially a member of the crew from the moment of outGating there. For the first two months, ship's time, she was not legally adult and therefore is listed as an apprentice/trainee at two-thirds of basic pay. On reaching her eighteenth birthday by Earth time she was given a straight crew rating with all responsibilities and normal perks.

Since her Gating was unauthorized she is not eligible

*for the standard half-pay during Gate lag, but I don't
imagine that bothers you too much.*
    My best to both of you.

                                            Bill Flynn

Marnie hadn't thought her shadowy, irregular status
weighed on her especially. When Clancy told her the news
and posted it on the bulletin board it took a little time to sink
in, but after sleeping on it once she found she had acquired a
new confidence.

It felt really good. Even though Clancy informed her that
in all fairness her passage through the local Gates would have
to be recorded as two Earth years' worth of Leave Without
Pay!

She'd had, now, a total of three job tours in the Deployment
Vehicle but only brief tries at learning its controls; there were
always so many other things to be done that by the time those
were completed, Ptiba Mbente was impatient and granted only
a few minutes for practice purposes. The day after Marnie
learned she was officially crew, though, Ptiba being on watch
it was Eli Mainz who took Marnie and Paula Trent with him
for a full simulation checkout. And on this occasion, after a
long and sweaty stretch of helping move revised supply allo-
cations around the Vehicle, Eli gave both Paula and Marnie
enough hands-on time at the controls to get a reasonably solid
feel of the operation.

Deployment itself, for instance, was no simple matter; you
didn't just fire up the Traction Drive and pop out. First, all
the tests. On Virtual Thrust, crank the drive up to a fraction
short of redline max, then idle down. Unlock the landing legs
and lever them out two notches, enough to prove mobility
without damaging the bulkhead behind. While the copilot
checked out screens and instruments, making certain that all
units were operational and that their reports showed the DV
ready to emerge.

That emergence was especially tricky. The procedure had
been accomplished, Marnie knew, only by test prototypes in
high Earth orbit. And from nose cone mockups, not real ships.
The test DVs themselves were far from complete vehicles,
merely shells equipped with miniature drives and the ancillary
emergence gear under test; thus the partial or complete failures

of the first four configurations tested posed no real danger to the safely suited test personnel. The fifth version was duplicated for *Starfinder* and *Roamer*; *Arrow* carried the sixth.

Dutifully Marnie performed the simulated tests. Once the DV itself checked out operational, next came Disconnect & Displace. In flight the nose cone presented a solid shield to the barrage of particles. Yet once *Arrow* reached destination orbit that shield had to divide itself, along a circle of ten meters' radius, freeing the DV to push forward out of the ship. And to move its considerable mass an auxiliary force was needed: you don't fire off Traction Drive, even at low thrust, in a confined space.

So one button (now locked to simulation) cuts the magnetizing currents circulating to either side of the dividing line, one in the DV and the other in *Arrow*'s own hull, to end the magnetostrictive effect that has transformed a snug fit to a virtual weld and made the forward shield, effectively, an unbroken surface throughout the ship's voyage.

And with that action noted on the pilot's console, another switch allows liquefied gases to expand and catalytically ignite between the DV and the necessarily sturdy bulkhead behind it. A single-shot pistol, of large caliber but inconsequential muzzle velocity, yet according to the manual it would do the job.

From there it was a matter of navigation and maneuvering, things Marnie had practiced from the lesser aux positions in control. She enjoyed this runthrough anyway. Sitting in the actual DV pilot seat made it all so much more *real*.

"Too bad there's no good way to simulate docking," said Eli as they made their way back along the tunnel. "Either here or back aft, where the Vehicle can refuel *and* transship cargo."

There was a lot more to learn, Marnie realized. Always.

"Oh come on; Alton's on Ptiba's watch for two hours yet," Paula urged, so Marnie yielded and went to her friend's quarters for their usual ritual after a job or exercise: first shower, then refuel with a snack and chat like magpies.

Showering involved a lot of splashing and laughter—in Marnie's case, at least, a throwback to school days. And because since the first few grades she'd been in classes with kids mostly two to three years older, the difference between Paula's physical development and her own modest beginnings in that department didn't bother her any.

What did was that all-too-usual mishap, an eyeful of shampoo. "Time out!" and she ducked over to reach outside and grab a towel. Eyes dried, she turned for reentry but stopped short. From this angle, with Paula off to one side Marnie saw past the heavy spray to an upper corner of the large stall. And just below that corner sat a diminutive unobtrusive object—unobtrusive, except that it didn't belong there.

Marnie blinked; the thing was small enough to hold in a nearly closed fist and almost but not quite the color of the stall itself. Peering, she noticed a minuscule round spot, shinier than the rest, and then at one side, near the edge that met the wall, a tiny luminescent fleck of green.

Something joggled in memory; she almost recognized it. But then Paula turned from rinsing her hair and with one hand shunted most of the shower head's spray into Marnie's face. So for a while there it was Katy bar the door.

Not until the two were out and dried and nearly dressed, chatting away as usual, did Marnie's memory click. The gadget in the shower fit the description of the micro-vidcams Celeste's tame gendarme had used aboard here.

And dollars to dogmeat, that green light meant "Recording."

The jolt derailed Marnie's train of conversation; after some seconds she saw Paula looking at her with a puzzled exression, and said at random, "How's Alton getting along?"

"*That's* a coincidence." Now Paula came up animated. "I mean, he's always asking about you. Every time you and I do anything together he wants to know all about it—what we said, what we did, how you looked." She laughed, but not very much. "I swear, if you were a little older, I could get jealous."

If Marnie looked much of any way right now, she guessed it would be perplexed. But Paula didn't seem to think so. Reaching out to grasp Marnie's hand she said, almost pleading, "Hey, no! That wasn't a chop; I didn't mean it that way. I only . . ."

"Hey, peace out; I know what you meant. Just the idea of anybody jealous over *me*, had me stopped, there."

Seeking a way out of this cul-de-sac of discourse she said, "Well, his liking your friends is better than not, I expect."

But if Marnie thought she was off the hook concerning Alton Darnell, she lost that illusion right now. "Alton's strange, you know. Very creative—as a lover, I mean—but sometimes he gets some really eerie ideas." She paused. "And he broods too much. A whole year of him, on *Starfinder*, I was beginning to wonder about. So—I like it here a lot, but I don't think I could take being with him the full ride. And once back on Earth . . ."

"Well, you have to do whatever's best." But Marnie had heard enough; what she wanted was out of here, before the strange Mr. Darnell came home. More and more the guy sounded like a real gootz. Before she left, though . . .

"Excuse me a minute." She went into the bathroom, but not for the usual reasons. Once inside she stepped into the shower stall and yanked at the vidcam. As she'd hoped, it was only stuck on with a magnet and came free easily. She stuffed the small device into a pocket, paused to cycle the toilet for Paula to hear if the sound reached that far, and came back out.

"Well, I'm in line for a nap. See ya."

Heading toward control with his latest routine report for Earth, Allaird saw two people coming forward, baggage-laden, along the corridor. One was Amalyn Tabard, the other a stranger, a young woman. *Very* young was his first assessment; the next was that the slim newcomer's erect posture added to her moderate height. Other details began to register: oval face now flushed to high color, regular features, emphatic dark brows over grey eyes, honey-blond hair coiled high at the back of her head.

He stepped forward past the control room door to make greeting. "Amalyn," then, "Hello; I'm Clancy Allaird, temporarily in command. And you'd be . . ."

She met his handshake. "Trish Pembrook, replacing Estella Holms. For how long, they didn't tell me. But if it's the full tour—well, my parents and I said good-bye with that possibility in mind."

Clancy smiled. "Hadn't you better give shipboard life a longer tryout first? To see if it really suits you?"

"I was brought up on space work." She looked very serious. "And after all . . . to see a new *world*!"

"Welcome aboard, then." Her hand was warm but not moist. "Are you feeling all right? No wobbles from the jump?" And of course she'd be used to zero-gee . . .

Pembrook smiled. "None at all; I'll be fine."

"Good." And to Tabard, "You're seeing to everything?"

"Yes." She specified a room number. "All right?"

"Sure. Then I'll talk with you later, Pembrook." And he delivered his report packet to control.

Stopping by the galley to replenish her supply of fruit juice, Marnie encountered the new arrival getting the guided tour from Amalyn Tabard and sat briefly to talk with them. Trish, Marnie was surprised to learn, was barely eighteen by years experienced, and had actually been born later than Marnie.

Now how was that supposed to feel? Was she behind Trish in some way, or ahead? Well, she had nearly six years of growth before her that Trish had already been through. Oh well . . .

". . . my first space weld, outside and suited up, when I was fifteen." In high orbit, living with her parents on the partially assembled macroGate, that was. Marnie felt wonder; what a time it must have been. "And—"

But Tabard said, "Come on, Pembrook; we have to get you settled in. You kids can talk later; there'll be lots of time."

So Marnie collected what she needed from the galley and went to quarters. There she inspected the tiny vidcam. What she knew of such gadgets could be written on a little blue bean, so she looked for its make and model designations, cranked up the computer terminal and began search.

Finding its descriptive specs didn't take her long. Uh-huh, here were the function controls. In the drawer under the computer shelf she found the cord needed to patch the vidcam to her terminal input. Making sure that what she was about to see wouldn't be going out to any casual viewer on the system, she reverted vidcam access to zero and began Play. But after a few minutes she stopped it and took a deep breath, for calmness.

Not only had this peeper been recording Paula's showers (with or without her knowledge, Marnie had no idea); he'd also captured an incident when they'd had sex in the stall, standing up. The sound quality was nothing much, but every surprising word of dialogue came through intelligibly.

Well. Marnie took it back to zero again and set the terminal to Record. After a moment's thought she set up a non-listed file, tagged it "P.Tom," and resumed Play. There was Paula alone, Alton and Paula in rut, Paula, Paula, Alton achieving satisfaction all by himself, Alton with Paula as the latter performed services Marnie certainly considered "eerie" whether Paula did or not. . . .

Setting the play at double speed, soundless but time-saving as the terminal automatically switched bit rates to accept the data, Marnie ran it until she saw herself and Paula enter the stall; then in real time she watched, fascinated, as the two laughed and cavorted. It was all so totally innocent, nothing but silly fun with no murky connotations. But in company with what she'd just seen, it made Marnie feel uncomfortable.

At the end she found she'd watched for barely forty minutes; at normal speed Darnell must have nearly two hours of covert voyeurism here. Well, all right for him; she looked up how to erase a recording and wiped this one completely. Then—her own copy, in the P.Tom file?

No. It might just come in handy some way.

The signal at the door found her not quite asleep yet. Grumbling, she put on a robe and went to answer it. When Alton Darnell shoved past her and stood glaring, she felt some unease. But no surprise, not really.

Before she could speak he said, "You have something of mine. I want it."

In her own rooms, Marnie Allaird didn't intend being pushed around. Not by *this* one, anyway. "What makes you think so?"

"It's gone, and Paula didn't take it. She didn't even know it was there. Still doesn't; I know how to ask questions without giving anything away." *You go right on thinking that.* "So where is it?" He gestured away any denial. "Don't lie; Paula told me you were there. And nobody else was. So don't bother to tell me any more lies."

Marnie's eyes narrowed. "And just what lies do you think I've told you?"

"Why—" He was stuck, because so far she'd made no statements at all.

"If you want something, you'll have to say what it is."

"*You* know!"

"Tell me and we'll both know."

"All right. It's a . . ."

She didn't let him off easy: he had to specify name of device, make, model, the whole pouch of pasta. Then "Okay" and she walked over to the terminal desk, hoping he wouldn't read any significance into that location, and handed him the vidcam. "Now you can get out of my quarters. And don't ever come here again. For any reason."

For a moment Darnell seemed apprehensive; then some thought changed his look to smugness. "I suppose you're going to tell your dad I barged in here. Well, think twice. You did steal my vidcam."

So he had no idea she'd viewed the recorded action. Fine; leave it at that. "All you have to do is stay away from me."

The man had all the consistency of a flea. "Stay away? But I've been wanting to know you better." He gestured, waving the vidcam at random. "Hey, I'm sorry I blew up. It was just, finding this missing and all, I lost my head, sort of."

He stepped closer. "Actually I like you a lot. A girl your age—you know, the earlier she starts, the better it gets for her later on."

What in the—? What business was it of his when she started, and what did her periods have to do with anything? Get better? What was this boobatch talking about?

With a skunky grin he said, "I can help; I know how to make it easy and I'm really good at it. Back home I . . ."

Why had it taken her so long to see what he meant? And what kind of person *was* this? How had he made it past the psychologists?

Abruptly she stepped back. "That does it. You don't just leave me alone; you get yourself off this ship. Request transfer now, go to Earth. You—"

"Leave the ship? Oh no, you can't sell that one. Paula, she'd go with me. And that puts you shorthanded again, doesn't it? I don't think the captain would care for the idea."

He really didn't know what he'd done, how far he'd hung his butt over the edge; he still thought he had points he could argue. And: Paula would go too? Ha! But Marnie couldn't repeat Paula's complaints; for all she knew, they might have been nothing more than blowing off steam. Instead, "You just get off of here. Or . . ."

"Or what?"

"Or Captain Allaird gets a look at what you had in that vidcam and don't have now. It's . . ." *Think fast!* ". . . it's in a suspense file." She made a show of checking her wrist chrono. "In less than sixteen hours it pops up and beeps Urgent for him. I think you'll want to be off this ship by then; don't you?"

His face changed; he reached for her. "Maybe. But I'm on here *now*."

She dodged free; this was getting way past the gootz stage. Through suddenly-tightened throat she barked, "Hold it!"

"Like hell. You're all alike; yell a little at first, but then you love it." One hand clawed out to grip her shoulder.

She knocked it away. "Are you *crazy*?"

His eyes went narrow. "Don't you ever say that to me. I'll show you who's crazy. I'll . . ."

Unexpectedly her voice steadied, saying, "I'd better tell you something first." At her armpits sweat came so strongly she could smell it; it didn't smell all that good.

Seeing him pause, carefully she said, "There was a man, tried to do things to me. He didn't do them. You know Clancy smuggled me on this ship?"

"So? Why admit that to *me*?"

Breathing came hard. "You want to know why he had to? Because I was wanted in six states, for what I did to Carl Knapheidt."

Well, if Celeste's holovid plea hit network news, the search probably spread at least that far. And it was none of this muckhead's business that Carl had his tender parts hanging loose for the grabbing and was—now that she thought about it— probably spudded out of the real world and no return address.

Putting a name to the man, though, gave Darnell something to believe; he stepped back a little. First stammering as he searched for words, he said, "S-so you'd rather have me on Earth, telling the law where to find you?"

Her fear lessened; she still had trouble breathing, though. "They already know." Gulp. "Look, Darnell, officially I'm a crew member now. And besides, that statute of limits, you know the thing I mean, it ran out a long time ago.''

''Yeah?'' He thought about it, then nodded. Apparently reaching another of his amazing compromises with sanity he said, ''Well, all right I'll leave you alone. You probably wouldn't be any good anyway, acting so tightass and all. But you can't chase me off this ship.''

She didn't bother to say yes she could. Instead, ''No. But that suspense file can.'' Slowly, his posture sagged. . . .

When he was outside and the door locked behind him, Marnie went straight for the shower. But the way her legs began to shake, she had to sit down a minute first.

What was eating Alton, Paula had no idea. He'd come in, gone to clean up, and come back out hardmouthed and pale, asking questions that made no sense.

Then he'd gone storming out, cursing someone or other in a harsh monotone. That was nearly half an hour ago. And now the door banged open and in he strode. ''All right, we're getting off this ship, going back to Earth. Get our things packed; I'll go set it up with the captain.''

Not pausing to hear any answer he turned away. ''Wait!'' Paula stood, trying to grasp what was happening. ''What do you mean, leave? Why? *I* don't want to go; I like it aboard here.''

He came over and grabbed her shoulders. ''You like what I tell you to. Now get us packed.'' And again he left.

Shaken, Paula stood indecisive. Alton's behavior really *scared* her. He'd never hit her but once, and then cried and made promises she hadn't believed even at the time but were nice to hear. But one thing she knew for certain: she never ever wanted anything like that to happen again.

She didn't want to leave *Arrow*, either. But what to do about it? She needed to talk with someone. Not Marnie; this was too much to load onto anyone her age. Who else? Nicole Pryce, maybe. But the second officer would be on watch by now; distracting her there wouldn't be a good idea.

If only she could get into the local Gate, be nonexistent for the next two ship's months like Captain Tetzl and the rest. Alton would have to leave without her. But she'd never get anyone to activate the device for her. . . .

Oh the hell with it. If Alton was going to the captain, so would she. She packed, all right, but only her own things, including what she'd been issued here.

Then she took a last look around and left the rooms.

She found the captain in quarters. The only trouble was that Alton was there first.

"I don't understand." Clancy really didn't; he'd thought the two from *Starfinder* were settling in rather well. Certainly Marnie spoke well of Paula Trent. "Why do you two want to leave?"

Looking uncomfortable, young Darnell shrugged. "It's hard to say, sir. Expectations, I suppose. We signed for a year on *Starfinder* and got shanghaied to a different ship, where things aren't the way we studied for and we don't know anybody—the group we trained with, and all. So I feel—it's just that . . ."

"And Paula feels the same way?" The door chime sounded. "Just a minute." He stepped over and admitted Paula Trent. "Well, come in. Alton's just been telling me, you two want to leave us. I'm still not sure just why."

"He's lying. I don't know what's biting him, but one thing's sure: I like it on here, just fine."

"Paula!" Face reddening, Darnell stood. "You know what we agreed. Don't try to go back on it!"

"Sit. Down." Deliberately, Allaird made his tone icy. It worked; as if the air had gone out of his legs, Alton Darnell dropped back into his chair. "Now I want to hear more about this. Darnell, you wish to leave; never mind why, for the moment. Trent, you don't want to go with him. Could *you* give me a reason?"

"I'll give *her* a reason," the man snarled.

As Paula said, "Because this is a good ship; I feel at home here. And the way Alton is now, the way he's become, I'm afraid of him."

"You'd better be! I'll—" Standing, fists clenched and all control gone, Darnell ranted.

"Enough!" Allaird could still muster a good parade-ground roar. What in the worlds had happened to young Darnell? He'd seemed rational enough before. Well, whatever had driven him over the edge, Clancy saw no reason it should remain *Arrow*'s problem. Quietly he said, "I've heard all I need to. Mr. Darnell, your request is granted. Let's go."

"What—where—?"

"To the Earthgate. No, wait a minute." Sitting down at his terminal Clancy poked up about half a page of text, printed it out and put it in a wrapper addressed to Starship Personnel, NASA. "This goes into the Gate ahead of you. I'm recommending your termination as a member of the crewing pool, with prejudice. Details to follow. Now get your ass in gear, mister. The next chair you set it on will be two years later and in Earth's own good gravity. Now move it."

Alton Darnell still thought he had a voice here. "What about my things?"

"Trent?" Paula looked up and nodded. "Take your own gear back to your quarters. Pack his and bring it to Earthgate. Make sure you don't miss anything. The stuff'll lag you a few hours at Glen Springs, Darnell, but I'm sure you'll manage."

He marched the man straight to the transfer ring and took him inship, then along the corridor to Earthgate. All without pause, allowing his charge no chance to exchange a word with anyone they met who offered greetings. "Later," said Allaird to each and all, and that had to suffice.

At the Gate he sent off the papers, then said, "Get in; brace yourself for one gee." Then, looking only to see that the man was set for the jump, he activated.

Keeping in mind how pickish Nicole Pryce could get about Gating records, Allaird meticulously logged both transmissions.

Nicole's watch still had hours to go but Clancy needed someone to talk to. Back in his own quarters he put the beep to Marnie's. His call woke her but she seemed chipper enough, and accepted his invitation to lunch ". . . or breakfast, whatever."

His story, held until the coffee stage except that Marnie took decaf, didn't take long to tell. At its end he said, "I don't know; to me the young fella always seemed mostly okay. A little glib maybe, sometimes; a little too withdrawn, others. I never had any idea he was the kind of guy you'd see his wife with a black eye, she says she ran into a doorknob."

He paused, waiting for comment, but Marnie said nothing.

So, "Did you ever notice anything peculiar about him?"

Oddly hesitant, finally she said, "He seemed like kind of a gootz, was all."

"Gootz? What's a gootz?"

"It's, well—oh, *you* know . . ."

The funny thing was, he almost did. Gootz: a word coming out of nowhere to spread throughout every schoolyard in the land. Nobody could explain it but nobody had to, because everybody knew. Everybody the right age, anyway.

So he let it go. "Well then—did he ever give *you* any problems?"

"Umm." Another pause. "Nothing to speak of."

But for a moment there, Marnie's face became a mask; from behind it her eyes showed a recalcitrant twinkle.

Not really, of course. Eyes don't twinkle; that's book talk. Any more than they actually follow someone across a room (pitter-patter!). She must have blinked and looked aside some way, back and forth so the reflections changed.

"With Trish here," Marnie said now, "I guess the gender balance thing is *really* up the spout."

Oh hell; Clancy hadn't even thought of that aspect. All he could find to say was, "Maybe Eli's a latent polygamist." Then, "Polygynist, actually." And remembering, "Since he didn't have much luck with polyandry."

But Allaird had to pay for showing off his vocabulary by explaining the differences between the three terms. Still it was nice to learn his daughter didn't really know everything already.

Because sometimes he wondered.

Awake and fed, Marnie decided she'd better see how Paula was doing, and found her in the lounge talking with Trish Pembrook. Fine; together they gave Trish a quick overall tour of the ship. Then, after a full-gee exercise session, the consequent shower turned into a fair roughhouse—not hard enough that anybody might get hurt, but definitely some robust tussling.

All in all, Marnie found the threesome interesting and fun. For one thing, Trish's presence inhibited any discussion of Alton Darnell, and for that, Marnie was profoundly grateful.

Back in her rooms, though, she began to wonder. She'd seen

it with others and had it a time or two herself: when two friends team up with a third, all of a sudden there's a competition nobody asks for and nobody wants, each to be everyone else's *best* friend and not become odd person out.

Well, she'd just have to watch out for that. Because there was something she'd thought about but never had occasion to try: if you decline unwelcome competition, you can't be a target.

As if Clancy didn't have enough on his mind, Earthtush brought word of an impending VIP visit, due to materialize within hours. "Senator Wallin, huh?" Allaird shook his head. "Hadn't realized the old gentleman was still with us. He must be . . ." and found he had no idea of the man's age.

Wallin was no longer a senator, hadn't been for years since he stepped down in favor of Bill Flynn, but he still carried the courtesy title. He was the man who had, back when he headed the space committee, witnessed the historic Three-fingered Annie fiasco of the first Traction Drive breadboard demonstration, seen the device's possibilities, and ramrodded the empowering legislation that produced first *Jovian-II* and then the starships.

Since retiring he'd served as consultant and watchdog for Flynn—a roving emissary, more or less. Allaird knew the man had begun a tour of at least one of the other ships, maybe both by now. So it was no surprise that he'd come here. Or shouldn't have been, if Clancy weren't so preoccupied with other matters.

Stopping by the lounge he found Phil Henning and Pilar Velez pretty much at leisure, and asked, "Could you two check out the VIP rooms right away, see they're ready for company? Just the essentials; the frills can wait until our guest picks what he wants. Okay? I'll appreciate this a lot."

They hadn't reported back when Gina Todisco called to announce the senator's arrival, but Clancy didn't worry. The hospitable formalities of greeting would take up the slack.

Heading inship to meet the man, Allaird wasn't sure what to expect. Would he be ambulatory, wheelchaired, or what? Vaguely he remembered hearing that Wallin had had a couple of bouts with bad hips, successful surgeries, and heaven knew what. With that question on his mind he was unsurprised to find, when he met the group approaching along the corridor, that the senator hadn't come alone. The woman alongside him, whose arm the old man held lightly, stood at medium height. Thin, somewhere in her late forties by Clancy's guess, she had a pleasant expression on her somewhat triangular face. Curly brown hair, shortish, was showing some grey; not bothering to hide it could indicate any of several attitudes. Being comfortable about herself was the one Clancy hoped for.

"Senator. Clancy Allaird, temporarily commanding. Welcome aboard."

Wallin freed his hand to shake Allaird's. "Thank you." He turned toward the woman beside him. "Maxine Durand, my keeper." Clancy nodded to the woman as Wallin continued, "She's been on *Starfinder* with me, then *Roamer*, and now here. Where, if you'll agree to it, we intend to stay for some time."

"I'm sure . . ."

Wallin interrupted. "We can talk about that later. For now, let's visit your galley. Habgate transit shouldn't make a man hungry, there's no reason for it. But I generally am."

"Yes, sir. This way, then."

Standing aside he saw that notwithstanding his age, Senator Wallin had a good mastery of Velcro in zero gee.

". . . not even sure myself, how old I am by time actually experienced." Over coffee, his snack finished, Wallin looked around the crowded table. "Earth time's easy; just check the current date and subtract. Which gives me eighty-six. But what with Gating and time dilation, that number doesn't mean much. And the other one's hard to keep track of."

Clancy thought about it. "Uh—your first trip, you went to *Starfinder*, then direct to *Roamer*, and back to Earth?" Wallin nodded. "Do you know how long you were gone, by Earth time?"

The senator's scowl indicated concentration. "Yes. Nine years and four months, almost exactly."

"Okay." Including three jumps. And now Gating here to *Arrow* . . . "All right—say forty months' total stay on the other two ships." At ten to one . . . yes. "The way I make it, you dropped three years on shipboard, total. And four times through the Gates." Clancy beamed in triumph. "You arrived here, then, with eleven years difference in your two ages. Or close enough.''

Wallin mustered a pretty good grin himself. "Seventy-five, eh? That's not so bad. This one uncle of mine . . ." He came back to the subject. "And so now all I need, to keep myself up to date, is to use your twenty-five ratio as long as I'm aboard."

He leaned forward. "Tell me this. How much longer, ship's time here, until *Starfinder* approaches destination and begins decel? Because at that point I'd like to Gate aboard her again. Arriving when they've been in orbit several months, and have had a chance to learn something about their planet."

For a moment the sheer scope of this man's plans set Allaird back on his heels; then he considered the problem. *Let's see now.* Clancy's trouble was that once he began to get the numbers straight in his mind, it went right ahead with them, so he didn't think to stop and use the pocket calc instead. "Okay; counting from the day we inGated here, we're now up to one-thirteen. The one you want is three-thirty-six. So you're looking for bed and board, sir, for—oh, seven and a half months, a little less. I expect we can manage that."

Wallin cleared his throat. "You won't have to. I can still do my timeses in my head too, captain, and I make it—oh, fifteen and a quarter years Earth time, near enough. And my own thinking is for Maxine and myself to bypass a number of those years completely, by means of your decelerator Gate. If you will be so kind as to allow us that usage."

Huh? "Of course, senator. You just let me know what you plan in the way of a schedule, and I'm sure we can oblige." This old boy was as full of surprises as a pothole in deep swamp. . . .

Marnie wasn't keeping all the numbers straight; for one thing, her father and Wallin were working from basepoints they both seemed to understand but hadn't stated aloud. She was fascinated, though. And now the senator said, "I'm worried about *Starfinder*. The last we heard on Earth, Rance Collier and his lady—striking woman, she is—had decamped to *Roamer*. And then Hayes Morton, who'd gone out with cadre 2–A as exec, messaged that Captain Tetzl and both her co-execs and three other people had all vanished, God knows where but it would have to be by one Gate or another.'' Under bushy brows he squinted at Clancy. ''I don't suppose you've heard anything, know what it's about?''

Marnie thought she'd burst from the effort of keeping silent, until Clancy said, ''Happens we have, and do. Those six came here, five unconscious and Fleurine Schadel with the dart gun that does that little trick—and did here, too. She took them through our loop Gate once; when she came out we thought we knew what to expect and were ready for anything, but we were wrong. She zapped our team in control and Gated again there. If we hadn't had remote viewer swatching, we never would have known who did it, or how. She took—let's see, it was Rozanski and Hanchett and Tetzl—back in with her, and grabbed our captain, too. Which is why I'm in charge for now.''

He paused, but Wallin waited, so, ''She left the 2–A couple lying there; when they came to I signed them on, since we were short one just then, by way of a gall bladder. Though we did get a replacement a bit later. One of those two is still with us; the other, uh, proved unsuitable and I sent him home.''

Allaird stopped; the senator shook his head. ''I should have paid more heed to young Collier; I'd worked with him on Earth when he did liaison for us with NASA and Gayle Tech and Dr. Habegger. And I was aboard *Starfinder*, you know, when Tetzl and her group arrived. Rance had misgivings; I think he'd had some kind of run-in with the woman, but he wouldn't say what.''

Clancy could guess, but kept silent.

''Hawh!'' Wallin gave a rueful snort. ''She had no use for *me*, no mistake about that; didn't bother to hide it much. But you don't pull the chain on a starship captain for personal satisfaction; maybe I leaned over backward for just that reason.''

He stood, easily enough in the light gravs. ''Next time those people pop out, I expect you can nab Schadel. Imagine you'd better just bung the lot off to Earth and let 'em sort it out there.'' Then, frowning slightly, ''How long until they're due, anyway?''

Having figured that answer some seconds earlier, Marnie

couldn't restrain herself from giving it. "Roughly sixteen days. About six hours less, actually."

Without turning his head the old man peered sidewise down his nose at her. "Pretty quick there, young miss. We haven't been introduced, have we? But I think I've heard of you." Then to Clancy he said, "Changed my mind. I'm going to stick around and see what Schadel has to say for herself."

He grinned like a wolf. "And Old Iron Tits, too."

XI

Interest in the upcoming reemergence of the *Starfinder* quartet, even the imminent retrieval of Ellery Dawson, was upstaged by the news from Earth. At first Allaird thought it had to be a flat-out hoax. "The Intruder? Some kind of huge alien ship, just barging right in on the solar system? *Eating moons*? What grade of gullible do they think we are?"

But hour after hour, over the next day and then a second one, more bulletins followed. Keeping up wasn't easy, and keeping the action straight was impossible.

At the Earth end, of course, it was months passing, not days. And maybe on that scale it made sense. Not here, though.

Especially the incredible-seeming finale.

Which was the only part that did make sense to Marnie. As she listened to the latest discussion, this one in the lounge, it finally came clear to her that the alien ship, the Intruder, wasn't really bigger than, say, one of Saturn's moons. The ingestive orifice itself was slightly smaller in diameter than the orbiting macroGate sent in desperation to face and challenge the hurtling construct. On the order of eight hundred feet across, if she had that part right.

But from that opening issued an immaterial trumpet-shaped field, glowing with the impact of spaceborne particles. It was this field that sucked in space-time, matter and all, presumably converting some matter to energy before spitting it all out the other end, since every major ingestion produced an increase in the thing's ability to accelerate. Approaching the inner system its velocity grew to equal and then exceed that of the Earth in orbit. "So that the macroGate," Clancy commented, "really had to pour on the coal, to intercept before the Intruder could gobble up the moon. Well, they're assuming that was the target; Earth was just plain too big for it." He shrugged. "But what happened then, I don't understand at all."

Senator Wallin nodded. "Because they're not telling us the whole story." He looked at the readout sheet he held. "As our macroGate neared the Intruder, this says, the ingestive field flickered and died, so our construct landed—or maybe docked—face-to-face with the thing's forward orifice. The aliens' drive gave one hellacious burst of thrust and then went dead."

He set the sheet down. "After that, all we're told is that maybe the whole huge ship died also. Crews are working to get into it and find out."

"And that's everything?" said Nicole Pryce.

"Officially, yes. Bill Flynn sent me a note saying that it wasn't our highly touted crew of experts that did whatever was done. The real credit, he says, goes to Anne Portaris. If the brass-bound brains ever declassify the information."

"Portaris?" Clancy frowned. "I have the highest respect for that lady, but what could one person do?"

"Beats me," said Wallin. "I have no idea."

But Marnie did! She knew she should keep it to herself, yet she couldn't. "Sure you do, Senator!" He stared at her. "You were there. The very first time."

For long seconds the old man's face went blank; then he began to laugh. "Oh hell yes! She told you about that, did she?" And, "Yes of course; that would work. And no wonder they're not spreading it around. You keep your lip zipped, young woman." But then he shook his head. "No, that's silly. As silly as classifying the information in the first place." He looked around. "But until the lid comes off officially, we don't tell it outside this ship."

Given his go-ahead nod, Marnie related how the misaligned Traction Drive prototype gave Three-fingered Annie the nickname she so detested. "It aged her finger a hundred years in less than a second. I bet she fiddled the macroGate's drive, so it did the same thing to the Intruder."

Clancy looked dubious, but he didn't argue.

From one corner, Phil Henning spoke. "You know—if putting the fields out of phase one way speeds time, then the other way would slow or even *freeze* it for whatever was in range. So she could have done that, too, if she'd thought of it."

Wallin shook his head. "Could, yes—but to what purpose? You'd be spending full power just to delay the showdown. And when you let up, you'd be right back where you started."

Henning blushed. "It was just an idea."

The senator blinked. "And very innovative, too. Don't let *me* throw cold water on good thinking."

Visibly, Phil perked up again. "You know? I'm going to check theory and figure how she did it."

Marnie's next waking came feverish and nauseous, her gut cramping unendurably. Chauncey Ng's diagnosis was fast and simple: "It's some kind of flu bug—and a mean one." Between shaking with chill and burning up, heaving her socks up and suffering the most agonizing and interminable diarrhea she'd ever known, Marnie couldn't disagree.

And that was before the uncontrollable coughing set in.

"How could she get this?" Sitting across a galley table from Chaucey Ng, Clancy knew he sounded accusatory but he couldn't help it. "She had her flu shots, and . . ."

Then he realized; ten years ago she'd had those shots. Not by her own time, but by Earth's, where each winter brought a new strain, some more virulent than others. And come to think of it, everyone aboard was in the same boat. But still, "Nobody's been having the flu *here*."

"I expect it's me." He hadn't noticed young Trish Pembrook sitting off to one side at a nearby table.

"How? You had your shots. You looked a little feverish when you arrived, but that didn't last."

"I was exposed, though. When I visited some of my family on Earth, just before reporting to Glen Springs. And had the shots afterward. So I did get a mild case, and must have been still carrying the bug when I got here.''

''Then how come nobody else has caught it?''

Clancy spoke too soon; a short time later Chauncey was called away to have a look at Paula Trent. And over the next few days the Djakarta flu, that had ravaged Earth two years earlier, began cutting a vicious swath through the duty roster.

Clancy himself got off relatively easy; whatever strain his own most recent shots had been for, must have been a near relative of this one. But for the next week and more, he and the few healthy people stood a lot of double watches.

When he got around to think of it, he sent Earth a request that new flu shots be Gated to *Arrow* every year as soon as available. To have on hand in case of need, any time new people came aboard with a fresh virus. It might work.

Both crises having passed—the two-year-old Intruder scare *and* the ship's freak epidemic—the continuing stream of follow-up stories from Earth began to get on Clancy's nerves. The Liij, the aliens in the Intruder ship (except that they called it something that translated as Environ) weren't dead after all. Sorely diminished, yes, but now with a chance to survive.

And the effort and resources that had been rushed into action to stop the Intruder were being diverted to help assure that survival—a tradition, Allaird reminded himself, that dated back to the Second World War. Human teams had boarded the Liij Environ, met the aliens and somehow talked with them, come to terms that enabled cooperation.

He wondered why he could muster so little interest in such momentous happenings; finally, after centuries of hoping and fearing and wondering, the human race had learned it wasn't alone in the universe. But Allaird found no thrill in that learning.

Finally he decided it was because this was entirely Earth's discovery. And he was no longer *of* Earth. That planet lay some eight light-years behind him; if at this moment he outGated to Glen Springs, he would have been gone approximately twelve years. By the time *Arrow* reached destination, there'd be no one at home he could relate to; his own daughter's classmates would be doddering or dead.

Most of the people onship seemed very hup-hup about the

whole historic smorgasbord: alien threat foiled, then Man finds Brotherhood from the stars. Well, something like that. Clancy envied them; they were having a lot more fun than he was.

Part of his malaise may have been from contagion; these days Nicole showed an unsuspected moody streak. Nothing Allaird could pin down: no fights or open disagreements, no obvious pitfalls to be carefully avoided. It was simply that she had, somewhere along the way, holed up inside herself. The way it was with Clancy, he really needed to get her out. But he didn't know how.

He waited until the schedule showed a time when both would be off watch *and* well rested, then subtly—he hoped— proposed they have a quiet meal together for a change. With as much enthusiasm as she showed for anything these days, Nicole agreed.

He scrounged through recent additions to galley supplies and assembled the makings of a festive spread. He fussed over the wine selection and finally set aside a bottle each of his two top choices. And well in advance he advised Marnie of his desire to be completely alone with Nicole for those few hours.

To Ptiba Mbente who had that particular watch he said, "I want a big favor. During your next shift, don't let anyone call me for anything that isn't a clear and present danger to the ship itself. Can I depend on you for that?"

"All the way." She looked curious but didn't ask.

So Allaird was all set. And nervous as a boy on his first date.

"Oh sure; I understand. You folks have a good time." But Marnie felt let down. Certain things were bothering her, and she'd been thinking it might help to talk with somebody.

This stuff didn't wear on her all the time. It had begun while she was sick—light-headed with fever and having altogether too much time to think—but physical recovery hadn't ended it. She'd wake up earlier than she wanted to, and these ideas would start in on her and she couldn't get back to sleep. Enough times like that could work up to earnest worry.

What chafed, mostly: why was it, what was it about her, that made these chicken hawks home in on her? Sure; in the very early grades, she and all the other kids were given the message that when some adult got predatory toward a child in a sexual way, *it is not your fault*. And if anybody went to put hands on you some way they shouldn't, *say no, and tell somebody*. She believed these things because on the face of them they were true. Still, though . . .

Carl's mindless attack had shocked her, scared her out of any semblance of calm reason. Yet after a time, inside herself she'd put it to rest. She knew she'd never encouraged him in any way because she could barely manage to be civil toward him.

So she'd come to terms with that calamity as an isolated event. But then here came Alton Darnell trying more or less the same damn thing! Well, she'd coped, come away with no thought of aftereffects. And all's well; right?

Except that in the back of her mind where she wasn't looking, the two incidents melded together into something nasty and painful. On the order of: anyone who unerringly attracts twisted men *has* to be sending out some kind of signal.

What Marnie needed was some fresh input.

But maybe Clancy wasn't the right one, anyway.

Then who was? Nicole was booked, Paula after Alton Darnell had her own stab wounds healing, Trish too new and too young, no other woman Marnie *knew* well enough. And no man at all.

Leaving a totally blank slate; Marnie had no one to talk with except herself. With a paradoxical feeling of relief, she made a cup of tea and sat down with it. All right . . .

Digging in one's head requires various tools, ranging from agonizing concentration to detached semitrance, all driven by the need to know and understand. Or, thought Marnie, shaking her head clear after a long and intensive bout of introspection, maybe it's all just a pile of crap. Either way she was stiff in the muscles and sweaty as could be. So, soaking out in a hot shower, she considered what she thought she might have learned.

Most of her effort, physical and emotional, had been toward freeing herself from this load of guilt or shame or bullshit. The results, in terms of logical answers, were quite concise.

Carl would screw anything that wiggled if it wasn't fast enough to get away.

Alton had a thing for young girls and here on the ship she was the only candidate available.

So all that applied to Marnie herself was, she was probably the only person unlucky enough to meet both of them in the same lifetime.

Warm and pink from the shower, she had the best sleep she'd had in days.

Why Clancy felt he was walking on eggs, he had no idea. Hey, this was Nicole Pryce, they were pretty damn well in love, and he had a menu coming up that would make a mummy drool.

Not being a mummy, Nicole expressed her appreciation less crudely. Dinner went well, she evidently enjoyed his choice of wine although they were only halfway down the first bottle by coffee time, and she spoke freely enough.

But only about superficial matters. He still had the feeling she was sitting on something he should know about, and he had no idea how to get at it, no way to read her thoughts.

Nicole seemed to read his, though. "Clancy? With all that's going on, back home, do you find yourself wishing we'd never left?"

Not you, too! Carefully, "What do you mean?"

"There's another race, another species, running loose in the universe. And back on Earth everybody's getting to know about them, some even meeting them. But not us."

Her face took on a stricken look. "Dammit, that's what *we* set out to do. And the stay-at-homes—it all falls into their laps, instead. They get to meet the aliens and we never can; the Environ has to be already on its way out of the solar system. It's not fair, Clancy—it's not fair."

She'd come up standing. He went around the table and held her, steered her over to the big sofa, gathered their cups and glasses to sit handy in front of them on the coffee table. Beside her, he thought first and then said, "If our people don't put Habgates on that Environ they're stupider than I think. Hey, once we reach destination and people get started on colonizing, assuming the planet-finder folks got the right info off their six-billion-mile scatter array, you and I can take a leave and go any damn place we want to. Earth, other ships' destinations which should be established colonies by that time, and why not this Environ thing too, while we're at it? So . . .''

Nicole shook her head. "We'd be back numbers, Allaird. Out of date. Museum pieces. Can't you guess how much Earth will change in—how long will it be? Seventy years? Close, anyway. You and I go back to Earth then, they'll be very nice to us but you bet your sweat we won't be considered operational. Ornamental is more like it. Charmingly quaint." She made a snarling face. "I'm not putting myself in that position. Ever."

Because she was simply adding detail to his own misgivings, Clancy had absolutely nothing in the way of rebuttal. Instead, "You think we made a mistake, coming on here?"

Abruptly she clung to him, face against his neck. It didn't feel wet, so she wasn't crying. "I don't know. I thought I had it all worked out before I applied for training. And during all the stages when people dropped out or got dropped, and I stuck. I came on here feeling great about it, and that's how it's been, until—until those goddamn *aliens* turned up. And now I just plain don't know."

His arm tightened around her. "You too, huh?"

As she pulled away to look at him he saw she *was* blinking back tears. "Damn you, Clancy. You could have said something!"

No I couldn't.

They were about five minutes short of going to bed with more enthusiasm than they'd had in some days, when Ptiba beeped the intercom. "Captain! You'd better get up here! And watch yourself; they're—" The speaker clicked off.

Oh bloody hell!

Sent by watch officer Mbente to see if any mail had arrived at Earthtush, Paula Trent was within a few feet of that terminal when its receiving space flared with color. Blinking against afterglow she saw three bulkily wrapped figures emerge, masked and goggled, each holding some kind of hand weapon.

"Hold it right there!" The man in the lead, the short one, waved his odd-looking gun. "Hendryx! Got a make on this one?"

"Just a minute." The one addressed punched buttons on a small hand viewer, then said, "Paula Trent. From *Starfinder*, cadre 2–A. We've got 'em, Marv!"

"Not yet." Marv came toward Paula. "All right, where's Tetzl? And how many of you are there?"

"I—she—" Normally level-headed, Paula was jarred totally off-balance by these looming gargoyles. "What do you . . . ?"

"Oh, get a move on." Marv gestured. "To control. Nobody's going to zap *us*; we'll take care of that department. Hendryx, Feldman, watch our flanks."

Numbly Paula led the way. She hadn't even checked for mail.

When Ptiba saw Paula being herded at gunpoint she grabbed at the intercom and yelled for Clancy Allaird, but within seconds her hand was knocked free of the talk switch. "All right," said the short man, after his colleague's viewer correctly identified Ptiba and Coyote Benjamin for him. " You belong here. Now who all's aboard that doesn't? Tetzl's people. Besides this one."

His gesture indicated Paula; Ptiba said, "It's not her doing; she was brought here. And others. One's Gated back to Earth already: Alton Darnell. And the rest . . ." She gestured toward the local Gates. "They're on ice in there."

Peeling off goggles and hood, the short man exposed a ruddy face and incongruously cheerful expession. "So you folks took care of Old Iron Tits all by yourselves? Looks like we've had a trip for nothing."

"Not exactly," said Clancy Allaird, entering.

Having no idea what awaited him, Clancy approached control warily. Once he saw the strange getups with only one man's face showing but no guns actually pointing at anyone, he stepped inside. "Those suits will come in handy a few days from now; she's put the watch to sleep twice, so far. But it's not Tetzl; it's Fleurine Schadel. Tetzl's out cold, along with Jimmy Hanchett and Cleve Rozanski. And," he remembered, "our own captain, Ellery Dawson." With that, he introduced himself.

"Marv Corby," said the short man. As the other two shed their own masks and goggles Allaird saw they were younger than he'd expected: Dean Hendryx blondish and thin-faced, Neola Feldman his opposite in both those respects. Corby turned to Paula Trent. "Look, I'm sorry I acted so rough. We didn't know what to expect here; you see?" And then to Clancy, "Schadel, huh? That's a poser. Any idea why?"

"She didn't say." Putting a little irony to it. "Anyway, you must have some ideas yourselves—or you wouldn't be here. Did you get word from *Starfinder* or from *Roamer*?"

Corby chuckled. "From Rance Collier. He and Su Teng went through *Roamer* like a dose of salts, got home just in time for the big Liij fracas." He sobered. "So we knew Irina Tetzl had her own cadre set up to take *Starfinder* all the way in, and intended to Gate unwanted replacements elsewhere. We couldn't know where she'd taken over and where not, so we had to put a containment team out to each ship. I drew this one."

"Well," said Clancy, "somebody has to get lucky. I don't suppose any of you commandos could use some coffee?"

And quarters, and bedding, and spare clothes, and some smooth-soled shoes to wear on the living areas belt . . .

For a start, after consigning Corby's preliminary report to Earthmouth, he led the way to the transfer ring.

Refreshed, Marnie dressed and fixed herself a quick snack from the fridge before reporting for duty at Ship's Supplies. As she passed the common-facilities corridor she saw Clancy escorting three bulkily clad strangers. For a moment she paused, but Pilar was expecting her so she kept going. Whatever was going on, she'd find out later.

Cheerful as usual, Velez gave greeting and handed her a list: towels, bedding, and the like. "Round up this lot and take it along to the VIP suite, would you? If nobody's home it might be a nice touch to do the beds, but if they're in, just make certain they know where the stuff's kept. Okay?"

"Sure." Assembling the items didn't take long. They made a sizable bundle but not a heavy one; a bit awkwardly but with no great effort she packed it to the rear transverse, along it and past Earthmouth, then forward two doors to the suite itself.

She touched the door-chime button but heard nothing from inside. In case they had it turned down she rapped gently; still no response, so she let herself in with Pilar's passkey and found no one present.

Rather tidy people, the senator and his companion: a few

things lying around here and there, but not much, and no dirty dishes. The bathroom door was ajar; she placed clean towels on the racks and put the reserves on the proper shelves, then carried the other things toward the bedroom.

That door was closed, and now as she approached she heard sounds from inside. After a moment she stopped, embarrassed and undecided. Because she knew sex when she heard it.

This was louder than daddy with Celeste years ago, when they'd all have to share a hotel room at one of his departures or arrivals and she was supposed to be asleep but wasn't, yet. But not a patch on the whooping of Celeste and Carl who seemed determined to entertain passing motorists.

Nonetheless it was unmistakable, and Marnie wanted out of here before her intrusion could be noticed. But—oh jeez, it would be anyway: the towels. No help for it; she set the bedding on the bathroom counter, grabbed up the used towels, and made for the door posthaste. As she reached it, behind her came the sound of indrawn breath.

She didn't look back. And obviously there was no point in trying to close the door silently.

On her way back to Supplies she thought about the situation. Not the fact, surprising to her, that Senator Wallin at his advanced age was still doing it, but the other part. Why had her accidental intrusion evoked obvious distress? She *hadn't* meant to spy, and she simply wouldn't say a word to anyone about any of it. If that wasn't good enough, too bad.

After all, they could have put the bolt on.

She found Pilar issuing the same kinds of supplies, plus clothing, to the three strangers, and was co-opted to do a little gofering for the cause. Between tasks Marnie listened, and after a while had a fair idea of the containment team's agenda. Marv Corby, the short guy in charge, barely acknowledged when Velez introduced her; he was too busy talking, concentrating on the point at hand. The other man, Hendryx, did smile and shake her hand, and the round-faced woman Neola Feldman now and then engaged her in fragments of conversation.

Clancy showed up shortly before the issue was complete, and all six of them pitched in to carry it to the quarters Allaird assigned. Marnie, it turned out, had part of Corby's things, and as she piled them on a bed he said, "Thanks, Marnie. I appreciate the help." So he'd been paying more attention than she thought.

She grinned. "Sure," and left with Pilar, who headed not for Supplies but to the galley. Break time. After the skimpy breakfast, Marnie enjoyed a couple of biscuits with her tea.

Until she saw Maxine Durand walking straight toward her.

Oh crap! Marnie's solar plexus hit free-fall as the woman approached, tight-lipped and aggressive, stopping so close that Marnie had to look up to see her face. "I need to talk to you."

So Marnie was stuck. First, though, "You'd better get on back, Pilar; I'll be along when I can." Because even if Durand didn't want privacy for this, Marnie sure did.

As Velez cleared earshot the woman sat. "I think you owe me an explanation."

All right, tell it straight. "I had stuff to deliver. Nobody answered the door—chime or knock, either one. Your—" Durand tried to cut in but Marnie wasn't having it. "*Your bolt.* It was off, so the passkey worked, should have meant nobody home." She paused, but now the other seemed willing to listen. "When I heard different, I got out as fast as I could."

"Is that all?" Not quite so rigid now.

"Except that I haven't said anything, and I won't."

With one deep breath the woman relaxed. "Thank you. That's what I needed to know." Puzzled, Marnie probably looked it; Durand said, "People make jokes, cruel ones. It's not fair."

"No'm."

"And . . ." The woman gestured. "A child—I was afraid you'd be telling . . ."

"I won't; I already said that."

"Yes." Durand nodded. "I'm sorry I misjudged you."

"That's okay." It wasn't, not entirely, but what can you say? Anyway, the senator's companion had backed off now, so let go of it. Marnie stood. "I have to get back to Supplies now."

Without waiting for an answer she walked out fast. At least now she knew why being overheard was such a big crisis.

To Pilar Velez's questions she said only, "Just a mixup, was all; nothing important. Forget it."

* * *

"You don't need any barricades or anything," Allaird said. "There's three of you and one of her, you padded against the darts and her not. You may want to spread out a little, divide her attention, but frankly I don't see how you could flub it."

"He's right," said Neola Feldman. With the bulky "armor" off, now as they sat in the lounge the youngish woman no longer reminded Clancy of a teddy bear. Strongly built for her height, but not chubby. "This job's a cookie." Dean Hendryx nodded.

"I know," said Corby. "I want to make certain, is all. For instance, what if some of the others are awake by now?" Then he realized, and shook his head. "Yeh, yeah; instantaneous for the subject transmitted. For a minute there, I forgot."

"Easy enough," Senator Wallin said. "Gates do get confusing."

The exchange gave Clancy an idea. "Our vidcam record, Schadel and the others out of one Gate and into the other, it's all in the computer. You want to be really prepared, let me show you something." He called it up on the room's large-screen entertainment terminal, skimmed to the flare of disappearance, and backed up a couple of seconds, freezing Fleurine Schadel in combat-ready crouch. "See there? I figured out where she's watching; she's primed for anybody coming in that door."

"So?"

"When they outGate again, she still will be."

Corby nodded. "Right. One of us should be there, to hold her attention while somebody else pots her from the side."

A bit like shooting fish in a barrel, Allaird thought—but wasn't that what Security was all about?

"The important thing," said Wallin, "is to bring this hidey-hole business to a halt. We want some answers out of those people. I know I do." And no one argued otherwise.

Corby wasn't done fretting; his optimistic face disguised a world-class worrier. "Let's be sure we have all the IDs right. Dean?" Hendryx passed him the hand viewer. "Now then; Jimmy Hanchett, you said? Are you sure? Take another look."

This was a waste of time and Clancy said so. "Why bother? They're all in the monitor copy; you can check 'em yourself."

He backed up and reran, freezing and zooming for better

view when one and another face appeared clearly, until Corby nodded. "Okay: Schadel, Tetzl, Hanchett, Rozanski. With your Captain Dawson. Trent and Darnell left flat. Only it's not Darnell."

"You mean he was some kind of impostor?" Nicole sounded dubious. "Then where's the real one?"

Rising to pour a warmup for his coffee, Corby grinned. "He never existed." Settled again, he said, "You're a cabinet secretary, see? And your nephew's going to the slammer, this time for sure. So you pull strings with some people who run the Federal witness protection program. The setup's unusual, but luckily the kid has some useful ship skills. Because your brother had him sent out on macroGate work one year, up where his hobby couldn't get him in trouble. So our possible political embarrassment jumps bail and disappears, and Alton Darnell with a full set of stamped credentials shows up just in time to fill in for I forget who got real sick all of a sudden. We suspected something, but I didn't know for sure until I saw that picture."

He spread his hands. "Fourteen years later he comes back. Even if he's recognized, the statute's run out. Which it has, now; by the time we guessed what might have happened, it was already too late to get him back in time to indict him. And hell: on *Starfinder* he was cut off from his hobby, anyway."

Allaird cleared his throat. "What hobby?"

"Molesting young girls, right around puberty."

"I see." Clancy stood. "If you'll excuse me . . ."

"Oh hey—!" Corby yelled after him. "I didn't mean . . ."

But Allaird didn't give a damn what he meant.

"What's the *matter*?" Barging into Supplies and hauling her out of there with only minimal courtesy, hotfooting the two of them to her quarters and now closing the door behind them, Clancy wasn't acting like himself. Confused, more than a little angry, Marnie blurted out, "What's going on, anyway?"

"Alton Darnell." He sat, so she did too. "Something happened between you two. What was it?"

Oh boy. She and Pilar had pretty much run out of work, so that part was probably okay. But still . . . She answered,

"Nothing much; I said so already. And why's it important now?"

"The man's a known molester, that's why; picks on young girls, right about your age. So I want to know, did he try anything? And how far did it go?"

She hadn't intended to say anything at all, but now she had to. Well, "It wasn't like Carl; he never even touched me!" Only the robe, when he grabbed her shoulder. "All right, he said some stuff and I thought for a minute there he was coming at me—but nothing like Carl! And once I saw what he really meant, I sent him off."

"Sent him off?" For a moment his face went to pure doubt; then his expression cleared. "I guess you must have, at that; I never did understand why he wanted off the ship so fast. But what kind of leverage could you use on a man like that?"

So okay, tell him. Marnie smiled. "You."

Clancy didn't even try to argue. After a second he nodded. "All right; case closed. How about I heat up some pizza?"

It wasn't lunchtime yet. Oh, well. "Fine."

He overzapped it a little drippy. Messy eating takes longer; after a while he began telling how Alton Darnell was really somebody else's cover ID. It all sounded pretty much like "Simon Speer, Superspy" on the holos, but so did half the political news, especially speeded up twenty-five to one. So she guessed the story was probably true. Or near to it.

Since a variation in the fourth decimal place of *Arrow*'s velocity could shift its time ratio several percent, prediction of Fleurine Schadel's next emergence could hardly be exact. Using a grade of math Clancy could *not* do in his head, the main computer periodically integrated the effect of such fluctuations and adjusted drive thrust to compensate over the long haul, but these after-the-fact corrections didn't necessarily hold for a given interval.

So once again the local Gate vigil was set to begin well before action was really expected. Marv Corby hadn't anticipated the situation. "I thought we'd only need to hold Alert for a few hours." Well, it couldn't be helped. "So we'll do it with two instead of three. Each of us at the ready for eight hours on and four off. That should . . ."

Allaird cleared his throat. "Those suits aren't exactly tailored, are they? Why can't one of the regular watch use whos-ever's off guard duty? When the changes coincide, that is. Come to that, I'm pretty fair with handguns myself. And since the darts are harmless, there shouldn't be any hesitation, qualms, whatever, like you might expect from amateurs.''

The last part cleared Corby's frown. ''All right. Make those assignments in advance: somebody the suit fits *and* can shoot.'' Murky syntax, but Clancy got the drift.

So, twelve hours into the alert he put on the padded suit Dean Hendryx had just peeled off and learned how to get mask and goggles in place fast when needed. Coyote Benjamin and young Trish Pembrook, left unprotected, had their orders: when the Tush flared, get behind their consoles and hit the deck. Which, in zero gee, meant grabbing the proper hand-holds, swinging forward and around and down, and then hold-ing on.

After a couple of practice tries they had the drill down well enough. Even Corby, from his chair with its legs hastily spot-welded to the deck alongside the corridor door, in the ''target'' position, approved.

Then, same as the month before, it was sit and wait.

Playing anisotropic rotation pool with Paula Trent, Marnie fidgeted. She hated being left out of things. Paula had come off alert-status watch, relieved by Trish Pembrook of all peo-ple, and here Marnie was, stuck well away from all the ex-citement. Why, she couldn't even call Clancy on the intercom; orders were, none but official calls into control and those had better be important! She put too little stick into her shot; a vector product of forces nudged her slow-moving cue ball amiss.

Assessing the lie of the table, Paula shook her head. ''Let's cap it for now; this is no game to play jittered. I'm a little strung anyway, waiting through the whole watch for Schadel to pop out and zap or get zapped.'' She racked her cue; Mar-nie—glad to quit but not wanting to say so—followed suit. ''Why not watch some holo for a while? Or better yet, maybe just talk?''

Marnie didn't really want to. The run-in with Darnell had been hard enough to keep to herself; now, with what she'd learned from Clancy, there was just too much she had to ride herd on, not to say the wrong thing. But, "Well, okay."

While Paula got some coffee Marnie mixed juice with a fizzy soft drink, half and half, then added apricot sorbet to make a float. They sat at a small corner table, and after a brief silence Paula said, "I think I need to talk about Alton."

I don't. But, "What is there to say?" That was safe.

"Did I tell you, he came in at the last minute? He hadn't trained with us or anything. But my pairmate, Billy Jackson, got awfully sick. Just a couple of days before we Gated. They took him away to a hospital, and—here's the funny part—Alton was flown in the same morning. With all his shots up to date, his gear already issued, as if they'd known ahead of time that we'd need somebody. And he wasn't even on our list of alternates. So we had to do the group marriage thing again, and everybody took for granted I'd move in with Alton, so I did, because who else was there?" She shook her head. "But it was never quite right."

And no wonder! But the way Paula sounded, she thought *she* was to blame. Marnie sighed. "Look—I don't know how much I should say. But something we just found out: the guy wasn't a real crewman; Darnell isn't even his name. He's a bad apple in some bigshot's family, and they faked him onto your ship to keep him out of jail." She reached for Paula's hand. "None of this was your fault; you just got caught in the works, is all." Maybe not as badly as Billy Jackson, though; what had those people used to put him out of action? And for how long?

At any rate, "Just be glad you're done with it now."

Slowly, Paula nodded. "Yes, I am. And thanks for telling me." She frowned. "How did *you* find out?"

"Oh, I get around. Uh—like I said, I'm not sure I was supposed to say anything. So keep it between us; okay?" Then, "Oops! I'm due in the galley. Pete said if I was late *again* . . .''

". . . get her to give up without having to drop her," Neola Feldman was saying, "we wouldn't have to wait so long, to ask questions." It made sense to Allaird, but whatever Marv Corby intended to say was upstaged when the Tush flared, then faded to show Fleurine Schadel crouched before four limp bodies.

Miraculously, to Clancy's way of thinking, nobody got trigger-happy as the woman blinked, looked around, and lowered her gun. "Somebody figured it out, huh? Well, I couldn't blank the whole watch with only two darts left, anyway." She didn't seem particularly concerned, saying, "Fastest six years *I* ever spent. Or is it eight? In and out, I lost track."

"Six," said Clancy as Schadel reversed the gun and held it out by the barrel. Paying Corby no heed she walked to Allaird at the command console.

"You'll want this, I guess. Am I under arrest?"

Now Corby put in. "That depends on what you've done, what your actions add up to. I came out here to stop a takeover. But it was Irina Tetzl we were after, not you."

Schadel gestured. "Well, you've got her."

Corby nodded. "So I see. What we'd like to know is why."

One hand pushed back the frizzy blond hair. "Let's just say I got fed up with the bull bitch keeping every man on the ship on call for her personal harem. Decided I couldn't put up with three more years of her, all the way to destination. And . . ."

She stopped. "That's enough. I'll have to tell the whole thing for some deposition or other. Damned if I do it twice."

Corby looked like pushing, but Clancy spoke first. "That's our captain you've had on ice there. Until he wakes up, I have command. Welcome to *Arrow*."

He gestured toward the still-drugged quartet beginning to drift a bit in zero gee. "Do we haul these down to the belt, or wait and let 'em come along under their own power?"

"We take them," Corby said. "Except for your man, I want them under restraint when they wake up."

XII

Fascinated, Nicole Pryce watched as Irina Tetzl began to stir. Her shoulders moved, pulling against the bonds; her mouth formed an expression of protest. Then her eyes opened, slightly tilted and surprisingly pale. In seconds she seemed fully awake.

"What we must do next . . ." She stopped; the eyes widened. Nicole knew what the woman must be registering: *Arrow*'s main lounge, unfamiliar to her, and people she'd never seen before. As the reality of bound hands became apparent.

Tetzl shook her head. "What has happened? How is this possible? You will release me at once. I am captain of *Starfinder* and senior in date of rank to whoever commands here, so I assume charge of this ship until I return to my own."

No one answered. Irina Tetzl's audacity, her *presence*, had her audience on the ropes. For moments Nicole half expected someone to obey, until Senator Wallin said, "You're temporarily relieved of all duties, captain, until we learn a few things. And your tenure as *Starfinder*'s commander ended at least a year ago, Earth time. Since your arrival here from *Arrow*, you've also been through our local Gates twice."

"But I am in *permanent* command! I have assessed the needs of the mission and made firm decisions. You will not question . . ."

She looked at him more closely. "Wallin! Is this your doing? Who among my crew did you subvert?"

Then her face stiffened, taut with alarm. Her left arm jerked. "What is the hour? I had forgotten, lost track. I cannot see my timepiece, and . . ."

Marv Corby looked amused. "What difference does it make? You aren't going anyplace, just yet."

"You do not understand. I *must* return to my ship."

"I'm sorry, ma'am," said the senator, "but that's simply not possible. Not until we've straightened some things out. And I had nothing to do with what's happened; one of your people acted all on her own. Now let's get on with it."

Irina Tetzl sat even more erect. In measured tones she said, "I do not have to answer to any of you. And so long as you treat me as a prisoner, I have nothing more to say."

True to her word, she simply ignored further questions. So the focus of the interrogation moved on, to her companions.

Allaird had met Cleve Rozanski briefly during the *Jovian* days, himself preparing for his tour on the original *Jovie* while the other readied to command the second one. He remembered the man as an extroverted jock type, pleasant enough and apparently competent. But here Rozanski looked defensive and answered Wallin in monosyllables. And though records showed the outstanding job Jimmy Hanchett had done, taking over the shambles his cadre 1–A found on *Starfinder*, none of that ability showed now. The Canadian displayed all the presence of a kid in the principal's office, and a guilty kid at that.

Of course both men, and Tetzl for that matter, were totally at sea here; their earlier memories, prior to being drugged and Gated, ended twenty to thirty minutes before Fleurine Schadel turned their lights out. Finally Clancy said, "Fleurine, maybe you'd better fill these people in, and us as well, on just how you all got here. The events, I mean; the reasons can wait for a more official session."

He gestured to her. "Go ahead." Ellery Dawson began to move a little, but his waking needn't be waited on. . . .

After a moment when it seemed she might stubborn up, Schadel began. "There was a meeting, in Irina's quarters. Actually a setup to dart-gun the ones she'd decided to discard; Jimmy was supposed to bring them here, stick them in your local Gate, and return. It's no secret I didn't like any of this and a lot more. Anyway, when she started shooting, her first target ducked and the dart lodged in a chair arm."

Her grin at Tetzl, Clancy thought, really wasn't all that mean. Gloating a bit, maybe. "I pulled it out, and when Irina moved past me I stuck it in her neck and grabbed the gun.''

She swung her head around a little, giving Hanchett and Rozanski their fair share of grin. ''That's when I dropped everybody who might not agree with what I intended, and went ahead and did it. Told Benita Torres to inform Hayes Morton he was captain now, in case he couldn't figure it out for himself. Brought all three of you, and Darnell who was gung ho to join your tong, and his pairmate Trent so they might as well be together, and made it to here. And like the senator said, we've all been through the local Gates twice, since. That was to make sure her stretch as captain was well over and done with, before I turned loose of the situation. But I guess I lost track and maybe overdid it.''

She looked to Clancy. ''That what you wanted?''

It was Wallin who answered. ''Very satisfactory.'' Turning to Clancy, ''This matter is by no means settled, however. Until it is, I recommend a limited version of house arrest for all four of these people. Can this be arranged?''

''I don't see any problem. We can use some of the landing party space. Corby? Can you and your people maintain watch in the corridor there, just to keep everybody honest?''

Marv Corby nodded. Allaird continued, ''Rozanski and Hanchett can room together; I expect each woman should have single quarters.''

''Not necessarily,'' Schadel said. ''I don't hate her or anything; she just needed stopping, was all. Besides, you can see she's not feeling well; somebody should look after her.''

Tight-voiced, Tetzl said, ''It does not matter; if you keep me from my ship you destroy me.''

Nothing like a flair for the dramatic, Clancy thought. But it didn't sound as if Tetzl posed any threat to Schadel, either. So he called Pilar Velez to roust out quarters supplies for four, pulled the deck plan up on screen and assigned the pair of adjacent rooms handiest for the containment people to keep under surveillance, and sent the lot of them off in Corby's charge.

Then he poured himself a healthy jolt of sour mash over ice. Ellery Dawson was waking at last, and for that conversation he needed more than coffee.

''All right,'' said Dawson a time later, ''I think I understand most of it.'' He'd been shaken, and still was to some extent, to find himself transported from control to the lounge with no memory of anything in between, but was obviously trying to pull himself together. Now, ticking off points on his fingers, he said, "I've lost a month in the Gates; the intruders came from *Starfinder*, some kind of power play there but you have them in the box now. Senator, you and your associate came out on tour and ran into a mess; sorry. And Clancy, you say FTL comm didn't work, after all?" Allaird confirmed.

"And that we have two additions to the crew. Holms' replacement from Earth, and also one from *Starfinder* that you feel you can trust. If you say so . . . Although one smelled bad and you Gated him home. And . . ." He was running out of fingers. "Oh yes, the containment crew that came to deal with the intruders. But how did they know . . . ?"

Teams to all three ships, Clancy explained. "I see," said Dawson. "And now, what's your next move?"

Huh? "Why, returning command, of course. You're back now, so it's *your* move, wouldn't you say? I'll give you any backup info you need; that goes without saying. But from here on out . . ."

Looking uncomfortable, Ellery Dawson said, "I don't, uh, feel we should, uh, change horses in midstream. The existing situation—from its beginning you've had the reins in your hands." *Jeez*, thought Clancy; *one second I'm the horse; the next I'm the rider. Make up your mind.* As Dawson added, "So what I'll do, I'll pick up the rest of the command routine. Like the watch schedules, responsibilities like that. And . . ."

"Actually," said Clancy, "I've been delegating that stuff. Nicole has it pretty well in hand." And producing schedule charts people could understand, for a change!

"Well then—other areas of procedure. We'll work it out later, Allaird. Right now I'm a bit fazed; not too many minutes ago I was fired up, waiting for the intruders to appear. Now it's all over and I missed it. I need some time to relax."

He stood. "I'll be in quarters. Meanwhile, Mr. Allaird, you're in charge." He shook his head; Allaird heard him mumble, ". . . trouble with command, you have to make all the decisions."

As the returned captain left, Clancy's glare dared anyone to comment. Or at least that's how Marnie saw it, as he said,

"All right, what *do* we do next? Senator?"

Clearing his throat first, the old man said, "I think your captain's reaction gives us a hint. He's not only disoriented; he's in shock. And so are the *Starfinder* people, with the possible exception of Ms. Schadel."

His lips tightened, then eased. "Let's take a day to review the situation, then convene a hearing. With Bill Flynn's backing I still have considerable clout; any decision I make will hold up under review back home." He grinned. "It says here."

"Good enough." Clancy nodded. "I'd better get back now." His eyes widened in alarm. "Oh jeez! I left control without calling for a relief watch officer. Some commander!"

As he stood, Nicole caught his arm. "It's okay. I saw you were busy and alerted Gretel. She was due next, and by now it's her watch anyway. So relax."

He stretched, the way he did when tension got at his shoulders. "You're right." For the first time, apparently, he noticed Marnie, sitting off to one side and keeping quiet; she'd come in at the moment when Irina Tetzl had the room paralyzed, and used it to pick an inconspicuous seat. "Hi. Did you get an earful? What do you think of Old Iron Tits?"

"She carries an awful lot of drive thrust, doesn't she?" And in a strange sort of way: the short rumpled curls, tilted eyes and high cheekbones gave the woman a rakish gamine air, at odds with her true age. "What's most likely to happen to her?"

Clancy nodded toward Senator Wallin, now leaving with his companion. "It's his say-so. And I'm glad it's not mine; I haven't the faintest idea what the best decision is."

"I still can't figure how she did what the Schadel woman says she did," Marnie went on. "How could she boss everybody around, uh, in their personal lives, so much?"

Nicole chuckled. "How did she bring us all up short for a minute there, alone on a strange ship and tied to a chair? On *Starfinder*, remember, she commanded."

"And Rozanski, her own pairmate, was exec," Clancy added. "If he went along with it—and apparently he did, and Jimmy Hanchett with him—there's practically all your top brass leaning on the troops. There's nothing new about the abuse of power."

"Except," said Nicole, "traditionally that's been a man's

prerogative.'' She gave Allaird a wicked look. ''Nothing personal, of course.''

By now, Marnie knew the signs; they'd be going to quarters. ''See you later.'' Hungry, she headed for the galley.

Aaberg's watch was nearly over when her call woke Clancy. ''You might want to see this,'' she told him. Nicole was already dressing to report to control and relieve Gretel; Allaird decided he might as well go with her. He wasn't really tired, anyway.

What Aaberg had to show them was the record of a sensor trace, a bright line slanting down across the main screen's left upper area. Even replayed in slow motion it seemed to appear instantaneously; then, as *Arrow*'s own velocity took the ship past the phenomenon, almost at once the line slipped offscreen.

''What would you say that was?'' Sybiljan Baynor asked. ''Some kind of cosmic string?'' Over at the next console, Pete Larue looked interested but baffled.

Clancy checked the mass detector record and shook his head. ''Those things are supposed to be extremely massive. I see just the hint of a blip, coincident with the line's appearance, as if maybe something went by us very damn fast.''

''Just a minute.'' Backing the action to just before the line's initial appearance, she ran forward at the slowest speed the equipment could produce; then, as soon as it appeared, she froze the picture. Most of the line disappeared, leaving a short segment near top center of the view. ''This is roughly a microsecond frame,'' she said, ''so that's how far the whatsit went in that time.''

Right; like car headlights making streaks in time-lapse photography. ''Distance?'' said Allaird. ''From us to it, there?''

''There's no perspective basis,'' she began, then paused. ''Wait a minute. *Our* velocity, and the time the line takes to move offscreen when it reaches the edge of our sensor view.'' She frowned. ''I need to program a dynamic projection. To scale, time and space both. And then run it. Hold on.''

Clancy was still trying to establish velocity as a function of trace length; the decimal point kept getting lost so he gave it up, just as Baynor announced, ''Give or take a bit either way, I'd estimate that length at not quite a thousand feet.''

Times a million, divide by the feet in a mile: ''That'd be awfully close to c. Well, no reason the thing couldn't be doing just about our own clip." Clancy frowned. "There can't be anything of ours out here. You suppose we had a near oblique pass with some more new neighbors?"

"Wait a minute!" Gretel Aaberg said, "How about relativity, the Lorenz-whosis contraction?"

"Fitzgerald," said Sybiljan, smiling like teacher's pet.

"That's right." Aaberg nodded. "Then wouldn't the actual line be considerably longer than what we *see*?"

Clancy thought fast, then said, "Nope. The contraction's along the mutual velocity vector, isn't it? I *think* that's right. And we're seeing this from the side. Well, on a slant, actually, which skews any estimates we can make. But my guess is, we're running in just about the same league."

Since the line trace at the distance observed showed no detail, they were stumped for further data: spectrographic, electromagnetic, whatever. Only the line itself, stark and enigmatic. "At least," Nicole said, "they don't outclass us with an FTL drive, like the Liij. Or there'd be no freeze-framing a segment; there'd be just the whole thing all at once." She paused, then said, "If we could detect it at all."

On that note, as Eli Mainz and Gina Todisco arrived to relieve Sybiljan and Pete, Allaird headed back to quarters.

". . . coming at each other, both doing almost the speed of light," Gina was saying, as Marnie came into control to check the duty roster for her own next chores, "then our relative speed has to be *more* than c. So how can we see it at all?"

Nicole looked pained. "Relativity doesn't work that way; velocities don't add or subtract arithmetically." Puzzled was the word for Gina's expression. Nicole said, "Don't ask me why, but here's how it's figured." On an aux screen she set it up, relative velocity equaling V-one plus V-two, divided by: one plus V-one-times-V-two. "And the result can't be more than one. Meaning c, in these units."

Neither Gina nor Eli looked ready or able to absorb anything more, but Nicole went ahead anyway. "Also: in the case of radiation, moving at c, its arrival velocity is always c, no matter how fast a ship's going. And if one object up ahead is stationary and another is coming at us at our own speed, the difference between their velocities *relative* to us is a little less than one part in three million. Or about three decimal places short of any difference our instruments could detect."

Both looked dubious; Nicole said, "Check it out, any numbers you like." Marnie had seen this once, in honors class the month before graduation; she'd forgotten the equations themselves but the mathematical elegance of the concept still impressed her.

Now she asked, "What's this all about, anyway?"

Hadn't Clancy told her? No, she hadn't seen him since the lounge. So Nicole, bringing the sensor trace onscreen, filled her in. Marnie sighed. "Suppose we'll ever know who it was?"

Pryce shrugged. "Hard to say. But we're still pretty close to Earth, astronomically speaking." She paused. "Not much over nine light-years—nine-point-one, roughly. Which is to say, whoever it is, they're practically skirting our home turf."

Marnie looked again at the screen. "But not heading there. The slant. Right to left, we can't tell the angle for sure but it's way wide of approaching our system. And it points down." Through the ecliptic plane, she meant, and Nicole nodded. "So they won't pass anywhere near."

"Maybe that's good," said Eli Mainz. "Who knows what they're like?"

"That's not the way to look at it." Gina spoke with heat. "How do we know unless we meet them? And read your history, Eli. Maybe they're the ones to worry what *we're* like."

Marnie nodded. Gina had a point there.

When Allaird had the rest of his sleep out, he readied himself for a new day. With several hours free before his next watch, he decided to tackle a few loose ends. Amalyn Tabard answered her intercom; he said, "Okay if I come talk with Ellery a little?"

"I wish you would."

"Is now all right?"

"Make it five minutes."

So he did, and at captain's digs, Amalyn opened the door. "Come in, Clancy. Maybe you can get him to make sense."

What the hell? "Yeah." He looked across the room, to where Ellery Dawson sat staring at a decade-old holodrama running with the sound off. "Ellery?"

And again, louder, until Dawson looked around to face him. Clancy didn't like what he saw. "Ellery? Are you all right?"

The eyes tracked, the expression carried assurance, the hands were steady, but something didn't feel right as Dawson said, "And why wouldn't I be?"

Unanswerable question. "Fine. When do you want to pick up on the routine? Watch duty, and so forth?" Don't mention command. Not yet, anyway.

"Duty? Oh, yes. Well, after I report, I suppose, and make a few arrangements."

Maybe this wasn't going to be so bad after all. "Report, sure. Hey, why don't we go up to control and you can put that report together, and I'll Gate it off to Earth. Or—"

He saw Dawson begin to freeze. "Or we could do it right here, and I'll take it to control for the watch officer to process for you."

But Ellery Dawson shook his head. "Not that kind of report, Allaird. Be serious. *I* will report, at Glen Springs and to the Congress if necessary. When all scurrilous allegations have been laid to rest, then I shall Gate back here and resume my command responsibilities. In the meantime, please excuse me." Rising, he strode decisively to the bathroom and locked himself inside.

"Amalyn! What the hell . . ."

"That's what I'm asking *you*." The bushy-haired woman gripped his arms. "What's happened to him? Is there anything we can do?"

"I don't know." Clancy was thinking ahead; if Dawson went home, would Tabard go with him? And if she did, who'd be drive chief? Phil Henning knew his theory, all right, but to date he'd never had to show a grasp of practice. Gina and Coyote were adequate as techs, damn good in fact. But none of them were a patch on the drive chief Amalyn Tabard had proved herself to be.

So neither his thoughts nor his next words held much real concern for Ellery Dawson. "Amalyn? Where would *you* stand?"

It shook her, he saw, as she made a slow nod, accepting the necessities. "Yes, Allaird. You have to think of the ship first, don't you? Because Ellery isn't. And for the same reasons, if he Gates to Earth he does it alone. I'll stay."

Her mouth twisted. "I know he needs me; I know he'll feel I'm betraying him. And in a way I am. Maybe I failed him, didn't give him the support he had to have. He's a good man; it's not his fault things happened that he couldn't handle. But I can't leave you without a drive chief. Phil's a genius on the theory and Gina's thoroughly competent in all routine matters, but with due modesty, I'm the one who can twist the drive's tail and make it behave. That's why I can't leave."

Before he could answer, speak gratitude or praise or sympathy or maybe something really stupid, she said in very matter-of-fact tones, "So if Ellery goes, these will be your quarters?"

Without hesitation, "No. We're happy where we are."

"It's not entirely fitting . . ."

"It hasn't happened yet. First let's see if we can pry Ellery out of the john and talk some sense into him."

There was more to it than they were letting on; Dawson was sure of that. Their story sounded plausible enough: that after a period of intruder watch he could no longer recall, he'd been stuck by some sort of poisoned dart. Which rendered him unconscious and conveniently blanked memory for the previous half hour or so. Then, so they expected him to believe, he'd been put through the local decel Gates, and finally brought to the lounge where supposedly a group from *Starfinder* had been interrogated before being restricted to their assigned quarters. He hadn't yet seen any of these supposed intruders but had the fullest confidence that they could be produced for his inspection. They, or persons claiming to be such.

It wasn't good enough, that story. For one thing it didn't explain the accusations, the people talking behind his back. They didn't know he could hear them, but when he lay down, just at the edge of sleep, the insinuating voices began. At the bare limit of intelligibility they whispered of his failure, his incompetence, the charges he could be brought to face.

Well, they weren't going to get away with it. So far, he'd pretended to believe, to go along with the charade. Because he couldn't be sure just who was involved and who wasn't, and the first rule is, don't let them know you're onto them.

He'd slipped a bit, a few minutes ago, revealing to Allaird that he suspected conspiracy. But would Clancy be in on it? He'd never been pushy, never tried to muscle in on the prerogatives of command. Maybe he was simply an innocent, unwitting tool.

It made no difference; either way, Dawson didn't dare confide in him. Or even in Amalyn, whom he *knew* would never purposely betray him. In fact, he could no longer trust anyone aboard; that was why he needed to Gate to Earth, get to someone outside the range of the conspiracy. Only on Earth could he find safe counsel.

Looking into the bathroom mirror, rearranging his expression to one of full self-assurance, Ellery Dawson shrugged. Might as well get on with it.

Finally he answered the light, insistent knock. "I'll be right out."

"I don't see that we had a choice," Allaird told his assembled officers and chiefs. "He's convinced there's a conspiracy against him. For a couple of minutes, when we brought him face-to-face with Tetzl and the rest, I thought we were getting through to him. He recognized them, all right: Tetzl and Rozanski and Hanchett, at least. But then he said it was bigger than he'd thought, something like that, and got even more urgent about Gating home. So I wrote a formal memo for him to take along, saying I accepted command during the period of his absence but that it would revert to him when he got back here, and then we saw him into Earthmouth and sent him off. He didn't want to say good-byes all around, so we didn't push it."

And at Glen Springs, Nicole wanted to know, what would happen? Clancy reassured her. "While he was getting his stuff packed, what he wanted to take along, I Gated out a message detailing the situation; they'll be alerted. I emphasized that it's not a case of misconduct or malfeasance of duty; the man simply took a shock he can't handle just now, and needs help."

"What was such a shock?" asked Ptiba Mbente. "Several of us got zapped, the same as he did. It didn't put us looking over our shoulders for the bogeyman."

Amalyn Tabard cleared her throat. "That's because you

don't feel you're in over your head, unsure of doing your job right. Ellery hid it well, but I knew that was how he felt. And my guess is that being taken over, having his control preempted without his knowledge or even recall, was too much for him.''

And if anyone would know, Clancy thought, it would be she. ''As may be,'' he said. ''Now then—as long as Ellery was still aboard, technically at least, our own changed command functions were strictly brevet, no reclassifications needed. Now, though, I'm putting us in for official upgrades including pay. You're my First, Nicole. Gretel Second, Ptiba Third. Any questions?''

Mbente grinned. ''As DV commander I'm already paid at that level. As though I had anywhere to spend it.''

''Maybe I can get you extra for wearing two hats.'' She shrugged, obviously not concerned either way. ''Well, then, unless there's something more,'' he said, ''meeting adjourned.''

Toward the end of Clancy's next watch Dean Hendryx came into control escorting Fleurine Schadel, who looked worried. ''Says she has to talk with you, sir. Neola's holding down the corridor.''

''All right; what is it?''

No comb would ever tame that hair but apparently one had tried. Fresh clothing also helped Schadel's appearance. She said, ''Something's very wrong with Irina Tetzl.''

''What, specifically? Illness? Behavior?''

''I don't know. At first she wouldn't talk, then she asked how could I do this to her. She wasn't raging or even angry, seemed mostly hurt—and incredulous. Then almost despairing, but quieter and quieter as she went along, until she lay down and went to sleep. When they woke us for breakfast she wouldn't go, and she hasn't said a word since last night.''

''Another silence strike?''

''No.'' Schadel's face showed anxiety. ''You'd have to see her. I'd say, she's gone inside herself somehow. And she doesn't like it there, at all.''

''Hendryx!'' Clancy spoke sharply. ''Get back to that room. You or Feldman, one, stay in there with the woman. We don't want a suicide on our hands.'' Maybe he was overreacting;

he'd chance that. And to Pilar Velez at the right-hand console, "Ptiba's on next here; call her early if anything comes up." He turned to Fleurine. "Okay, let's go."

Hard to believe it was the same person. Dull-eyed and slack-mouthed, face strained with vague, abstract tension, Irina Tetzl looked nothing like the vital, commanding presence of the day before. Well, day and a half, strictly speaking. Or, Clancy's built-in calculator reminded him, five weeks on Earth.

He pulled a chair over to face her where she sat, slumped, on the bed. "Captain Tetzl?" No response, not the slightest.

"I told you, captain. She's shut off contact. I doubt if she even hears you."

Sparsely furnished, the room did have an intercom terminal. "Pilar? Locate Chauncey, get him to control. With his med kit, please. I'll be right up." Then, "Thanks, Fleurine, you did right to hit the alarm button. Can you watch her for a time now?" She nodded. "All right then; Hendryx, you take over outside again. And Feldman's free to go."

"Actually we're into her shift now."

"Whatever. And thank you both."

For the first time in quite a while he chafed at the slight wait for the transfer ring.

"Maybe there's something in the complete edition of El-lery's computer scrapbook," Clancy said, and called the for-mer captain's *Starfinder* crew material file up on an aux screen. That was why he'd had Ng meet him here; his room terminal didn't access Dawson's total file system. "Here, Chauncey, you'll know what to look for, better than I do."

Ptiba Mbente had indeed arrived, along with Edd Jarness and Trish Pembrook, to take the watch. Pilar hadn't left, though; apparently hoping Chauncey wouldn't be needed long here, she stayed, waiting. Probably out of luck just now, Clancy mused, as Chauncey said, "Who'd have thought it? This looks like the original unedited personnel files, medical and all."

"What's it say about Tetzl?"

"Hang on; it goes back a way." Scrolling the copy up, pausing, moving on, Chauncey clucked to himself, then said, "When she goes aboard *Jovian-II* she's taking something ge-neric, a long chemical name I don't recognize. Quite a lot of it, so maybe it begins to give her side effects. Because when they come back she gets switched to something else. Gametin-12. Ten milligrams, three times a day.''

He shook his head. "That's a stranger, too. Let's go look it up. In the book."

So, with Pilar accompanying them, Ng and Allaird went downship. Exiting the transfer ring they met Nicole Pryce. After a few words of explanation she came along too.

"No." Closing the reference book, Chauncey Ng sounded sure. "It's not even on the market now; erratic long-term effects."

"What's it for, anyway?" Clancy'd never heard of it.

"Depression, really bad cases. About fifteen years ago it looked like a big winner. After a time, though, it did too good a job; besides building a tolerance, it gave a pretty good imitation of chronic manic syndrome. If you know . . ."

Nicole nodded. "Sort of. High energy, conviction of infallibility, logical abilities enhanced but judgment iffy."

"Something like that." Chauncey was looking through Supply readouts. "Looking to see what we have, that might . . ." Mumbling, he turned pages. "Anyone acclimated to *that* formula, she'll go through ordinary antidepressants like popcorn. And just coming down off it, no wonder she's crashed like all hell. Here, I'd better get out some tranks. Sedatives too, maybe."

Those he had at hand. "Had to dig some out for your ex, that time, Clancy, so I remember where they are." He brought out a packet. "All right then; I'll check my stock for antidepressants. Haven't had any call for such stuff, but the list shows a few things. Provided just in case, I guess. God knows where those cartons may have got themselves, by now."

He'd find something or he wouldn't. Clancy and Nicole headed back toward the room where Fleurine watched over Irina Tetzl. As they passed the corridor leading to the VIP suite, Senator Wallin hailed them. "Allaird? I think I'm ready for our hearing. How soon can we set it up?"

Clancy sighed. "Not right away, senator. I'm afraid it isn't a good time."

"Why? What's happened?"

"Irina Tetzl seems to have swallowed her own head."

Wallin frowned, then he nodded. "If you say so. Just let me know when she pukes it back up."

With Neola Feldman opening the door for them, Clancy followed Nicole into the room and looked around it. In one chair Fleurine Schadel sat alert and watchful yet seemingly relaxed. Still sitting on the edge of a bed, Irina Tetzl stared blankly into something Allaird was glad he couldn't see.

Nicole went to her. "Here. Take this. It'll help until Chauncey finds something better." Accepting the pills in a limp hand, with an autistic jerk Tetzl put them to her mouth, choked them down without water, and sat gasping.

It was unreasonable, Clancy thought, to expect any quick or definitive reaction to the medications. Nonetheless he sat waiting until, after some time, Irina Tetzl raised her head and actually looked at something visible and real: Nicole Pryce.

"Thank you. I will sleep now." There was no vitality to the voice, though, and when she lay down Clancy was reminded of an old rag doll, left out in the rain all week.

So the next day when he asked Marv Corby how Tetzl was doing, the answer surprised him. "Your man Ng gave her some stuff, late yesterday, that seems to have brought her around. If you call it that. Now she's demanding a court-martial."

Checking the time, Allaird said, "I'll tell the senator. I expect we can start right after lunch." Sitting on his utter astonishment so Corby wouldn't see how much he was shaken up.

To Clancy's way of thinking, Rozanski's testimony and Hanchett's had been displays of total pussyfooting, neither man willing to admit anything with regard to themselves, Tetzl, or who shot Abraham Lincoln. Obviously disgusted with both men, the senator excused them ". . . for now, but don't think I'm done with you," and called Irina Tetzl.

Sitting to one side of the lounge, now closed to all but the participants and designated observers, Tetzl shook her head. "You have not yet heard from my accuser, as is proper. I wish to reserve my own statement for last."

Shrugging, Wallin said, "All right. Fleurine Schadel?" She moved to the chair facing him. The senator wasn't bothering with any swearings-in, saying at the outset, "You're on your honor, all of you, as ship's officers. If that doesn't bind you, neither would a few extra rituals.''

Now he said, ''In your own words, tell us how Captain Irina Tetzl, in your opinion, violated regulations and the ethics of command.''

Schadel frowned. ''I'm not sure what actually busted regs and what just abused them. You were there when that cadre arrived. She demoted Jimmy Hanchett, sent out as exec and then named acting captain after Maggie Sligo got hurt, down to watch officer. So her personal stud Cleve Rozanski over there could have the slot. Not supposed to have captain and exec from the same cadre, but a lot *she* cared. Rance Collier made her give Jimmy back his job, sort of, but only as co-exec. And she shuffled the watches, that were set to give pair-mates the most off-duty time together, to do the exact opposite.''

Pausing, she bit her lip a moment, then continued. ''This crew group marriage thing, now. She used it to have as many men as she could round up, all at once.'' Her glare aimed more toward Hanchett and Rozanski than Tetzl herself. ''I think Cleve even helped her; where I come from, it's called pimping. And Jimmy got hooked early; she'd do all the things decent women won't.''

Clancy blinked; he'd never considered versatility indecent.

''Collier was the only one even tried to hold out,'' Schadel went on. ''Not that Su Teng would've fried him for it.'' She giggled. ''Told me once she'd said to Rance, go ahead and prong the silly slut, in her left ear if that's where she wants it.''

Irina Tetzl looked offended, but Fleurine wasn't done yet. ''Just about anybody could've led Dink Hennessey around by the weenie, and the two younger guys never had a chance. Anyway, regs or no regs, she was playing Nookie Monopoly with loaded dice and I got damn well fed up.''

''I see,'' said Wallin. ''And were there any legally certifi-able violations? Of regulations, obligations, duties?''

''You damn right. She and some of the others set up a real fancy plan: instead of Gating home when their year was up, they'd stay on the ship all the way to destination and run the colony there. Stash incoming cadres and dissidents into Gate lag and so forth. No point in my wasting time spelling it out;

they put the whole thing on a datacap. And I have a copy with me.''

She brought out a small packet. "Play it yourselves."

Irina Tetzl stood. "You need not. I admit to all it contains. I should like to make a statement of explanation. Not of excuse, for there is none. And then, pending court-martial which I feel to be justified and necessary, I shall agree to resign my commission under whatever terms you choose to set.''

XIII

No longer did Tetzl have the commanding presence of her first appearance here; to Clancy she seemed a bit subdued, maybe even unsure. Yet she spoke calmly and with dignity. Unlike the tortured look she'd worn during her lapse into depression, now her overall expression was one of acceptance.

". . . difficulties stabilizing medication levels during my first mission," she was saying. "Back on Earth from *Jovian-II* I underwent various tests, after which Gametin-12 was prescribed. And then I was assigned to *Starfinder* as captain, in cadre 1–B. It was, I see now, shortly before we Gated aboard that the drug first began to distort my logical perceptions. This substitute your Mr. Ng has found for me is not adequate for long-term stabilization, as perhaps you may notice, but it has given me a regained perspective."

"Isn't there quite a lot of time in there, between missions, unaccounted for?" asked the senator. Then, "No, I forgot; you Gated both ways, off *Jovie* and onto your new ship. Sorry; go ahead."

"I will not apologize for my sexual intensities; they are a part of me and this was well understood by my superiors. Nor for the ways in which I sometimes prefer to exercise them.

We are not living in the days of the Puritans. I do regret misusing my position to coerce others into indulging those preferences, and realize no apology can undo those impositions. One matter, though, I must make clear.'' She leaned forward. ''All that time, I had total confidence in the rightness of my actions.''

She spread her hands. ''How could this be? Simply because I was most faithful, most dutiful, in following my prescriptions exactly. Had I been irregular in those matters I would have known enough to suspect my own judgment in some areas. But my superiors also had full knowledge of my medical condition. Relying on their assessment and diagnosis I put complete trust in the medication, and thus in the quality of my decisions.''

Irina sat back again. ''Now to my usurpation—my attempt, rather, to retain command of *Starfinder* to destination and afterward. I very much wanted to oversee landing, exploration, and eventual colonization.'' Her smile held sadness. ''I still do—*and I am well qualified*. But now, as before the onset of my aberration, I realize I had no right to *take* the role. If I could have waited and served on that cadre, I would have—but then, twenty-five years later, I would have been much too old.''

This one, thought Clancy, *lays it on the line*! Now she said, ''Originally I had a different plan. Between the return home of my cadre 1–B until departure of 4–A which *will* be privileged to see and explore a new world, eleven years must elapse. I had thought to apply for at least one, perhaps two inspection tours of various ships, each consuming four years in Gate lag alone—and then ask for command of 4–A itself.''

''Too bad you didn't stick to that idea,'' said the senator. ''It just might have worked.''

''And I fully intended to do so.'' She nodded. ''But as time passed, my values shifted. At first I avoided excess in my personal desires; reason reminded me of limits to be obeyed. Then gradually I came to feel that *I* knew best, after all. Any and all self-questioning only confirmed that conviction.''

Gaze shifting, she stared at the deck before her. ''And the rest, you know. With no further excuse I say again: my bout of incapable judgment requires me to resign, under what terms you may set. Following which, I will expect court-martial as is my proper due.''

"Of course I reserved my decision," Wallin said after Corby took the *Starfinder* quartet away to their rooms, leaving only ship's officers and chiefs in the lounge. "It takes some thinking, Allaird. Court-martial's out of the question; we're not a military outfit and never were. I may not even accept her resignation; after all, the woman's overall record is outstanding. In her right mind she's a brilliant organizer, and the hushed-up flap over some horny didoes aboard *Jovian-II* also buried an incident of rather heroic improvisation, when that ship got into a nasty jam.''

"I hadn't heard anything," Clancy said.

"That's what I was just saying." Wallin made a sour face. "There's no problem with the two men; they're Gating home this very day. Rozanski gets the boot, no question about that; he had to know something was terribly wrong, and made no effort to stop it. Hanchett—well, the train was already rolling when it got to him. Being summarily demoted knocked his props out, too. I think I'll just send him back without prejudice, let him hunt a new job in the agency on the basis of what his record shows.''

"And what about Calamity Fleurine, the gunslinging gal of the spaceways?" Nicole looked more serious than she sounded.

Leaning back, the senator yawned and stretched. "Now that's a poser. Technically I suppose she mutinied, though if anyone ever had justification to pull the plug, she did. But I expect you all noticed, when it comes to testifying, she doesn't exactly put her best foot forward. I'd hate to see what a starchy inquiry board would do to her at an official hearing.''

Clancy saw the old man's point. "Could she be returned to *Starfinder*?"

Wallin thought about it. "What's the time factor?"

After thought Allaird came up with, "Right now by Earth time it's about seventeen-point-five years since that ship lifted out. Cadres 2–A and 2–B are aboard—well, 2–B and whatever Tetzl and Schadel left of 2–A. If she Gated back there soon— let's see . . .''

Keeping track of Gate lags and time dilations wasn't easy,

but after a minute or so Clancy said, "She'd find 2–A nearly ten months along in its year of duty, and 2–B about four."

"And all of them complete strangers," said Nicole. "Except the 2–A people she'd barely met. I don't think . . ."

"You're right," said Wallin. "She'd have no place there. And some of the crew might resent the disruption she caused."

"Well, there's no hurry," Clancy said. "You can think about it. And it strikes me, no one's asked her what *she* thinks."

"True." Wallin nodded. "Maybe she'd just like to go home and forget it. Which is something I could probably arrange with a little finagling. Meanwhile I do have to decide about Tetzl."

"Sure, Amalyn," said Marnie, sitting at an access console in control. "What is it you want to look up?" This was a good day for Marnie; Ptiba Mbente was letting her sit regular watch duty for the first time, logging sensor data and running calculator checks on time-distance readouts. Tricky stuff, but she thought she was getting the hang of it pretty well. And now Amalyn Tabard, the drive chief no less, was asking her help.

"Captain Dawson's files on the *Starfinder* crew. I want to see Fleurine Schadel's."

"Anything in particular? I could find it for you."

"No, that's all right; just call it up and turn me loose. I don't want to intrude on your work."

"Okay." Once the heading came onscreen, Marnie moved to another station and picked up where she'd left off. Time dilation had been running a little high, she found, but now the drive had eased off for a while to even things out. Carefully she blocked out the sections of graphs and readings needed for the daily summary and saved the result into permanent record.

That job done, she went to get a squeezebulb of juice from the dispenser. As she operated the device, Tabard came over and said, "Thanks. You can have your regular place back now."

"Any time. Did you find what you wanted?"

Amalyn nodded. "I think so."

"Anything important?" Well, she *was* curious.

"Yesterday Pete asked me to take them their meal tray, her and Tetzl, and we got to talking. Work talk. I just thought I'd check the record, see if she's as good as she seems to think."

"Is she?"

"I wouldn't be at all surprised."

As Tabard left, Marnie wondered, good at *what*? But she hadn't thought to ask, soon enough.

". . . would have done, Clancy, if *you'd* been on that ship?"

The trouble was, Allaird had absolutely no idea. Bringing their special tea to Nicole who'd stayed in bed after, he handed her a steaming cup. "When? At what point in my life? Come on, Nicole! That stuff on *Starfinder* all happened during our early days on this ship. I couldn't be here and there both, dammit!"

"Yes; but if you *had* been?"

"And if the dog hadn't stopped to sniff, he'd have caught the rabbit."

"No, really. You were first male alternate for that cadre. What if you'd been called in? Think about it."

"I could have been, yes. Well, in that case I'd've been paired with someone. And group marriage or no, that's how I'd have kept it. It may sound trite, but one woman at a time is all my life has room for. Or ever had."

"But if you were paired with Old Iron Tits herself. If Rozanski were the one you replaced. How would you handle *that*?"

"Not very well, probably." He tried to imagine it. "I suppose, if she brought other men in, I'd move out."

"And just be alone?"

"Those duty tours are one year each. I *was* alone, after the divorce, a lot longer than that. Mostly, anyway."

So the tea went fast, and interaction resumed. As Clancy thought, briefly, how lucky he'd been to escape that whole mess.

After Clancy left quarters, wanting to put in some full-gee exercise before dinner, Nicole considered what he'd said. With most men she'd known, she'd have listened through a screen of skepticism, straining to detect the points where sincerity got lost behind self-deception or downright misdirection.

But not with Clarence Allaird. It might get a little awkward sometimes, but there was something to be said for a man who simply did not lie.

Not even to himself, if he could help it.

Marnie always enjoyed having dinner and spending an evening with Clancy and Nicole. And since the new First had begun scheduling the watches, these events came around quite regularly. Often enough so she felt included. The rest of the time she was quite content mingling with whoever hit the galley, or now and then simply snacking in her own quarters, either alone or sometimes with Paula Trent or Trish Pembrook, or both.

Although Paula was spending a lot of time lately with Eli Mainz; she wouldn't say whether anything was serious yet, but Marnie thought it might well be getting that way.

Today was a family occasion, though, and Marnie was glad of the chance to talk about what was going on: the people from *Starfinder*, their fates as decided by the senator, and so forth. But then, still at table though finished dining, the three were barely into those subjects when Wallin himself came visiting; with him arrived Amalyn Tabard and Fleurine Schadel.

As Clancy made extra coffee the others rearranged chairs for a more comfortable grouping. When he had everyone supplied, he said, "Is this business, or social?"

Wallin chuckled. "We have a proposition for you. Fleurine would like to sign on here. In Amalyn's place."

Clancy looked first surprised and then dubious; Schadel said, "Look, captain; I'm not a troublemaker by trade. The thing on *Starfinder* was different. I—"

"I understand that. And I think I know why Amalyn would like to Gate home. What concerns me are your qualifications. As drive chief, I mean. How do I know . . . ?"

Amalyn Tabard cut in. "I'll vouch for her. I checked into Ellery's file on that cadre. On the practical end, she was one of the top Traction Drive people available."

Clancy looked to Schadel; she said, "That's right. What we had was a team: Rance Collier carried the theory and I knew how to apply it. Like which wrench to use where, to tune what."

"Just about the way it works between Phil and me," Amalyn added. "Anyway, I've been quizzing Fleurine, and we went back to the drive room—with Marv Corby chaperoning in case she tried to hijack us through a black hole or something!—and we went over the control systems for better than two hours."

Her nod was emphatic. "Take my word for it, captain; I wouldn't make the recommendation if I weren't sure."

Frowning, Clancy turned to the other woman. "Sign on, you say. For the full tour? All the way to destination, not just a year's hitch like *Starfinder*'s?"

"Yes. By now there's nothing I want on Earth. Anyway, they set the year limit because much longer at point-three gravs, you might not readapt. You have the full-gee ring—and just trying it out, I see I've got a long haul getting back in any kind of shape. But I will."

"All right," said Clancy. "Tell you what: the next few days, Schadel, you take over. Tabard, you observe and keep a log on her work. Then in—oh, say a week—we can . . ."

"No!" Amalyn Tabard could be firm when she wanted to. "A week here is half a year for Ellery. As long as it was necessary I was willing to stay. Now it isn't. So—"

By merely clearing his throat, Wallin got silence. "We can obtain an evaluation right now. Allaird, get me Irina Tetzl on the intercom."

Nobody asked Marnie, but she volunteered, "Makes sense to me." Clancy's glance toward her seemed more approving than not. He made contact as requested, then yielded to the senator.

Wallin kept matters brief and to the point, first having Tetzl call Corby, on duty as hall guard, in to talk. "I want to see Captain Tetzl here in the exec's quarters." And, "No, she won't need an escort, just directions." And gave them. Shutting off the comm, he said, "She's no threat here, and showing a little trust should have her in a cooperative frame of mind."

A few minutes later when the woman entered, to Marnie she seemed a bit cautious but largely self-possessed, though not with the somewhat overpowering presence she'd shown at first. Clancy offered her a chair and then coffee before Senator Wallin began, "I realize you and Fleurine Schadel have had your differences. Can you disregard those and give me an objective opinion of her capabilities as a drive chief?"

Without preliminaries Tetzl went to the main question. "Her grasp of theory is not profound, but practical knowledge as good as one could ask. With support from Collier on more esoteric aspects—and it was rarely needed—she kept *Starfinder*'s drive in perfect working condition. Am I objective enough, senator?"

He didn't answer directly, but did thank her. And then, "What do you say, Allaird?"

Clancy paused before asking, "Amalyn? You sure Phil can carry the theory end?"

"He's been doing. And," partly to Fleurine, "he's easy to work with. Quiet, usually, but never tight with information."

Marnie watched her father make up his mind; a moment before he spoke, she knew his decision. But not how he'd state it.

"Tell Ellery we miss him."

"How could you say that?" Nicole asked later, when they two and Marnie were alone again. "You don't miss him and you know it. And here I was thinking how nice it is that you never lie."

"I didn't," Clancy protested. "I never said we missed him; I just asked Amalyn to tell him we did. Make him feel good, and all. Why not? It doesn't cost anything."

"So you got her to lie *for* you."

"Nope. Merely to repeat what I told her to say."

Nicole fumed. "*Somewhere* in there you're causing a false statement to be made. But just where?"

"Where the other dollar goes, when the bellboy keeps two."

That was a slippery misdirection problem; Marnie never had figured it out. So she gave up on this, too, and they set to speculating what the senator had in mind for Irina Tetzl.

Marv Corby didn't like it. "Schadel here, she's facing mutiny charges; senator, you can't just let her off the hook."

"I can and I have." Holding court in the lounge for perhaps the final time, Wallin spoke without heat. Clancy envied his ability to hold calm; amiable appearance notwithstanding, Corby could be irritating when he got wound up.

"But my job's to take her back to Earth, take all of them. And a full-dress board hearing there might overrule you."

Snort of laughter. "Who you going to get on that board, that I don't outrank? Or if I don't, Bill Flynn does. And I've Gated him a full report." Overriding Corby's efforts to speak, the old man said, "You're not putting Captain Tetzl on trial, either. The person responsible is whoever failed to overhaul her prescription back on Earth, when it came out that Gametin-12 was unreliable. But hell, you know as well as I do, how easy it is for details like that to get lost in the system."

He continued, "I've ruled that she's on emergency medical leave, and that Fleurine Schadel acted in the knowledge that such leave was necessary, for everybody's good. Schadel's reassigned to this ship, duration yet to be decided. And Jimmy Hanchett," looking to where that man sat glumly, "is returning for a new assignment since his designated tour on *Starfinder* ended six years ago and his absence in the meantime was caused by circumstances beyond his control." He looked down his nose at Corby's rebellious expression. "These things are in my reports. You won't want to try to mess with my conclusions."

Corby sighed. "Would you mind telling me what I *am* supposed to do? And what happens to Tetzl? Sainthood, maybe?"

"A whole lot of testing, medical and otherwise, to decide if she gets medical retirement or a new assignment." Irina didn't look especially thrilled at the prospects, worse though they could have been, but she made no protest. "You and your team may *escort* her to the proper facilities at Glen Springs, just as you will escort Mr. Hanchett to report for reassignment." Hanchett didn't seem pleased, either. Even though his ass could be in a very binding sling indeed if Wallin so chose.

The senator leaned forward. "However, you will *conduct* Mr. Rozanski to the local administrative office where he will be discharged with full pay, including severance allowance, but also with prejudice. He will not work for this agency again."

Of course, Clancy reminded himself, the six years of unauthorized Gatings wouldn't be paying anyone a nickel, let alone the normal half pay for Gate time.

Sullen, Rozanski looked up. "Hey, why pick on me? Irina called the shots and she gets off free. Outside of our little circus there I did my job, stood my watches. I—''

''Like hell you did!'' Fleurine Schadel was feeling her oats, Clancy decided, as she flared at the big man. ''You and Jimmy right from the start, almost, and practically all the men later, she'd haul you off watch or from anywhere you were, to get her daisy-chain workouts. You did your job the first six months, yes. But once she took over, if you sat in control *half* a watch it beat your average. Don't tell me about standing watches; between the two of us, I'm the one did that chore.''

''If you want a board hearing, Mr. Rozanski,'' the senator said quietly, ''it will be arranged; you may plead your case. I doubt its results would be as generous as the terms I offer. But if that's what you want, I'll withdraw my report and you're on your own.'' No response. ''Decide now, if you please.''

The man hesitated. Then he gave a lopsided grin. ''Aw hell. I fucked up, right enough. It's just, I'm not the only one, except to get screwed for it. You call that fair?''

''The only one could've helped stop it, too,'' said Schadel. ''And you know it. With you backing her up, though, nobody else had a chance against the two of you, captain and co-exec. Especially after you hooked Jimmy in. Wasn't for Rance Collier you'd still be gangbanging, the whole pussy-whipped lot of you.''

For the first time this session, Hanchett had something to say. ''I'm sorry, Fleurine; I've already told you that. Look: you're really staying on here, sending me back alone?''

'' 'fraid so, Jimmy. You left me alone often enough, back on the ship. And what the hell, you're Gating with *Irina*.''

That woman looked over. ''At the same time, only.''

Which pretty well summed matters up. After a pause Corby said, ''Look, senator; I didn't mean to be insubordinate or anything. I made my objection, you overruled it which you have every right to do, so now I carry out whatever orders you give, and no funny business. That's the fact.''

Wallin smiled. ''Thank you, Mr. Corby. You're within your rights to express your opinions. And I had no serious doubt of your reliability.''

''Good enough, sir. All right; how long's it going to take to get everybody's stuff together and hit the Gate?''

*   *   *

For no particular reason except that she felt like it, Nicole Pryce went with Clancy to see the group off to Earth. The senator came too, with Maxine Durand in attendance. The group from *Starfinder* had very little tack, only what they'd been issued here on *Arrow*, so Corby and Hendryx and Feldman weren't burdened with anyone's gear but their own as they escorted Tetzl and Hanchett and Rozanski to Earthmouth. Amalyn Tabard was still packing, and would Gate separately when she was ready.

At the Mouth, though, no one seemed eager to get going. As Clancy brought the Gate to activation, Irina Tetzl stood gazing around as if memorizing this corridor and its equipment. When Allaird looked up she said, "Though neither of us intended I should need your hospitality, still I thank you for it. Also, my appreciation to Mr. Ng, whose aid enabled me to understand and clarify my position. And, senator . . ."

Her expression was hard to read, but mouth corners and tilted eyes hinted at a nascent smile. "Your understanding impresses me; I hope to repay your trust."

Looking embarrassed, Wallin said gruffly, "That's what I'm counting on."

No one else had much to say. With a grunt that probably meant "Let's go," Marv Corby set his duffel in the Mouth; at his gesture, the others followed suit. Looking away to avoid the flash, Pryce saw only the color flare reflected from bulkheads. And less than a minute later the second one, sending all six back to Earth.

Wallin heaved a sigh. "Well, now we've got some elbow room again. Anybody want to visit the lounge and join me in a drink to that?"

"You mean *besides* the macroGate components?" Edd Jarness was saying. As Clancy led the group into the lounge, the backup pilot looked over briefly, then turned back to Coyote Benjamin. "I don't think so, Ky. Where are you going to find room for all that stuff?"

"How about astern? There's a good-sized area free there. If they change the design a little—mount the nodes slightly outboard instead of just inside the tail-end perimeter—the usable space goes way up."

Jarness frowned. "You're talking about the DV docking area? Isn't that likely to cause problems?"

"Docking, sure—but that's at destination. If my gadget's not dropped off by then, they simply move it. Look, Edd; all we need is a life-support hulk that can be programmed to decelerate and find itself a stable parking orbit. With living space and Earthgates and the makings of a bigger pair, to bring out a DV for landing and recon . . ."

Losing track of what Nicole and Maxine Durand were saying while the senator listened patiently, Allaird stepped over to ask Coyote, "Recon of what? Did I miss something?"

Benjamin grinned. "Maybe. Have you noticed that since we passed belts of higher density—the interstellar gas—we find more stars, sun-class and dimmer, than showed up from Earth?"

Right. In this direction there seemed to be more particle-ridden volumes of space than *Starfinder* had reported encountering. Not dust clouds, exactly, but definitely the equivalent of obscuring fog. And the less spectacular members of the stellar population were now appearing in larger numbers and at closer range than anyone had expected. Still, "And so?"

"That ship that crossed ahead of us on a skew course," said Coyote. "It had to come from somewhere." Allaird nodded. "So maybe we might pass near its home system, or some other place it has roots down. And it would be nice to be able to drop off a recon package, instead of just reporting the place for some other ship to scout, if and when."

"And he thinks he's figured out how," said Edd Jarness.

"Not us," Ky protested. "I have no idea how we could get the necessary stuff here and set it up; nobody could possibly work outship at these speeds. But later ships . . ."

"I'm listening."

So Benjamin told it. Astern, tucked safely between the drive nodes, affix a mobile space station, stocked with supplies and equipped with computer-sensor control. Nearing any planetary system, "Well, any that looks really promising," drop it free, programmed to decelerate at whatever gee force was needed and establish a prechosen orbit. "Then it signals Earth. People can Gate into it, and haul out the components to build a junior-grade macroGate. Two-way, of course, like the big ones. Bring

a DV or two through *that* one. Supply barges, too. Presto:
instant landing and exploration facility.''

Well, hardly instant. But compared to sending out a whole
new ship . . . ''And if they don't have occasion to drop it off
en route,'' said Clancy, ''it could come in handy as a research
station in the destination system. Yes, this is definitely worth
suggesting to Earth. And the report goes in over your name.''

As Allaird moved over to fix himself a valedictory drink,
to toast the ending of *Arrow*'s involvement in *Starfinder*'s
problems, he felt good. Nothing like having a bunch of original thinkers on the crew. . . .

Unlike Ellery Dawson, Amalyn Tabard clearly relished having a going-away party. ''I hate to leave,'' she told Nicole,
''but in a way I feel *responsible* for Ellery. I keep thinking I
may not have been supportive enough—that if I had, he might
have been able to handle the things that threw him.''

''Oh for heaven's sake!'' Almost angry, Nicole protested.
''You're not his mommie. The man worked his way up to
captain, after all. You'd think he could stand on his own two
feet.''

''And with a little more help, maybe he can again. I have
to go find out.''

''If you say so.'' Nicole poured herself one more drink than
she'd ordinarily have had. ''Anyway, you know we'll miss
you.''

More than half the crew, nearly everyone who wasn't on
duty of some sort, trooped upship to Earthmouth to see her
off. The good-bye song had it that she was a jolly good drive
chief, which nobody could deny.

Nicole hoped Schadel would be another one.

Working out alongside Clancy in the full-gee ring, Marnie
found the idea of dropaway outposts ingenious enough, but it
wasn't as though it had anything to do with *this* ship. Her lack
of enthusiasm seemed to disappoint him, so she tried to work
up some interest. ''What happens is, the first crew sets up a
DV-size Gate, and they haul macroGate components through
that, so then they can get a real ship there with just Gate lag?''

''That's about it.''

''But with us, all we can do is log the coordinates and tell

Earth." As he nodded, she had an idea. "Hey, if we happen to spot something good near the *far* end, some ship could come through our macroGate and get to it a lot faster."

"That's right."

"Well, I hope we do." By now she was panting a little; with all the commotion brought aboard from offship, she'd gotten lax on her full-gee skeds. So she buckled down to work up a total good sweat, doing an extra fifteen minutes for luck.

When she headed for her shower she really needed it.

She was mostly dried off when the chime sounded. Putting on a robe she went to the door. Paula Trent was too wound up to make sense at first, but eventually, ". . . what *she* was doing there! Eli and I, I thought, pretty soon now, but here was this Schadel woman bold as her brassy hair and lying around in his bathrobe, no doubt what *they'd* been up to, and . . ." Paula seemed determined not to cry, but it was getting close.

"Here, sit down. Fix you something?" Coffee was quickest; when Paula was sipping at the hot cup Marnie said, "You hadn't yet, though—you and Eli?"

Paula shook her head. "No. I didn't want to hurry anything, like last time, and after all I'm not married into this ship yet. I wasn't quite sure, you see. Eli's nice and all, but not good-looking like Alton, which was really about all there was to him so I shouldn't put much stock in that, should I? And heavy—Eli, I mean; it took a little getting used to. But I really began to think, you know, and now *this*."

"Yeah." Now this. "You want me to talk to anybody?" What she'd say, Marnie had no idea, but it seemed the proper offer.

"I don't know." A shrug. "What is there to say?"

"What did you say to Eli? Ask him if he's made up his mind or just browsing?" Strange, talking this way to a grown-up woman like Paula, but it did strike Marnie as a reasonable question.

"I—I don't think I said anything much. Just pardon me for intruding, something like that, but real sarcastic. And stared her up and down, and turned around and got out."

Mmmmm. "They're still there, you think?"

"On my way out she said something, she was due on watch

anyway, so stick around." Sniff. "I didn't, of course."

"Course not." Might've been better if she had? Well, maybe not. "Any ideas what you do next? Talk to somebody?"

"I'm not sure; I'll have to think about it." Paula finished her coffee and waved off the offer of a refill. She stood. "Thanks for listening, Marnie. It's helped." And she left.

Marnie herself said nothing, to Clancy or Nicole or anybody else. She snacked alone in quarters, thinking about the situation. None of her business, but Paula was her friend and couldn't seem to handle it on her own hook. So when the next watch ended, Marnie loitered in the corridor outside control until Fleurine Schadel came out, then moved to walk beside her.

"Talk with you a little?" A few questions couldn't hurt.

The woman looked around at her. "Sure. What about?"

She was definitely heading for the galley. "Let's get sat down first," and as Schadel loaded a tray Marnie got some juice and a few crackers, then followed her to a small table.

"Okay, shoot. What's on your mind?" But then, "Marnie, isn't it? Marnie Allaird. How come you're aboard here? I mean, a kid your age."

Tell it straight? Yes, but short. "Stepfather trouble. No other family to be with, so here I am. And very glad of it."

"Good enough." And again, "What's on your mind?"

No way to ease in. "You're deucing out my friend Paula."

Schadel blinked. "She came to you with it? Well, all right. Eli's the only unattached man on the ship. I asked him was he paired up and he said no, not exactly. So I made my play and he took it. How long's this Paula been . . ." Smiling, she shook her head. "Oh sure; my last trip through the Gates plus the few days since we all came out again, a little over a ship's-month, figuring your time ratio. So." She spread her hands.

"So, what?"

"So all that time she didn't take him, and he's been left alone I forget how long he said. And even at your age, maybe three–four years shy of being interested yourself, I expect you know about how men get. Women too. Just because she was letting him go to waste whether he liked it or not, why should I?"

There was probably an answer to that but Marnie couldn't think of one, as the woman continued, "He's a little young for me, sure, and not much for looks. Nice kid, though." She leaned forward. "But I don't have a collar on him. We went to bed a couple of times today and maybe it'll happen some more. But neither of us said anything about moving in together."

"Yes, but you've . . ."

Fleurine shook her head. "You say to your friend Paula, if she wants the guy she better tell him. I kind of like him myself, but stealing from babies isn't my style so she gets her chance if she wants it." Done eating, she stood. "Tell her." And walked away to dump her leftovers and clean the tray.

Leaving Marnie totally free of the dislike she'd felt earlier. Plain speaking always did get to her.

Clancy Allaird purely hated mucking around in other people's personal problems. He'd thought he was done with that but here came another mess; Paula Trent wanted to leave the ship.

She hadn't said why, exactly: just that she'd stayed to fill a vacancy but Trish Pembrook was here to do that, so . . .

When he tried to pump Marnie about her friend's motives she shook her head. "I don't think I should say; anything she told me was just between us. You see?" But Clancy wasn't totally obtuse. Item: Paula had her nose out of joint. Item: Eli Mainz was strutting around like a young rooster. Item: Fleurine Schadel was no shrinking violet.

And continuing item: the crew now consisted of six couples, Eli Mainz, and three adult women. Plus Marnie, who did not as yet enter into the mating equation and thank God for that! So with Nicole on hand for backing and Senator Wallin as a witness or maybe just for the hell of it, he called the four leftovers in for conference. He didn't really think the subject matter was suitable for his daughter, but she dropped in unannounced and he wasn't about to embarrass her by chasing her off.

He waited until everyone had seats; this was no social occasion so he offered nothing in the way of refreshment. Hoping his internal glare didn't show on the outside, he began: "Normally your private lives are none of my business, but when they lead to my losing ship's personnel, that's a new ball game.''

He aimed his gaze at one and then another, looking for a sign of reaction. ''Somebody tell me what the problem is.''

It worked. Eli said he hadn't *meant* to hurt Paula but Estella was gone nearly three months now and Paula didn't seem to know what she wanted and he just . . .

Well, sure. So, had he made his mind up yet? Nervously, Eli Mainz eyed both women. ''I've tried to, but . . .''

Paula said she'd thought better of him than that: sniff.

Fleurine looked rueful. ''Here I promised you I'm not trouble, skipper, and now look! It's just—well, *Starfinder* wasn't exactly Monogamy Lane. I didn't mean to hurt anybody.'' And what was wrong with sharing, a little?

Paula Trent didn't believe in that sort of thing. ''If that's how it is, I want to sign out and go home.''

Nicole Pryce spoke. ''Even before Eli makes a decision?''

''He had his chance, just now. And anyway, he's *shown* it. This woman barges in and grabs him, and he . . .''

Schadel flared. ''You had a month start and didn't take him. If you had, I'd've honored that.''

''Easy for you to say *now*!''

''All right, Trent,'' said Clancy. ''You're relieved of duty. I'll give you a commendation on your job performance to date, with a rider noting your susceptibility to personal difficulties. You do realize, your departure leaves us shorthanded again.''

''No it doesn't!'' Glaring at her sometime friend, Marnie said, ''I can stand watches now; I've been doing it, some. So just go on, if you have to! Who needs you?'' As she herself bolted from the room, a step or two ahead of tears.

Looking stricken, Paula Trent said nothing. Clancy felt sorry for her, sorrier yet for Marnie, but what could he do? ''The rest of the proceedings won't concern you. So if you'd rather, you can go and get packed to leave.''

Nicole put a hand on his arm. ''But there's no hurry, Paula. Take all the time you want. And we'll have a party, too.''

Allaird shrugged. ''Sure; why not?'' And then, to Trish, ''How about you, Pembrook? Being another extra. You have any problem with that?''

Grave-faced until now, the young woman smiled. ''If I were back on orbital work I'd be doing the young crowd social stuff like everybody else. But not sex, I think; not any time soon. It ties you to somebody, and right now I like being independent. Having friends, but not just one special person.'' She shrugged. ''I want to stay on, clear to destination. There'll be all sorts of people coming then—for landing and recon and starting the colony. And I'll still be under twenty-one. Plenty of time.''

Until she changed her mind, anyway. Maybe she wouldn't; Allaird could hope. He stood. ''Then I guess we're done here.''

Fleurine said, ''You're not going to rap my knuckles or anything?''

''What you did, nobody'd told you not to. I wish you hadn't, because I hate to lose Paula here, but done is done. I will say, though, that this ship isn't *Starfinder*; so far as I know, existing relationships are pretty stable. I would take an unkind view of anyone coming aboard new and messing with them.''

After a moment she nodded. ''I hear you.''

For the first time, Wallin spoke. ''That's very wise.''

To Allaird's considerable relief, the group dispersed.

With her door propped open just a mite, Marnie waited until people began to come out of Clancy and Nicole's digs, then gave it a few more minutes before going to punch the chime at Paula Trent's door. When Paula opened and then stood back, Marnie took it as invitation to enter; once inside, she said, ''I didn't mean any of that, back there; I'll miss you a lot. I was just so *mad*. You said you were going to talk to Eli, and then you just . . .''

Paula hugged her. ''I did talk with him; it didn't work out. He said if we moved in together it would be just us, nobody else. But until we do, what he does is his own business.''

''And you didn't want to. Move in, I mean.''

''It was blackmail!''

Not exactly; maybe close to it, though. Which, coming from Eli Mainz, surprised her. Well, being alone since Estella left must have been harder on him than anyone realized. ''And there wasn't any other answer? He wouldn't dicker, at all?''

Paula moved back. ''I didn't try; I couldn't. Look, maybe you're stronger, maybe you could go head to head with some-

body, stand up for yourself. I can't. After Alton, guessing so
badly, what kind of man he was . . .'' She shook her head. ''I
don't have any confidence left; how could I?''

''Oh, c'mon!'' Marnie thought back. ''You didn't even *pick*
Alton; you said so, remember? You picked—uh, Bobby Jackson?''

''Billy.''

''And then got Alton dumped on you instead. That's not
exactly your fault, Paula. So quit hitting yourself. You want
to go home, all right, do it. But don't go whipped.''

''I am, though. The captain's sending a report on me, remember? All about how I can't handle my personal problems.''

Yes, there was that. Well, ''Maybe I can do something.''

She hugged her friend and left.

''Oh all right,'' Clancy said. ''I'll just say, she had some
unusually tough breaks here and I'm sure she'll manage fine
in her next assignment. Okay with you?'' It had better be!

''It's the truth, too.'' Marnie wasn't giving away an inch.
''Neither of those guys were her free choice.''

And come to think of it, she was right, there. ''Yeah. Well,
I'm sorry to lose her. I guess you two made it up okay?''
Because he'd been a little worried they wouldn't, with Marnie
left to regret it later.

''Oh sure. I just—well, she explained, and all.''

''She came to you?''

''I went there.''

Clancy nodded. ''Right move. Don't be afraid to reach
out.''

''I'm *not*.''

''Yes, I know. Give us a hug?''

The next day Paula Trent got a good turnout at her sendoff.
Waiting for Earthmouth to activate, Marnie said to her, ''I
know staying in touch won't work very well from Earth, the
time difference and everything.'' Paula aging, if she stayed
home, more than two years for every month Marnie lived. *And*
the four years, at Earth end, of round-trip Gate lag. ''But hey,
you can let me know when you go out next, and where.''

''Sure.'' The equipment was ready; Paula stepped inside.

"Goodbye, Marnie; thanks for everything and have a good trip."

The Gate flared. Marnie missed Amalyn Tabard; she'd miss Paula more. Losing people was no fun at all.

XIV

Clancy had barely relieved Ptiba on watch when Senator Wallin came into control with Maxine Durand. Allaird's watch crew, Pete Larue and Trish Pembrook, paused from check-in to see what was up, but Clancy frowned and they got back to business.

"Hello, senator. You have a message to go?" Because that was usually the errand that brought him here.

"Just word of mouth; note it in your own next report." He sat at an idle console. "Remember I said Maxine and I intend to bypass considerable time in your local Gates? After this Tetzl thing was settled? Well, we're ready to start. And the message is, just tell Earth where we are and when we'll pop back out. Not that they can do anything about it, after the fact."

"Well, sure. When do you want to start?"

"How about right now?" Wallin's brows tilted.

"Oh hey." Pete Larue interrupted. "If you're heading into deep freeze, you got to let me feed you up first. After watch, now, I can set up a spread you won't forget for a while."

Wallin chuckled. "Thanks, Pete. Matter of fact, I'm hungering right now. Which is exactly how I want to feel in twenty-nine days and the odd fraction when we're due out. So just note the time when we Gate, and in case we stay out a while before Gating again, be prepared to set the table accordingly."

And of course, Clancy reminded himself, there was no point in Wallin or Durand carrying anything along. Because literally, by their perspective, they'd be gone no time at all.

"If anything comes up that you think I should know," Wallin said, "post a note for your watch officer. If there isn't, we might just loop on through a time or two before we have that meal. If you'd authorize the watch to work the Gate for us."

"Sounds reasonable," said Clancy. "See you in a month. Or a few seconds, depending on how you look at it."

So he Gated them, to emerge a bit over forty-two thousand ship's-minutes futureward, and logged the departure accurately.

"One of these days," he said to Pete and Trish, "maybe we can settle down to just herding this ship where it's going."

Marnie liked the responsibility that came with standing watches, but the Deployment Vehicle was her real love. Lately she'd been concentrating her studies in that direction. And every time she drew DV inspection as her offshift chore she ran as many simulations as Ptiba or Eli would allow: first deployment itself, then piloting and navigating. And now, with more free time than usual at the end of an inspection that went quickly because nothing needed more than minor adjustment, Ptiba brought up the sims for landing the Vehicle. Edd Jarness, the other team member today, already knew the routine, so Marnie was granted most of the sim time.

"Once you're into atmosphere and slowed enough to need thrust to stay aloft," Mbente said, "it's time to point your tail toward the landing spot and switch to your rear viewers." In the pilot's seat she moved controls; on the screens, the simulation showed what her moves would have accomplished, as the ground "below" swung up and the rear sensors took over to show it rushing past and nearing rapidly.

"You've got three outboard sensors pointing aft," Mbente explained, "plus the heat-shielded one at center stern. Now when you get down close, the drive nodes churning stuff up, that center one's blinded by dust and so forth, no use to you. So you'd better pick your spot well and remember what's to avoid if anything, because there's no rechecking at the last minute."

The way she was saying this, sounded as if she expected

Marnie actually to do a landing. Most likely it was just her way of speaking. Still, though . . .

She watched Ptiba through two "landings" on different types of terrain; it didn't look too hard. Then, "Okay; you try it," and suddenly the sim gear grew horns and a tail; it did the flipover well enough, but after that she couldn't get it to do *anything* quite the way she wanted. Coming down the first time she was dropping too fast and had to redline the drive to keep from crashing. Second try, she didn't kill her side drift fast enough and could have tipped the DV over at touchdown.

Ptiba kept her look noncommittal; Marnie said, "One more; okay? I think I'm getting it," and Mbente nodded. So this time Marnie killed most of her vee, vertical and tangential both, while she still had altitude, then spotted a nice flat place and let down slowly all the way. Before Mbente could comment, Marnie said, "Yes, I know that was poor fuel economy. But at least I got it down soft. With practice I'll find out how much faster I can let it drop and still stay safe."

Ptiba cleared her throat. "The trouble with sims is, they can't show you how it *feels*. The seat of the pants thing, and I mean that literally. The indicator shows what kind of gee force you're using on decel, but it's not the same as feeling it."

"I guess not. Still, sim practice can't hurt."

"Take a couple more right now," said Edd. "While you're hot." So she did. She didn't manage anywhere near top efficiency, but each try bettered the one before.

Despite what Marnie had told her and Clancy about Fleurine Schadel after Paula's story ceased to be confidential, Nicole still felt edgy in the woman's presence. She guessed it was the track record: drugging and kidnapping five people, including three officers, off *Starfinder*—and then, within a very few days of her arrival here, disrupting a tentative pairing. The question in Nicole's mind was, what would she do *next*?

So when Schadel approached her and Clancy at table in the galley, mentally Nicole zipped up her parka to await the storm.

Clancy didn't seem bothered. "Hi, Fleurine. Settling in okay? Any problems?"

At his gesture she joined them, setting down her coffee cup and a plate with two biscuits. "Just a lot of studying to do, but Phil Henning's a real help. It's the differences, I need to learn.'' The sophisticated control system with its more finely tuned feedback loops. The impressively greater drive power, redlining at six gees rather than two. The higher thrust necessary to maintain vee against particle resistance at greater speed, thus the increased fuel usage. And so on.

"But that part's all right; I'm getting it. Something else worries me, though. The Gating through decel, at destination.'' Sure, most of the crew went in twenty-five ship days before the five gees would take over, so as to come out a few hours after that thrust ceased. And a small team stayed on until just before decel began, to swing ship and aim its decel course precisely; that detachment would arrive roughly twenty-one months after the first group, because *Arrow* would be back to normal time then. "Which means Eli made a bum pick,'' she said, grinning. "Drive chief's one of the last-minute team, and he isn't. But hell, there'll be all the new people there before I come out. I expect I'll just have to start looking again.''

"And that's not what worries you," Nicole commented.

"Nope. It's what the lead group might run into." She scowled. "I grant you the circuitry's good; nothing should go wrong. But nothing *ever* should, and it usually does anyway. What scares me: suppose decel doesn't cut off on sked? Oh sure; besides the timing, it's set to cut by proximity to our goal star. But still—what if they Gate themselves into five gee and can't climb out of the Tush? What happens to the first arrivals when the next ones come through? Ker-*splat*? And how long does it take to starve, in five gee?''

Clancy chuckled. "You know something, Schadel? You're paying your way already.''

He didn't look worried. And maybe he wasn't.

Allaird was pleased that his call for council, in the lounge after dinner, drew a fair crowd. Aaberg and Baynor and Ng had the watch; nearly everyone else with technical interests showed up. Discussion moved fast; there was no disputing that here was a prime case of holes in the safety net.

Sybiljan wanted to cut thrust using a pressure-sensitive strip all across the back of the recessed Tush concavity. "Five gees should certainly push a person against it hard enough.''

"Nah," said Pete Larue. "It's cute but it's fancy. Just put

a manual switch where it's easy to reach. I mean," he corrected himself, "*possible* to reach, in five gee. Like as far toward the back as we can get it."

"You'll have to recess the unit," said young Trish Pembrook. "Anything that sticks out into the field . . ."

Trish was full of surprises. Earlier she'd come up with the answer to another problem: the possibility of someone out-Gating before the previous arrival had vacated the Tush. This could only occur if decel hadn't ended on time, what with inGating intervals stretched by twenty-five at the receiving end. But just supposing someone couldn't climb free: "They found something out once, by accident. Just before I came here. It never hit the news, but a cousin of mine worked there and wrote me."

An experimental Gate setup, located in a basement, got flooded and stayed that way during a time when several large test objects were due to appear. Just in case, the area had been hurriedly evacuated. But nothing happened, and only when the receiving terminal was fairly well drained did the test specimens emerge. "Making a bit of a splash. Quite literally, Rudy said."

Now how, Clancy wondered aloud, was that possible? "If one time quantum in Aleph space is two years here . . ." Well, maybe it was some other aspect of the balloon effect that stonkered their try at FTL communications.

"They got an opinion from Dr. Habegger," Trish said. "Something about how at the quantum level the limits are fuzzy. He said he couldn't think of anything that would shorten the duration, but given an impediment at the receiving end, it could stretch. Too much, he said, and the stay in Aleph might be two quanta. But this delay was too small to hit that limit."

"As may be," said Clancy, whose grasp of quantum theory was hazy indeed. "Let's get back to backup." So Pete and Coyote volunteered to test out, in the one-gee ring, a structure to be installed between the Tush and the control console, that a person could *climb* under decel thrust. "We can rev the ring up heavier," Allaird added, "and carry weights when we try it."

With that much settled, he tried once again to beat Marnie at anisotropic billiards. She won all three games.

*   *   *

The "climber" didn't work out; nothing scalable at multiple gees could be made the right shape to reach the console. "There isn't room for a ramp, or steps, at an angle a person could drag himself up," said Pete; Clancy took his word for it.

They settled for redundant systems: two manual turnoff switches, another operated by pressure as Sybiljan had suggested, others by body capacity of anyone appearing in the Tush or beams of light interrupted for the same reason. "So it's not just a belt and suspenders holding our pants up," Coyote commented. "There's also the staple gun and the glue."

"Better'n having your bare ass hang out in a cold wind," said Fleurine. It wasn't the first time Allaird saw Eli Mainz wince at one of her remarks. Maybe the boy had bitten off a chaw with more tang than he was used to.

With time, he might acquire the taste. He'd better.

On Nicole's watch, a few hours before Wallin and Durand were due to reappear after their first ship's-month in the Gates, Sybiljan Baynor said "*Oh*-oh!" and called Pryce over to have a look. "The computer puts the radiation source at under two light-years, roughly eighty degrees off our course at this point. That's after relativistic correction for our velocity."

Right; at this speed, so close to c, the entire forward view shrank to a smallish circle at center front; computer analysis could spread most of that out to an approximation of true positions. Where Sybiljan pointed now, the screen showed a reddish yellow star. Not a terribly bright one, but maybe it could have planets, at that. Nicole scowled. "What kind of radiation is it?" Not the star's own, she meant, but the anomalous bursts.

"Very low energy; except for the pulsing, the scanners wouldn't have noticed it. At our velocity it comes in about like hard X-rays. But slowed down, unDopplered the best the computer can guess, it could be close to our own space comm frequencies."

Sybiljan frowned. "The modulation patterns aren't at all obvious. This could be digitalized voice on a multichannel system, or some form of TV, or just plain computer language."

"And of course there's no way we can decode it."

Over at another console Phil Henning looked up. "I've done a preliminary analysis, but all it tells me is that there *are* patterns. Good as our computer is, I don't think it can handle the magnitude of parameters this problem carries."

"Not with all the chores and data it's already stuffed with," Nicole agreed. "Well, let's record a good batch of samples, leave them Dopplered up to save datacap space, and Gate the whole teaser back for Earth to chew on."

She reached for the intercom. "Meanwhile I'd better see if Clancy wants to do anything else about it." As she wondered, whatever happened to titles and last names on duty?

Allaird held off and met Nicole and her team in the galley; he was hungry and they'd be, too. Once seated, and with the edge off his appetite, he asked questions, and after a few minutes said, "How come we haven't spotted this before now?"

"Partly view compression," Sybiljan said. "Anything near the center has to be pretty evident or we can't get definition on it, and this star isn't. Also, until quite recently it's been more or less in line with a fairly bright cluster a long way off. But now . . ."

"Yes." The stellar object's color put it to the cool side of the sun: spectral type K, maybe? He couldn't remember whether the qualifying numbers ran up or down. Anyway, "How hot would you say, Phil? Four thousand Kelvin, maybe?" To the sun's six.

"I'd say forty-five hundred. Hot enough for life, and certainly old enough." Because the dimmer stars aged more slowly. "So," Henning said, "what are we going to do about it?"

Easy answer; Clancy said, "Take all the readings we can and feed them back to Earth for future reference."

"You mean we're not even going to try to investigate? When it's obviously some kind of communication signal?"

"Absolutely not."

Phil Henning stood. "I think we need to call council. This question's too important for snap decisions."

Allaird suppressed his irritation. "Fine. The lounge, in two hours. Everybody welcome, and the watch can attend by intercom." He got up and walked out. Nicole followed.

* * *

With Clancy's tacit permission, Marnie went along to the meeting. She hadn't entirely understood the reasons he'd spelled out to Nicole for his decision; maybe they'd come clearer in the inevitable debate.

After Allaird stated the question, Henning led off. "Here we have an unquestioned sign of intelligent life, and . . ."

Clancy heard him out, then sat with apparent patience Marnie didn't believe for a minute, while others spoke on both sides of the argument: Edd Jarness and Nicole on Clancy's behalf, Sybiljan and then Gretel Aaberg on intercom supporting Phil. A few people who held no real opinions took several minutes to explain why not before Allaird said, "Okay, that should be most of it. Now here's why we're going right ahead with the mission as planned."

He had his points numbered. One: the six billion mile Array gave destination a ninety-five percent chance of planets; the ship's sensors couldn't tell about this star, even from a mere two light-years. Two: sure it was theoretically possible to program *Arrow* to come to rest near the star at orbital speed, but ". . . along with straight-ahead decel we need a side vector; half the distance on accel, the other half brakes. Unmonitored, that's too many variables, too much chance for error."

Three: Gate lag. Suppose the system *is* inhabited by spacefarers. The ship sits there empty until the crew outGates, ". . . and by that time the supposed derelict's being taken apart by curious natives, and we pop out into no air."

And he hadn't even had to bring up the idea of hostiles.

"So we set decel to *get* there in two years." Phil.

Two-B: If this star *didn't* turn out to be an acceptable alternative destination, more than two years would be added to overall mission length. And the risk of navigational error was by no means lessened. No one even suggested doing lower decel on a crewed basis; although *Starfinder* and *Roamer* were built to live in during accel as well as cruise mode, *Arrow* was not.

Phil wasn't done, though. "Still, isn't it worth the risk, when we *know* intelligent life is here?"

Clancy smiled. "Even if that were true, I'd have to say no. But all we can say for sure is that somebody's been here, or sent something here. This isn't where that ship came from, the one that slanted past us a time back; wrong direction.''

He leaned forward. ''Do you want to chance screwing up the whole mission schedule, maybe just to find a goddamn *beacon* somebody planted?''

And there were still three points he hadn't had to use!

Seeing Phil Henning grin capitulation, Allaird relaxed, then started at Nicole's nudge as she said, ''Isn't the senator due out, about now?''

Overdue was more like it, but variations were nothing new. They got up to control to find Wallin and Durand chatting with Gretel and Chauncey and Pilar. After greetings the senator said, ''Pete's alerted to set up that dinner; I want to hear about this planet we're not investigating.''

So, downship to the galley, where Clancy had eaten recently and now settled for coffee as he explained. Finally Wallin nodded. ''Makes sense. But something puzzles me. What do you do at destination if it turns out the Big Array was wrong?''

The question surprised Clancy, but on second thought he realized the senator had been off Earth when those options were worked out. ''We don't stop there.'' Wallin's heavy brows raised. ''It's the final checkout team that inGates just before decel begins. At that time we're roughly a tenth of a light-year out, plenty close enough to spot worlds and even get some sort of horseback evaluation. If it doesn't look good, no decel—and four–five days later the full crew's on hand to hold council.''

And the possible choices? ''There are three alternate stars listed in the mission directive, in case destination doesn't pan out. Or if we've spotted something that looks better, on the way in, we can opt for that. Backtracking if need be.''

Maxine Durand frowned. ''But doesn't *turning* the ship imply acceleration of a kind?''

''To any extent, yes,'' Clancy said. ''Small turns we just swing ship a little and let gas resistance reduce forward vee while normal thrust adds a side component. Bigger ones . . .''

He beckoned to Ptiba Mbente at the next table. ''Your DV training covers maneuvering better. Want to explain?''

''All right.'' The slim woman cleared her throat. ''Steering a ship around in free space takes more than just pointing it where you want to go. You have to reduce your initial vee vector and build a sidewise component, sometimes even partway backward.''

The two visitors looked blank; she continued. ''Say you want a right-angle turn, from north to west. The simplest way is swing, point *southwest*, and hold thrust until instruments tell you the course is right. Well, for any turn, just point toward the center of the arc, bisecting the angle. At ship speeds, of course, it takes considerable time and distance, and everyone has to Gate: some early, to come out as soon as the accel's done, and some late, to check everything just before it starts.''

The senator's eyes narrowed. ''What happens to velocity?''

''You come out with just what you had going in. But it's not constant throughout.'' Ptiba's forehead wrinkled. ''Okay, it's like a ballistic trajectory; the middle of the turn is the top of the arc. And time ratio goes *way* down, along in there.''

''But safe in Gate transit, the crew's not affected,'' Nicole reassured everyone. Assuming everyone got the timing right . . .

''There's a more general formulation.'' Sitting at the edge of the group, Eli Mainz sounded nervous. ''For when you don't *want* the same vee coming out. From the same point of origin, lay out your initial and final velocity vectors to scale, just a couple of arrows. Then run a third from the head of your starting vee to the head of the other. That's your delta-vee, course *and* magnitude. Dividing by your accel gives the time required.''

Ptiba laughed. ''Is *that* what I missed, going on leave the weekend my kid brother got married? Thanks, Eli.''

Wallin sighed. ''Personally I hope you can get by with only minor course changes. And settle for the assigned destination.''

Clancy could drink to that, and said so. ''But not for a while yet. I have the next watch.''

Wallin and his companion spent an evening socializing in the lounge and a night in their quarters, reporting to control before breakfast. ''Coming out hungry, having a meal first thing, I like it,'' the senator told Nicole, who as watch officer readied the Gate. Then, ''See you next month,'' he said, and once more the two went nonexistent with respect to *Arrow*'s universe.

Bill and Mara Flynn were home celebrating his fifty-sixth birthday with a few friends when Allaird's message faxed in from Glen Springs. When he heard the little extension chime *ting* he excused himself from table and went to see what was coming in.

He came back with the flimsy in his hand. "Charlie? How close is *Nomad* to Go?"

Charlie Sprague, Flynn's liaison with ship preparations, looked up. "They're a couple of months behind, you know; that last set of change orders is more work than anyone expected. So it'll have to be set for higher accel, to get up to speed before the crew outGates. Still well below redline, though. Why?"

"Because we may want a whole new set. Have a look at this. Our gang on *Arrow*'s had another brainstorm, and this one looks very good indeed."

So *Nomad* was rescheduled to leave nearly a year late. It would need a new crew, because the assigned group had already inGated. That Tush would have to be replaced and brought to Earth; its crew would emerge to find they hadn't gone anywhere.

Because *Nomad* was going out with a scout pod affixed to its stern, a navigable space station designed to find orbit around a possible future colony world and wait for a recon team. Coyote Benjamin's idea had definitely made a hit, back here at home.

With some improvements. This pod would nestle in an oversized single-purpose Tush; if and when it detached to scout a planetary system, word would be sent back, and four years later by Earth time a replacement would appear in its place. As with the originally suggested model, airlocks would allow crew members to enter and program it as needed.

"What I like about this part of the job, Mara," Flynn said when the plans were firmed, "is that someone's always coming up with a better idea."

If it wasn't one thing fretting her, Marnie thought, it was something else. With Paula Trent gone, Trish Pembrook was becoming a closer friend and confidante; she and Marnie did many of the same things Marnie and Paula had done together.

So today, showering after a bout of full-gee exercise, they'd got to roughhousing in the familiar way, but after a little while Marnie realized she was getting excited. At first she couldn't figure out what was going on; then a specific tingling gave the answer. Embarrassed, she pulled back. "Let's stop; that's enough."

"Too rough? I'm sorry; didn't mean to."

"No, it's all right. Look, I'm tired. You mind . . . ?"

So Trish left. Marnie hoped her feelings weren't hurt; none of this was Trish's fault, anyway.

Marnie had discovered orgasm quite young, more or less by accident, lying awake at night and feeling miserable because of the divorce. It made her feel better, and of course she had no idea what it related to—not until SexEd at school a few years later, and then the "facts" seemed quite unreal to her. Or maybe just unlikely.

It had been a year or so before Celeste found her at it. She didn't raise a fuss, just said, "Well, I guess you won't grow up frigid," whatever that meant. And, "Don't get too taken with this; it's not healthy to overdo things, you know."

She didn't say where to draw the line or anything; Marnie decided to save that pleasure for special occasions. When she felt especially bad—or, oddly enough, especially good.

But here on the ship, somehow she'd forgot about it almost entirely. Until now.

And now was what bothered her. Because excited wasn't the right word; aroused was. And where did she come off, getting aroused by wrestling with Trish Pembrook?

Most women responded that way to men, some to women, a few to both; that's what the books said and Marnie believed them. Not that she thought about that stuff much. But despite her bad experiences with Carl Knapheidt and Alton Darnell, she'd always assumed she'd be one of the majority.

If she weren't, she supposed that would be all right, too. But how was she going to *know*?

It wasn't in Marnie's nature to swallow her anxiety and hope it would go away. At Carl's house, fearing him while Celeste ignored her worry, she'd had to do pretty much that, but this was different. Her first impulse, to talk with Clancy, met an unexpected emotional roadblock; somehow she just couldn't. Trish? She was level-headed and all, but somehow discussing this disturbing reaction with the person who occasioned it was more than Marnie could tackle.

Well, she trusted Nicole, certainly. So when Clancy relieved his roommate at control, Marnie hung around until she had the chance to ask her for a private talk.

In captain's digs, stumbling a little from embarrassment or maybe just confusion, she tried to tell what had happened to her. ". . . and I never thought anything like that, so what does it mean?" Intently she stared at Nicole. "What do I grow up to be?"

She couldn't read Nicole's expression, as the woman said, "You've never felt that way with anyone before?"

"I don't think so. And why Trish?"

Pryce shook her head. "I don't think it's Trish. Tell me, how do you suppose you'd feel if it were a boy, instead?"

"In the *shower*? Oh, come on, Nicole!"

"Roughhousing. Wrestling. Physical contact and exertion, breathing hard. Overall physical stimulation." She overrode Marnie's protest. "Your glands don't know what you're doing or who you're with, that's got your heart pumping faster. They react because you're growing up and they figure it's time they did." She spread her hands. "I think it's just that simple, Marnie. A perfectly natural reaction. If you don't want it to happen, then avoid the situation. And if it does, you're not obliged to do anything about it. Not unless you want to."

"I really don't!"

"Then that answers your question. You'll grow up to be who you are."

"Whoever *that* is." Because . . . but no, she didn't want to discuss Carl or Alton. Not now.

Instead, Marnie skipped to a new worry. "I don't want to hurt Trish's feelings, either. So how . . . ?"

"Hmm. Could you tell her that physical contact makes you uncomfortable right now, so let's ease off it for a while?"

"I guess so." Marnie stood. "Thanks, Nicole."

"Any ol' time."

It was two days before Marnie felt up to confronting Trish,

and then she didn't have to. Somehow, Nicole's explanation of her reaction seemed to have defused it.

Five days after its first sighting, the Beacon system lay abeam, about two light-years off. The patterned sequences of radiation had ceased for a while, then returned briefly; Clancy agreed with majority opinion, which labeled them beamed signals intercepted by sheer chance. "Probably in-system comm, and we've run across some that overshot and came on past." Since no more such chance encounters occurred, the point was moot.

Not so were the indications picked up by Ptiba Mbente, late one watch. "That's drive field activity," she told Allaird when he relieved her. "No doubt about it. It's a little different from ours and I wish I knew what that difference means, but out this far the emissions arrive too faint and blurry to tell much. No doubt of it, though: those are drives operating, out there."

At such distance, of course, locating discrete sources of the fuzzy wave packets was a pipe dream. Predictably, Phil Henning reopened the idea of changing the mission to explore here. For a moment Clancy seriously considered the proposal, then shook his head. "The programming now would be a little simpler," he said. "Just decel to an approximate stop, swing ship toward the system, then speed up halfway and slow down the other half. But all the other objections still hold. No—log this new data in and Gate it home. We're staying on sked."

It had been some time since anyone aboard talked about the alien Liij very much; still, it seemed strange to Nicole Pryce that Fleurine Schadel took so long to pick up on the occasional mention. When she did, her questions came fast, and Nicole tried to fill her in as briefly as possible.

She had a better feeling now for this woman who had grabbed opportunity and taken her chances; the blunt directness no longer made her uncomfortable. Now Fleurine shook her head. "Damn. If only I'd been there in control, instead of Margrete and Benita, when Rance made his play. I could have been home with him and Su, right in the middle of all that excitement, and seen this Liij business for myself."

Shrugging, "But then Irina Tetzl would still be riding high and mighty, dumping new cadres off to here and to *Roamer*, and Earth still wouldn't have any idea what was going on.''

''Not exactly,'' Nicole corrected her. ''Corby sent a team to *Starfinder* too, don't forget, and I'm sure that group out-Gated as ready for a skirmish as his team did here. What you accomplished was to put that ship back to normal quite a bit sooner.''

''Yeah. Well, I guess it was worth it, then.''

Two months out of prison, Carl Knapheidt didn't feel like a free man. What he felt was, simply, lost. Seven years under Bolton Graef's protective domination had atrophied his capacity to think for himself. Bolt was nowhere near the worst he could have drawn; after the first days, teaching Carl his place here, the big man never again screwed him dry and hurting. Within a month Carl was coming too—not always, but now and then.

And with Bolt around, nobody else messed with Carl. Killers were a dime a dozen in the place and Bolt was only Murder Two—but he'd done it wired on PCP like a case of dynamite, wrung the man's neck, turned his head straight backward. Some of the heavies said they didn't believe it, but nobody ever tried him. So Bolt didn't have but a couple of fights on his record here, from when he was new and had to show who he was, and would probably get out near the short end of his ten-to-fifteen.

Bolt never loaned Carl out for favors, the way some did. What was his was his, nobody else's. And besides, that way neither of them was going to catch anything evil.

Most likely it was Bolt who planted the shiv in Carl's kit, though, just before he was due up for parole, so he did the full seven years. Bolt acted sympathetic at the time—patted Carl on the back and said he was better off staying inside, anyway. ''I keep ya safe, bunkie,'' and in most ways he really did.

Wouldn't let him do dope, for one thing, even though all kinds of stuff circulated in the block. Made him work out, too, get in shape a little. ''Somebody catch ya, I ain't around, ya gotta show some mean.'' Twice it paid off; Carl didn't win, exactly, but they didn't take him, either.

When the release order came, Bolt shook Carl's hand. ''Gonna miss ya.'' Carl mumbled along the same lines but was mostly just being polite. Because now he was going out and free, and *do* some screwing instead of the versa kind of vice.

Somehow the family law firm had sheltered Carl's home and a certain amount of capital investment from the Treasury Department's confiscation policy in drug cases, so he had a familiar place to stay. It needed some work, but what didn't? After the month it took him to make up his mind, Carl got most of the first floor, enough to make a reasonable suite of living quarters, cleaned up and generally rehabbed; if he was going to have people in, he'd need to show a little better front.

He also needed new clothes; he hadn't slimmed down all that much in the middle, but workouts and plain work had rebuilt muscles he hadn't felt since college; his old suits were too tight in the shoulders.

Ready as he'd ever be, then, Carl set out to a club he used to frequent. Name and management and decor had all changed, but the type of clientele hadn't. He took a tall blonde home with him; she wasn't as young as he'd have liked, but neither was he.

An hour later he took her home, period. After seven years he was habituated to one specific form of sexual stimulation, and the woman wasn't equipped to provide it.

He'd heard enough con talk to know it wasn't like this with everybody, and not necessarily permanent. What he didn't know was what to do now. Except, it wasn't going to be drugs.

He found himself missing Bolt, after all.

As chief medic at Glen Springs, Dr. Max Harbin had a right to his air of authority. It did get on Bill Flynn's nerves a little, though. Now the man cleared his throat. "Well, you've interviewed her, senator. What do you think?"

"She seems fine to me, but I'm not the expert. What's your opinion?"

They can never keep it short. Harbin rehashed what Flynn already knew: Irina Tetzl's brilliant but erratic career, the events leading to the present situation, the diagnoses, the treatments, the progress over more than a year and a half. Finally he got down to basics. "Laser surgery, for the small anomalous cyst, corrected the glandular imbalance, obviating any need for further medication as maintenance. And the ensuing enzyme therapy has effectively stabilized her condition.''

"So you're saying she's fit, now.'' This was the question; he already knew, Flynn did, that she'd been through a full retraining program for the proposed new assignment.

"I am.'' The doctor's throat needed a lot of clearing. "There is one side effect. The matter has never been discussed, but the patient will most certainly have suffered a significant reduction in sex drive.''

Bill Flynn kept a straight face. "You say there have been no complaints.''

"That is correct. Neither from the woman herself nor from the man she's living with at present.''

"Then I don't believe you need mention it.''

In Irina Tetzl's case, the development was hardly likely to pose a major problem.

Sometimes a month could go by pretty fast. When Marnie reported to Ptiba Mbente's watch, along with Pete Larue, it surprised her to find the note saying the senator and Maxine Durand were due out again within the next few hours; of course the inevitable slight velocity changes, with their effects on time ratio, made exact prediction impossible. At any rate the two emerged about an hour before the end of the watch.

Wallin's idea was to Gate again immediately, but Ptiba talked him out of it. "Little party going on, downship. You really ought to go look in.'' So he and Maxine headed for the transfer ring.

Marnie wished she could, too. Well, it wouldn't be long now.

"Come on in, senator, Maxine.'' Clancy waved to the newcomers at the lounge door. "Pardon us for not waiting.''

Actually he'd completely forgotten their schedule. It was posted in control, but this was his day off. Now nearly a dozen of the crew were gathered, drinking lightly but snacking like wolves. "What's this all about?'' Wallin asked.

"I got a raise,'' said Coyote Benjamin. "And a bonus. They're using my idea, on *Nomad*. As a start, anyway.''

Then he had to explain: the navigable Gate-bearing pod, livable once it reached orbit, to be dropped off at any likely planetary system. "Only they're mounting it astern *in* a Tush, so they could send a replacement when the first one leaves."

A little more discussion and Wallin had it straight. "That's good thinking. And the credit's all yours?"

"Not the Tush part. But yes; Clancy—Captain Allaird—gave me all the glory, in his report."

"Hell, it was your idea," Clancy grumped, remembering how Ellery put *his* name all over the FTL comm suggestion, which he'd had nothing to do with. Oh, well; it hadn't worked anyway.

"*Nomad*," the senator said. "Which one is that, now? And so, how many years would it be?" Because the starfleet schedule, so far, was one new ship every four years. "*Starfinder, Roamer, Arrow* . . ." Counting on his fingers. "Damn, I forget!"

Clancy knew, but he needed a moment to remember. "*Scout, Falcon, Nomad.* I think that's as far as we've heard."

Again Wallin and Durand stayed "overnight" before going back into the Gates. After that, though, unless there was something to catch up on, for the next several Gatings the senator planned merely to say hello and pop right back in again.

Clancy didn't bet on it. There was always something. . . .

XV

On the west coast Celeste Malvieux, as she called herself now, weighed her options. In the nine or so years since she'd returned to Earth and fixed Carl Knapheidt's clock so it probably ran backwards if at all, Celeste had starred in several imaginative self-productions before a breathless world. Or just plain not breathing; sometimes she wasn't sure which.

Waste not, want not; although Marnie couldn't be found,

Celeste felt no obligation to force that information onto the department that paid her child support money every month out of Clancy Allaird's salary. It was nearly three more years before the checks stopped, with a curt note stating that Margaret Clarisse Allaird now being a crew member aboard the starship *Arrow*, support payments to Celeste Allaird Knapheidt were summarily discontinued and previous overpayment would be reimbursed according to the following schedule, which Celeste threw in the wastebasket with suitably profane comment.

That was when she scrapped all her previous surnames and picked a new one. By now she knew a CompuNet raider who could validate Social Security numbers the government hadn't really issued, so the dipsydoo went easier than one might expect.

If the bastards couldn't find her, they couldn't collect.

Since her venture into space she'd been married twice: three years to a tabloid publisher and almost as long to a sports promoter, both notably shady dealers. She wasn't sure why she picked men of that stripe; maybe it was that no matter what she did to them, she didn't have to feel guilty. The thought of Clancy Allaird still bothered her sometimes. Marnie *was* aboard the ship with him; Celeste knew that much, at least. Maybe it was best, after all. Even for herself.

She'd also learned of Carl's release. For a while she worried: would he come after her, try to get even? But the private investigator reported that Knapheidt had become more or less a hermit. "Hardly ever goes out. Orders in a few hookers, every so often. Both polarities."

So he wasn't broke, after all. Just bent a whole lot. On consideration, Celeste didn't begrudge him a little salvage.

Right now she was deciding whether or not to marry Keith Henry Rasmussen III, an ambitious financial predator enjoying a somewhat advanced stage of youth and skilled in the art of living off corporate carrion after he'd killed it himself. She had cut Keith out from the attentions of a covey of younger and crisper bods because she knew and demonstrated more tricks in bed, and even after forty he was still naive enough to think anyone could be unique in such respects.

All in all, Celeste firmly believed that any man who could be pussywhipped deserved to be.

On the one hand Keithums was a total swine, no question.

On the other, you had to keep in mind the grade of trough he presided over. . . .

Marnie never abandoned her study schedule entirely, but some of the happenings aboard had cut into it pretty badly from time to time. After the *Starfinder* people Gated home, though—all except Fleurine, anyway—she got back into the routine better.

Besides her general studies, Marnie was trying for a working knowledge of various shipside specialties; nearing the biological age of twelve and a half, she could imagine no future more desirable than becoming a ship's officer. Maybe even captain someday, if she got lucky. What such an assignment would mean in personal terms, she hadn't yet considered. . . .

So about a week after the senator's second visitation from the local Gates, noting that this was day two hundred ten of *Arrow*'s crewed progress at full velocity, she cranked up her quarters' computer terminal and took stock.

She knew about as much about operating the Deployment Vehicle as could be learned without actually flying the little beast. In the ship's control room she could read, log, and interpret the indications on instruments reporting from *Arrow*'s outside sensors, and use them to determine velocity and position figures for the ship; thus she knew they were now closing on fourteen-point-five light-years from Earth, and was able to figure what the Earth date "really" was. Roughly, at this point, fourteen years, seven and a half months since Clancy had Gated her out of Glen Springs.

Now she was working toward qualification as drive tech, third. All her knowledge was operational; to manipulate controls and evaluate observations responsibly she didn't need the fine points of how the innards worked. And that's how it would be with the drive, too. She wasn't alone in learning new specialties; Clancy encouraged versatility. And most were hitting the new areas of technique at much that same level. Not everyone had to know *why*—but in case of need, *how* was essential. So Marnie settled down to put in some time and really learn.

It was, she thought, as she called up the basic drive control files, one of the better ways to keep from getting bored. Now then: the proper method of adjusting interfield phasings . . .

*   *   *

After nearly seven shipboard months of recurrent crises, Clancy Allaird enjoyed a few weeks of relative quiet. Nobody arrived, nobody left, nobody had any problems that couldn't wait until he'd had a proper breakfast. The way a ship *should* run.

He didn't mind the puzzles that came from outside. In fact he welcomed them as breaks in routine; peace and quiet didn't need to be monotonous.

Like the triple-star system well off the ship's starboard flank. It didn't seem to have any planets, none that could be detected from here, anyway, but the small reddish luminary rode in a Trojan orbit with respect to its brighter consorts.

From what Clancy remembered, the mass ratios between the three had to lie within rather narrow limits for the layout to be stable. It was Phil Henning who dug out the math for those equations and then ran mass-luminosity curves to prove the three stars could do what they obviously *were* doing.

"You just go down there, Knapper," Sarbo said, "and take the tour and pay attention. Chita here goes with you, she tapes the lecture and keeps track of how they work the fucking Gate."

So with Conchita Ruiz riding herd on him, Carl went to Glen Springs, to the starship-crewing center. Three times in two days, in the guise of interested citizens which maybe wasn't too far off the mark at that, both suffered through the guided tour. The flare of colors accompanying the disappearance of several cartons of supplies impressed Carl; nothing ever impressed Chita.

Returning, they reported back to Azi Sarbo, a shirttail relation of Slide-action Cartiere's and now sitting high in Slide's vacated saddle. "No real security," Chita said. "Not even any metal detectors. You draw down on the tour guide while she shows you how the Gates work, you say send us off or we blow you out." She shrugged. "Couldn' be easier."

Sarbo frowned. So did Turk and Laszlo; monkey see, monkey do. Two slabs of men: beside them Azi looked like somebody's kid. Didn't sound like one, though, as he said, "What about it, Knap? My little cousin, she's too optimistic, you think?"

Not real cousins; this was the fiction that Slide-action's people were all "family." Hell, they weren't even Mafioso—but you didn't say so out loud. Carl said, "It might not be as easy as it looks." Then, at Chita's glare, "There was an armed guard, remember, that followed the group around."

"Yeah, sure, the old guy." Chita snorted. "Had his holster flap buttoned down the whole time, so the piece don' fall out."

"Just the one?" said Sarbo. "Nothing more, you saw?" Not inside the building, no; Carl had to shake his head.

"So we go with the job as set, and this is our out, after. We play tag with those Gates until the statute time's up."

Laszlo nodded; so did Turk. The seal of approval.

Carl wasn't even told what the job was. Which was fine by him; all he wanted was to get paid for his little spy act and go home. But Azi wanted differently. "Naw, Carl; you gotta be down there and get tour tickets. For five, because you coming with us. So you're not around later, to answer a lotta questions."

Shit; he might have known it would go like this. And just when he was getting his sex straight again, well enough to try it on somebody besides hookers.

Knapheidt hadn't looked Sarbo up; he'd never heard of him. But Azi spotted Carl's release in the news, recognized the name from Slide's list of clients, and came around to see if he could market a little something. No damn *via*; dope had been Carl Knapheidt's downfall once and that was plenty.

But Azi also had a handle on commercial sex in the area, and it didn't hurt Carl's dealings along those lines to be known as a friend of the boss. So he went to a few of Sarbo's parties and accepted some favors he thought were freebies.

Now he was finding out they weren't.

When the tour group entered the big Gates room, Carl took a hitch in his breath and a firm grip on his sphincters. This was going to be a bitch, but no help for it.

He'd had to change the tickets once, from early afternoon to late, because Sarbo called from upstate, got hung up in transit and running behind schedule. Always something . . . ! For a minute there he'd thought maybe this was his chance, take just four tickets and say that was all he could get, so he wouldn't have to go in the Gate. But he got to thinking, you never could tell, Azi might just shoot him instead. So he signed for the five. Not his own name, of course.

The way it went, Chita would have known he was lying anyway, because the tour group turned out smaller than usual, maybe fifteen. Still hoping, Carl tried to hang back toward the tail end, but no luck; if Turk wasn't flanking him, Laszlo was. Both heavy in the midriff with all the loot stashed in money belts.

About halfway down the long room now, everybody gathered around the third Gate in the lineup, the guide was saying, "... were moved into space, to macroGate Two, for several years until it was decided the precaution wasn't necessary after all and they were brought back again. This Gate, now, transmits to *Arrow*, our third starship, and you'll note by the indicator panel that it's been rendered operational. I have no departures scheduled, so presumably it's a supplies requisition. Now ..."

As she turned away, Azi Sarbo dropped a quarter; it bounced ringing on the floor. In moments, Laszlo and Turk had moved out to cover the group while Chita jerked Carl toward the Gate. She was half his size, but he went along because he had a pretty good idea what she'd do if he didn't.

Grabbing the guide's shoulder, Sarbo gave her a shake that jarred her carefully arranged red hair loose to stand out in disarray. "Hold still!" And, "Everybody down! On your faces, hands behind your head."

The guard fumbled at his holster. "Leave it sit, soldier! You may be good, but we're five to one." Four, really; Carl wasn't packing. But he admired Azi's tactic; let the man keep his pride, easier for him to give in.

Now Sarbo shoved the woman toward the control panel and backed into the Gate area itself, motioning Laszlo and Turk to join them. "All right, lady; send us out!"

"But I—I can't do that!"

"You said it's up and ready; hit it. And anybody comes after us, they get blasted. Now move it! I'm still here thirty seconds from now," aiming at her, "you're dead."

"Wait! I—all right, I will. But it takes longer ..."

"Start."

Where was the goddamn U.S. Cavalry when you needed it? Carl didn't want to go; he didn't even want to be here.

Wait a minute, though. *Arrow*? That tricky little cunt Marnie! Sixteen years ago now, a little over, maybe; Carl hadn't forgotten, though. And a story on the holo: "... youngest member of a starship crew ..." By God, he'd ...

As the air thickened with flashing color, Carl heard Sarbo's gun fire. But no sound of the bullet striking.

"How the hell could it happen?" Bill Flynn was mad clean through. "Don't we have any security down there?"

On the other end of the line, the director of Glen Springs both looked and sounded whipped. "There was a guard in the Gates room, but he was badly outnumbered. Senator, you have to realize, there's simply no precedent; we've never had any trouble before. Not since the Earth First protesters, over at the Cape when the *Jovian*s were under political attack. And that's ..."

"A long time ago. Yes, I know. Well, it's not your fault, Roger. But what are you going to do about it?"

"What *can* I do? The ringleader said they'd shoot anyone who went through after them, and at twenty-five to one, between the five of them they could guard the Tush for *months*, by our time. And they could wait spread out, flanking whoever arrived. Sitting ducks." He paused. "We can't use assault methods, throw in a grenade first, anything like that—even if we didn't kill some of our own, by mistake, we could damage the ship."

"Then you're saying we can't send anyone at all, for any reason, until Allaird gives word it's safe to do so."

"I'm afraid that's true, senator. We can still provide supplies, of course."

Flynn's imagination beat at the bars of the situational cage. How big was the water supply line? Send a man through in a diving suit? But how the hell could he get out of the tank?

He shook his head. "All right, Roger. Keep me posted."

Two days later Flynn approved sending a team after all. Specially equipped and bearing very special instructions.

At least the media didn't know. Not yet, anyway.

*   *   *

It was Fleurine Schadel who guessed that the rather spectacular explosions appearing on the rear sensors, while *Arrow* was passing a double star system not terribly far off the port beam, were some sort of super-thermonuclear floating space mines. "Radar fuses," she insisted, "and we got close enough to set 'em off. But long gone before the buggers could react and blow."

"You're probably right," Clancy told her. The round trip beam transmission time wouldn't be enough to get the ship out of range, but no detonating mechanism could avoid a few milliseconds worth of inherent delay, and at *Arrow*'s velocity it didn't take much of that to spring them on past, free and clear.

Predictably, Phil Henning wanted to go investigate, but realized it wasn't feasible. "No, we really couldn't chance the ship being discovered and none of us out and awake." True . . .

There was some question as to whether certain sensor traces indicated ships traveling between the twin systems. "I'm certain they do," said Sybiljan Baynor. "But it's not Traction Drive as we know it, and as near as I can tell by the readings, nothing's pushing even half of c."

"Not in our league, then," Clancy concluded. "And they act mean, to boot. So," he said to Ptiba, "I guess you know what to put in the log summary for Earth, regarding these systems."

"Maybe you'd better tell me."

Allaird grinned. "Don't send out the welcome wagon."

Too bad he couldn't give that advice to the nearer neighbors, back at Beacon System. He tried figuring how many light-years behind them those planets were, but decided he'd have to look it up in the log. And then forgot to.

A little over two weeks into Wallin's latest hibernation, Nicole coming tired off watch brought Clancy an envelope. "Something from the personnel office." What now, she wondered. . . .

"Let's see." Reading quickly, then he handed her the sheet. Boiled down, it read that Irina Tetzl having received corrective medical treatment was now fully certified for duty and would arrive aboard *Arrow* to serve as supernumerary watch officer for a period of approximately ninety ship's-days. After which she would Gate to *Starfinder* on rendezvous with relief cadre 4-A, and take command as that ship began its long deceleration. She would be accompanied by her pairmate Nathan Brandt, drive chief for the cadre, who would meanwhile assist *Arrow*'s chief.

"On the other hand, if she screws up, it's back to Earth," Nicole summarized. "Do you suppose she might?" She frowned. "I'm not sure I like our being guinea pigs on a test run."

Allaird shrugged. "What the hell, Nicole; that's what these entire missions are."

He was right, she realized; belatedly they kissed hello.

"What's she like, so far?" Senator Wallin asked. As Clancy had bet himself, the third emergence was running true to form; during this period in the Gates, Irina Tetzl and Nathan Brandt had arrived, and the senator had to see what was going on.

It would be Tetzl, of course, who concerned him. Like Clancy himself, Wallin had no qualms about the large ruddy-faced man who accompanied her. Quiet except for his rare contagious laugh, Brandt hovered near his pairmate like a shaggy, protective teddy bear. Or so it seemed to Allaird.

"Stick around and see for yourself," Clancy said now. Due on watch in less than an hour, Tetzl should be stopping by the galley, any minute. "Here, have some more coffee."

And soon she did arrive. Alone for once, and now Allaird remembered that Brandt would be inship, getting a guided tour of the drive area itself. Once Irina had her tray ready she came and sat beside Clancy, across from Wallin and Durand. "Yes, I am come back, you see." She smiled. "Ten days past, arriving here, Nathan and I. In another eighty, slightly less perhaps, we go on to *Starfinder*. Conversion to drive thrust living mode will be complete or nearly so; we join cadre 4-A to commence and carry through deceleration to destination orbit."

As talk continued, Clancy watched the senator absorb the differences, some obvious and others more subtle, from the last time they'd seen this woman. Well, appearance. Top to bottom: grey hair no longer dyed blonde, still sheared at sides and back but no longer curled above, just shortish and slightly

wavy. Paradoxically the change made her face look incongruously younger. That face a bit less lean, more solid, and a
similar shift in body proportions; she wasn't what you'd call
stocky, Clancy reflected, not by any means. But with the excesses of thyroid and adrenals curbed, Irina Tetzl's metabolism
no longer burned away everything but the vital core of her.

She spoke quietly, not so intense as before her treatment.
"We are all lucky my unlawful attempt was foiled. I have
been studying the changes that must be made, to convert *Starfinder* for living under one-gee deceleration." She shook her
head. "I had not even considered the difficulties involved.
Although conversion should be largely complete when we arrive, operation of the ship will be tremendously different from
what I knew. But back in Earth orbit we trained on simulations, so I am prepared."

Her presence might have lost some impact, but the loss
made her a lot easier to be around. Now, finished with a light
breakfast, she stood. "I am due for watch; excuse me."

Watching her brisk, no-nonsense exit, Senator Wallin raised
an eyebrow. "That's not the Old Iron Tits who used to worry
the hell out of me. I think it's going to work."

And in the days following Wallin's fourth local Gating,
Clancy found no reason to contradict the old man's judgment.

As the air lost color, Carl still didn't hear any bullet strike.
Blinking, he saw no mark on the bare walls before him.

He felt a push, then found himself drifting out of the Gate
recess and grabbed for something—anything—to hold onto,
but by now nothing lay within his reach. "Hey—!"

His slow spin had him facing away when Sarbo barked out
"Everybody hold onto who's next to you. Don't panic, Knapper; we'll get you in a minute." Then "Goddammit Turk, you
puke and you'll eat it!" Maybe not the best way to put the
admonition, but when Carl's drift faced him around, Turk
wasn't erupting.

Somehow Azi got the others strung out hand to hand until
he himself reached the control chair and managed to get
seated. Then Chita, Laszlo holding her by one foot, swung out
far enough to catch Carl's outstretched arm, and shortly everyone had a handhold for anchor. "About time!" said Sarbo.
"Now then . . ."

From around a corner only a few feet away came two women. One was slim and very dark, the other stockier and older, with hair like a blond, shaggy mop. Both stopped, eyes wide and expressions frozen. "Hold it right there!" Sarbo yelled. He wiggled the gun. "You come over here, blondie, and *you* stand right where you are 'til I say different."

His brow wrinkled. "How the hell do you *walk* in this place?" Then he nodded. "The shoes, right? Okay, take 'em off, you," to the blond. "Chita, see if they fit," because sure as hell none of the men could get into them.

The blond held onto the control console as Conchita tried the shoes on and took a couple of uncertain steps; Carl expected her to fall or float, but she didn't. "Hey, they work, yeah."

"All right; we'll get us some more. You!" to the black woman. "You go bring 'em back, enough to go around. You do that and not one damn thing else, if you want your friend here with all her parts inside where they belong. You got me?"

"I think so."

"Then *get*!" Now back to the older woman. "You got a squawkbox around here? Talk back and forth around the ship?"

She gestured to a corner of the console. "That's the intercom. Who do you want to talk to?"

"I don't; you do. First, how many guns on here?"

She stared at him. "I haven't seen the inventory."

"Well, it don't matter; anybody comes at me, you get it first and then we shoot up your damn Gate. So they won't. Call your captain and tell him we're in charge now. And why."

She reached across and pushed several buttons; Azi scowled. "What the hell you doing?"

"I'm not sure where he is; I'm calling broadcast."

"Well, get to it."

She cleared her throat. "This is Fleurine Schadel. At Earth-tush. I need to talk with Ellery if he's awake for once."

The woman who answered sounded surprised, or maybe cautious. "I don't think he's available right now."

"Then get me Old Iron Tits. Maybe she can help."

If this was how starship crews talked about their officers,

Carl thought, it didn't say much for discipline.

Something else bothered him, too. Azi'd shot his damn gun off. The bullet hadn't ever gone spang: there or here either.

In control Marnie looked up, startled. *Old Iron Tits*? And wanting to talk with Ellery Dawson? Had Fleurine blown a feedback loop, or what? At the main console Nicole spoke again. "I'll call her right away," as Ptiba Mbente passed the door carrying an armload of Velcro shoes.

Talk switch off. "Ptiba? What are you doing with those?"

"They're wanted," and the DV commander kept right on going.

Fleurine was speaking again. ". . . five of them, one a woman, they say they're taking charge of the ship. They have guns. If anybody tries to stop them, they say I go down first and then they destroy the Gate here. After that, God only knows."

Nicole frowned. "You might warn them to be careful with the guns. Breaching the hull could be extremely dangerous to all concerned."

Marnie stared. Breaching the *hull*, here in the operations tube? Then she realized, intruders might not know any better. And it couldn't hurt to keep them a little nervous. . . .

Again she listened to the intercom. In the background someone barked out something largely unintelligible except for the obscenities, and Fleurine said, "We're coming to control and they'll tell you in person, what they want. Schadel out."

"What's she trying to do?" Clancy said, entering fast and breathing hard. "*Ellery*, for Pete'sake! And . . ."

"Maybe she's giving you the chance to be here without their knowing you're captain," Nicole said. "It could be an edge."

Marnie missed whatever was said next. Because grouped behind Fleurine and Ptiba shuffled four men and a woman.

Four strangers and Carl Knapheidt.

Instinct bared her teeth. Her breath hissed.

Seeing the man who had tried to violate his daughter shattered Allaird's restraint. "You sonofabitch! What are *you* doing here?"

"Watch your mouth; we have the guns." But all Knapheidt waggled was a forefinger.

The little guy, the one who looked like the brains of this sideshow if they had any, did wield a handgun. "Shaddup!" He pointed it at Clancy, not in menace but to indicate who he was talking to. "You the captain here? Ellery, is it?"

No point in glaring at Fleurine. Allaird said, "Captain Ellery Dawson cannot be with us at this time." Then, losing all semblance of formality, "What the hell do you *want*?"

Small Stuff nodded. "Now you're talking. We're taking a tour, see? Go through these Gates you got, one ship and then another, it's two years a jump, am I right? Well, I'm pushing for about ten years worth of that, then we go home and they can't touch us, the statute runs out."

His smile was pure sarcasm. "Any objections?"

Before Clancy could answer, a voice said "I see no problem." He turned to see Irina Tetzl come in, carrying something that resembled an ornate gun. But it couldn't be; there weren't any!

To no one in particular she announced, "From the intercom, I believe I understand what is necessary." Then, with apparent icy calm as Nathan Brandt loomed silently behind her, "Now to which ship would you prefer to go next?"

"Well . . ." The little nervy guy stuck his jaw out. "What's our options?"

"The ships are *Starfinder* and *Roamer* and—" Suddenly she seemed confused; she stared at the local Gates as if she'd never seen them before, then at Clancy, back to the Gates and again at Clancy, this time glaring at him. "No! I see what you are thinking, but you cannot unleash these persons on Eden colony. It is a fragile experiment, they are not prepared. You must not . . ."

Totally bewildered, Allaird tried not to gape.

"Hold it!" The little man worked up a smug grin. "Eden colony, huh? In there?" He pointed. "Tell me about it."

She set her lips primly, then said, "An unbalanced concept; you would not be comfortable. Barely the fiction of governmental structure. Also, the men outnumbered six or seven to one, by women; hardly an equitable arrangement. So you see . . ."

The smaller man laughed out loud. "We'll take it." The

swarthy-complexioned woman, Clancy noticed, gave him a look of pure hatred. He ignored her. "All right, let's get on." And waved his gun again; the gesture was becoming monotonous.

As the other four moved at Irina's gesture to the local Mouth, Carl Knapheidt said, "One thing, Azi." He lunged at Marnie. "This kid here, she comes along."

"Like hell!" Infuriated, Allaird forgot the guns. But Knapheidt already had the girl by the arm, pulling her with him into the Gate's operational area.

Bracing to dive in after Marnie no matter what, Clancy stopped at Irina Tetzl's overriding shout. She raised the pistol-grip object and toyed with its trigger, evoking a threatening howl that rose and fell, nerve-grating. She said, "I do not recognize the hostage principle. Release the girl, sir, and you may leave." Her grip tightened.

Carl turned and twisted, moving Marnie back and forth in front of him. "Ha! You can't get at me without hitting *her*."

"I do not need to; the small, bossy one is a better target."

"Now wait a minute!" the man Azi yelled; as the heavy object swung to point at him, he stood frozen.

"The matter is not negotiable." Tetzl's smile held pity. "If you cannot control your own people . . ." With the others seemingly paralyzed into deadlock, the gun thing wound up its scream. "Choose!"

"All right!" Frantically he jerked Marnie loose from Carl Knapheidt, pushed her out and away, then drew himself up and leveled his gun. It shook a little. "Now send us to Eden!"

"With pleasure," and Nicole activated the local Gate.

Unprecedented obtrusion into plenum-major of highly kinetic mass from previously disruptive dimension packet produces not merely pain but physical damage neither quickly nor easily restorable. Due to normal state of admixture, impacting causes injuries to be widely shared, spread among many.

It is determined that the mass, small in comparison to its destructive capability, obtruded while suffering such rapid change of point group loci as to escape the boundaries of dimensional overlap during the single moment between intrusion and withdrawal. Thus disruption is not confined, as previous effects have been, to point-groupings within extrusion itself.

The cause of such extreme kinesis remains inexplicable; a hypothesis arises, that such phenomena may be specific to the particular sub-plenum producing cross-dimensional interaction. Previous study has shown this grouping to be a normal array of paired vectors defining six directions in all. Divided equally, as expected, between spatial and chronal.

Unexpectedly, however, the sub-plenum proves to harbor development of volitional entities which exist unadmixed and lacking capacity for intercommunicative osmotic liaison.

All this from exostudy; to observe *within* the vector sub-set requires an unforeseen modification, deliberate limitation of a sensory extension to the dimensional packet in question. With some misgiving, decision accretes to essay such experiment.

"Fleurine said Old Iron Tits was needed," Irina said, "so I performed her as best I could remember. Was I credible?"

It wasn't exactly the word Clancy would have chosen, but he nodded anyway.

"Jeez!" said Fleurine Schadel. "All I was hoping was you had another of those dart spitters. And just zap 'em."

"And why Ellery?" Nicole asked.

"Hey, I asked if he was *awake*, didn't I? Figured you'd catch on, I had company that didn't know any better."

Arms around Marnie, Allaird made a puzzled scowl. "What kind of gun is that, anyway? I've never seen anything quite like it." And where could Irina have found the thing?

"Why, a cordless torquing wrench. Men such as those, I felt, would not recognize such a tool; a gun is what they would expect, so that is what they saw." She smiled. "I improvised, myself, these large gunsights of iridescent foil. Anodized."

"Well . . ." Words really did fail him. "Thanks."

"You are quite welcome. And now," said Irina Tetzl, "we must think of the details of the enclosure to be built here."

"A cage, yeah." Clancy nodded. "Let's don't forget the sign on the inside. To let the senator know it's not for *him*."

Having Gated a report to Earth, Allaird was spotting measurements on deck and bulkheads, showing Pete Larue where to cut away deck covering and begin welding plates in place, when the six men came charging into control, reasonably skillful on Velcro. Helmeted and goggled above bulky garments, they carried large bore handguns. "All right, freeze! Bandits and everybody else. Now, who belongs here and who doesn't?"

Oh bloody hell; straightening up, Clancy gestured toward the local Mouth. "I'm Clarence Allaird, captain. Your bandits are all safely in local Gate lag; we're setting up now for when they come out again. I'm afraid you've had your trip for nothing."

The man in front took off his goggles and pushed the helmet back. "Believe me, that's not bad news. We've got softnose slugs with only target loads, but the skivvy was, hit one piece of equipment by mistake and it's up on charges. What a way to run a manhunt." He put his hand out. "Mel Hobart."

"Welcome aboard, then. Would you all like something to eat before you Gate back? Least we can offer."

"That would be nice. So would getting out of these damn Impakt tunics. But, you're sure you don't want us to stick around, just in case?"

"For a month? Two extra years, Earth time? Besides, it could get a little crowded, and not much for you to do, waiting."

Advised that reassurance had already been sent to Earth, Hobart and the rest did have a meal, followed by a brief tour of major points of interest. Then, after much expression of mutual good wishes, they Gated home.

"Now," said Clancy, "maybe we can get back to work."

When would they realize, back on Earth, that Gate lag and time dilation tended to make rescue missions obsolete before they got here?

Never jinx your luck, though; Allaird crossed his fingers.

"Damn near pooped my pants, I guess you know," Wallin said, seated in the lounge and sipping coffee. "Came through the Gate expecting our usual cheery welcome, and here we're in a *cell*, lit up so we can't see for glare. Tell us a bit more, of what happened. And how this is supposed to work."

So Clancy told it, and Nicole took up the explanation. The marauders would have no choice. "They drop their weapons, their clothes, everything, down that slot into the bin outside the cage. The vidcams up in the corners cover their actions, and the glare keeps them from spotting the cameras."

"And bareass with no guns," the senator said, "you don't figure these goons to pose much of a problem."

"No." Clancy shook his head. "Though they might be able to damage the Tush, if they get panicky and try some shooting before they give up. We don't know just what could happen in that case; early tests along those lines were inconclusive, one way or another. So you'd better not use these Gates just now."

Wallin made a face. "You're saying we need to stay out here in ship's time, until after that bunch of hoods emerges?"

"Course not," Allaird said. "Any reason you shouldn't pop off to Earth for a few days, say hello and come back? By that time, all this will be over and done with."

"You know, it does sound good," said Maxine Durand.

"I'd like to check on something first," Wallin said. "I'll see you in a little while." A half hour later he returned, a bit flushed in the face. "All right. I just wanted to try out on the one-gee ring a little while, see how it felt. I guess I haven't got too much out of shape to hack it for a few days."

So after a night's sleep and some minor packing, the two Gated off.

"Let's see if I've got this straight," said Fleurine Schadel. "This guy, you really owe him the axe; you want to cut him too short to hang up. You'd like to know his soft spots."

Marnie nodded. She'd tried to find ways to ask Nicole, had come to realize Trish couldn't help her, and lacked the nerve to approach Irina Tetzl. But on the face of it, Fleurine knew a few things about getting one's own back. Thus, "What can I say, so he'll wish he'd never seen me in his life?"

"I don't know enough yet; what's he like?"

Carefully editing her story to tell much of Carl Knapheidt but next to nothing of the terror he'd put her through, Marnie prospected for information. Just a few more days now . . .

Chita Ruiz screamed. "Azi! How they *do* that?"

Snarling, Sarbo said, "Sonsabitches! Switched the Gate someway, sent us back. Wonder which slammer . . . ?"

Then Carl noticed. "Hey, we don't weigh anything. We're still in space." Which ship, he wondered? It didn't matter;

wherever they were, bare panels enclosed a small area containing only the single Gate. There was a slot, not quite two feet wide and maybe five inches high—but behind it, less than a foot away, lay more blank metal. Turk banged on the small door; on this side it had no knob or handle, and it rang solidly.

Lazslo cocked his automatic; Azi said, "Yeah, come on, everybody. Maybe we can blow ourselves a hole through."

"Wait." Carl put a hand on the little man's arm. "You want lead bouncing around? You'll shoot one of *us*, is what."

Sarbo nodded. "Awright, put it up, Laz. We gotta . . ."

From behind the metal came a voice. "Listen good, in there. If you want out, do what I say, do it now, and do nothing else."

First the guns, then the clothes. Sarbo railed, but there wasn't any choice; finally, cursing, he gave in. Carl was mildly surprised; Chita had better knockers than showed with clothes on.

She'd practically had to beg, but finally Allaird let Marnie stay for the bandits' ignominious release. He grumped more than a little. "It's not decent; they'll all be naked," and made dire hints that before he sent Carl Knapheidt back to Earth he just might want to pat him down flat like hamburger.

Ignoring that part, because arguing would only make him madder, Marnie said, "Sixth grade, we had a field trip to a nude beach; the only thing not decent was the shape some were in."

Under lowered brows he stared at her. "Why do you really want to be there?"

"I owe Carl something. And this is my last chance."

He looked even harder but didn't ask any more questions.

After Chauncey Ng retrieved the guns and clothing and so forth from the outside bin, he gave Allaird his choice of weapon to wield as power symbol. Clancy picked the big Mauser; he had no idea whether he could hit the broad side of a barn with it, and didn't care; the thing was for show, here, not to use.

Then with Edd Jarness covering from one side and Coyote Benjamin from the other, Ng opened the cage and motioned the five crestfallen raiders to come out. Seeing who they faced seemed to put them into something resembling shock.

A sorry bunch, thought Clancy. The two big muscle guys hadn't said a word and looked to share the IQ of iceberg lettuce. The little one was trying to convince himself he was still tough with no gun and no clothes. The woman would have been attractive if it weren't for her wholly feral expression.

And then there was Carl Knapheidt; Allaird put a lid on his feelings and said, "Make it march, commandos; you don't have to give the shoes back until we have you in Earthmouth." The smaller man protested, but Clancy simply waved the Mauser.

Coyote led the way. Corridor aft, right turn onto the transverse, and here we are. Allaird said, "Tell 'em your clothes will be along in a while." Maybe an hour, maybe a month; he hadn't really decided. The guns, no hurry at all. "Now get in there, settle toward the back, and toss the shoes out."

Those things done, Clancy stepped near Carl Knapheidt. "You know something, you sad sack of shit? I'd like nothing better than to kill you. Maybe twice."

"Clancy!" From behind him, Marnie's voice came urgent. "He's mine; remember?"

Now what was she planning? Nothing physical, certainly. He said, "Sure. Just don't make too much of a mess." And enjoyed watching Knapheidt's cheekbones burn red against suddenly pale skin. This was getting to be fun. And Nicole was primed to activate the Gate on his signal.

Stiff-legged, Marnie stalked up near the uneasy group. "Carl? Remember the bathroom?"

"Now look! I didn't do anything, I didn't hurt you, I—"

"Shut up." Spoken quietly. "Remember what you said?"

"No. No, I don't think so. What do you mean?"

She pointed. "Why do you call it a cobra, Carl? It's not even much of a worm."

Activate.

When the color flare died, Clancy said, "Marnie, whatever gave you the idea to say *that*?"

"Fleurine. I asked what's the worst I could do, and she said that'd pop him like a balloon. Do you think it did?"

"I wouldn't be surprised."

              *   *   *

Later that day, as Pete and Edd were dismantling the cage preparatory to restoring the deck covering, Allaird remembered to fish the clothes out of the bin and Gate them off.

It wasn't too much later. Maybe a week by Earth time.

XVI

"Voted you out? How the hell could they?" All these years, Bill Flynn thought, and Wallin was still as cantankerous as ever; the old boy hadn't changed a bit. Of course conserving time at twenty-five to one made a difference. Not to mention Gate lag.

Until Flynn mentioned the recent election, they'd been having a great reunion. Mara had never met the old senator, and neither she nor Bill knew Maxine Durand, but at the Flynns' summer place the four had been getting along very well.

But now Wallin's dander had risen and Flynn was hard put to explain. He tried anyway:

In the latest major election their party lost the presidency on a last-minute tabloid smear. "It was utterly ridiculous, but made a big splash and there was no time to refute it."

"But how did that reflect on *you*?"

Well, Flynn's term ended on an off year, "and you know how it is; you lose the presidency, it hurts the whole party. Then somebody brought up the Glen Springs raid again. Even though Allaird handled it beautifully and security's been tightened a lot, I was still the guy who was letting pirates take over our starships." He shrugged. "Some years it's just turnover time."

"So how does this leave the program?"

"Not too badly off. In the past two months I've pushed to fund everything I can as far ahead as possible, and irrevocably.

But Jocelyn Waymire, who'll be taking over my committee chair, she's a nitpicker—sees wasted money in every item she can't understand in a ship's report, and firmly believes in economizing by cutting everything straight across the board.''

Wallin's lips pursed. "Now where have we heard *that* before?"

But the evening was too fine to waste on talk of the long-ago president who was never sure whether he was still making a movie or not. "Forget it," said Flynn. "I still wield enough clout to wangle a liaison spot that gives me full access to agency workings, and some good backdoor leverage."

And then, "So tell me: you're fresh back from *Arrow*. Would you say for certain that Tetzl's dependable now?"

"She'd better be. It's *Starfinder* Maxine and I are joining, after Irina's brought the ship down through decel." He grinned. "From the report Allaird sent you, the woman still has plenty of moxie. Tricking the bandits into the local Gates, and all. I wish I'd been aboard, and out and around to see that."

"Be glad you weren't. People could have got killed."

"But nobody did. Bill, how about one more shot of that sour mash? And then I'm ready to get some sleep in. This gravity of yours can get tiring when a man's not used to it."

The next day Flynn saw them off to Glen Springs, on their way back to *Arrow*. A little over four months later he went down to the facility himself, to observe as armed guards took the unexpectedly unclad starship raiders into custody.

Still searching for a retort to Marnie, Carl was caught off balance as gravity jolted him to the floor. He got up slowly, looked at the welcoming committee as it broke into startled laughter, and decided that not counting prison, this might be the most humiliating moment of his life.

That distinction didn't hold for long, though; matters speedily got worse. Clothed hit-or-miss in a hurry, the group rode manacled to the nearest courthouse. The trial must have been scheduled in advance; the judge ran it like a railroad. Two days later Carl and Azi and Laszlo and Turk were checked into a high-security prison.

His first impression was, maybe this one wouldn't be too bad. On the third day, though, he was allowed out into the exercise yard, where a weathered hulk of a man walked over to him. "Well, if it ain't our old friend the Knapper. Slide's sure gonna be glad to see you."

Losing his front teeth hadn't made Jambones Tully any prettier.

As Clancy saw it, Irina Tetzl and Nathan Brandt deserved a notable sendoff to *Starfinder*. The party, put together with Nicole's help, came off quiet yet festive.

Any antagonism between Irina and Fleurine had been erased by the crisis with the would-be pirates. Now Schadel, allowing herself an extra couple of beers—well, it *was* her free day coming up—leaned across Eli Mainz to ask the other woman, "You're ready to tackle command again, then? You feel confident now, sure of yourself?"

For a moment Tetzl pursed her lips; then she said, "No. Not entirely. I do find myself with doubts. But . . ."

Shrugging, she smiled. "In a way, those uncertainties give me a new kind of confidence. Because I do *not* now have that feeling of omniscience which led me to excesses, I can put a firmer trust in my own judgment. And the unsureness makes it certain that I shall not become complacent."

Her words gave Clancy an unexpected jolt. He blinked, then found himself saying, "I'll be damned! Irina—I'd never thought it out myself, consciously, but that's pretty much how it feels. A little uncertainty *does* keep us on our tocs." And too bad it had never worked that way for Ellery Dawson. . . .

"I thank you for the validation."

To Allaird's other side, Brandt was caught between Phil Henning who was trying to explain a fine point about exciter tuning, and Fleurine who now turned to put an oar in, saying, "Look, you can analyze field vector phase lag 'til it comes out your ears. But all you really need to do, Nate, once you have the frequencies right, is fuzz your tuning a little. Broaden it. So on the scope the peak widens into two. Just barely, with a tiny dip between. Then if it drifts either way, that little bitty rise kicks in extra bias and centers you again. Got it?"

As Brandt nodded, Henning said, "That's all well and good, Fleurine, but it doesn't address the *reasons* we . . ."

The big man laughed. "I'll study the text readouts, Phil; I

really will. But meanwhile I appreciate knowing this short-cut."

A bit later, more than half the crew escorted the pair and their gear to the *Starfinder* Gate. Clancy said, "Pop us a message, will you, as soon as you've looked around and assessed conditions? So we'll know you got there okay—which you will, of course—and what the status is. And mainly, just to keep in touch."

"I shall."

Several handshakes later, color flared and faded. Schadel said, "I never thought I'd say this, but I'm going to miss that woman."

Bill Flynn's packet containing the news that he was soon to leave the Senate for a liaison post ". . . but don't worry; I'll still be in touch and help keep an eye on things," also brought word of the trial and sentencing of *Arrow*'s five "space pirates."

Marnie was curious but Clancy got it first, commenting to the group idling in the lounge as something caught his fancy. "One thing they never did figure out," he said. "Apparently the little guy fired his gun just as the Gate activated at Glen Springs. But the bullet didn't hit anything there—and it sure didn't spang off the bulkhead *here*."

"They're certain he did fire?" Nicole.

Fleurine Schadel looked up. "There *was* a kind of echo; remember, Ptiba? Just as we came around the corner?"

Mbente shook her head. "I don't recall it." Her eyes widened. "But there was smoke at the gun barrel! Only a wisp; I'd forgotten. It puzzled me for an instant, but then the little thug started making threats and I forgot all about it."

"So where'd the bullet go?" Marnie asked.

"Maybe Dr. Habegger's Aleph continuum," said Ptiba Mbente.

It was as good an answer as any.

"Gating tomorrow. See you soon," read Senator Wallin's message, and sure enough, about an hour later he and Durand arrived, to spend a final two weeks or so aboard before going on to *Starfinder*. "You wouldn't receive an arrival notice from Irina by then, would you?" he asked.

Visiting in captain's digs, Marnie watched while her father checked time rates on his terminal, then said, "No. The way you've planned it, you leave about the same time she gets there. Unless you want to reschedule."

"I don't think so. If everything goes right, they'll have been at destination something like nine months when we pop out. Time to assess the place, scout the planet if there is a good one, maybe have their macroGate up and running. Or if not . . ."

"That was never made clear in the news releases," Nicole said. "Do they simply leave all the control and residence configurations in thrust mode, go back to accel, and head for Point B?"

The old man shrugged. "What would be done about living arrangements, I'm not sure. But they'd still set up the shipshooter, the macroGate, so that later missions can leapfrog out with a big head start. And plant enough radio telescope satellites to make up an understudy to the Big Array, looking for other possible goal stars. They wouldn't have cranked up again yet, to go on to their own next-choice system—but Maxine and I can't afford to wait around for that option anyway."

He went silent, but now he'd roused Marnie's curiosity. "So what would you do then, sir?"

Wallin peered at her. "That could take some thinking." He turned to Clancy. "Is *Roamer*'s ETA in your files?"

Punching keys, after a moment Allaird shook his head. "No data here, to speak of. But we don't need it. I happen to remember, that ship's on a forty-two light-year jaunt. *Starfinder*'s is thirty-one. And ships go out every four years."

Except for *Nomad*, Marnie remembered. But it had lifted away on higher accel, to come close to regaining sked. Anyway . . .

"So," Clancy was saying, "*Roamer* reaches goal about fifteen years after *Starfinder* does. Earth time."

The senator was counting something on his fingers; then he nodded. "Besides a final jump to *Roamer* itself, we'd have only about ten more years to bypass, by means of Gate lag. If we wanted to go see what that group finds."

He stood. "Well, thanks for the talk. You know, when we Gate off to *Starfinder* I may get homesick for this ship."

And when they did leave, Marnie felt as though she were losing a favorite uncle.

He wouldn't be back, either. Not out of necessity, at least. A month after Wallin's departure, word came from *Starfinder*:

Arrived to find conversion for deceleration complete. Beginning that process immediately following final checks. From a half light-year out, prospects appear most favorable. Thank you and good wishes.

Irina Tetzl

The day following arrival of Tetzl's message marked the crew's first anniversary aboard *Arrow*. By ship's time, of course; at the anniversary party Clancy tried to avoid thinking of the quarter century that had passed on Earth.

Twenty-seven, if you included Gate time, he heard Edd Jarness saying. Fleurine Schadel laughed. "I'll see that and raise you seven. Good ol' cadre 1–A inGated nine months before *Starfinder* lifted out." Allaird missed Edd's comment, but Fleurine said, "Go ahead, look it up. But of course I sneaked in six more years Gate time than you have." Edd's turn to laugh.

As Marnie, playing some kind of anisotropic table game with Trish Pembrook, laughed also. Still nearly two months short of her thirteenth birthday, biologically speaking, while back home she'd be—what? Almost thirty-nine, for God's sake!

Clancy shuddered, then felt a wry amusement. If this were either of his two earlier assignments, the ones that fell through, he'd be done with his shipboard hitch and back on Earth with only (*only?*) a fourteen-year displacement. As was, though, he was roughly twenty-five light-years from Earth with another forty-five or so to go, which would have him inGating for decel in something like seven hundred days from now.

Well, minus the point-one light-year decel distance. And the twenty-five days before decel began. And—oh, the hell with it. The computer in his head was too beat for a good readout; when he had time, he'd check with the one that never tired.

Anyway, thirteen of the crew's original sixteen members were still here at first year's end; not too bad an average.

Young Trish was filling in well, and now Marnie was handling most of a normal adult crew member's load and seemed to feel good about it.

How Clancy Allaird felt was very damn lucky.

Marnie knew the older ship's fifteen Earthtime months of decel was only about eighteen days on *Arrow*, but an extra twelve elapsed before the *Starfinder* Tush brought another message.

Maxine and I lucked in, here. One world looks utterly glorious and another may be habitable under duress. We intend to stick around for a time and have notified Bill Flynn not to wait up. We thank you for all the hospitality. Look us up sometime.

                                                                    Wallin

Well, who knew? With the Gates and all, maybe she could, at that. But not right away. For now, her place was on *Arrow*.

What the Beaconsetters looked like made no real difference to anyone aboard; still, Marnie thought, it was interesting to view. Phil and Sybiljan dropped by the galley for a snack while she and Clancy were having breakfast; all agog, Phil began telling it. "We've kept fiddling with those signals, you know, just for fun. Well, we isolated a subcarrier in their overall emission package. Digitalized frequency shift with a quintary code—two positive values, two negative, plus zero shift. Anyway, the *pattern* looked like video."

"I thought we'd never solve the scanning protocol," Sybiljan put in, "but it's sort of a diagonal crosshatch, interlaced; not what you'd call efficient, but it's their choice. Anyway . . ."

"You want to come see?" Had Phil ever shown such eagerness?

In an instrument test room near control, the two showed off their findings. "The colors probably aren't anywhere near right," said Sybiljan. "If it's supposed to be color at all; first off, we tried the marker pulse groups as digital sound, but that didn't work, so . . ."

They all stared. The picture was oval. Behind the central

figure could be seen oblong shapes, reddish against a mud-colored background, that were probably electronic equipment of some kind; blinking lights seemed to be a universal necessity.

But that figure! More or less chartreuse with streaks of a clearer green, only a head and upper torso appeared, plus the extremity of one gesturing limb, divided into three stubby, flexible tendrils. There was no neck, only a widening of the head to the picture's bottom, and where that widening began, so did some sort of covering garment, grey and showing no texture.

And the head? "What *would* you call it?" Clancy asked.

Consensus was, a guppy. A great big guppy, with a high forehead and rudimentary antlers. The guppy mouth moved, and Marnie wondered what sounds it made, that they weren't hearing. "Are you sending a copy of this to Earth?" she asked.

"Wouldn't you imagine they've already figured it out?" Sybiljan said.

"So what?" said Clancy. "It can't hurt to let 'em know we're on the stick here, too." He grinned. "You two, I mean. I sign the reports, but this is strictly your brownie points."

Marnie hurried off to tell Trish Pembrook.

As near as Clancy could figure it, day four-twelve was Marnie's thirteenth birthday, biological. So far she was showing only hints of approaching physical maturity, mainly the rapid disappearance of puppy fat, revealing the good clean lines her face and body would carry in adulthood.

She said, when he hinted, that she didn't want any big party, so he and Nicole put on a family spread in their quarters. He put the word around, though, and when other people dropped by, two or three at a time, Nicole had party snacks to bring out. So before the evening was over, straddling a change of watch, Marnie got her good wishes from everyone and obviously enjoyed them.

That celebration coincided with another, less personal one. Word came that *Starfinder*'s macroGate had received its first loads from Earth: first a large supplies container held waiting in the huge Mouth area for Gate activation, and then the first personnel carrier to take an explorer team out to another world.

It all did seem to top off Marnie's shindig pretty well.

The next day, though, she came to Allaird's quarters holding a message sheet and looking solemn. "It's Celeste. She's dying, and wants to see me."

Dying? But it'd be four years, since that message was sent, before Marnie could get to Earth. So how . . . ?

"Gates. At the hospital." Of course. "They'll be putting her through twice. With some time between, to allow for me getting my things together and clearing away here if I need to. But Clancy . . ." She was troubled; he could see that.

"You don't have to go if you don't want to."

"Yes I do. Clancy—how old is Celeste now? I mean, when she sent this?"

He thought. "I'm not sure; I don't know if she ever told the truth about her age. But if she did . . ." Hmmm. "When you and I left Glen Springs, Marnie, she'd've been thirty-two by her own count. That's a bit over thirty years ago, but Celeste Gated twice. And then there's Gate lag on your message. So—call it fifty-six."

"But that's not old!"

"Does the message say why?" Why she was dying, he meant.

"Nothing I understand." She showed it to him; all it said was Eckhardt-Cray Syndrome and he'd never heard of it either.

He shook his head. "Well, if you feel you have to go, let's think about what's required. I'll give you a set of official orders to show at Glen Springs, to issue you an ID that reads Legally Adult; you'll need that. And an authorization card to draw on your service credit account. Now, your clothes are sure to be out of fashion . . ."

She didn't care about any of that; she just wanted one last family dinner and to be on her way. But she might later, so Clancy saw to it that she wouldn't be found wanting.

She didn't cry before inGating, but he damn near did.

Attempts at sensory observance within the offending dimensional array prove unavailing; previous measures in pursuit of preventive isolation render that sub-plenum relatively opaque. More rewarding are glimpses into the combined packet, basic sub-continuum plus intrusional overlap. But here, mass aggregrations in a state of continued obtrusion prove to be relatively simple nonvolitional matter structures; to study masses that may be of importance it is necessary to scan intrusions of only momentary nature. To this end, sensory apparati of only two dimensions are insinuated therein. Thus, basic patterns and operations of sub-plenar volitionals may be sensed both externally and internally, by mere surface-to-surface scan mode and without impinging on normal function.

One apparent threat proves to be less than first estimated. After many intrusions of mass objects of first and second order, suddenly masses of much greater magnitude transfer through expanded dimensionality. Unease results, until it is observed that loci groupings made capable, by whatever means, of emergence and withdrawal of such masses, invariably display obvious signs of imminent obtrusion. Given reasonable caution, they pose no risk.

Older, sure—blond hair grey at the roots, lined face bare of makeup, body thin under the hospital smock—but not deathly looking. Seeing Celeste in the chair, Marnie was reminded of all the heroines with Holo Stars' Disease; you knew they were dying because the story said so, but they never looked it. Still, though, "Hello, mama." As if Carl had never existed.

Celeste stared. "My God. You haven't changed at all." And then, "Aged, I mean. Oh, you're different. Grown-up, someway. Like you know what you're about, now. How long is it? For you?"

She didn't act like wanting a hug but she got one anyway. "A year, a little more. I just had my thirteenth birthday, bio."

"Bio?" Celeste shook her head; no matter. "Do you hate me, Marnie? Was I that bad a mother? Except for Carl. But I didn't mean—I never meant . . ." Her expression hardened. "And I fixed that bastard's wagon for you. I . . ."

Hearing what Celeste had done, Marnie reserved her own news of Carl for later. ". . . and I'd ditched him earlier, before I went out looking for you. Where the hell *were* you, anyway?"

Marnie told her; Celeste nodded. "I thought so. But I couldn't stay and wait. The warrant ran out, or something; you never can trust those damned lawyers."

She was nowhere near done talking; Marnie put her own questions on hold. "I'm so sorry. Carl, I never knew how bad he was. Let myself go dopehead, so you had to run, be stuck out in that crazy place instead of having a good life. Marnie . . ."

Crazy place? Good life? Suddenly Marnie realized: Carl was the best thing that ever happened to her! If not for him she'd have gone to her nice school and got a nice job and married some man maybe nice and maybe not, and by now she'd be sweating her own kids going wrong—and would never see much of *anything*.

"Mama. I'm fine. I love it on *Arrow*. Lately I stand watches like any regular crew member. We're crowding thirty light-years from Earth. I've seen—oh, I've seen so much! Even a flatscreen picture of some intelligent alien person; we don't know if he lives where the beam came from, but there he was." She considered. "Or maybe she."

Celeste blinked. "And that's what you want?"

Damn right! "Yes, mama." And now her own anxieties, that she'd stewed with all the way up here on the bullet train, needed venting. "Mama? How is it you're dying?" *You don't look it*.

"You tell me and we'll both know." Celeste's laugh was half cough. "It's something they don't understand much. Breakdowns in the central nervous system. I'm on a pacemaker already; pretty soon I'll need another gadget to tell me when to breathe. All anybody knows is, it happens to people who used too much of one kind of dope I got into when I was with Carl. The doctors think it kills immunity to a virus everybody has but normally it can't hurt you." She looked defiant. "Hell, nobody *told* me."

Then, plaintively, "I wonder if Carl got it too." So Marnie told of the raid on *Arrow*, the fiasco it had become. And Celeste laughed. "He couldn't get anything right if you tattooed the directions on him. Can't even stay out of jail."

Then she sobered. "I should talk. Marnie, you haven't asked what I've been doing. Or why. But I'll tell you anyway. You know, when I was a kid I had to know how to get mean, just to hold my own. Maybe I never learned to let loose of that. Well, for a while I did; when you were little I was nice, wasn't I?"

That much was true; even with the slutting around, Celeste had done a pretty good job of parenting. And until Carl and his drug hobby, none of the boyfriends had ever given Marnie any trouble. Swallowing a lump, she nodded, as her mother said, "I think maybe I used all my nice up, then; there couldn't have been a helluva whole lot of it. Tell Clancy I'm sorry; it was my fault and not his, but I couldn't let him know that so I hit first." Marnie had no idea what she was talking about. "After that I didn't really try too hard to pick decent men, not like they're all that easy to find anyway. One sludgebucket after another, Marnie. And finally one too many. When the grand jury caught up with Keith Rasmussen my name was on all the evidence papers. He'd say here sign this honey it's just routine. So I did two years upstate and that sonofabitch drew probation."

She sniffed. "I don't have the strength to get him myself. Or the time, probably. But I have money Keith never knew of. And neither did the grand jury, those sanctimonious pimps! I've set up a trust, for an agency to nose into everything he does and fink it in. Sooner or later . . ."

She must have sensed Marnie's withdrawal. She said, "Honey, that's just a part of my bankroll. Hey, you get the most of it. Wherever the hell you end up."

As if that mattered . . .

Marnie endured the rest of the afternoon, a dinner, and all evening with her mother. Then, with apologies, she fled. She felt very sorry for Celeste, and several times during the visit almost recaptured the love and warmth she'd felt throughout most of childhood. But then the older woman would say something, express so much hoarded venom, that Marnie was repelled.

It didn't help that she saw parallels between her mother and herself. With Celeste it had been a molesting stepbrother—or more than one? Marnie wasn't sure. Not the stepfather, though. Only when Celeste ran, she had no place to go. . . .

But right now, it was Marnie who had to get away. She promised she'd be back, so she'd keep that promise at least once before returning home to *Arrow*. But not right now.

Okay, who or what *did* she want to see? Not a whole lot. The hour or so she'd spent in one medium-sized city, sightseeing in the time between arriving by bullet train and catching a commuter hopper to Garnetsville where the hospital was, had made her uneasy. She wasn't sure whether people had changed or she just wasn't used to them any longer.

Nor they to her; right off the bat she could see she looked like a freak in today's company. Not only her clothes, either. Her hair, except for medium bangs, was a little past shoulder length these days; she wore it tied back at the nape. Whereas the apparent norm for girls in her own age group and even young adult females was asymmetrical, such as beginning stubbled at one side and tapering out to wind up with a long straight fall at the other.

And that was only one variation. Her own appearance drew not only stares but giggles. And at first, being unused to Earth gravity except for exercise sessions, she probably did look awkward in her movements. Standing or walking for very long still tended to tire her, somewhat.

Well, she didn't plan to be here long enough for any of this to really get to her; for the time being, let 'em snicker.

On Clancy's suggestion she'd obtained some addresses and phone numbers before leaving Glen Springs. Now, prior to departing Garnetsville, she began trying the numbers.

Estella Holms wasn't available; Marnie spoke greetings and good wishes into the answering machine, but could leave no number for a return call.

She hadn't looked closely when she collected her short list; now she realized that although a state line intervened, Ellery Dawson and Amalyn Tabard resided quite near Glen Springs. So she'd wait until she headed back there to make that call.

Considering the passage of time, Marnie hadn't been too optimistic of finding Anne Portaris still alive. What she did find, surprised her: a little more than two years earlier, Portaris had returned from a visit to the macroGate now positioned near Clancy's discovery Niflheim, and then Gated off with a research team for a tour of the Liij Environ. Which was to say, the portions modified for humans to inhabit, or where, suited against lethal alien atmosphere, they could safely venture. Marnie shook her head; here was one enterprising woman.

Were there any others, *not* on her list, she'd like to get in touch with? She thought back to school friends: Jeanne Russo for instance, or Natalie Londus? Then she shook her head. They'd be in their *forties*, for heaven's sake! Not that she had any prejudice against that age group—but how could grown women, with families of their own, relate to someone they'd known thirty years ago as children, who was *still* a child? They'd view her as some kind of weird specimen under glass. No, it wouldn't wash.

She wished she'd been able to locate Paula Trent. Sure, it had been something like twenty years since Paula left *Arrow*, and Marnie had had only a couple of brief notes from her. Still, though . . . But the records showed that several years ago Paula Trent had disappeared. By joining the Siblings of Devotion. Persons entering that cult not only changed their names; the group refused to provide any link between new identities and old. Bereft relatives and various governmental entities had essayed legal challenges, but since the Parenting Committee paid all debts of members when they entered, including tax liabilities, there wasn't much of a legal handle for the courts to turn.

Which left one name, a man she really wanted to meet but felt diffident, despite Clancy's reassurances, about approaching. Oh well. She shrugged and punched the number, located in a suburb of the nation's capital.

"Yes?" For the first time, the booth's screen lit. The woman pictured was somewhere in her sixties; good bones kept her handsome, and the soft shade of her brown hair looked natural whether it was or not.

"Hello; could I speak to Senator Flynn, please?"

"Why, yes. May I tell him who's calling?"

"I'm Marnie Allaird. Captain Clancy's daughter. I—"

The picture switched, to a man whose face bore lines more cheerful than not, and freckles that had faded to muddy tones. "So *you're* the gal all the rumpus was about. Back on Earth now, are you? For how long? Will you come see us?"

Well, yes. Sure. Of course. Not to mention, gladly.

". . . this *power* Captain Tetzl had," Marnie explained, "even when she was actually pretty much out of control. That part didn't show, you see." The Flynns wanted to know more about various happenings on *Arrow*; she found herself enjoying the spotlight and hoped she wasn't saying anything out of turn. "I only saw her that way for a few minutes, a couple of times—but wow!" And to the next question, "Really changed. Very able now, Clancy thinks, but not—not *imperious* any longer, if that's the right word."

Satisfied about Irina Tetzl, Senator Bill had other things on his mind. Fleurine Schadel, the Beacon system, the bandit raid: Marnie filled in details as best she could. Yes, Carl Knapheidt was the same man he'd met, the stepfather she'd fled (she didn't say why, because the details were none of anyone else's business), but the invasion of *Arrow* wasn't aimed at her; Carl was part of a gang of robbers using the Gates for a hideout. "Well, it didn't work. You should have seen Irina bluff all five of them with a cordless torque wrench!"

At dinner she got the impression that they thought starship crews lived on freezepak rations. Actually the charbroiled salmon, delicious though it was, would have been nothing out of the way for Pete Larue—but Marnie didn't say so.

After the meal, with some time left before she had to leave, Flynn was saying, "So my old mentor's going to settle down on Tetzl's Planet. You know, ever since the voters dumped me I've intended to Gate out somewhere, look around, see for myself what it's like on a ship and maybe a destination world."

His smile looked wistful. "But you see, I've never dared be gone four years; it took me nearly two Senate terms to nag Jocie Waymire into shape where I can trust her not to hamstring the starship program." He sighed. "What do you think, Mara? Would you like a little tour? Young Scott could handle my desk for a time—permanently if need be."

The woman smiled. "Bill, I thought you'd never ask."

Back at Glen Springs, next morning Marnie wrote a message for Clancy, to the effect that she'd be Gating in two days and that the Flynns would accompany her, to visit on *Arrow* for a bit before going on to see Senator Wallin. Which would allow him a couple of hours to have the VIP suite put in shape for guests.

On the phone, Amalyn Tabard sounded glad to hear from her. ". . . meet you at the depot and we'll have dinner somewhere nice." So Marnie spent the middle of the day nosing around the facility, especially the Gates room, and asking questions. Also she took some time browsing in shops outside the base, picking up a few gifts to take back: for Clancy a watch with an auxiliary scale that could be set to keep an approximation of Earth's calendar (if vee stayed relatively constant), a bracelet for Nicole, and a geometric puzzle that should keep Trish busy for a while.

The minicab got her to the train in plenty of time—not a bullet, this one, but a stop-and-go commuter run. At the station it took a moment to recognize Amalyn; her hair, now with a few grey streaks, sprang rebellious as ever but wasn't long enough to do much about it. Her face hadn't aged especially, though.

After the hugs, Marnie looked around. Tabard said, "Ellery couldn't make it. He . . ." Then she shook her head. "He *wouldn't* come; he won't see anyone from the ship. Here in the administrative group he's achieved a respectably high position; you'd think he could take pride in that. But . . . oh come on, Marnie. Let's go have some tea, and talk."

So Marnie found herself telling some of the same stories she had the day before. Knowing most of the people involved, Amalyn tended to ask different questions, but still it felt more like a recital than not. Later, after a tour of the pleasant suburban area in Amalyn's minicar, they had dinner, reminiscing in general about old times aboard ship. Then, after a pause, Tabard said, "I'm thinking of Gating out. To the colony, maybe, if they say I'm too old to work a drive room." And before Marnie could ask, which she didn't intend to do, "With Ellery or without him."

"Well, I guess you have to make up your own mind." But after that, Marnie couldn't put much steam behind her request for Amalyn to say hello to Ellery from her ". . . and, and everybody."

Slow trains weren't ideal for sleeping, but that was Marnie's easiest routing back up to Garnetsville so she rode one anyway. A hotel near the hospital included a wing of minimal cubicles, bunk and bath, catering to hospital visitors at hourly rates; she checked in at five a.m. and topped off her sleep quota before making the promised return visit to Celeste.

The trouble was, they'd said everything that needed saying; now they couldn't find anything in common. Celeste plain wasn't interested in *Arrow*; she'd been there and the memory was bitter. And her own reminiscences, rambling and hard to follow, all dealt with hope and betrayal. Worse, in many instances it seemed obvious to Marnie that her mother had been the offending party, but in Celeste's eyes all blame lay elsewhere, now and forever.

Though to be fair, at least half the time she was probably right; Marnie couldn't help wondering how she herself would have turned out, given the bad start life had handed Celeste. But the sheer mass of resentment began to overload her own feelings.

Lunch, before Celeste got caught up in her litany of grievance, wasn't too bad. And Marnie stuck it out through most of the afternoon. But when Celeste mentioned staying for dinner and Marnie realized the meal was two hours distant, she said, "Oh, I'm sorry; I *have* to catch the next hopper." Looking at her mother, Marnie sighed. "Mama, I wish I could stay . . ."

"No you don't; you don't like me and why should you? I'm not anybody you'd want to know." For a moment Marnie saw Celeste shrink from the truth inside her; then she rallied. "Thanks for coming, though; it's good to see you're turning out all right. Even if it is taking you hell and forever to get past puberty!"

"Mama, I—I *did* love you," was the best Marnie could do. Good-byes said, she left to catch the hopper and then connect with the bullet train. She was heartily glad to get back to Casual quarters at Glen Springs, happier yet to rise the next day, have breakfast, meet the Flynns who arrived when they'd said they would, and all inGate together.

Planar sensory scanning of sub-continuum's volitionals during obtrusion gives rise to puzzlement: similarities and differences alike resist categorizing, yet to build any semblance of understanding, such knowledge is requisite. A serendipitous mode of investigation opens when one volitional which has been studied earlier obtrudes another time. In the interest of thoroughness, redundant scans are undertaken before withdrawal is allowed; microstructure and responsive patterns are templated at extreme detail. In result, sensory access to the sub-plenum appears feasible; even interaction may be attempted.

In that event, however, preparation must be extensive.

"Well, where the hell *is* she?" Clancy's initial shock at how much Bill Flynn had aged was washed away by frantic fear. "You sure she didn't step out at the last minute?"

"Couldn't have. At least, I don't see how." Shaking his head, Flynn seemed dazed. "She was standing between Mara and me, arm in arm." Mrs. Flynn—Clancy hadn't met her before—nodded in agreement. "And all that color flared up," Bill continued. "I'd seen it before, of course, but not from the inside. And then . . ."

His shrug denoted pure mystification. "Here we were, and Marnie wasn't. Clancy, we just don't *know*."

And that's how it stood. Query to Earth meant a two-month delay, but Allaird sent one anyway. While waiting, hoping Marnie *had* left the Gate before activation, a brief holdup inGating for some unknown but valid reason, and would arrive soon.

But she didn't. Mail came from Earth, and miscellaneous supplies, but no Marnie.

So a time that should have been pleasant, filled with good reminiscences, ran tense and anxious. Until Bill and Mara Flynn, mouthing sincerely polite words but with obvious unease, Gated off to *Starfinder* and the planet named for Irina Tetzl.

Another three bad weeks passed before Marnie outGated.

When the colors rose up, something powerful flickered through Marnie. Like a convulsive shudder. When the hues faded, and gravity with them, the Flynns were gone; she stepped out of the Gate to find herself standing alone. In moments Clancy, followed by Nicole, came striding full bore along the corridor from control; he looked furious about something.

What . . . ?

"Where the hell have you been? Two *years* . . ."

Moving away from the Gate recess, she shook her head. "The Flynns. Senator Bill, and Mara. Where . . . ?"

He came to hug her then, but still sounded angry. "You're

saying you were with them? They appeared right on schedule, a month ago. Two years, by Earth time. They've gone on, to *Starfinder*. Marnie—what happened?"

Two extra years? She'd been in the Gates for double the usual lag time? Half-dazed, Marnie tried to answer her father's question. "I don't know. Except that this time, Gating, I *felt* something. That's never happened before; not to me, anyway."

"Nor to me. What was it like?" It was Nicole's turn for embrace; her voice carried curiosity, not accusation.

A chill, running all through her? A jolt of electricity, like when she was ten and her study lamp shorted to its metal base? Neither one fit exactly, but they were the best comparisons Marnie could think of.

With only puzzlement in his face now, Allaird asked, "Could the *Gate* have screwed up some way?"

Nicole frowned. "I can't think how. Clancy, the program's been Gating people—and things, too—on and off ships for over forty years now. Not to mention all the other applications, on or near Earth. And there's *never* been a malfunction, let alone one like this, doubling the normal Gate lag." She gestured, throwing up her hands. "I have absolutely no idea what could have gone wrong. All we can do is log every Gating carefully and see if it happens again."

"I guess. Well, I'll advise Earth, for what that's worth. Wallin and the Flynns, too, while I'm at it." He put an arm around Marnie's shoulder. "Then we'll have to see what's in the larder, that'll fill in for fatted calf."

Still confused, Marnie settled for being glad to be home.

Confusion came from other sources, too. Clancy and Nicole, apparently, had kept the mystery of Marnie's disappearance pretty much to themselves and the Flynns. A few others knew, but the rest seemed to think she'd simply stayed on Earth longer than expected—and at twenty-five to one, wondered that she hadn't changed more.

Unsure of what she should or shouldn't say, Marnie tended to answer direct questions truthfully but to pass off casual comments with noncommittal answers; in consequence, it seemed that several contradictory versions of her late arrival were in circulation.

Well, she wasn't going to post a bulletin. Things would just
have to sort themselves out.

She did take pains to give Trish Pembrook the true story—
and then regretted it, because Trish was fascinated; questions
kept coming, long after Marnie had run out of answers. Finally
she said, "That's all I *know*, Trish. Let it go."

Once again she had the anomaly of having been away only
briefly from people who hadn't seen her for much longer. And
once more, also, the strangeness wore off quickly.

The routine of standing regular watches helped, but it was
several days before she remembered to hand out her homecoming gifts. Which were gratifyingly well received.

XVII

As things settled down better, Marnie thought to report on
her other contacts—or lack of them—back on Earth.
"Estella was listed, and her machine message didn't mention
anyone but her, so I guess she lives alone." She'd intended
to try again, but somehow forgot. "And Anne Portaris . . . you
can't believe . . ."

"Yes we can," Nicole said. "We got a packet from her."
And Marnie stared at pictures of the alien Liij in company
with suited humans, including Anne, or sometimes in the human areas and wearing breathing masks themselves. "She's
been around—skipped at least twenty Earth years, Gating back
and forth." So she'd be a *lot* younger than Marnie had
thought.

"And so Paula's disappeared into a cult," Allaird commented, "and Ellery into a mental hole and pulled it in after
him. You think Amalyn'll Gate out by herself?"

"If he won't go with her," said Marnie, shrugging. "Like I said, I didn't see him at all."

With everyone brought up to date, Marnie headed out to report for galley duty.

One unwelcome disclosure came later. With all the other hassle, no one remembered to tell Marnie she'd received mail while in Gate lag; only by accident did she find several items in a lower, otherwise empty drawer of her desk. One came from Garnetsville, and it should have been no surprise to open it and find notification of the death of Ada Celeste Rasmussen, a little over three years after Marnie had last seen her.

Yet somehow the news caught Marnie off guard. So did the fact that it made her cry. Not for long, and perhaps not for the death itself; she cried, more likely, for the life her mother had lived. Maybe for the good fortune Marnie had had, that Celeste had been denied. And since that was none of Marnie's own doing, her grief purged itself more easily than first seemed possible.

As good as her word, Celeste had left Marnie a considerable sum of money. What good it would do her, she had no idea, but at the computer she wrote a letter of acknowledgment to Lawrence Crane, the attorney named as executor and trustee of Celeste's will. At least her mother had dumped Maurice Fitzhugh.

For no reason she could pin down, Marnie's next thought was of Carl Knapheidt—and what she'd realized, in Celeste's hospital room, about his true effect on her own life. Impulsively she composed another letter.

Carl Knapheidt:

You didn't intend to, but you made me run away to the best place I could possibly be. Now that I know this, I don't hate you any more. I forgive you and I hope that when you get out of prison if you aren't already, you don't do anything to get sent back.

Margaret C. Allaird

Since she had no idea where to send it, she pulled up the earlier letter and added a postscript to Mr. Crane, asking him to locate Knapheidt and arrange delivery of the sealed enclosure.

Before sending any of it she showed both items, along with the word of Celeste's dying, to Clancy and Nicole. The note to Carl sent Clancy's eyebrows up, then he grunted; Marnie didn't actually see anything, but guessed that Nicole had jabbed an elbow to his ribs. As to Celeste, both made consoling comments, but Marnie shook her head. ''I've cried already; thanks.''

''Sure,'' Clancy said, one arm around her. ''Let's all have dinner together, okay? In—uh—about two hours?''

''Fine,'' said Marnie. ''I can get hungry by then.''

''I'll see what Pete has in, that's special,'' Nicole added.

Two months later came word from Lawrence Crane. Marnie's letter had been hand-delivered to Carl Knapheidt at a downscale retirement home; family money or not, apparently he was still consistently on the cheap. He was at the time in his third year of parole and not in much of a position to break it, due to inmate-inflicted injuries suffered during his second incarceration. Crane's letter concluded: ''He read the letter in our representative's presence and rather vehemently rejected the opportunity to reply. I must decline to quote him directly.''

Yeah. I bet. . . . Well, she'd done *her* part.

Over the six months following Marnie's arrival Allaird found no evidence of further Gate malfunctions; finally he had to file her delayed emergence in the corner of his mind where nagging mysteries defied total forgetting.

Shipboard routine ran smoothly; velocity and position checks maintained their normal libration around the ideal nominal conditions of constant vee and stable time ratio, and if crew members had any personal problems they kept them under control. Or to themselves, at least; Clancy would settle for that, any time.

The only event of general note came close to midway of the fourth of those months: day 603, in fact. In the *Roamer* Tush appeared a brief message announcing that ship's approach, after decel, to its destination system. Allaird didn't recognize the captain's name and didn't expect to; this relief cadre would have matured more than a generation past his own time. What he found interesting was that time lapse sensor scans during the decel approach had located several planets, although orbital distances hadn't yet been pinned down too well. *Stay tuned . . .*

Arrow was now traversing a region of space in which the stellar population was on the skinny side; since passing the system that greeted visitors with space mines, the ship had come no nearer than several light-years to any but very dim stars, and only two of those. "Not much chance of planets," said Sybiljan Baynor. Nor enough high-energy radiation at such luminosities, Clancy gathered, to catalyze organic reactions in the seas those nonexistent planets probably wouldn't have, anyway.

So he wasn't too surprised when no ships or beacons evidenced themselves. Nor disappointed, either. A little peace and quiet suited him and Nicole just fine.

An hour before her next watch, Marnie's alarm brought her awake from vague, uneasy dreaming. As she sat up, the blurred, rasping voice from her dream—a familiar one, it seemed to be, but somehow distorted—still droned at her.

Marnie shook her head. This was a real sound, not a dream. But where did it come from? Her sound system was turned off, and besides, the hoarse murmur didn't come from that direction. And it wasn't the intercom, either. She brought the lighting up; the voice ceased, and at the same time she saw something unfamiliar, sitting atop a chest of drawers.

No, not just sitting. Emerging, swelling up. As she stared the bulge grew, forming itself into a sort of bust: crude at first, then with features differentiating, refining themselves in shape and color and texture, into a neck supporting a head.

Her head.

A forlorn shred of common sense insisted she was still dreaming; at the same time her critical faculty rendered judgments. The hair wasn't real; that part was actually a solid mass, contoured and colored to look like hair. Why the illusion failed, Marnie wasn't quite sure. But it did.

The eyes stared blankly; the lips, slightly parted, did not move. Not even when, quite clearly now, they spoke to her.

In a pretty close match to her own voice.

* * *

With a string of polysyllables, some few making recognizable words, the approximation of Marnie's voice went on for
perhaps a minute. Then it paused, waiting.

"What *are* you?" Talking to some kind of plastic construct,
was she? Marnie shook her head; as the simulacrum mimicked
the movement, she had a thought. A very wild one, not just
off the wall but past any edge she could imagine. "Was it
you, that messed with me during Gate lag?" Well, one of the
words she thought she'd recognized, was "dimensions . . ."

No answer; try again. "Where are you from?" All right so
this was crazy; it was also *happening*, and not threatening her,
so why gootz out? Unresponsive, the head-thing kept silent.

Actually, only one question mattered. "What do you
want?"

The answer came as unintelligible gibberish, with only occasional recognizable words or phrases. ". . . volitional . . . extrusion . . . sub-continuum . . . excess kinesis . . ." Marnie
shook her head. "No! Try to make sense!" Because she was
pretty sure this was real. Which meant she wasn't crazy, and
whatever was happening here, it had to be important.

So she repeated, "What is it you *want*?"

Employment of a structural simulation of subject volitional,
including samplings of its primary communication mode,
evokes no meaningful content from it. At next, then, surface-
dimension sensors make insertion, to within the volitional itself. By adjustment, these may achieve response at nearness,
in this sub-plenum so lacking of overall contiguity.

A sort of gauzy film, barely visible, reached from the
strange head to her own. Again, as when she Gated from
Earth, a great chilling shudder struck through her. First came
the wordless conviction that indeed she'd had previous contact
with whatever this was. Then, over and through the droning,
enigmatic tones, her mind perceived word sequences that
seemed to hesitate and then form—or else dissipate before she
could comprehend.

Still more confused than frightened, she did her best to follow. All right; the context seemed to be, why didn't she stay
in her own space instead of invading *its* space? So this mental
ventriloquist dummy was from the Aleph-plenum, sure

enough; had to be. "We don't mean to. It's how we get someplace fast; we didn't know you were there."

The same question package reran several times but never
quite the same. So Marnie also varied her answers, phrasing
the idea as many different ways as she could devise. Then she
thought to visualize what she meant; she brought into recall
an illustration she'd seen: people inGating, passing through a
vaguely depicted interspace and emerging at the far end.

Finally the head nodded. How did it know to do that? The
same way it mimicked her looks or voice; it just did, was all.

Then the questions changed—not only content but tone.
More urgently, it asked of something that had—emerged? im-
pinged? broken free? run loose?—and caused much harm.
Only once, apparently, but the creature(?) seemed highly concerned about it. Wanted to know why, how, for what reason.
And if it would happen again, keep on happening, continue
from this beginning. Overtones of anger, here. And threat—
but a threat totally unclear, incomprehensible. So she tried to
ignore that part, to concentrate on what this was all *about*.

Content of response cannot be adjudicated in full certainty;
while the sensory projection is designed, from scannings of
the volitionals' own operational sequencing processes, to provide interface between disparate concept configurations and to
operate at sub-continuum chronal rate, accuracy of transposi-
tional mode can be assessed only by later analysis and behav-
ioral result.

Initial exchange gives moderate basis for encouragement.

Why it took her so long to understand, she couldn't say;
when she did, the answer was obvious. The damned bullet,
fired by Carl Knapheidt's boss bandit; it wasn't here *or* at Glen
Springs. Ptiba had guessed Aleph-plenum; apparently she was
right. Marnie tried to explain; it was an accident, mistake,
error. Trying to visualize something in aid of meaning but
without much luck. Anyway: it was not on purpose (in fact,
she wasn't sure the precise timing *could* be achieved on purpose, but that idea was too complex to convey here). Not
meant, not intended. Not to be repeated, won't happen again,
once and once only. Apology, sorry, regret, grief (well, that
was a little strong, but still on the right spectrum). And . . .

She wasn't sure whether the chime came from the door or the intercom until she heard Gretel Aaberg's voice. "Marnie? It is your time to be here for watch. You are all right?"

She'd been talking with this thing for an *hour*? And until now, hadn't noticed hunger rising. "I'm sorry. I—I'll be there in a few—as soon as I can, I mean." Because the chilly shudder came again; her intent to move somehow blocked itself.

She cut the circuit. "Look—I *have* to go. If I don't . . ." No change; she tried visualizing again. "People will come busting in here." Clancy, red-faced and furious, waving—oh, inspiration!—a great big *gun*. Oops, maybe that wasn't a good idea after all; she'd said the bullet was a one-time accident. Deleting the gun from her imagining, instead she gave her father huge fists and a set of fangs.

So when the film withdrew, and she looked around and saw him entering in person, for a second it jolted her that he seemed quite his normal self.

Marnie didn't answer the door. But Allaird could hear her talking to someone, so being in a hurry he barged right in. And then didn't see anyone else here. "What's going on?"

Her voice seemed to come from two places at once and neither made sense; she herself stammered and the other source uttered a string of nonsense syllables. Looking for that one, on the dresser he spotted a fairly lifelike bust. Something new; if she'd brought it back from Earth, why hadn't he seen it before?

The head turned to face him; he recognized his daughter's likeness. "Hey—not bad!" A *clever* toy.

As he walked over for a closer look, Marnie said, "No! Wait!" but he'd already reached it. For a moment he touched a surface that tingled like something vibrating at high frequency; then, under his direct and sober gaze, the bust begin to shrink. Oddly, the neck dwindled to nothing, leaving the head floating above a bulge of the surface below, each diminishing at a deliberate rate until both vanished altogether.

"What the hell . . . ?"

Her look wasn't exactly accusatory but it came close. She took a deep breath. "Clancy—you're going to have trouble believing this. Because I can't quite swallow it myself."

* * *

Withdrawal at advent of second volitional was itself of non-voluntary response mode and is deemed unfortunate. Yet exhaustive scrutiny of experimental results may be of utility at this chronal juncture; since action may not be undone, it must be accepted as though intended. Advisability of similar future experiment is reviewed; necessities govern decision.

Partial replication of the volitional successfully drew and held attention. Earlier scannings are now studied more thoroughly; perhaps a more ambitious effort may prove superior in accrual of information and restraint on volitionals' actions. To this end, communications exchanged are subjected to examination and analysis; subsequent attempts must be given more accuracy.

Successive problems from this dimensional sector, measures taken in alleviation, and nowtime status: all are reviewed from beginning, and evaluated. Adjustments have been made to accommodate both momentary and continuing intrusions from this troublesome sub-plenum into contiguous vector grouping, and it has been shown that the degree of its spatial-chronal curvature narrowly obviates any true peril from reverse chronal impulses. Advent of greater-order masses, first seen as danger, proves to be only a minor disturbing factor. But cessation of latest infringement, the loosing of high-kinesis mass outside the boundaries of artificially produced fields within the delineated combination of sub-plena, must depend on agreed restraint by the volitionals themselves.

The one approached seemed comprehending, yet among the noncontiguous, how can any one have decisive control over actions of many? Should adverse demonstration be required to obtain the necessary concurrence of all, unfortunate for the volitionals.

"Swelled up out of the furniture and tried to talk with me; I *told* you. Then when Clancy came in, it went away." She'd told about the communication, too, what she thought she understood of it, over and over. But the group—most of the crew, gathered in the lounge now—kept on asking questions until, on balance, she'd just as soon be talking with the golem again!

"But didn't go back the same way," Edd Jarness put in. "Wasn't that what you said, Clancy?"

Allaird nodded. "I didn't see it come up. But leaving, when the head got small it just shrank in place, not connected to anything. I can't see how . . ."

"I can." Trish Pembrook stood beside an upholstered chair; from behind it she reached a hand up. "Watch." As she lowered the hand, first her wrist went out of sight, then the palm. With only her fingertips showing above the chair back, she paused and wiggled them. "See? No visible connection."

Allaird snorted a quick laugh. "Okay. Ptiba, Marnie says you called it right about the bullet; apparently it raised hell in Aleph and these things are mad about it. Understandably."

"I *told* it, that was an accident. And seems to me the timing'd be so touchy it couldn't be done on purpose, but I don't think I could have explained that to the . . . whatever it was. Course, I don't know how much it understood, of what I did say."

"Yeah," said Clancy. "And that worries me. Look; I'm going to hand Earth a full report on all these anomalies. Your double Gate lag, Marnie, and then this—this *apparition* we saw. Or whatever we want to call it."

"Alephant," said Trish.

Clancy's brows pulled down as he peered at her. "What?"

"Inhabitant of the Aleph continuum. Alephant. Why not?"

Allaird shrugged. "Why not indeed?" But Marnie bet herself he wouldn't use the term in his report.

She lost.

What with the Alephant mystery, Allaird got behind on reading his mail. It was Nicole, when he came to relieve her from watch, who jumped him about it. "You could at least check out the dispatches from *Roamer*."

Yeah sure; feeling harassed and realizing he shouldn't, Clancy said, "You're right; pass 'em over."

He read into the document a couple of pages, then shook his head. "They say it looks as if all three of the Triad Worlds lie in the star's habitable zone. Now how can that be? Orbits far enough apart not to interfere with each other, you'd think the incident radiation energy differences have to be prohibitive. Seems to me it'd be hard to place even two, that would have water consistently in the liquid phase."

He looked further along in the paper; maybe *Roamer*'s destination was a multiple star system with tight spacing. "Don't they say anywhere in here, what the layout is?"

Nicole shrugged. "That must be in an earlier report, but I don't find it anywhere. We could ask."

"Maybe I will. Okay, the board's clear; you're relieved. See you when I get off here?"

"Right." She left. After checking sensor logs, then finding nothing urgent in the line of ship's functions or personnel problems, Allaird called up graphic mode on a side screen and began trying to work out a planetary system, configured around a reasonably durable sun, that would accommodate three worlds in a habitable temperature range.

He didn't have much luck with it.

As acting chief of the Habegger Memorial Labs at Gayle Tech, Dr. Alynn Hastings took her work seriously. Now she reread the summary of her researchers' reply to a report from Captain Clarence Allaird, aboard *Arrow*, detailing certain anomalies with regard to Habgates and the Aleph continuum.

It began fairly well, she thought. ". . . find no reason why, if one quantum of time in 'Aleph' approximates two Earth years, our Gatings should uniformly match that continuum's quantum points. But this caveat assumes that time quanta throughout an entire universe are always 'in step.' Such an assumption is not necessarily valid. More probably, the advent of matter from our universe into theirs initiates a uniform time quantum step within the bounds it occupies. Experimental data support . . ."

She skipped ahead. Comment on the young Allaird woman's inexplicable doubled Gate lag steered clear of the kind of bold speculation Hastings liked to see, the sort that often led to unsuspected truths; instead, it waffled.

She checked the names appended to that section; Moss and Krueger definitely needed spinal transplants. So did the team assigned to derive some sort of theoretical basis for the strange "visitation" related by Allairds junior and senior. Granted, that group had little to go on; still, something other than "insufficient data for speculation" would have been nice. . . .

All right, on to the bullet thing. Although enjoined from re-creating the ballistic situation, Grant Hume had done a number of experiments with local-return Gates; what did he say here?

". . . exact boundaries of the Gate effect having never been sharply defined by previous experiments, several approaches . . ."

Yes, all right—but most of them didn't work. Or didn't prove anything. The color flares foiled any attempt at catching on camera the cutoff point of, for instance, a jet of liquid spurting from within the Gate. Colored smoke was useless because the air in the Gate recess didn't go anywhere anyway. (*Why?* Even after decades of usage, there was a lot nobody knew about Habgates.) And . . . grumbling, she set several more sheets aside, before she saw something interesting.

One of Hume's assistants had conceived a new line of attack. Slim rods of various materials had been utilized: wood, plastics, numerous metals as well as nonmetallic compounds, each extending from the Gate's surrounding inner surface and reaching toward a central point, the lot arranged in a dense, uniform pattern. Further, from a framework facing the Gate recess a similar pattern of rods also extended into the space under study.

A picture taken before Gate activation could have been labeled "Porcupine Hollow." The After pic was quite different. Inside the recess, floor and curved shell alike showed every rod, regardless of its composition, sheared off cleanly at the surface delineated by the tips of the Gate's activating circuit elements, arranged in the usual array of interlocking polyhedra.

No surprise there. But the rods reaching into the Gate from its open front told another story. Those truncated ends defined no smooth surface, but a randomly wavering boundary. And not all stubs were neatly cut; some ends featured a ragged, eroded look. "In other words," Hastings mused, "without a physically enforced boundary, Gate fields tend to waver a bit."

Skipping to the report's final page, she shook her head. No definitive summary, just more hedging. Though the conclusion to be drawn was clear enough. Frowning, she added a few lines herself, wielding her stylus to print in letters large and bold.

"SINCE THE UNBOUNDED FIELD AT THE OPEN FRONT OF A HABEGGER GATE IS NEITHER STEADY NOR PREDICTABLE IN ITS EXTENT,

THE EXPECTANCY OF AN OBJECT ESCAPING AT HIGH VELOCITY DURING A GATING CANNOT BE CALCULATED."
ALYNN HASTINGS, D.SC., HABEGGER LABS

It probably wasn't what Captain Clarence Allaird wanted to see, but he'd simply have to make do with it.

The first few days after being startled by her arcane visitor, Marnie endured a mild case of the jumps. When nothing more of that sort happened, gradually she felt at ease again.

Not that she was ever frightened; it wasn't that kind of experience. Just on edge a little, a case of "what next?" Two months later, her unease long past, she sat with her family in captain's digs while Clancy quoted parts of the report from Earth. It wasn't exactly worth the wait, and he said so.

"You have to realize," Nicole put in, "we didn't give them a lot to go on, really. And they did devise some ingenious tests, investigating the projectile problem."

"With no answers." Allaird wasn't mollified. "If this Dr. Hastings hadn't put her note on the end, I could still be searching through all those pages. Trying to find out whether there might be some kind of answer in there *some*where."

"Well, she did do that much, at least."

Clancy grinned at his shipwife. "I know. I'll send her a thank-you note, too. Her personally, not the Labs crew." He paused. "Maybe that Hume guy, too. He and his people seem to have done a lot of work, even if he didn't have the nerve to say out loud that it adds up pretty close to zero."

Disappointed by the short shrift given her own personal experience with the Alephant, Marnie said, "I have something for the gootz who wondered if our family has problems with hallucinations." Clancy's brows lifted. "Ask him if the closed mind is dominant or recessive in his."

It got her a pretty good laugh, at that.

Coming off watch, Allaird woke Nicole when he entered quarters; then he set up the coffeemaker. By the time he'd showered she was fully alert and fit to talk with. "I think I know how those Triad Worlds work,'' he told her. ''Not all the way, but mostly.''

''Well, that's nice,'' Nicole said. ''Do you get a prize?''

Repartee aside, though, he knew she did have some interest in the puzzle. ''Latest report still doesn't spell it out,'' he said, glopping up a fresh piece of toast with three kinds of jam, ''but we detectives know how to work with clues. Okay, there can't be even two independent orbits in the star's habitable zone, let alone three. But there's a *big* momma rolling around that track. So either two of the Triad are moons of the major rock—maybe tide-locked and leapfrogging—and the third's in Trojan position sixty degrees off, or the other way around.''

''Other way? Oh—a single moon, and the pair riding in the Trojan slot. But why can't you tell which?''

He handed her the readout sheet. ''Because the guy who wrote this thing probably composes tax forms for a living.''

After a moment she nodded. ''Or bank loan contracts.''

Clancy was going to expand on the possibilities of the Triad system when the intercom signaled. ''Yes? Allaird here.''

''Clancy?'' It was Marnie. ''Could we talk a little? I mean, is this a good time?''

He looked to Nicole; she nodded. ''Sure. Come on over.''

''. . . all of a sudden it feels so final,'' Marnie was saying. ''Because of Trish, really. She just got word her father's dead. See, it's nearly forty-five Earth years since she saw him. And she's been in touch with her folks; not like Celeste and me, with no contact for years there. So Trish hadn't *thought*, until now. And her mother, she'd be nearly the same age, so it can't be much longer. With the time ratio and all.''

Clancy wasn't sure what her point was. ''I'm sorry about your friend.'' First he'd wondered why Trish's loss would trigger Marnie when Celeste's death hadn't, but her words explained that. ''Would you like one of us to talk with her?'' What he could possibly say was a total mystery to him, but still . . .

''No, she's going to be okay. Thanks, though.'' Then, after a pause, ''It's me, really. Clancy . . . I'm *lost* to Earth. It's not even there for me; I don't know anybody back home.''

All over, it seemed, she shuddered. ''I feel so cut off.''

Going around Marnie's shoulders from one side, Allaird's

arm had to counter and slip Nicole's coming the other way. "You're not alone, Marni Gras."

"Bloody right not," said Nicole.

"You—you both feel it too?" Did she sound a little better? Clancy sighed. "Long since; hell, I forget when it was."

"I don't," Nicole said. "When word came in about the Liij; remember? It was all Earth's celebration and none of our own."

Clancy nodded. "Yeah, that's right. Anyway, I knew Earth had no part of me any longer, and that it went both ways. And it hurt, sure. But we did come here on purpose, didn't we?"

"All of us," said Nicole. And looked as if she meant it.

Marnie considered, then nodded. "Maybe not at first. Because I didn't know, then. But I do now." She frowned a moment before her expression cleared. "All right. The ship's my home and it's a good one. At destination—well, the colony could be it, or maybe even another ship. I'll have to wait and see."

So she'd be all right. With any luck at all. Anyway, thought Clancy, destination was no longer a matter of the far future. Today was number seven-fifty of the ship's crewed period. The first contingent would inGate, twenty-five days before the onset of decel, in just about nine more months.

During chronal progression ensuant to the partial success in exchange of meanings with the noncontiguous volitionals of the erstwhile troublesome sub-plenum, caution is maintained. Further experiments await additional study, at nowtime undertaken.

Analysis of the direct sensing within and adjacent to the sub-plenum itself produces information priorly unknown. Volitionals of the greater plenum neither design nor require devices of nonvolitional mass for manipulation of continuum parameters; thus, such objects in the sub-plenum are a source of bafflement and, early in attempted cognizance, even dismay.

Within a relatively short chronal period, however, the devices under study become capable of being understood, and a strange fact is observed. Whether by purpose or by random accessibility, in expanding to obtrude outside their initial sub-continuum the volitionals have opted additional dimensions of less than optimum utility. In particular, the chronal-prime vector of the annexed grouping is maximally disadvantageous to the volitional's stated purpose of moving between noncontiguous loci with minimal chronal displacement.

Alteration of such choice would appear a facile solution. Yet *within* the sub-plenum, it is soon realized, exists no viewpoint from which to make selection. Nor means of doing so, without guidance from outside the entire dimensional packet.

Two opinions conflict. Positive: could these other volitionals somehow be given capability to elect such choices, obtrusions would each have lesser effect on the overall plenum. Negative: were their devices altered to be of more efficient chronal utility, usage would increase greatly. Overall effect in the greater plenum is a matter of contention. Ergo, effort toward providing such capability waits upon further evaluation.

When Marnie turned fourteen, bio, three weeks after Trish reached twenty, *Arrow* had been running crewed for better than twenty-eight months, ship's time. And although Marnie herself had missed roughly four of those in Gatelags, still she'd done enough actual living to change considerably from the girl who'd been first aboard the ship. For one thing she wasn't chubby now; instead she definitely wore woman's shape. Nothing flagrant: modest breasts and a round little butt; once past some early embarrassment, all in all she rather enjoyed the effect.

By Earth's calendar, though, she had inGated at Glen Springs a bit over sixty-one years ago. The compulsion that drove her to calculate that figure was something like needing to scratch an insect bite; she dreaded the answer but had to know it anyway. Sitting before her terminal she stared for a few moments, then shut down the screen. Clancy and Nicole were putting on a spread for her; it wouldn't do to show up late.

Once she got there she shook her somber mood quickly, and enjoyed the party a lot more than she expected. After all, in five more months subjective she'd go into the local Gate— and next thing she knew, pop out to see what lay at the far side of *Arrow*'s decel period.

Assuming Clancy picked her for the advance contingent. She started to ask him, but he was busy talking, so she dropped it.

* * *

". . . wanted to get back to her on that," Allaird said. "But I didn't get the chance before she left for watch. Anyway, Nicole, why don't we figure out the listings now, while we have a free shift together?"

"Just so it doesn't take too long," and Clancy appreciated the implication.

He put the roster onscreen. That file displayed all the important parameters: individual specialties, pairings, the lot. After looking for a moment Clancy said, "The original idea, back at Glen Springs, was for half the crew to go ahead and the other half wait 'til the last minute."

"And?"

"That might be dumb. When we outGate at destination, after decel, won't we want as many as possible, to get things moving?"

"I think you're right," Nicole said. "All we need staying behind until decel is the core group best suited to set it up."

So Clancy started moving names and their associated data blocks around on the screen. And after a couple of mild arguments with regard to qualifications, he and Nicole agreed on a pair of assignment rosters. "Unless somebody raises a really valid objection," Nicole hedged.

"Valid, or violent?" She grinned, and Clancy hit printout.

"I've listed pairs together," he said, "regardless of rank. Easier to keep track of who's who."

ADVANCE PARTY:

Clarence Allaird, captain, pilot/navigator
  with Nicole Pryce, first officer, chief habGate tech
Ptiba Mbente, third officer, DV commander
  with Coyote Benjamin, drive tech
Pierre Larue, galley chief, ship's service maintenance
  with Gina Todisco, drive tech
Chauncey Ng, navigator, galley specialist
  with Pilar Velez, supplies chief, galley aide
Trish Pembrook, instruments and maintenance backup
Margaret Allaird, cadet (drive, DV, navigation)

DECELERATION OVERSIGHT GROUP:

Gretel Aaberg, second officer, instruments
   with Edd Jarness, backup pilot
Fleurine Schadel, drive chief
   with Eli Mainz, backup (DV, navigation, habGates)
Phil Henning, assistant drive chief (theory)
   with Sybiljan Baynor, instrument chief

"I'm shorting the stay-behinds in the galley department," Allaird said, "but it's not my fault how everybody paired up. And I don't see how we could ask either Pete and Gina or Chauncey and Pilar to split up, all that time."

"Only twenty-five days for the decel party, but twenty-one months for the advance team," Nicole said. "Are you going to suggest it, anyway?"

"Not unless somebody insists. Of course, maybe we'll get some gripes anyway, on other grounds. But I can't see why."

As it happened, several seemed surprised at the assignments but no one complained.

With destination so imminent, the last five months dragged interminably. When day ten-twenty finally neared, Marnie felt there should be something in the way of ceremony. But there wasn't even a need to pack for the "trip"; they'd be coming right back into control, after all.

What they did have to do first, a seemingly endless task, was button down everything loose in preparation for decel. They couldn't bring the rotating belts to rest yet, of course; that was a job for the six remaining, who would also secure their own quarters and control. But everything else needed careful evaluation and treatment. Luckily there were lists to follow.

To ease the decel team's plight, Chauncey Ng prepared and stored a supply of varied meals designed to mitigate the monotony of standard ration packets. "Space 'em out a little," he said, "so you don't run out too soon." On a quick guess, Marnie figured everybody got one special meal per day. Of course, those who wanted to could try their hands at cooking up their own treats. . . .

Eventually, after good-byes which for obvious reasons

meant more to the advance team than to the others, the ten forerunners lined up and went into the local Gate two by two. "I feel like Noah," Clancy said, stepping into the recess hand in hand with Nicole. "Or maybe one of his chosen animals."

What with the brief Gating intervals, Marnie and Trish as last in line departed only a few minutes later.

Janine Crewes worried. As new director at Glen Springs she was barely getting the feel of the place, and here came the agency saddling her with new developments. "Aren't we going to be a little late with this?"

On the phonescreen Dr. Alynn Hastings looked younger than her age. "Can't be helped. The tests started when they started; you can't rush Gate lag. But by sending pre-activated units in knockdown form we can have habGate capability to the destination world itself, at least two years ahead of schedule."

Janine frowned. "They'll be preparing for decel by the time these arrive. Do you really think they'll have time for all the extra work?"

"We'll hope so. If not, they can install while orbiting."

"Which would delay launch of the Deployment Vehicle."

"That's the chance we take," said Alynn Hastings.

To Fleurine Schadel the ship seemed empty; the half dozen still aboard came nowhere near giving it a lived-in feeling. Over the remaining days she checked and rechecked drive parameters until she could have recited them in her sleep. If anything went wrong it wouldn't be *her* fault! To Fleurine's relief, Phil Henning checked her results out clear, all the way.

Roamer had reported a strong possibility of planets from half a light-year out. Well, their star didn't sport a dust halo about five times as wide as Pluto's orbit. Here at maybe a tenth of a light-year, all *Arrow* could make out were some fuzzy indications that didn't prove much. Still, the general feeling was that prospects looked good.

Everyone seemed satisfied, in fact, except Sybiljan; more than not, the instrument chief was seen frowning over her work. Finally in the galley she explained her worry. "The mass detector figures don't jibe with our vee/distance reckoning. And they're out of line with the observed values for luminosity—magnitude, if you like—of our destination star. According to the mass spotters we're closer than we should be. By quite a bit, in terms of slow-end velocities."

"Of these instruments," said Gretel Aaberg, "in which do you place the greater trust?"

Baynor frowned. "I have to vote with the massers. Over our entire route there've been so many fluctuations in velocity and time ratio; we try to cancel them out, but the reckoning's still approximate. And our luminosity readings: variations in vee can screw up the relativity corrections. So to be on the safe side I think we have to start decel sooner than the schedule reads."

Since for obvious reasons the ship was aiming between one and two A.U. wide of the star anyway, Fleurine couldn't see how a little long or short in the distance figure could hurt a whole lot. But that, after all, was Sybiljan's department.

"I have to leave word," Baynor said. "This change we're making, for the advance team. So if things aren't the way they expect, they'll have some idea why." Only when she'd punched her message into the main console terminal did she sigh and relax. "We're starting decel nearly a hundred and fifty-eight minutes ahead of plan. That's almost sixty-six hours at the far end. Luckily the glitch wasn't in the other direction; we wouldn't dare correct for it." Because *delaying* decel could have the advance team emerging into five-gee stress. Safety switches were all well and good, but obviously Sybiljan didn't want to take any chances.

Over the last few days before inGating, the six finished the job of preparing for decel. Then, carefully, while Sibyljan crosshaired three major reference stars, Edd Jarness operated the twin pairs of yaw thrustors, one to initiate rotation and the other to stop it, swinging ship until *Arrow*'s nose aimed directly back along the ship's drive wake. Not until the rear sensors, now spotting the three beacons, confirmed the move's accuracy, did Gretel Aaberg pronounce turnover accomplished.

And so finally, with everyone lined up and waiting, Fleurine rechecked all her settings including the delay needed to allow all six to Gate safely, and punched the decisive button.

"Geronimo!"

*　　*　　*

As the flare died, Marnie saw control crowded with those who had preceded her, mostly looking bewildered and talking at cross purposes. Moving away from the Gate she turned to see the screen that seemed to have everyone's attention. Along with a few dim specks appeared one bright object, pea-sized in this depiction. It didn't look all that interesting, but . . .

Reaching Clancy's side she grabbed his arm. "What is it?" And what's wrong with everybody, but she didn't ask that.

"It's our destination star." His voice sounded dead flat. "Something screwed up. We've finished decel, all right. And come to rest, nominally. But about forty billion miles short."

XVIII

"**I** make it closer to forty-four," said Trish Pembrook. She was, Clancy noted, one of the few people shaking off surprise to investigate matters. "And now that we don't have to correct for relativity any more, I think the reading's pretty solid."

"How's it look for planets?" said Coyote. "From here we should be able to detect something."

Pembrook shook her head. "A couple of big ones, nothing useful. Oh wait—a little guy, but it's two–three A.U. out if the scale's accurate, and that's not necessarily the limb; even with our own sun that's deep freeze, and this one's dimmer."

"You mean we drew a blank?" Pilar's tone was shocked.

"Not necessarily," Allaird said. "What we want may be too near the star right now, from our angle, to get definition." Moving to the master console he took some sightings of his own. No comfort; in the matter of distance yet to go, Trish was as near correct as made no difference.

All right, what had gone wrong? Before he could ask for ideas, Nicole said, "Here's something. In the log. Sybiljan says the mass detectors showed us as being closer than we should have been at that point. Just about as much too close, as we actually fell short."

Slaving an aux screen to Nicole's terminal, Clancy read the same text. "Yeah. The masser contradicted our reckoning and sightings, and she went with it." He shook his head. "I can't blame her for that. But the fact is, she guessed wrong."

And why? Clancy pulled up the sensor scans, starting from the advance team's inGating, and set up maximum-speed viewing. "Trish? Would you bird-dog this for me, see if it gives any idea what caused the error? I need to call council. Down in the lounge, assuming the belt's up to speed. So let me know, there, if anything useful shows up." Because control was too crowded for quiet confab, and no one seemed ready to leave.

Trish was busy at the monitors and most of the others were making more sound than sense, so when Clancy and Nicole cut Ptiba and Coyote out of the herd, Marnie followed. Along the corridor, into the transfer ring, and on to the lounge. Actually she'd been in this place less than an hour ago by her own subjective time, but the barely noticeable film of dust on things made a liar out of that perception. Though actually, now that she thought about it, *Arrow* had been left uninhabited for only about ten weeks, ship's time.

Clancy drowned a couple of ice cubes in sour mash bourbon and no bones about it. "All right, folks. Before we tell Earth we've screwed up, however that happened, let's figure how to fix it." He cleared his throat. "We're an awkward distance out from destination. Nearly ten times the Deployment Vehicle's round trip range. But for the ship, only about thirty days under accel and then the same on decel, assuming we use one gee throughout. The trouble with that is, *Arrow*'s not configured for occupancy under thrust. The earlier ships were, but we're not."

"Then how were we supposed to get into orbit?" Pete Larue sounded argumentative. "Nobody could come out of decel right on the money; there'd have to be some jockeying, a few million miles here and there, getting up speed and then stopping.''

"But that's all short-term," Nicole said. "Swinging ship, hitting drive briefly, coasting, then slow again. Most of it's in zero gee; everyone straps in for thrust. And we'd feed out of the daily supplies stores on this deck, nothing that would need cooking. No real problem for only a few days of maneuvering, overall. Not two months, though; we couldn't manage that."

Allaird made a grimace. "Sure we could. We can do *any-thing* if we have to. But running ship for that long, in a one-gee field sideways to our entire layout's orientation—well, it's not my idea of fun."

Frowning, he looked around. "Any good thoughts?"

Ptiba raised a peremptory hand. "The emergency plan."

As Marnie saw Nicole's eyes widen in recognition, Clancy shook his head. "Tell me."

"The modification they proposed," Ptiba said, "while we were about halfway through training. In a fix like this we don't live in the ship proper. We slave the major controls to the DV and camp there while we home in to make orbit." She shrugged. "Strapping all those circuits will take some time, but . . ."

"Oh shit!" said Clancy Allaird. "I knew I missed a few things, coming in late. But I didn't know it was this bad."

Then he grinned. "Okay; where do we begin?"

Relief barely had time to replace Marnie's anxiety when the intercom brought Trish's voice. "The bugger factor just showed, captain. Want to come see?"

So they traipsed back upship, to control. It wasn't so crowded now; Trish explained that Pete Larue had press-ganged some people to go down and put the galley back in service. "Enough to get by with," she said. "Anyway, here's our problem."

Along with the rest, Marnie looked. Frozen onscreen was the destination star, smaller than in present view; dimly visible alongside it sat a smaller object. "There's our glitch," Trish said. "I have some tentative figures."

The findings were clear enough. This big, dim hunk of stuff, about a sixteenth of the sun's mass and correspondingly lacking in luminosity, lay about fourteen light-days this side of the

destination star. "Right in front of it, as we approached?" said
Nicole. "That's an unlikely coincidence."

No. Not directly in line, but too near to be distinguished
separately, from where *Arrow* rode when Sybiljan had to make
her decision. And the combined mass reading, taken to be the
star's true mass as determined from its luminosity, brought
destination an apparent forty-four billion miles closer. Which,
out of the overall five-sixty-six indicated by dead reckoning,
seemed plausible enough. "She did the right thing," Clancy
said. "Even if it turned out wrong."

"Something else," said Trish. "Let me run the view ahead
to now, max speed." And as the star ahead grew in size and
its companion, more than two hundred billion miles nearer,
slid off the side of the screen, another change occurred.

"The damn thing bent our course," Clancy complained.
"Even if we weren't short, we'd be off by a bundle."

"Well," said Chauncey Ng, "from this far out, there's no
problem correcting."

"So like you said before," Coyote Benjamin put in, "where
do we start?"

"Well, for one thing," Clancy said, "we're still pointed
bassackwards, looking through our rear sensors." He gestured
to Ptiba. "You want to crank up the yaw thrustors and swing
ship? At this stage our heading doesn't have to pinpoint; just
stay in the regional ecliptic and aim—oh, ten to twelve
minutes of arc off one side of the star. The right, make it, so
we go *with* planetary motion, not against it." Because every
system they'd seen spun the same way Earth's did. "We can
tune finer at turnover. I'm going to quarters now and get the
manual onscreen, study up on how we haywire the DV to run
piggyback."

It took Ptiba quite a while to get *Arrow* lined up and not
drifting in yaw. When Marnie got tired of watching, she went
to see if the galley was on line yet. She settled for sandwiches.

Nothing, thought Clancy, was ever as easy as it looked at
first. Thrust mode emergency operation for *Arrow* class ships
had indeed been a late modification. The manual's Controls
chapter said the adaptation package was in place, its circuitry
installed to allow operation from the DV by flipping a few
switches; tests said it wasn't. "Usually it's the paperwork that

arrives late," Allaird grumbled, "and I like it better that way."

So they'd have to improvise. The schematics in the manual's Appendix D were some help; at least they showed what was supposed to be connected to which, between ship and Vehicle. They also showed an ample number of trunks which did not in fact exist; Clancy found a mere half dozen spares, with perhaps as many more available if nonessential telemetry functions were shut down.

His key personnel here were Pete Larue as ship's service maintenance expert and Trish Pembrook who had done considerable installation work, learning her way around macroGate circuitry. "Routine stuff, that was," she downplayed it. "Just hook up the right colors where the drawing says to."

Still, it was her suggestion to dig out a telemetry carrier system, one terminal for each end, and multiplex it into one of the screen feed cables below the video band: instant trunks.

On the other hand, if it hadn't been for Pilar Velez knowing Supplies backward and forward, the others could have searched for days without finding those terminals; it took her twenty minutes.

Not for the first time, Allaird blessed whoever had picked this crew. Well, mostly . . .

Enough tools and paper were spread around to look like a real installation job by the time anyone thought to check for mail from Earth. Dear God, there could be nearly a two-year pileup! What Clancy was called to see dismayed him even more: a stack of large crates, complete with bracing to prevent movement, nearly filled the Tush recess.

By intercom to control and galley he rounded up enough muscle to begin clearing the Gate terminal, securing the containers to bulkheads with StikTite-equipped lines. But no sooner did they empty it than the fields flared and another load appeared.

There were five in all. And so far he had no idea what they were for. But with the last batch came a pile of papers, not as bad as his original expectations, yet more than he liked to see.

He took the stack back to quarters and began sorting: one routine, the next nonessential, one needing answer but no

hurry, a misroute, item too late for action, comment on a recommendation he'd almost forgotten. Was it Gatelag that triv-
ialized all these things to him?

And then he hit the jackpot.

"Obviously," said Nicole, "they hoped to get this here in
time to be installed before decel. Maybe Sybiljan starting early
threw the plan off." She'd heard Clancy wind down from
defaming the genetic inheritance and ancestral morality of
whoever dumped this load on the crew so late in the game; it
was time to tune in his constructive mode.

He wasn't quite ready for that. "She hit the button less than
three hours early, our time. How could—?"

Then he shrugged. "Never mind. Somebody misfigured our
schedule; it happens a lot. Anyway, we're supposed to clear
some space in one of the lower DV holds—one of three that
outload directly, using the landing legs as ladders when the
Vehicle's grounded—and install this pair of Earthgates. *I* don't
know what Glen Springs expected; I do know what they're
going to get. Delay." Because all this gear couldn't be moved
and put in place with *Arrow* under thrust. So heading in toward
surveillance orbit would have to wait until after the new chore
was done.

"Would you like me to ride herd on this one?" Nicole
asked, knowing he had his hands full planning approach to
the system, gathering data, and making out reports to go to
Earth. "Ptiba's busy with the controls-switching protocol; if
she can take some time out to show me where things ought
to go in that hold, I should be be able to take it from there."
After all, who was the Gates expert around here?

He nodded. "Yeah, that'll be fine; thanks. Pick whoever
you need for the heavy hauling. Including me. After I get this
one report in, a little mindless labor sounds like a nice break!"

Marnie got the clipboard with the shipping checklist on it
and the job of keeping track of what was to be moved when,
so at first her time was spent near Earth Tush, pointing out
which items should go next. "Pretty soft," said Coyote, as he
and Clancy released a set of StikTites and began maneuvering
another large crate over to the longitudinal corridor before
moving it forward to the nearest major cargo hatch.

He was grinning, though; Marnie said, "We all have our specialties. Yours is muscle." Both men laughed.

Somebody back home, and more likely several, had done their homework. Hold Eighteen, the specified installation site, contained a fair amount of boxes small enough to be transferred to the ship proper through the rear entrance. Those were fastened safely to the forward side of the major cargo hold bulkhead, and in the space thus cleared Nicole saw to the unpacking of the Habgate components.

The takedown models were well designed; once a few quick welds had the bases in place, assembly was like solving a rather simple jigsaw puzzle. Sooner than she or Clancy expected, the units sat alongside their power unit, ready for activation.

"These are the new type," she explained. "Once the Tush is on line there's no two-year wait before anything outGates, because that part was done back on Earth. *Then* the Gates were disassembled for shipping. So once we crank it up, it produces."

She put that step on hold; first, Clancy wanted to be sure the ship's controls were fully multipled to the DV. At either end, master cutover switches determined the configuration. In alternate mode, *Arrow* could be controlled from either its own main console or the DV's, the latter being disconnected from its normal functions. Reversing the switches put everything back to standard. At the DV controls Nicole watched as Ptiba in chief pilot's seat operated her controls according to Clancy's intercommed instructions. After a few minutes he said, "It looks fine from here. Can you call up all the sensor data you need?"

"Everything I can think of. Would you like to come check it out, just in case I'm missing something?"

So Clancy did, and then put the console inactive, "to avoid any accidental use until we're ready to move up here." He turned to Ptiba and her team. "Good job, all of you."

So then it was time to do something about the Earthgates. Everyone at hand trooped down to Hold Eighteen.

Putting his own thoughts in order, more than telling Nicole and the others anything they didn't already know, Allaird began: "At Glen Springs they've had their end on the line ever since they sent these, probably—and a test object sitting there in the Mouth. So once we activate the Tush, we start receiving. And we can't have that, stuff piling in here, until after the Vehicle lands. We can fire up our Mouth and send them something, but no message that could be useful in time."

Pilar Velez, delivering an extra tool kit Clancy had requested, said, "Two months round trip; no, that wouldn't be soon enough."

Before Allaird could correct her, Ptiba did. "It's not two months any more, Pilar. We're down to zero vee or near it; there's no time difference now. Four years there is four years here, too." And Clancy saw the reminder jar more than one of Ptiba's audience. It's easy to forget such things. . . .

But enough for today's lesson; he cut in, saying, "So anyway, either we hold activation on the Tush until the DV's sitting groundside, or . . ."

"Or we could let them send the first load and then just leave it in there to plug the Gate," Nicole finished. But then she smiled. "As a matter of fact, though, I have a better idea."

Along with everyone else Clancy waited, until she said, "It's out of the question to ice any of us in the local Gates. Too wasteful of personnel. But with all ten living on the DV control deck, privacy's going to be hard to come by, even with plastic curtains hung to screen off pairs of bunks. And over a two-month period, that could get wearing."

"So?" Chauncey Ng looked and sounded totally baffled.

"So we've got bunks for how many? Two dozen? Intended for the first exploration teams, when they show up. Except that now it appears some will Gate direct to the surface. Anyway—to repeat, we have very little privacy. I move we preempt the Tush with a couple of the extra mattresses and a bedside stand . . ."

She waved a hand. ". . . with a bar console right alongside. Some plumbing would be nice but I'm not sure it's practicable."

Coyote Benjamin laughed. "Our very own motel room? I like it." And, he went on, they could have a symbolic room key hanging alongside the main screen; if it wasn't there, the room was currently taken. No problems . . .

Assured that crew-usage water was stored forward and thus

"above" Hold Eighteen, Chauncey said, "Don't worry about the plumbing. And I'll highgrade some zero-gee fixtures from one of the maintenance relief stations on the equipment decks."

Zero-gee? Then Allaird nodded. Sure, they'd be under thrust most of the time, but what about when they reached orbit? Or during turnover, for that matter. And he was fairly sure Supplies didn't stock any spare convertible units. Safety first.

The Mouth flared and vanished its test object the moment activating power was applied; the Tush remained safely blocked by its installed furnishings.

Another two days' work and everyone could move into the DV. Button everything down, make sure the Vehicle's larder was stocked sufficently, everybody pack for two months of camping out, and what do you suppose we *forgot*? But before the residential belt was brought to rest, there had to be one last party. Mild, but festive. After which, the belt was secured for thrust mode and all ten of the advance team abandoned ship for life in the DV. Almost three weeks after they'd outGated.

Clancy looked nervous, Marnie thought, as he prepared to commence accel. For one thing, this wasn't his familiar control console; the pilot's display here differed in more ways than she liked to think about. But she saw him shrug and knew what he must be thinking: *All right, let's do it.*

On the console's keyboard and switch field his hands moved; Marnie felt the drive's hum, then a slow push building from the deck below until it seemed she stood on Earth. For the next month, Velcro shoes would be superfluous; *Arrow* had begun to move, to build itself enough vee to pay attention to.

About a month's worth. Then it would be swing ship and slow again, to see if they'd come more than seventy Earth years to discover anything worth the finding.

Arrow's unwanted course change and residual drift velocity had little effect on the ship's schedule. A few hours under drive thrust corrected those aberrations. The only real delays— hooking up the DV remotes and installing the new Gates—

were straight out of Earth by way of Glen Springs.

Nicole wished Clancy would look at it that way.

Living up to Earth's expectations didn't bother her a bit. If they wanted to make changes they could take the consequences. But Allaird tended to shoulder the burden of other people's responsibilities; it wasn't easy to talk him out of it.

It wouldn't be so bad, she thought, sitting chief pilot and halfway through her watch, if they had more chance to relax in private. It was lucky she'd thought of the Gates Motel; that refuge was a real life saver. But with only a crew of ten available to keep a ship running 'round-the-clock while largely barred from most of it, no pair could duck out and hide for very long at a time. Maybe an hour, tops. Nobody pushed you to cut your privacy breaks short; your sense of obligation took care of that. Or else Clancy's would. But the haywired intercom link was only used if someone was really needed topside, and such occasions were rare. Even then, usually it was just the buzzer, which also brought up a red light. Meaning, ". . . when you're ready to talk."

So most of everyone's time was spent right here on the control deck. To each side, four of the five lower bunks had been deployed: all the outside pairs, leaving the middle spaces clear. The resulting quartet of two-bed enclosures—and also the single lower bunks, one on each side of the latrines-shower complex, assigned to Trish and Marnie—were screened off by plastic curtains. At least they were opaque enough to dim the lighting for sleepers.

But still, Nicole thought, this was just like . . . like *what*?

Unexpectedly, from beside the pilot's console Marnie said, "You know what this arrangement reminds me of? Summer camp. I haven't felt this jammed since Celeste sent me off there when I was ten." As Nicole looked around to her, Marnie gave a muffled laugh. "Only then it was just girls."

"Yes." Before Pryce could say more, the young woman turned away, leaving Nicole to her own thoughts. Such as that her comparison would have been to camping out in a phone booth.

Decision to essay additional communication in the subplenum cannot implement itself at current chronal juncture unless a different volitional is approached, for which acclimatization must again proceed from beginning stages. The volitional previously encountered has become difficult to engage due to the onset of varyings in its spatial/chronal parameters, previously constant although extreme. Lack of constancy renders dimensional synchronicity uncertain; although a tentative contact attempt is made, no affirmative result ensues.

Resumption of communication effort must delay further.

Marnie didn't really mind living with a bunch of people, guys and all, running around not too careful about wearing enough clothes; it took a little getting used to, was all. And the fact was, the shower cubicle provided no place to hang clothing, not even a robe. So you left your clothes by your bunk and came out of your curtained area wearing a towel; once inside the shower stall, you could reach out and hang it on the door handle. Not exactly the last word in convenience, but the system worked. If you weren't too prissy about coverage when a towel slipped. And after the first two or three days, seeing that no one else seemed to care much about such lapses, neither did she.

Except to keep from having any of her own.

With everyone on hand if needed, immediately available at all times except when taking a Gates Motel break, Clancy had simplified the watch assignments: four six-hour shifts of two people each, exempting Pete Larue and Pilar Velez, who shared the responsibility of setting up four meals per day and took care of a few other housekeeping chores. Minor ones.

Clancy and Nicole and Ptiba sat chief pilot; the fourth, Marnie knew, would have been Eli Mainz as assigned DV backup, but his pairing with Fleurine put him with the decel group. When Clancy left it to Ptiba to choose a new backup, Marnie expected her to name Trish; instead, she got the nod herself. "Marnie's worked at it longer, practices at every opportunity," Ptiba explained. "I think she deserves the chance."

So, six hours out of every day, Marnie took over at the chief pilot's console. A figurehead, sure: if anything important came up she was expected to yell for one of her seniors. But still it felt good. Except that only one-quarter of each day were she and Clancy and Nicole all off duty at once, and odds had it that at least one of them would be sleeping.

Marnie's watch partner was Chauncey Ng. Gina Todisco rode shotgun for Clancy, Coyote for Nicole, and Trish for Ptiba, each sitting co-pilot although that console now handled only navigational and other sensor data. The communicator's seat sat empty except for visiting purposes, since nobody was out there to communicate with.

It all went pretty smooth, Marnie felt, except that she could have used a little solitude now and then, or even the chance to talk alone with just one or two others. It took her a time to notice that some of the crew tended to go down to the Gates Motel a lot more often, and stay longer, than the wish for sexual privacy could possibly require. Never more than an hour or so, but still and all . . .

Further, it wasn't always paired couples or even just two people, and yet Marnie sensed no feel of intrigue or excitement. So the next time Clancy and Gina relieved her and Chauncey Ng, Marnie picked up the "room key" and went over and woke Trish up.

"Let's go down and have some coffee, and talk."

Trish blinked. "Down to the Motel?"

"Sure."

"*Us?* What's everybody going to *think*?"

"That we can use a little privacy like anybody else. What would you expect?" And once she got over looking surprised, Trish grinned and nodded.

Following nearly a week cooped up with nine (usually) other people all day *every* day, the quiet hour Marnie and Trish talked together seemed like a real vacation. After that she let no day go by without taking a period of respite: either alone or with Trish or whoever was free that she felt like inviting.

One of the first was Clancy, who expressed chagrin that he hadn't thought to ask *her*. "Sorry, Marni Gras; somehow it just didn't cross my mind." Then he smiled. "Well, you know what they say. The first billion miles are the hardest."

And of course the slowest, occupying the initial six days and fifteen hours under thrust. By contrast, Allaird told her now, ". . . in just the last *day* before turnover we'll cover roughly one-point-four billion."

"That's the t-squared in the constant-accel equation, right? Really builds up fast." Another question surfaced. "How much time dilation do we get, this time? At peak vee, I mean."

His brows lifted. "Come on now; you can figure that yourself. One gee for—oh, call it thirty-one days."

Well, sure she could. "All right; I make it just about point-oh-double-eight c." And switching functions on her hand calc, "Now that square root, of one minus the square . . ."

But her father stopped her. "You want the easy way?"

"There is one?"

"Hit your trig tables." She did. "Find vee in the sine column." Marnie nodded. "Time ratio's the secant."

"Straight across, just like that?"

"Kee-rect."

Marnie felt her frown build. "Why don't any of the books tell it like that?"

"It's not dimensionally correct according to Saint Albert; he used some imaginary values the calcs can't handle. But for our purposes, it gives the right numbers."

She checked her reading. "And this one's less than four parts in a thousand. Not enough to bother with."

"The computer will, though. The difference isn't much for time, but distance is affected too. At midpoint of this run, I put the possible error at up to eighty-five million. Which cuts no ice at that stage, but could eat time at the slow end."

Clancy stood and stretched. "We've held this place down about long enough. Somebody else probably needs a getaway by now." He moved toward the door. "Sorry, hon."

Marnie followed. "It's okay; I'm ready." Out in the central well, as Allaird began the long ascent, she said, "Hey, I *like* it on here. And everybody aboard, too. It's just . . ."

"*All* the time," his voice came from above.

"That's right." Then she needed her breath for climbing.

As *Arrow* neared the end of acceleration and approached peak velocity for this leg of the trip, relativistic sensor error began to build. Just as Allaird had told Marnie. But from the DV, he found, computer correction wasn't all that easy to come by; under normal conditions the Vehicle wouldn't need it. But the fact was, as he said louder than he intended, "Those morons at Glen Springs didn't give us that part of the hookup!''

What a man really hates at such times is the calm voice of reason. As, how could they guess there'd be an error so big that we'd require that sort of thing? You need to keep in mind . . .

"The hell I do! All I need is to get the goddamn readings!''

He could have taken them during the zero-gee period at turnover, sure. But that would use up *time*, not only the readings themselves but clambering back and forth to get them. And whipping along at more than sixteen K miles per second, an hour's delay could screw up his distance-accel calculations.

So, taking Trish Pembrook along because with Estella long since invalided home and Gretel Aaberg heading the decel team, Trish was the group's remaining instrument specialist, and Ky Benjamin because he was an all-around capable tech and in top physical shape to boot, Clancy headed down the ship's thrust-begotten gravity well to its normal control room.

Even with the sturdy and well-designed lifelines he'd had installed, the job bore no resemblance to fun. Neither getting to control nor working there.

If anything, the latter was the worse. Effectively, acceleration had tipped control over on its butt, with the local Gates at the gravitational bottom. "Seated" at the control console Allaird was actually lying on his back, facing straight up with no support for head or shoulders and a difficult reach to most of his knobs and switches. Not a situation, he found, for doing good work at any length.

So he did the job in short bursts, pausing between to sit up on the seat back and lean against the console top. Trish, he noticed, did much the same. But Coyote Benjamin, always the free thinker, sprawled across two adjacent seatbacks with his upper body slanting up to his console, held by a sling of line under one arm and across his neck to loop over the console casing.

When Clancy was done, he found he could just as well have gone with his horseback guess in the first place.

The climb back made the rest of it seem easy.

*   *   *

Turnover came on Marnie's watch, but she had no expectation of doing the job herself and she was right. Clancy didn't take over until he needed to, though. Standing beside chief pilot's position, first he said, "Mark your heading, Chauncey; enter azimuth and declination for three reference stars, besides destination, of course."

Marnie stared; he was certainly taking this ship reversal more seriously than the earlier one. Well, he'd have to; that time they'd floated almost at rest. Here at more than sixteen thousand miles a second, things would be a lot more critical.

When Chauncey signaled "okay" the captain said, "Everybody not shod in Velcro, grab yourselves a handhold." Then he turned to Marnie. "Start cutting drive. Bring it down slow, about one percent a second. You don't need to be exact; close is fine."

Checking the thrust indicators against the sweep second hand on her watch, she ran the cut only a few seconds over Clancy's nominal figure. He said, "Thank you, pilot. My turn now," and she moved to a position beside the seat, using her Velcros *and* a handhold for stability.

Chauncey clambered over to the communicator's position, making way for Ptiba Mbente to co-pilot; on this maneuver, apparently, top skills were indicated. When Ptiba was settled in, Clancy said, "All right. Just so *everybody* gets to learn something this time, I'll tell it as we go. First I open up one pair of yaw drivers: they start us pivoting and the opposing pair stops us. Ptiba—tell 'em what you're watching for."

As Mbente began, Marnie felt a slight sidewise push and saw the starfield on screen begin to move accordingly. "What I have is a gyrocompass reading that has to do a one-eighty degree swing. First our rotation speed builds up, pivoting—uh, that should be enough, captain." The push ceased. "Okay; you cut thrust at about twenty degrees, so . . ."

"So now our swing is just coasting," Allaird said, "and we wait. When we have that same angle left to go, I use the other pair to leave us riding steady but pointing backward."

It seemed longer than it probably was, before Ptiba called, "Now!" and the deck pushed the other way. After a time she said, "Five degrees," then "four," "three and slowing," a pause, "ease to half," and finally, "cut!"

"Switching main screen to rear view," Clancy said, and the

view changed. "How do those reference stars line up?"

Close, but not exactly, and the view still inched sidewise a little. "Well, I want our star about twenty-two minutes of arc off our course, anyway. Putting us off to the side about Mars distance, heading in." By cut-and-try, a nudge one way and a smaller one the other, over the next minutes Allaird refined the ship's attitude until he was satisfied.

He freed himself and got out of the seat, gesturing to Marnie. "Crank up your drive, pilot. Same rate as before."

So, gauging her thrust buildup the same way she'd done the shutdown, this time she came in within a second. "Well, we're halfway home," said Clancy. "The rest is all downhill."

Marnie hoped he was right.

His people must have been more worried about turnover, Clancy thought, than anyone had let on. Or maybe they didn't realize it themselves until after; he certainly hadn't. Yet now that it was all over, he had to admit he felt more relaxed.

Maybe it was that on any trip the turnover maneuver was supposed to happen only once. That's how it had been with *Starfinder* and *Roamer*. Allaird had no clear idea where the next ships had been sent—*Scout* and *Falcon* and *Nomad*—nor whether they'd got there yet. And after those he'd purely lost track. According to the projected skeds, by now there should be close to twenty starships launched, maybe even some of the rumored Boomerang or Bootstrap versions, whatever the hell *those* labels meant. But one way or another he'd missed seeing the reports.

Well, now it was a month to destination. Also it was over an hour before he was due to relieve Marnie as chief pilot.

He caught Nicole's attention. At her nod, he reached over and picked up the Gates Motel room key.

Although subject volitional's degree of spatial/chronal interdependency continues to alter, that relationship itself becomes of lesser magnitude and impediment, perhaps approaching a level at which contact may be possible previous to volitional's full return to parameters of spatial/chronal constancy.

For this venture, it is hoped, greater similitude may be

achieved between the volitional and the sensory extension presented to it. Preparation accretes.

As *Arrow* approached destination, daily routine scan of the sensor view began to confirm, with increasing assurance, the identity of dots on the screen as planets rather than something else. Size and apparent mass Clancy found not too hard to peg; orbital distance and sidereal period needed longer observation.

At luminosity about point-nine of the Sun's, the star massed slightly less than point-nine-seven on the same scale. Apparent size wouldn't be all that different even at close range, but this sun's light was definitely softer, more yellowish.

Following a flip remark of Coyote's, people began referring to it as Sol-junior. Or just plain Junior. Clancy had thought of calling it Target. But he hadn't spoken up soon enough; the bandwagon got away from him. So he went along. In his next report to Earth he stopped using "destination" in preference to the star's numerical designation, and just wrote "Junior."

What the hell; he had four solid years before anybody could tell him not to.

"Well, just where do we *want* to find a world?" Close to midpoint of a watch trick, Marnie put the question to Chauncey Ng.

"Hmm. Well." He was stalling, she could see, while he ran some numbers on his aux screen. "For the same incident energy that Earth gets, it should ride at not quite point-nine-five A.U." He paused; she nodded. "Something, not a whole lot, over eighty-eight million miles."

"How tight is that figure?"

"There would be some leeway; after all, parts of Earth are more hospitable than others. How much margin depends on a number of factors: depth of atmosphere, assuming we're lucky enough to find one that supports life. Axial tilt. Lots of things."

"But so far, nothing's showing?"

"Not that's suitable," said Trish. Lounging back in the communicator's couch, she recited the list to date. The two biggies, one heavily ringed and both well supplied with small-ish moons, riding at roughly five and eight A.U. The smaller one, first spotted by Trish herself, at the vicinity of two-point-six A.U. and receiving less than a seventh of Earth's incident energy flux. "Of course it's big enough to grow itself some internal heat." Since the speedy orbit of one of its closer satellites indicated its pull at nearly two gees.

"There's a couple more in tighter," she added, "but from here we can't tell *how* tight. On our closer approach, as our angle shifts we'll get a better idea."

Marnie frowned. "How come both the earlier ships had their planets nailed down from a lot farther out?"

"I'm not sure," said Chauncey. "I think it's because they could run crewed all through deceleration. There are a lot more kinds of test observations than we have rear sensors; they could switch instruments and check whatever they wanted to, change to catch whatever they needed at any time. And over a full year, too, coming in from half a light-year. We, though—we pretty much have to set up the more obvious choices and let them ride."

With only ten days and roughly two and a quarter billion miles remaining until the end of scheduled decel, Marnie hoped something turned up before too much longer.

A week later, with Junior about a quarter billion miles away and thirty-four degrees to port, Clancy got up to find Trish waiting with some figures for him to look at. She was patient, though, allowing him time to start on his coffee. Then, "I finally got enough readings to pin orbital data down, and we are about as lucky as anyone could get. Look here." She pointed. "The little world's much too far in, but this next one . . ."

Looking, he felt his brows raise in pleased, unbelieving surprise. Orbital distance nearly point-nine-four A.U., a year of something like three-forty Earth days, maybe two-seventy of its own which appeared to be roughly thirty hours.

Okay then: incident energy level maybe two percent above Earth's; definitely favorable for H_2O to exist in liquid phase. And the distance/period ratio of the major moon gave the planet close to three-fourths Earth mass.

As Marnie came to look, too, his own muttered calculations took over. Triangulating from their slantwise approach gave him fairly accurate distance and thus the planet's real diameter. When he put all quantities in terms of Earth = one, surface gravity came in at just under point-eight-five. "Or in that ballpark," he added.

"And one more thing," said Trish. "You see . . ."

"Damn right I do. *Atmosphere!* And hi-mag shows whirly streaks, like Earth's. I think we're looking at breathable."

"What do you want to name it?" Marnie asked.

He thought of the odds. "How about Straight Flush?"

It didn't surprise Marnie that her father took a leisurely breakfast and began his and Gina's watch shift before he moved to the communicator seat and put the latest findings into a report for Earth. When he finished, he called her over. "You want to run this down to the Motel and Gate it off?"

"Sure. But Ptiba and Coyote are there right now." She checked her timepiece. "Should be out in a little while."

Clancy nodded. "Right. There's not that much hurry." He moved to his normal chief pilot's position.

Marnie slid into the communicator seat. "Do we know much of anything about conditions on this world?"

"Some guesses. From spectral and thermal readings, among others, we *think* the planet has lots of water and not much axial tilt. Which could make things interesting, living there."

"Interesting, like in the Chinese curse?"

He grinned. "Maybe. At two percent over Earth's incident energy, anything near the equator's going to be hothouse country, if not oven. And a light tilt means no polar ice caps, possibly seas there instead. So . . ."

After a moment, she saw it. "There better be some land masses around the middle latitudes, or we're in deep."

His answer was cut off by the shriek from the central tunnel: Ptiba's. And then the sickening thud.

Lunging to the guard railing, Marnie looked over. About halfway down the shaft, Coyote Benjamin seemed frozen to the climbing handholds as he stared upward. And at the bottom, Ptiba lay crumpled; whether she breathed or not, Marnie couldn't tell.

But it took her a moment to notice any of those details.

Because what Coyote was gazing at, the thing that had probably startled Ptiba into losing her hold, was a human figure floating in air as if the full gee of decel didn't exist.

And looking all the world like Marnie herself.

XIX

"Get to her, Ky!" Clancy's voice broke the frozen moment. "See if she's all right."

Ptiba, he meant, not Marnie's double. Except, Marnie realized as she slithered over the rail and began her own descent, with no thought but to confront the apparition, it wasn't really all that close a match. Better than last time—for what could this be but the Alephant? Yet the clothing, copying what she'd worn at the previous visit, wasn't real, wasn't separate; surfaces merely changed, at appropriate folds and bulges, from the look of skin to that of fabric.

The hair was a better imitation than before, but she doubted anyone could run fingers through it. Even the long bangs she'd been growing out when this—creature?—first appeared, but had worn brushed back for some time now.

As she came down even with the whatever-it-was, she realized that now it simulated the whole of her. Floating in air a few feet away was a lifesized Marnie Allaird doll, its somewhat stiff facial expression seeming to indicate surprise. Well, that's what it would have seen, to copy. . . .

As Chauncey Ng descended past her, to join Ky in seeing if Ptiba could be helped, she looked into her would-be double's face. "What are you doing here? What do you want?"

"Contain of your harm, keep from us." This version's lips moved when it talked, but not in sync with the sounds. "Have more your talk nowtimes. Seek cause your choice chronal vector."

"Our what?"

The brows made a stylized frown. "Invaded sub-plenum have three. From adjacent vector space, you utilize not best effect . . . effective?"

There had to be meaning here. But what? Marnie shook her head.

The thing paused. Stiffly and awkwardly one hand reached out; instinctively she tried to duck away, but fingers touched her forehead. Smooth and without temperature they tingled against her skin; then came a very odd feeling, totally painless, of something *entering* her head. Not the fingers: their stubby ends still rested on her brow. But something that sent tiny effervescent spurts of tickling sensation behind her eyes.

She heard sounds: unintelligible voices, tones that rang sharply, a crisp roar of white noise. Colors burst across her sight; was this thing *Gating* her? She felt her muscles sag, and desperately fought to hook an arm over and through the loop of a protruding handhold.

Then came a flooding, a mighty flow of wordless meaning, as all the sounds and pyrotechnics faded to silent black.

By the time he got past the pilot's console, Allaird was third in line. He swung over the rail to see two Marnies about half-way down and Chauncey past them, still descending fast. Huddled at the bottom was Ptiba Mbente, with Ky kneeling beside her. Well, he and Chauncey would have to cope, there.

Clancy knew which Marnie was which because the real one couldn't float in one gee. So the other was the Alephant. When it reached to touch her he repressed a cry of warning so as not to jar her further, and started down as fast as he could go without missing a hold.

He saw Marnie begin to sag and moved to get there faster, before her weight could pull hand and lower forearm free of the precarious leverage she'd obtained—and barely made it, his right hand under her arm and holding her against his thigh while his left on the metal handhold above began to ache with strain. One foot found support, the other scrabbled uselessly.

Leaving him absolutely no way to fend off the thing that had zapped Marnie. Well, try talk! "Don't touch me. You see what happened to her.'' She was breathing, though. ''We *fall*, you see, if we pass out. And if we fall, we get hurt. Damaged. So just stay back and we'll talk. Okay?'' Feeling like a little kid chattering to his teddy bear, but what else could he do?

As the intruder's hand came away from Marnie, between the two a translucent sheet of film stretched briefly, then pulled thin and snapped, vanishing. Or did it resorb into the hand? Clancy shook his head. Pain shot along his arm; he couldn't hold this weight much longer. ''Somebody help me!''

''I'm coming!'' Nicole. Pete yelled something, too. But before either could get there, the Alephant moved. Nodding as if in reassurance, it put one arm under his where he held Marnie and the other around his opposite thigh. Clancy tensed against whatever had knocked Marnie out, but nothing happened. The Alephant rose, just enough to ease strain from his upstretched arm. Releasing that hold he reached to free Marnie's hand and wrist from the metal loop, then took a better grip as his other foot also found purchase. Now, if he had to, he could hold a little longer. As he stared at the apparition, fright fought disbelief; he said, ''If you'd just tell us what you want, we'll do what we can.''

He saw Nicole stop her descent level with him, a couple of feet away along the tunnel wall; Pete Larue took station on the other side. ''Are you all right?''

''Later.'' Again he spoke to the outré manifestation. ''What is it you want here?''

It gestured toward Marnie. ''This one know of need now-times, tell noncontiguous volitionals.'' The Alephant moved jerkily, like a holo on fast forward. ''Sensing extension must to end. Spatial/chronal accommodation fails. Retract is occur.''

''Come on, Pete,'' Nicole said. ''It's safe, don't you see?'' As the two moved to hold Allaird and Marnie, the imperfect likeness pulled free. It began to shimmer and dwindle, contracting toward its midpoint.

''Thanks for your help.'' For no particular reason Clancy found himself yelling the words. ''I appreciate it.'' The shape kept shrinking until a tiny image vanished with a pop and sparkle. Leaving Allaird not the only one to stare in silence.

Mumbling nothing intelligible, Marnie began to move slightly. ''We have to get her up top,'' Nicole said.

Clancy was about to lose his handhold. ''All right; can you

take her now?'' And waited while the transfer of weight was made.

''Aren't you coming?''

''Priorities,'' Allaird said. ''Marnie's all right physically. Shaken up, I'd expect. Let her lie quietly; when she comes to, give her some water. And call me. Right now, though, I need to get down and see how bad Ptiba's hurt.''

He waited to see them begin to raise her safely, then made his way hand by hand down the long tunnel. Absolutely refusing to let his mind dwell on the apparition he'd just talked with.

It didn't look good, Clancy thought. Mbente, her breathing shallow, looked paler than he'd thought her natural melanin could allow. Above her left eyebrow swelled a nasty, gashed lump, and that shoulder lay hunched unnaturally inward.

She lay with her head in Coyote's lap; Chauncey Ng fussed around her right foot and ankle. ''How bad?'' said Clancy.

Without looking up, Chauncey said, ''Just above the ankle, both bones fractured. Collarbone. Wrist. Concussion.'' Now he paused in his work and faced Clancy. ''That's the obvious stuff. If I had my gear from the ship I might find more.''

He sounded angry, but Allaird knew it was nothing personal, just fury at the fates for doing this. ''Is it safe to take her up to the deck? Can you work better there?''

Ng shook his head. ''I don't want to try it. Not for now. Just moving her into the Motel bed is risk enough.''

So that's what they did. Pilar drew the first shift in attendance, to call for help if she thought it needed. Then, with Allaird's okay, the other two men mounted an expedition into *Arrow* proper, to bring back as much of Chauncey's medic apparatus as was applicable—and feasible to move.

For perhaps the sixtieth time, Clancy did the fifty-five–meter climb. It never seemed to get any shorter. . . .

''Whether we can move her up here,'' Allaird told the group, ''depends on what Chauncey discovers. One thing we do know: Ptiba won't be in shape to take this DV down to scout the planet.''

That was all he would say; Marnie was stirring and it was past time he saw to her. Lying on the communicator's couch, partly curled up and partly sprawling, she began to move her head from side to side.

He put a hand to her cheek. "Marni Gras? You okay?"

The movement stopped; her eyes opened, then blinked. "Daddy?" She frowned. "Clancy, I mean." Then, "Is it gone?"

"Yeah, it is. Kept us from falling, first, though. How do you feel now?" And "Can you tell us what happened?"

A nod. "I think so. It wasn't trying to hurt anybody. Ptiba must have thought it was me in the air and tried to grab me. Then when we tried to talk, it couldn't get the words right so it went in my head some way, and . . ." She shrugged. "I guess I passed out."

"You sure did. How do you feel now?"

"Okay." And sounding surprised, "Great, really." With a quick motion she sat up. "But I have to—I have all this stuff I don't understand, that I'm s'posed to say. Maybe you better tape it; my hunch is, I'll be lucky to get it straight, even once."

"You're in the right place for that." Clancy hit a switch. "Go ahead, while it's fresh." Not that any of this made sense, he thought, but might as well play out the hand.

So she began.

"Volitionals utilize nonvolitional mass devices, manipulate parameters, obtrude from sub-plenum into contiguous dimensional array. Harms ensue, can be averted by continuum adjustment. But small mass of excess kinesis obtruding beyond usual loci brings great damage extent. This volitional"— Marnie indicated herself—"designates mass as error singular. Recurrence mandates corrective measures, possibly unfortunate to sub-plenum."

As she paused to catch her breath, Clancy stared in wonder. Then, "This and adjacent sub-plena are each of normal six-vector array, half spatial half chronal. Yet in obtruding, volitionals choose least efficient chronal-prime over two of superior merit; either would lessen chronal component of spatial displacement event produced by volitionals usurping loci of contiguous sub-plena. It is desired to ascertain bases for vector choice."

Abruptly Marnie shook her head. "The rest—I'm losing it. Something about we can't see from in here, how to make a choice. From our universe, not the ship. And they can't show us, from theirs. And maybe they're not sure whether they *want* to, but still this one came to tell us about it.''

"And that if there's any more bullets flying loose in their space," said Pete Larue, "we get our butts kicked!"

"Sounds that way," Marnie said.

"And nothing else?" said Clancy. "Can you get any more?"

"I think that's it." She put her feet down, and stood. "If anything new pops up, I'll tell you. But right now, isn't there something to *eat* around here?"

For now, at least, further discussion did seem futile.

"I guess I just flanged out, Nicole," Ptiba said. After nearly a day of semiconsciousness and restless sleep she had come awake with a seemingly clear head, and Chauncey Ng said she was fit to answer questions. So, "Out of nowhere there's Marnie holding onto nothing; I thought she's *falling*, so I grabbed, and from there it was a rough ride."

Nicole agreed; a free-fall drop would have killed Ptiba. She must have tried to clutch at every hold within reach; going too fast to stop, still the contacts slowed her enough to save her life. But at the expense of several assorted fractures.

With the readouts he'd brought from his med files, Chauncey managed a good job of setting and immobilizing; his spray-on splint casts weren't as neat as the readout illoes showed them, but he kept them light and compact; they worked. The collarbone, not the wrist, had Ptiba's left arm in a protective harness.

Nicole considered the setup. "It's only about forty hours until our vee and position should be at nominal end of decel. Ptiba, nobody expects you to try co-pilot then; someone will have to fill in. But if we got you topside, do you think you could sit alongside and advise?" Looking to Chauncey: "If you feel she can be moved safely . . ."

Ptiba nodded; Chauncey Ng said, "She can if we do it right," and explained what he meant.

The sling Ptiba lay in, Clancy thought, resembled a cross between stretcher and hammock. Lines from each corner met a few feet above and spliced to the main rope. Up at the deck, he and Coyote manned that line while behind them Pete Larue took a bight around two of the main monitor screen's supporting legs. Below, Chauncey and Pilar stayed with the sling, climbing carefully as between them they kept the burden riding steady.

Clancy had cut decel to half a gee, trusting the computer to tell him how long and how much he'd have to run it high, to compensate. Still the process was slow and strenuous, everything done on command and in small steps. Before the ascent was half over, Allaird had sweat running from his forehead and down his sides. "Check your cinch, Pete; everybody rest a minute." But then they took it to conclusion, bringing Ptiba through the gate in the protective railing and carrying her to her own bed.

Mopping himself off partially, Allaird went to stand over her. "You okay after all that?"

Mbente's smile looked shaky. "As good as before, not saying a whole lot. But yes, and thanks for the lift up."

Clancy touched her forehead; she didn't feel feverish. "Think you can observe and advise, when orbit time comes?"

"As things stand, you can count on it."

And granted any luck, Clancy felt, things might stand. For now, he set thrust at one-point-two gee to get back on sked.

Two days later the intercom sounded and a strange voice yelled at him. "Where is everybody? We're stuck here at the Tush with about a gee pulling aft, and aboard ship, nobody answers. If you're not in the Vehicle we're up shit creek!"

It was the first echelon of the arrival team, of course: a gang of twelve, under the agitated leadership of one Ketch Garber. When Earth's Gate to the DV refused to transmit, after a time the brass decided to send Garber's crew through the regular Gate. And here they were.

"We had a problem," Clancy explained. The false mass reading, placing *Arrow* billions of miles short after normal decel, "so we had to move up here, where things are designed for living under thrust, to home in." Then the delay to install the DV Gates. "There just wasn't any way to warn Glen Springs. We plugged the Tush and hoped somebody would get the message."

He heard some low-voiced cursing before Garber said,

"How early are we? We can't manage *here* very long, you know. There's no johns we can get to, even if anybody could shit sideways to the gee field. And we'll be getting hungry pretty soon."

"Yes, of course. But I can't cut thrust now; we're too close, couldn't make it up in time. And you couldn't reach the galley anyway; the belt and ring are both locked down."

"If we have to, we can follow this bulkhead around to the far side and Gate back."

"No, don't do that." This guy would shoot *four years*?

The trouble was, safety lines for climbing had been run only as far aft as control. But there was more line available. "Hang on a minute." And to Coyote, "How about we wake Pete up, and you and he go down and string line to these people? It's going to crowd hell out of us up here but it's only for another two, three days." Ky thumbed an okay so Clancy reopened the talk circuit. "I'm sending a couple of men down to get climbing lines to you. We already have them as far as control, so it shouldn't take long. Then you can come up here. Meanwhile, relax."

As he turned away, Pete Larue came over, still half asleep and suitably grumpy. "We better bring 'em by way of daily supplies reserve. We didn't stock this can to feed that many."

"Good point. But we're not all that far from orbit, Pete. And then we can spread out again."

Twelve more people, though. Well, that's what the double deck bunks, unneeded until now, were for.

But except for the Gates Motel, there went the last semblance of privacy.

Marnie didn't mind the disruption; she found the influx of new people exciting. At first she couldn't get the names down; Ketch Garber was the only one she knew for sure. Round-faced and sandy-haired, Garber stalked the deck with the stride of someone a foot taller, and wasn't at all like the petulant voice on the intercom. "Finding thrust on, and the place deserted, gorked me out," he said, obviously now ungorked.

Whatever that meant.

Eight men and only four women, this team: certainly no pairoff operation. Nicole explained, "They're not set up to live as a group for any length of time; they'll be part of a much bigger community soon. So balance doesn't matter.''

Right; ships were different.

One way and another, waiting for the end of decel, every-body put up with everybody else. After the first excitement of meeting, the new group tended to stay cliqued up. Mutual ground was missing; Marnie found no one in the lot who seemed interested in much that she had to say, and their own discussions might as well have been in another language. When she stopped to think about it she realized that these people, all early twenties to late thirties and first time out, had been born at least five and in some cases more than six de-cades after her own birth, and grown up in a culture she'd never known.

Was this how it would be with the colonists? Probably.

She'd long since quit keeping track of Earth fashions, and when it came to clothing, issue jumpsuits didn't change much. Other items did: these women wore their hair quite short and noticeably thinned, wispy halos with the scalp showing through; monkey fur, the fad was called. Marnie declined one young woman's generous offer of a fashionable make-over; if she wanted to look gootzy she'd pick something original.

The men tended toward brush cuts, "white sidewalls," and what Clancy called Fu Manchu mustaches—except Garber, who wore a shaggier look and no whiskers at all. Which did make him easy to distinguish from the rest.

Crowding or not, *Arrow* slowed toward its planned position.

With Ptiba out of action, Trish Pembrook would have been next choice to fill in as a fourth watch officer, but short of drafting Pete or Pilar into unfamiliar duties, she would lack a co-pilot. Instead, after considering other options Clancy cut the daily schedule to three eight-hour shifts—with Trish stand-ing relief, as Gretel Aaberg had done earlier in the trip. But nominal end-of-decel was due on the watch where he'd be the one relieved, so when that time came, Allaird waived the offer. "I may want to do some fast improvising here. Still, though . . .''

He looked across to Gina. "Would you mind if Trish sits shotgun for this part?'' She wouldn't; Pembrook took the seat. "All right; now we have to change heading and give ourselves a little boot. So we can coast down the gravity well toward Straight Flush, on a curve that'll match vee to make orbit.''

Well, she *looked* as if she understood. As Gina and Marnie helped Ptiba into the comm couch to act as observer/adviser, Clancy watched his indicators and prepared to set course and time his thrust, for rendezvous with Straight Flush.

The closer he got it the first time, the less he'd have to correct for, later.

Marnie knew the factors involved in approaching orbit: the star's gravity well, the planet's vee, and of course the ship's own speed and position which were the only items subject to pilot control. Slowing orbital vee dropped you starward and vice versa; the converse was that aiming out would slow you, et cetera.

Clancy had to come up behind the planet on the outside and do a little juking to match its speed. How he would put it all together to achieve orbital capture was less than clear to her, so she spent most of the next hours at the edge of the co-pilot's couch, watching.

She had to sleep sometimes, though, in the upper bunk she'd drawn because Trish won the coin toss. And waking from one of those naps she found an unaccustomed hush and no weight.

The drive was idling, one notch above standby. Two months since accel began, forty-four billion miles out, *Arrow* rode in orbit around its destination planet. Straight Flush.

A lucky thing, Allaird thought, that all the small auxiliary Traction drives, for attitude control and rotation and reverse thrust, were controlled in the same pattern he'd learned for the earlier model ships. And that Trish's telemetry carrier idea had given him enough channels to operate them all from here. He'd tried to bone up from the manual, but there hadn't been time for more than a quick scan. And yet he'd done the job with no really major setbacks. *Thank heaven for a retentive memory!*

After a bit more futzing around than he'd anticipated, using the attitude drives in various combinations, Clancy had the ship in temporary surveillance orbit, slightly more than a planetary radius out. He'd tried for a four-hour period, but by the time he had his orbit stable and mostly circular, an extra fifteen minutes or so sneaked in. The difference, he decided, wasn't worth messing with.

For now, *Arrow* pointed outward from Sol-Junior, to put Straight Flush on the forward screens during daylight observation while he picked a promising area for first exploration. Some attitude changes would be needed then, but nothing more; as long as the DV was shuttling down and back he wanted to stay in close. Once past that stage he intended to move out to synchronous orbit above that chosen spot, in preparation for assembly and activation of the macroGate.

But that would come later. The macro crew hadn't arrived yet and Clancy hoped they didn't for a while yet. As soon as he had position stable enough to put his main drive on standby, he set his people and Ketch Garber's to unbuttoning *Arrow* for zero-gee living. The belts revved up to point-three gee; the transfer ring was freed to operate; galley and living quarters were made usable again.

It seemed chintzy to put the arrival gang into the barracks-type housing provided for them, what with crew quarters vacant. But Clancy didn't intend to encroach on the preserves of the decel group, still Gating, or on the move-ins who still kept stuff in their original quarters; after all, his troops had put in three solid years aboard this bucket and earned a few perks. Still, maybe he could work something out. . . .

Of the twenty regular-quarters rooms, four had been spares all along. And let's see: Amalyn Tabard's old space lay idle, and Coyote had cleared his in favor of Ptiba's, Phil Henning the same with Sybiljan, and Fleurine with Eli. The other three couples maintained dual bases, and of course Trish and Marnie roomed separately.

Well hell. Even excluding the VIP suite which was going to stay just that, and captain's digs which he'd never got around to move into but you never could tell—and besides, that terminal accessed too many command functions to let strangers play around with it—eight spaces should be plenty.

He put the motion to Garber; the man said, "Do you have any rules, such as who's allowed to room together?"

Allaird was *not* going to get involved with other people's ideas of propriety. "They're in your charge; you make those rules. Mine are simple: no messes and no trouble."

Ketch Garber grinned. "Pretty much like mine. Thanks."
Well, you have to check. . . .

With *Arrow* no longer under way, watch duty as such became a one-person chore and largely a formality; charting the planet and gathering data from it were the major efforts. Marnie spent more of her waking time in control than elsewhere, sometimes in the nominal watch seat but mostly at whatever instrument console might be free, soaking up every bit of available information.

Possibly due to the lack of polar ice caps, the surface of Straight Flush was about ninety percent water. For the most part its land areas were archipelagoes rather than continents, but in the northern hemisphere one mass formed an exception. Spanning slightly more than forty degrees of longitude, its outlines resembled nothing more than a crooked and grotesquely widened fleur-de-lis laid upside down, sprawling from roughly seventy degrees latitude to barely past thirty-five. Its three ranges of hills or mountains—difficult to evaluate from up here—were broken by slanting gaps, saddle-shaped passes, and in one case a large water-filled depression that might have been a meteorite crater. Nicole Pryce called it Lake Dimple and the name stuck.

The central range's northern end dropped abruptly to meet a huge inlet. Most of the coastline, in fact, ran jaggedly and deeply indented. So that while extremities reached over a considerable span, computer integration of the area when properly projected put it at not much over two million square miles.

"About two-thirds the size of Australia," Clancy commented. And no one thing else showing above water covered a quarter as much. There were quite a lot of elses, though, lying in scattered streaks along that surface—enough to make up ten percent of the world's total area, give or take a little.

The matter of tides audibly concerned Jenice Raible, a short, dark-haired woman who seemed to be Garber's prime aide. The vast clear sweeps of ocean allowed tidal bulges to move almost unimpeded, and of three noticeable moons, one appeared to mass almost half that of Earth's satellite. Much smaller, though: about eight hundred miles across. "So it's denser than Earth," Jenice said, "by nearly ten percent."

A chunk from the core of a planet destroyed in some un-imaginable catastrophe? Who could know? But it rode nearly two hundred thousand miles out, and finally Raible calculated its tidal effect as something under three-fourths of the moon's on Earth, and quit worrying. Even though those effects *had* slowed the planet to a thirty-hour day. On the other hand this could be a very old world; dim stars last well.

Marnie decided not to mention that the tidal tug was being resisted by only eighty-five percent of Earth's gravity. She told Clancy, though; he laughed and said, "Don't stir her up."

Straight Flush wore a deeper atmosphere than Earth's. Spectrographic readings showed nothing overtly toxic and a fair share of oxygen, fitting well with the land's predominant bluish green tinge, which everyone wanted to interpret as vegetation. With axial tilt so slight, no obvious winter-summer differences were expected. Or observed.

As to animals, no clues appeared. And if intelligence or civilization existed here, it didn't go in for night life; darkside observations showed only shadow. The sole exception was a patch of glare glimpsed, on one pass, through cloud cover. But the first time a clearing wind pattern revealed the area to daylight scan, it turned out to be an equatorial island, now mostly blackened. "Forest fire," guessed Clancy. Or some equivalent. At least it bolstered the vegetation hypothesis.

"Well, unless somebody's down there rubbing two sticks together," said Coyote, "get braced for electrical storms."

"Wouldn't we have seen something?" Gina asked.

He only shrugged. No one else had an answer, either.

Nicole turned over to face Clancy. "We have all the information we can get from here; you know that." The sudden switch confused him; in quarters and off duty for a change, they had been catching up on the benefits of privacy. She said, "How much longer are you going to hold off sending the Vehicle down?"

And why? She'd know, of course, but she wasn't saying it: Ptiba wouldn't be healed enough to operate the DV for some weeks, Marnie was next best qualified to land that can, and Allaird dreaded sending her off to do it.

Failing to outwait Nicole, finally he said, "Yes, I know; I

have to, don't I?'' His sigh came out ragged. ''I'll work out a mission plan tomorrow. All right?''

''Fine.'' Pause. ''I'll help.''

So then they could get back to catching up.

''We can program an elegant trajectory in the computer,'' Ptiba said, looking serious, ''but figuring modifications on the fly might give you trouble. You may be better off, Marnie, doing it the simple way.'' Like, by hand? Well, maybe . . .

''We're down to human-scale velocities and distances here,'' Mbente continued. ''Just over thirty-eight hundred miles out, tangential velocity a hundred eighty-five miles a minute. So, tell me your easiest way to ground safely.''

Hmmm; all right. ''Kill the tangential and drop.'' Clancy's map readout showed the target, the smooth, gradual slope up to the rim of Lake Dimple in the Eastern Range, at latitude sixty. With surface rotation speed in the bullet train range, nothing hyper at that end. ''How fast do you want me to get down?''

Ptiba frowned. ''Choose your own leeway, and this time fuel's no object. Oh, say you shoot for three hours. In any case, we set launch time to put your target somewhere near position when you get down there. Now tell me the rest.''

So Marnie spelled it out the way she saw it. Except for a few minor corrections, Ptiba approved.

Ready or not, next day the DV was going for a spin. Lake Dimple would be clearing the morning terminator about two hours after *Arrow* did, giving nearly maximum possible daylight for this initial recon. It could hardly get better than that. . . .

Disengagement and separation went by the book; with the magnetostrictive seal released, igniting gases made the Vehicle shudder, buck, then pop smoothly out. Using the attitude thrustors Marnie turned the little ship ninety degrees by the gyro, checking against the planet's image on a starboard view.

Eight and a half minutes of drive thrust killed tengential velocity. In the rear screens *Arrow* dwindled. For a moment Marnie watched. Suddenly it all seemed very final; there went the ship and here she was, with two of her crewmates and Ketch Garber, with three of his. On the way down, all by themselves.

As she swung the can to point tail down, Ptiba's voice came. ''Looking good.''

From the comm seat, Ky Benjamin acknowledged. "Vehicle falling free now." About five minutes and sixty miles later, surface-reflection radar showed drop speed at fifteen hundred miles an hour. Marnie kicked in her drive thrust control, slaving surface radar through the computer to hold that speed until further notice. Coyote relayed the figures to Ptiba.

Sitting co-pilot, Trish said, "Check me on this: we watch for how the target area's lining up and tilt to drift whichever way we need to." Because launch timing would bring Lake Dimple around close, but no bullseye. "So when do we start real decel?"

It wasn't critical; fifteen hundred was well within the speed range of executive jets. Of course those didn't make their runs straight down; slowing, their passengers weren't bucking gravity head on, *plus* a Vehicle's own retardant thrust. And Marnie intended keeping total decel forces down near one gee; no point in subjecting passengers to more when she didn't have to. Which meant that near the surface she had only about fifteen percent of that to play with, drivewise. So, "After two and a half hours of drop, a little less. At about a hundred miles up."

Over the comm circuit Ptiba said, "That sounds right. Gives you some leeway, too. Where's your target by now?"

Trish checked. "Thirty degrees to go yet, close as I can make it." Marnie nodded; that guess fit the planned timing.

Which left her with over two hours to wait, doing nothing but watch instruments while the planet's gravity field, fully perceptible at constant drop, grew too slowly to really notice.

Construct containing the volitional earlier studied and simulated has reached relative spatial/chronal stasis. Indicated is further approach to this volitional, to ascertain surety of ending undue kinesis emergences. At execution, however, sensing extensor finds volitional in parametric fluxion. With cautionary reference to damage of other volitional at last previous enprobement, essayance is deferred.

If the computer knew its stuff, Marnie's arbitrary hundred miles gave her a margin of about seven. "Which should be plenty," Ptiba reassured her. The satellite that was *Arrow* would be setting soon after the DV grounded; Marnie felt grateful for the contact now.

Reaching for the drive control she nodded to Coyote.

"Initiating decel thrust," he reported, and everyone's apparent weight grew to Earth normal.

Marnie kept tabs on the radar; altitude and drop speed both stayed close to the numbers she wanted. Target lay a few miles north and west; she tipped the Vehicle's nose that way and watched the eastern shore of Lake Dimple creep toward bullseye.

Except to his own people, Ketch Garber hadn't talked much. Now, turning to Marnie, he said, "Once we ground and you button down, I'm in charge; remember that."

Well sure; he and his group ran the tests, the first emergence (if any!), and whatever unlading he deemed advisable. Marnie had no problem with any of that. Coyote, though, swung around to say, "We're not there yet."

Garber's expression went blank; he stood, saying, "I'll be down below, Hold Eighteen. Clearing away stuff around the Gates so we can get them out, and up running. Come on, troops."

"Just don't clear out the Tush," said Ky. Frowning, Garber straddled over the railing, not bothering to open the little gate, and disappeared down the tunnel. The others followed.

Keeping her voice mild because she didn't *like* being steamed at Coyote Benjamin, Marnie said, "Why so gritty with him?"

He shrugged on one side. "Didn't care for his takeover tone, I guess."

"Well, I'm the one he was pushing. If anybody. And if it starts to bother me, I'll take care of it."

Coyote blinked. "How old did you say you were?"

"What's that got . . . ?" Oh well: "Uh, two–three months short of fifteen, the last I counted. Why?"

"I guess I was thinking your age makes you a kid. And that maybe Garber was into the same mistake." He grinned. "Sorry."

"No fret." Shaking off the distraction she turned back to the board. Drop speed was tapering toward zero, with a safe margin of altitude remaining. And the target area . . .

"Maybe you're growing up other ways, too. Are you?"

What the hell? Swiveling to look at him she said, "Could you please shut up while I land this thing?"

At exec jet altitude and dropping like a leaf, Marnie had time for a good look below: the Dimple Lake crater rim sloped away steep at first and then flattened off. As the ground grew closer she saw treelike growth, interspersed with clearings.

One big one looked fairly level. Checking to make sure the landing legs were fully spread and locked, she tilted enough to sidle directly above the spot she wanted, and eased down. Impact was barely enough to jar; she cut drive and hit the "Level" button, then waited while the uphill leg creaked, its bottom segment telescoping enough to counteract the slight tilt of the ground beneath.

Ignoring the blue-green foliage in the side screen views, she turned on Coyote Benjamin. "*What* other ways?"

"Huh?" He blinked. "Oh. Well, I just wondered, you growing up and all, if having no boys around . . ."

In front of Trish he was asking her stuff like this? "Let's say, I'm in no big hurry."

His sigh, then, sounded like one of relief. "Well, that's good. No reason you should be. I just wondered . . ."

So it was all right; friendly curiosity, nothing more. "And I'm okay, thanks for asking but you didn't need to. Let's go see what Garber's finding out."

Trish stayed, to keep touch with *Arrow* while contact held.

"The air's heavy, all right," Ketch Garber said. "Nearly one-point-five atmospheres. Jenice tested a sample; it's okay to breathe, nothing toxic and no anomalous particulates."

"Not even pollens?" Coyote asked.

Garber looked at him, but both voice and expression had been friendly this time. "Apparently not. She pumped air through a filter and caught practically nothing."

"So where is she?" Marnie asked. For here in Hold Eighteen only Ketch and one other man labored at clearing the Gates for offloading.

"Outside, she and Harley both. Taking samples. Don't worry; we haven't seen anything out there that moves, and she has a wideband soundblaster just in case." The impact of one of those things would derail the purpose of a charging rhino.

Relaxing, Garber smiled. "Your aft airlock, down there, worked just fine the first try. Compression rate's perfect, Jenice said on the intercom; about as fast as you can do it without discomfort."

Marnie had forgotten the airlock comm set. Oh well; she said, "Would it be all right if we went out for a while?" If Garber needed boss treatment, why not?

It seemed to work. "Sure. Stay close, though. We'll be ready to winch out the Gates soon, along with their prefab housing, and we'll need everybody on that. Except your watch, of course; we should keep contact with the ship."

Which had set behind the planet's bulge by now, anyway. Never mind; Marnie and Coyote headed down to the airlock. Instructions said not to let native atmosphere into the ship yet, so they had to pump it out first and refill from the tanks.

The heavy air outside, carrying a fugitive scent neither mint nor sage but suggestive of both, had a sensuous quality. The lesser gravity added to the effect; *Arrow*'s two months at one-gee were recent enough that her muscles hadn't forgotten.

Yellower sunlight somehow gave the feel of artificial lighting; okay, ignore that. Underfoot lay dark soil, firm but not rock-hard. Stringy dark green tendrils, punctuated by bulbous purplish growths, crisscrossed the immediate area—while all around the open space clustered thick, gnarly trees of a sort; above the bottom sections of ribbed trunks she saw masses of rather blobby bluish green foliage.

And why, she wondered, did all this feel more like a holo set than an actual new world? All right, look around. Less than a hundred yards upslope, the rim of Lake Dimple rose against a patch of clear sky, deeper-colored than Earth's. Marnie turned to Ky. "Let's go up and have a look."

"Why not?" Moving fast enough to run short of breath they climbed, threading their way among closely spaced trees, then clambered as they came to the rocky crest, until they topped it and saw the lake beyond. Marnie gasped. From orbit it was an oval blue dot; the readout said forty miles along the major diameter. This barely rippling purpled reality took her breath.

Coyote said, "Good place to begin a colony," and she nodded. Too far from shore to make out any details, she saw water spurt up. A splash, or what? For several minutes they watched, but the effect didn't repeat.

From downhill came Garber's shouts. Time to tote that bale.

He had the hold's main hatch opened out, a winch crane arm unfolded and protruding, along with the hoseline that had pumped quickset from an inboard tank to fill pre-fab plastic forms and make a large floor slab, starting only a few feet from a landing leg. In a vague way Marnie had known these things existed, but preoccupied with the jobs she really needed to learn, she hadn't paid much attention.

If Jenice Raible wasn't back aboard the Vehicle she had to be still scouting, as Ketch Garber directed Hartey and Bourne, the other man, in assembling the panels he winched out to form outside walls and partitions. With only the front wall and that area of the roof left to place, Ketch signaled a break and climbed the landing leg, leading the way back up to the hold.

There wasn't much left of the Gates Motel, but Garber hadn't dismantled the refreshment bar. He'd only moved it over out of the way, and now fresh coffee scented the heavy air. As to that, Ketch said, "This hold is now part of the outdoors; we don't use its tunnel entrance again until we've bled this air to space on the way up." It sounded overly cautious to Marnie, but so did the airlock procedure and to the same end, so she made yessir noises and nodded.

She was rinsing her cup when Trish on the intercom said, "Marnie? Come on up. Captain Allaird wants you right now."

Garber said, "I'll go with you."

"I know how to work the airlock. I just did."

"I need some papers from up there, anyway."

Anyway? Well, if it made him happy . . .

XX

" ▪ ▪ ▪ **a**s soon as they can spare you," Clancy said. "The macroGate crew arrived; we're up to here with people. And they can do only so much before they'll need some help from the Vehicle. How much longer . . . ?"

Garber gestured his wish to speak; Marnie nodded. "We have quite a bit of offloading left to do, captain. We'll want our quarters secured, supplies and all, and the Gates up and running, before we're left to ourselves down here. It shouldn't take more than a few hours, but at this stage I'd really prefer not to rush matters, and maybe screw up some way. So—"

"Agreed," said Clancy. "Marnie; keep me advised?"

"Sure. I'll come back up here every so often."

"You stay here," Ketch said. "No offense, but we're into muscle work now and Pembrook's bigger." He tried, it appeared, to look apologetic. "Anyway, you'll need to plot your climb back, won't you? The timing and all?"

He was right both ways. "Okay, Trish; you're relieved." And Marnie turned back to the comm panel.

"About that ride back," she began. "The window for a straight shot, up or down—it only comes around every five hours and a dab. I'd figured on using that: push up a way, then cut drive and coast to your orbit. Matching the tangential during that part, so all you'd have to do is talk me in to dock."

Clancy couldn't see her shake her head; the movement came by reflex. "Lifting off just any old time, I don't see quite how to plot it. For one thing I need daylight."

"Not exactly," Allaird said. "The *ship* should be out of

339

shadow, sure. And for about five-sixths of our orbit, it is. But night or day down there doesn't limit when you can lift.''

Ptiba came on the circuit. "Marnie? Just let us know when you can pull out of there and I'll give you the computer's best idea for a rendezvous sequence. You may get up here and have to chase us or wait for us, but don't worry; it'll work okay.''

"If you say so." Then, "Any reason I need to stay at the board here just now?"

Clancy said, "I guess not. Why?"

"Muscle or not, maybe I can help out some, down below.''

One by one the Earthgates components were lofted out to the floor slab and hefted into place: the power supply all in one piece but the Gates themselves partially disassembled, though by no means as fragmented as on arrival. At the Tush, Garber pulled a unit before clearing away the mattresses. "What's that?" Coyote asked.

"The key matrix. If you didn't want anything outGating on you, I'm surprised you had it plugged in.''

Marnie looked at the recess it had come from. "There's no hatch like that on our other Gates.''

Ketch shrugged. "Older models, I guess." So that's why Nicole hadn't known she could keep the readied Tush deactivated.

Now, with both Gates assembled and the building fully enclosed, he replaced the unit. "Okay; time to open for business." Immediately the colors flared, then faded to present a small table, holding a tray with a dozen wineglasses. After Raible and Bourne cleared the things away, nothing happened for about ten minutes; then the next flare died to reveal a coldpack. The note on it read, "Take a break and have some champagne.''

Jenice Raible laughed. "That's what you call good labor relations.''

Eventually all the arrival team's supplies and matériel were offloaded and taken indoors. A little flushed from the wine, Ketch Garber seemed inclined to complain forever that some of his working gear, in the crates evacuated from the Vehicle to the hold behind in order to make room for the Gates, had been forgotten and left topside, on the ship. Seismic and geothermal instruments, things like that.

Coyote Benjamin cut into the tirade. "Bitching won't get the stuff down here. You'll have to wait for the next run and that's all there is to it."

It wasn't the best note on which to part, but what the hell. Garber did manage a grin when he shook hands good-bye.

"How'd you ever think of doing it *this* way?" Now that Marnie following Ptiba's orders had the Vehicle on course, hurtling free and slanting retrograde, with a velocity that seemed far too great for her purpose, she wanted some answers. While she waited, she punched Hold Eighteen's hatch open—releasing the heavy Straight Flush air, except for a few bottled samples for Chauncey's testing, into space. Then she resealed and allowed the hold to fill from the Vehicle's own tanks. Over comm, Ptiba said, "We were too far out of orbital phase for a normal approach. Either to chase us down or vice versa. And waiting for better position would take too long. You're not the only one saddled with new troops chomping at the bit."

"So you're going to shoot out past our orbit," Nicole added, "and then drop back. All your trajectory from there to apogee and down again will be slow speed, very light gravity pull; that lets us catch up to you. Then all you do is kill vertical drop and add tangential vee to match us. Easy pickings."

"If you say so." Late explanations were better than none, but working in the blind since takeoff had her edgy. All right: she tried to check what she'd been told against what her instruments were saying: from present height and vee and vector angle, how close would the DV's ballistic trajectory meet *Arrow*'s orbital passage? And at what vee, what slant?

Marnie thought back, to the lesson on how to make turns. This one cut tighter than a right angle and required considerable change in vee. The equations were simple; she plugged in some sample numbers, approximations, letting the computer cope with the sines and cosines while she called up Eli's graphic with the three-arrowed triangle. It was good enough for a starting point, a template, so she saved it to use later.

From there, nothing to do but wait and see what the real figures would be, going into that turn. Nobody said much.

It all worked; she brought the DV down to *Arrow*'s orbit and riding ahead just a bit. Clancy had said, "I'll swing us to

run bassackward; you dock aft," and that's how it went.
Working aim and distance by her rearview screens, Marnie
juked her yaw and attitude thrustors while she used the forward trio to close the gap but not too fast, making sure the
landing legs had reduced their splay to point slightly inward
and meet the tapered socket at *Arrow*'s stern so the DV could
slide in and make seal.

A bit of residual yaw threw her aim off; correcting, she
overcontrolled and had to thrust forward, clear of possible
damage. Again she tried slowing. But now her alignment
drifted off at least a yard, so she . . .

Damn it all. New to the maneuver, she simply couldn't
manage precise control of alignment and closure rate at the
same time!

She was beginning her third try when Ptiba said, "Marnie?
You'd better switch to multiple and let me bring you in."

What? "You can run it from there? Why . . . ?"

"Later," said Clancy. "Just make the switch, please. Same
as when we were running the ship from there."

"Right." Then, feeling her face flush with embarrassment,
Marnie watched as the DV met its docking recess almost perfectly, jiggled only a little, then slid smoothly in to nest against
the aft airlock bulkhead.

She had no instruments to register that the landing legs were
secured, nor that the pressure collar at the socket's rim had
inflated to form an airtight seal—but she didn't need them.
The collar wouldn't inflate until the legs *were* locked, and
stern sensors showed air pressure behind the Vehicle.

Good enough. Feeling let down by the ignominious end to
what she'd considered a successful mission, Marnie went
through her shutdown checklist before following Trish and
Coyote down the tunnel and into the ship proper.

". . . slight modification," said Ptiba, "to allow the transfer
of control function the other way." Showered and wearing
fresh clothes, Marnie and her recent crew sat in the lounge
with the DV commander, along with Clancy and Nicole, all
munching and sipping refreshment. "We hooked the trunks to
a pair of wideband transceivers; from here to the surface the
round trip delay's only a few milliseconds, so that's no problem, and . . ."

"But why didn't you tell me, before? And—and you could have taken over the landing, if you'd wanted to."

"Why should I? You were doing fine, and you had seat-of-the-pants contact; I didn't. Up here, docking, that wasn't important; all I needed was visual and computer input."

Mbente leaned forward. "Look, now. Docking's tricky." Marnie couldn't argue with that. "It takes practice. Which none of us, somehow, ever thought to try to give you. I'm not sure how we could've, anyway. No sims program could handle all the thrustor combinations; it'd take up more chip space than the Vehicle's computer has to lend out."

"Then how'm I ever going to learn?"

"Later, probably," said Clancy. "When the Vehicle isn't all booked up. Because first we have to get the rest of the arrival team's stuff down there. And then the macroGate group has dibs on the DV. Near as I can tell, that bunch was *born* impatient."

That team, all forty of it, seemed to take over the entire ship. Before meeting them, Marnie had wondered whether their getups would differ from those of the arrival team, and how. Only when she saw them did she remember that *Arrow* was on straight Earth time now, one to one; the two groups had Gated out no more than a few days or weeks apart.

Some did stand out. For one, a crew chief named Bet Carou, a tall woman who looked very black except by comparison with Ptiba Mbente. Energetic and plainspoken, Carou—along with Tyran Galer the team leader and Kyle Ferris his *segundo* who stayed quite aloof from ship's personnel—ignored the fashion fads followed by most of the contingent.

The ship's former air of quiet, which had sometimes given Marnie a feel almost of loneliness, she now recalled with longing. "You can't go any place," she complained to Nicole, "without a herd of them stampeding at you. And *noise . . .*"

Trish didn't mind at all. She'd worked on a macroGate installation; for her this was like old times, and now she put some of her free time into helping out. "Wiring and plumbing, that sort of thing's already in place for each fin section; just needs a few final hookups. Right now we're getting up partitions, stuff like that. And bringing some gear outship from the central holds, to install."

But this phase of the effort wouldn't last forever. And until the DV was available to lend some nudge power for the heavy moving, the twelve fins couldn't be levered out, joined, and unfolded to form a circle. So that the macroGate could function.

Eighty hours after its first launch, with *Arrow* and Lake Dimple in roughly the same relative positions as before, the Vehicle popped free again and decelerated into drop mode. Again Marnie sat as pilot and Trish co-pilot, but Gina Todisco had replaced Coyote, and along with the remaining eight of the advance team rode Clancy and Nicole.

Cargo contained not only the misplaced crates but also components for more pre-fab buildings. Breaking such things down into sections small enough for Gating hadn't been deemed feasible. Of course that decision had been made perhaps seventy-five years earlier; maybe methods had changed since then.

And so it proved. With more confidence than before, Marnie set the Vehicle down over near the edge of an area cleared of trees and brush but now surprisingly cluttered. All around she saw structures that had never ridden *Arrow*, and people swarming between them. They reminded her, somewhat, of an ant farm.

The Gates she'd delivered had been working overtime.

Leaving Gina in charge of the grounded vessel, Clancy told her, "While we're gone, the outer airlock hatch stays closed. Keep the aft sensors onscreen so you can see below. Intercom Station LL of your switch panel is on a landing leg; if anybody wants to talk, use it. But nobody comes aboard unless one of *us* is there to okay it."

Nicole Pryce frowned. "Are you worried about something?"

"Nope. We don't need tourists, is all."

Down inside the airlock he bled the higher pressure in slowly. "Chauncey says this air is okay; we don't need to keep it out of the ship. But coming back inside we'll pump down to one standard atmosphere before letting it mix."

He lifted the hatch and descended the ladder. When they were all down, he turned to Marnie. "Do you see the original building you helped put up?'' Because whoever was in charge would probably be where the Gates were.

She hesitated, then pointed. ''Over there, I think. They've built more onto it.'' Turning, she led the way; Clancy followed.

To be stopped at the major entrance by a uniformed guard. ''Would you state your business, please? And show some ID?''

Moving to the front of the group, Clancy said, ''Clarence Allaird, captain, *Arrow*. Where's Ketch Garber?''

''The advance team leader? I have no idea. Out gathering specimens, perhaps. Could someone else help you?''

''Sure. Who runs the show now?''

''Uh—I'm afraid Administrator Villereal's rather busy. Perhaps one of her assistants. One moment.'' The man talked into what looked like a wristwatch and maybe was, listened to a voice Allaird couldn't make out, and said, ''Mr. Bryan will see you. Mr. Roland Bryan. Second door right; identify yourself to his secretary.'' Turning away, the guard paid him no more attention.

At Allaird's gesture the others followed him inside and through the door specified. The thin young secretary, a person of indeterminate sex until Allaird spotted the telltale Adam's apple, gave a quick glance up and then pretended he hadn't, even when Clancy stood directly across the desk from him.

So Clancy kicked the desk. Gaping, the fellow stared. ''You got a minute? Captain Allaird to see Roland Bryan.''

Fingers on a keyboard. ''I'll see if you're listed . . .''

''Listed, hell! You were just talking to the guard about me and you know it. Now is Bryan here or isn't he?''

The intercom switch must have been open; a voice said, ''Send him in, Sibley.''

''There's more than one,'' the youth was saying. Too late; motioning Nicole and Trish and Marnie to precede him and leaving the rest to follow, Allaird opened the door.

Behind a larger and more luxurious desk sat a comfortable-looking man of about forty, sporting sleek brown hair and a ruddy face. Rising, he reached out a hand. ''Captain Allaird?''

''Mr. Bryan. Yes, I'm Allaird. Checking in. And these

are . . .'' He introduced his own party. "And these eight here belong to Mr. Ketch Garber's team.''

"Yes. Well. That's fine.'' He called Sibley in and told him to escort that group to the advance team's quarters; Clancy didn't really know any of them but bade them a cheerful good-bye and good luck anyway.

"Here, have seats,'' Bryan said then. And when they did, "All right, captain. The macroGate's on line then, I take it?''

What the—? "Afraid not. We had a setback, navigational glitch. Not the decel contingent's fault, but it put us back over forty billion miles and two months. Didn't Garber tell you?'' Slowly, affability leached out of Bryan's expression. "And another thing. Glen Springs dumped your direct Gates on us while the ship was in decel and uncrewed. That didn't help.''

Roland Bryan shook his head. "Excuses. The bane of an administrator's life. Oh, I'm sure they're valid—or at least, that I'm not technician enough to prove differently. But it does seem hard. Here we work our fingers to the bone, getting ready to oversee the colonists, and you tell me the landers face even more delay; lacking the macroGate we won't receive many colonists and couldn't accommodate them if we did. Not without the necessary heavy equipment.''

"You seem to be doing all right,'' said Nicole. "I saw at least several hundred out there. That's a start.''

Bryan looked pained. "This group consists of colonial *administrators*, and service personnel. Not farmers and the like.'' He turned back to Clancy. "You will return to your ship and deploy the macroGate immediately. Until that is done, there's no point in my giving you your further orders.''

Clancy stood. Placing both hands flat on the desk he said quietly, "My orders come from Glen Springs. I signed on for this trip—we all did—and once the macroGate's up and running I'll either contract for a new mission or I won't. Do you read me?''

"And supposing your mission's been extended?''

"Unilaterally?'' *Don't make me laugh.* "Look, we're wasting time. As you say, the macroGate's behind sked.'' At his gesture, his companions stood. "I'll keep you advised.''

At the door, exiting last one out, he turned. "If there's anything else, call me. Clancy Allaird. I'll be upstairs.'' And started toward the entrance. The guard there, again listening to his wristwatch, gestured for Clancy to stop. Not likely; he brushed on past and kept moving.

Until he reached the DV and opened intercom station LL. "Gina? Pop the airlock hatch and drop the ladder."

Marnie hadn't seen her father this pissed off since Glen Springs when she told him about Carl. He pumped airlock pressure down fast and opened it to the tunnel before the two fully equalized, then climbed as if pursued.

When everyone had joined him, up on the control deck, he moved to the pilot's seat. "I am going to lift this contraption like a bat. Everybody strap in." Once they did, he hit the go button hard; drive thrust plus gravity pull registered over two gees on the meter, and Marnie felt every dyne per gram of it—assuming she had her units straight.

Radar showed the Vehicle well above *Arrow*'s orbit before Allaird cut drive. Grinning, he executed a smart end for end, did a little computer checking and once again hit the drive hammer. This time for only seconds; then he leaned back and smiled. "Now we drop gently to meet *Arrow* and match vees. Marnie, would you like to take over?"

So she did. At near approach she saw that again the ship had been swung tangential to orbit and stern first, making the docking maneuver as easy as possible. She expected Ptiba or somebody to do that chore, but Clancy said to go ahead and try it, so she did. Now, surprising her, he seemed to have all the patience there was. After six botched tries he still didn't declare her preempted, and on the seventh she hit the jackpot.

Not pretty, but she got the bugger in there!

Right, thought Clancy; give her a chance and she'll come through. "Nice going, Marni Gras." Sensor indication showed air in the chamber behind; he said, "Why don't we go grab a shower and meet in the galley? Celebrate our first contact with the natives, or something." He saw Nicole smile at the mild sarcasm.

As he waited for the others to precede him down the tunnel, the intercom sounded. When he answered, Chauncey Ng said, "Captain, some woman groundside is on screen here. In control. Wants to talk with you."

Cleanliness had to wait; catching up to the others he said

he might be a while so go ahead and eat, and went to respond.

Chauncey motioned him to an aux screen; looking, he saw a tall woman, swarthy with grey-tinged black hair coiled at her nape above a colorful flowing dress. "Captain Allaird?" So the circuit was on visual both ways. "Carmela Villereal, chief administrator. I understand that you visited our headquarters today and left somewhat dissatisfied. Has Roland Bryan been doing his White Man's Burden trick again?"

On screen, Villereal's office looked not especially plushy, but comfortable. Clancy said, "He made it clear he's no mere colonial; he *administrates* things, whether they need it or not. If that's what you mean." So far this one seemed friendly, but he wasn't ready to snuggle and be pals. Not just yet.

"An ancestor of Roland's served in India before it achieved independence; he never forgave Lord Mountbatten. I'm afraid the man sees our work here as a sort of British Raj revival."

"And you don't," said Clancy. "Good. But that's as may be. What's this about him giving orders to ship's personnel? Such as me personally." Tone polite, but his feathers still bristled.

"I'm afraid I don't read everything carefully enough before initialing; there's too much going on. Roland Bryan slipped one past me; he gave notice to Earth that the colony world New Empire is now officially in charge of *Arrow*'s further operations."

Allaird gave a snort. "Including fuel and supplies? Glen Springs is going to die laughing." Or was that facility, too, now run by ambitious memomeisters? And—*wait* a minute! "New Empire? What the hell . . . I mean . . ."

"I thought it a bit pretentious myself, but the senior staff voted to confirm Roland's choice, so I agreed."

Okay, take no prisoners. "Your senior staff was a bit late. As captain of the discovering ship, with the crew's agreement *I* named this world, some time ago when we first made orbit. You can tell Mr. Roland Bryan he'll be doing his administering on the colony planet Straight Flush."

Was Villereal suppressing a smile? "By protocol, captain, you're entirely correct. But how many messages have you sent, imprinting that name onto the official consciousness? Roland and his group produce documents by the ream, each under the letterhead of the New Empire Colonial Administration. As a practical matter, sir, which name would you expect to prevail?''

Clancy took a deep breath. ''As a practical matter, I suppose I can't afford to give a damn. After all, there won't be word back from Earth for another four years. By which time I'll be long out of here.'' The *hell* out, he thought but didn't say.

Now she did smile. Clancy liked the effect; it helped her rather plain features. ''Your realism becomes you. May you and I, then, cooperate in our mutual concerns?''

''You and I, yes. But . . .''

''Code your calls and messages CV-One; that channel bypasses Mr. Bryan. Who is, I have been thinking, perhaps due for reassignment. If indeed my authority still includes such measures. And I rather believe it does.''

Allaird grinned. ''Lady, you've got yourself a colleague.''

The picture blanked. From behind him, Marnie said, ''I like her, too. Can you come eat now, or do you have to shower first?''

He shrugged. ''Oh hell; I'll eat dirty.''

Before he went, though, he printed out a message to be Gated to Earth. He made only a minor point of planetary nomenclature but was quite vehement on the subject of who he took orders from. It might not do much good, given Gate lag, but at least he'd be on the record. Eventually.

Each day now, Marnie took the DV down with another load to the colony. Until Chauncey Ng agreed that Ptiba was fit to pilot the small craft; once she took over, her greater skills in jockeying the craft allowed for considerably augmented loads. With the DV hanging tethered just clear of *Arrow*'s stern, suited members of the Gate crew hauled crates along the tunnel and lashed them to fittings on the vessel's hull. Ptiba could manage atmospheric entry and landing with such unbalanced overloads; neither Marnie nor Trish felt up to it, just yet. But either or both could spell Mbente, piloting the DV in space. So the schedule went to two a day; within a week all colony-destined materials were out of *Arrow* and down where they belonged.

Shortly afterward, everyone strapped down while Clancy nudged the ship out to synchronous orbit. Very gently, so that the rotating belts needn't be secured, he took it up. Twenty thousand miles higher he eased off even more, giving Lake Dimple time to come into position on the daylight side. Not directly under *Arrow*, but close for longitude; from an equatorial orbit, of course, the colony lay to the north. Then he jockeyed for synchronous stability and again aimed the ship at Straight Flush.

Next came transfer of macroGate materials from the central hold to the outer fins. Tagging along with Trish Pembrook in the overall group, Marnie helped carry some of the less bulky items and then acted as tool monkey for Trish, taking care to follow instructions and avoid getting in anyone's way. She wasn't all that comfortable working in a crowd, but staying inship and seeing nothing of the new developments didn't appeal, either.

Time came when a pair of fins had to go vacuum, the air pumped out because during partial separation and realignment no seal could be kept anyway. With forward mountings disengaged, the fins would be pivoted on their rear hinges to angle out from *Arrow*'s hull until the forward tips could be pulled together and secured. When that part was done, *Arrow* would resemble some strange flower with six curved petals.

In achieving this configuration, the DV was essential.

Clancy didn't want Marnie working vacuum at all, but after a lot of argument—with Nicole unexpectedly on Marnie's side of it—he compromised. "All right, you work with a partner at all times, and always *inside*. None of this out on a line stuff, you hear me?" And sounded pompous, even to himself. But she was so young, and he didn't know enough about outside work to coach her on it, even if all the new red tape gave him time to do so. And certainly he didn't want to trust that kind of training to these new macroGate people he barely knew.

Suits, he did know; *Jovian* had carried them. There had been periodic drills in their use, and during one equipment failure the entire crew had been forced to suit up in earnest. Current issue was somewhat improved: insulex body suits of thin membrane with an impermeable outer layer and an absorbent inner one, good for four to eight hours before sweat built enough to saturate. Back on *Jovie* they went clammy within the hour.

* * *

With considerable help from Nicole, Marnie got into the clinging suit; under it she wore only briefs and halter. With the ventral seam and relief patch sealed, all that remained was to clamp shut the semi-rigid collar, an oval that slanted back from below her chin to the crown of her head, and close the transparent facepiece. For now, she left the latter ajar; closing it would automatically put her on suit air and activate the short-range talkset. High on her back, the semi-flexible air tank rode like an oblong rucksack.

Trish knocked and was admitted. "Ready to go?"

"I guess so. Sure." Reassuring Nicole that yes she *would* be careful, Marnie followed her friend outship to the airlock serving Number Two fin.

Four others were waiting to use the lock. When all were inside and facemasks sealed, Bet Carou sprayed the chamber full of a pink mist. The crew chief's shoulder patch made her easy to spot. Now she said, "Watch for leaks; we always have to check for defects, the first time," but as the pressure dropped no telltale spurt from any suit disturbed the dissipating mist. Within seconds Bet vented the air, then opened the far hatch; the group clambered through, into the fin.

Except for the suit, Marnie decided, working in vacuum wasn't all that different. Velcro still held, and it wasn't as though the enclosure was noticeably open to space. It was not sealed, though, and holes appeared where fastenings were removed.

Suit air seemed tasteless somehow, and every voice on the comm net sounded directly in her ears; she couldn't tell where they really came from. The faceplate contours gave good visibility, but the suits all looked alike, with reflections obscuring faces. Unless you were up close and looking directly in, you couldn't see who was who.

But that was what the fore and aft nameplates were for.

Somebody wasn't reading those. Or didn't care. A woman's voice said, ". . . glad when we can move out of those barracks. Into the Gate, away from all those old crusties."

"Fifty years behind the times," a man answered, "and not a thought of catching up, trying to learn anything."

Somebody laughed; for a few seconds two or three talked at once before Marnie heard a woman's voice. "I'd bet there's one or two you'd like to teach. Maybe a little game of slut poker.''

Laughter. Then, ''Oh, get some focus! One of *those* deeks?''

''Shut your puker!'' Bet's voice, as Marnie saw the badged suit emerge from an equipment room. ''There's crewfolk helping, here. Though listening to you lot, I can't think why.''

Babble: it was just talk I didn't mean wouldn't want to no offense sorry didn't know just joking why didn't somebody *say . . .*

Until Trish's voice cut cold across the rest. ''The sooner you shut up and work, the sooner you'll get your wish.''

That remark put the stopper in; work resumed.

Pembrook wasn't in sight; Marnie went looking and found her in another compartment. Right now, she had no desire at all to mix with this macroGate crew.

Helping Trish move and place and fasten down various unit components, Marnie lost track of time until it was their group's turn for a break. After cycling back into the ship and opening faceplates, first came a john stop. The relief strip at the suit's crotch worked easily enough, Marnie found. Working so near airlock access, the suit's own built-in option wouldn't be needed.

In the corridor by the airlock sat a hamper Marnie hadn't noticed earlier. Bet Carou opened it to reveal snacks and coffee. No one seemed to have any problem taking refreshment in zero gee. Well, they'd have had practice at it. . . .

Following Trish's unspoken lead, Marnie decided that if any embarrassment lay in the situation, the Gate crew could carry it. Those four ate and drank in silence, not looking at much of anything, until Bet turned to Trish and Marnie. ''Look; these clowns were out of true, granted. Part of it is, they're a little scared of you. Maybe not scared exactly, but uncertain. It's like having their grandparents turn up as young people. Your experience goes back so far, and . . .''

''That's not how it sounded.'' Marnie kept her voice flat. Unwilling to show hurt, she shut up.

''Haven't you ever made fun of something that had you edgy?''

Well, maybe. ''All right, then. It's done with.''

"And you, Pembrook? Are you willing to forget it?"

"Depends. We'll see what happens."

Her answer ended both discussion and break. Reentering the fin, the six were just in time for all the commotion.

Pushing through the group waiting to go on their own break, Carou's half dozen had barely cleared the entrance hatch area when the screaming began. Marnie pushed ahead, and craned to see what was wrong. When she did see, laughter fought with alarm. And won.

Only a few yards ahead, a figure floated in vacuum, first at a slant and then pivoting upright: the figure of herself, simulated as best the Alephant could manage, and *just the same as last time*. No suit.

The macroGate bunch went total thalamus. Marnie tried to yell she was over *here*, but they were too much louder. Several were grabbing at the Alephant, trying to drag it toward the airlock and save its seemingly imperiled life. But they couldn't move it.

Of course not, Marnie thought. As an extension from the greater plenum the Alephant would be anchored there; pulling on the simulacrum couldn't budge it. Then after a few moments it did move, drifting at an even pace not toward the lock but to Marnie herself, its would-be rescuers trailing. When it came to face her, she saw its lips move.

Through vacuum, though she strained to hear, no sound came. Somehow, on the rigid features, frustration showed. Marnie spread her hands: *I can't hear you.*

This time she watched at close hand as the solid image, in the grasp of at least five frantically tugging macroGate workers, slowly shrank to vanishment.

"What was that?" "We thought it was *you*." "You acted like you *knew* it." "Is it something dangerous?" "A spirit?" "No, doppelgänger's the word." "How did you summon it?" "Can you call it up at will?" "What kind of powers does it have?"

In the lounge, she and Trish reporting to Clancy and a few others, Marnie shook her head. "That's the kind of thing they said, and finally I quit trying to explain. Those people don't think the way we do." She made a shrug. "If they really believe all that stuff, you'd think they'd be scared to death of me."

Nicole Pryce nodded. "According to the Glen Springs reports there's a trend growing, a retreat to superstition. It's happened before; I've read about it. But not in our time."

Clancy grunted. "I wish to hell they'd weed it out of the cadres they send *us*." He looked around the table. "Any other problems, dealing with the team?"

"You might say," Trish answered. "They got really snotty about us, about the crew in general. With everyone in suits, they didn't know we were there to hear it."

"They found out, though." Marnie chuckled. "And fell all over themselves, trying to eat it."

Looking serious, Clancy said, "If you'd rather not try to work with that outfit any longer . . ."

In nearly the same words, Trish and Marnie declined the offer: they could handle any situation the macroGate team could. So Clancy and Nicole agreed to let the matter ride.

Finding subject volitional barred to communication leads to withdrawal; although barrier layer is not impervious to sensory extension, to breach it might release and exhaust thinly-dispersed, compressible matter necessary for function of volitionals in this sub-plenum. Attempt will recur at further chronal interval.

When the first pair of fins was cleared to be pivoted out, Marnie wangled an observer spot in the DV. Ptiba popped the vehicle free and eased slightly out and back, trailing a bight of line with a tether to *Arrow*'s hull. In the rear screens Marnie saw suited figures haul in the tether and secure the main line through hooks at the front of each fin.

As the team members took stations inside, Ptiba edged the DV laterally away from the ship, pulling the fins' forward ends outward and together, ending at an angle of about sixty degrees to the hull. Then more macroGate techs emerged from the adjacent tips and joined their flexible hinges as far as those would mesh.

By the time Ptiba redocked, the operation had taken nearly two hours. Of course the team's part wasn't done yet.

* * *

In any project made up of repetitive stages, the first try takes longest; with practice, each step goes faster. Allaird knew all this, yet the pace of the first phase chafed on him. Only when all six folded arches angled out from *Arrow*, their tips in a rough circle over five hundred feet across, did he feel the macroGate project was truly under way.

The next phase, connecting the six pairs of fins end to end and expanding their formation into a circle, needed delicate handling. Through remotes to the control room Clancy watched as the aft ends of two adjacent fins were linked by tie lines, freed from the ship's hull, then drawn together and towed by gentle increments of the DV's drive thrust to an approximation of their final position.

None of this happened quickly, but practice again shortened the time of each succeeding move. Over several watches Allaird lost track of who was running the DV; Ptiba would need a rest now and then, so Marnie was probably doing some of it. And maybe Trish. For although the Vehicle redocked at intervals, none of the three had been back aboard *Arrow* since the operation began.

He didn't call to find out. Ptiba had made it clear she wanted no interruptions unless something important came up.

The last towing operation reverted to slow pacing, for now all fin segments were free of the ship; any sudden movement would be transmitted to the entire zigzag ring. While the mass of the overall construct was many times that of the Deployment Vehicle, any degree of motion imparted to it would need to be corrected. But finally the DV disengaged, leaving a sort of great flattened tiara floating as near to synchronous orbit as Allaird could gauge from control.

All that remained was to straighten the ring, and again towlines came into play. At one juncture after another, suited Gate personnel captured and fastened the DV's lines; then the Vehicle gently tugged, flattening the angle between segments until the two met squarely and could be secured. Then, when the lines were freed, the Vehicle moved to its next assignment.

It wasn't fast work, but finally the job was done.

Entering her quarters, Marnie felt ready to sleep the clock around. Except that she was still wound up. The bathroom

mirror showed a grime-streaked face; the braid she'd done
up—how many days ago?—was coming apart, and felt greasy
as she undid it.

While she undressed she sipped cold juice; the DV had run
out of it two days earlier, and during the hurried docking times
no one ever thought to restock. A good solid half hour in the
shower had her feeling both more relaxed and, to a certain
degree, refreshed. Ready for anything.

Well, almost. She wasn't really expecting the Alephant.

Agreed is that volitionals in the sub-plenum lack means to
sense choice of more utile chronal-prime vector, within adjacent dimensional packet, for purpose of spatial displacement.
Decision is that volitional should experience overall plenum
to greater chronal extent, enabling it to accrue understanding,
then return. No harm, it is felt, should result to any.

Subject is nowtime found communicatively accessible; sensors extrude to co-occupy volitional's coordinates, at all point-
loci restricted to only two spatial vectors, thus ensuring
nondisruptive admixture.

Interaction achieved, effort is applied to convey intention.
Unaccountably, excessive counter-intent ensues. Assuming its
cause to be incomplete comprehension, effort is repeated, but
resistance only intensifies.

Following further attempt to explicate intent as one of providing volitionals greater advantage rather than harm, sensory
extremities retract from subject into major extension, which
then itself withdraws.

Reactions of volitionals, it is evident, vary beyond predic-
tive comprehension.

XXI

The trouble was, Marnie was still shaky: not only when Clancy and Nicole called, but when they came to her quarters. They wanted to hear about the DV, and using it to position the macroGate. But for her those matters were, at best, on hold.

"That can *wait*. The Alephant came," and now she had their attention. "It wanted me to go stay in Aleph space a while, long enough to learn how the time vectors work, how to pick one that's faster. For the Gates. But . . ."

Clancy reached to squeeze her hand. "Doesn't it realize what that means in terms of time *here*?"

"I guess not. And how does it know I could even *breathe* there, or eat, spread out in umpty dimensions?"

"We don't know that's the case," Nicole objected.

"It was Dr. Habegger's best guess, though," Clancy said. "Anyway, did it try to *take* you?"

Headshake. "No, just persuade." She let out a shuddery sigh. "If I weren't so beat out, it probably wouldn't spook me so hard."

After a quiet family meal—with no coffee—she was loosened up enough to sleep.

As the macroGate moved toward operational status, Allaird monitored its progress by way of the info copies sent him by Tyran Galer over a data channel. Galer wasn't much for using voice/video contact, but punctilious about report readouts.

So after the Gate crew vacated *Arrow* in favor of their own duty station, Clancy kept tabs as Galer reported activation of its internal Earthgates, the outGating of supplies and materials and drive fuel for his maneuvering thrustors, and the like.

At that point Clancy moved his ship well away from the macroGate and watched the huge structure swing to point its central axis along its orbital path. *Arrow* sat directly in that path, but on the "in" side; any emerging ship, once Galer had his matrices plugged in and activated, would come out the other way.

In fact nothing *could* go through such a Gate the "wrong" way. On the Mouth side the asymptotically tapering fields converged on the Gate ring, centering the approaching ship; from the Tush, its own fields a continuation of those at the far-end Mouth, the force vectors converged further. Anything coming the other way would simply be deflected, by a cross-product vector force generated by its own motion, to pass outside the ring.

Due to Junior's unexpected dim companion and Earth's sending the extra Gates too late to install before decel, macroGate operation here would begin at least three months later than planned. But tacked onto the end of a nearly seventy-two year jaunt, that delay counted as rather small beans.

Returning from the exercise belt, Clancy entered quarters just in time to hear Nicole hailing him on the intercom. He answered, and she said, "Roland Bryan's been calling; wants to talk with you and he's in a hurry."

I'll bet . . . "I need a shower first. That slick-haired glory grabber can wait."

"Translation: you'll call as soon as you possibly can."

Allaird laughed. "If you want to put some jelly on it, okay." But it was a good half hour before he opened the circuit.

Bryan wasted no time on chitchat. "Galer's instruments indicate a planetary system about eighteen light-years past this one, roughly five degrees off your approach course coming in. You are to make your ship ready to undertake the flight to that system, where you will conduct standard recon and exploration and then return here. I am advising Earth . . ."

Sonuvabitch! "Now wait a minute. We don't have the parts for a macroGate any more; remember? You want to waste nearly forty years of a ship's working life, just *looking*?" Then an afterthought. "What does Villereal say about this?"

"As operations officer, such decisions are within my own jurisdiction. And I'll decide what's a waste or not. Certainly you'd carry a pair of Gates, to be utilized on the planetary surface." *If any* . . .

"I see." And maybe he did, at that. When in doubt, stall. "Well, I'd better call a meeting and inform my people. I'll get back to you."

Clancy didn't, though. Instead he got Carmela Villereal on-screen via her CV-One channel and brought her up to date. "How seriously do I have to take this empire builder?"

"Not so seriously as I must, it would seem. This is not the first overstepping of his authority, but it is by far the most flagrant." She frowned. "I'm afraid I was not entirely open with you, earlier. I have suspected, but without clear proof, the existence of a powerful cabal based on Earth, aimed at the establishment of a group of colonies under its sole governance. Although the starship program is and has been a UN operation from the start, this group is purportedly headed by Senator Howard Switzer. Howic the Howitzer, I believe he is called. A failed presidential candidate whose campaign tactics were abominable; now perhaps he seeks power in a new direction. The extent of his overseas affiliations, however, is obscured by rumor."

"But you think Bryan's one of the storm troopers."

"It would seem so. His latest move was to persuade Tyran Galer, out on the Gate, that Roland is the real power here and I'm some sort of figurehead." Then, abruptly, "What do you intend? Will you undertake this mission he proposes?"

"I was hoping you'd have some ideas. One thing, we're short nearly half our crew, including my drive chief. The decel team won't outGate here for another fifteen months—closer to sixteen, actually. We'd be a light-year out, by then—and ourselves still in Gate lag, leaving six people with an empty ship and nothing but our records to tell them where they're going or what for."

And there was more to it. "Ordinarily, I think you know, a crew inGates twenty-one months before launch, to emerge when acceleration's complete. It's idiocy to send a ship in the blind, totally uncrewed for a year after accel stops. I mean, do we want to trust the *programming* to take sightings and make the early course corrections? Hell, it could end up badly enough off target to add months to the trip." And remembering his argument back at Beacon World, what if some natives decided to dig into a virtually uncrewed ship? But he'd laid enough reasons on her. . . .

"Have you told Bryan any of this?"

"He wasn't listening."

"He doesn't. Allaird—I truly don't know what to suggest."

But as he spoke, Clancy had been deciding. He said, "Just don't endorse Bryan's orders, because I won't follow them. What can he do, anyway? The ship's up here and he's not; our fuel and supplies come direct from Glen Springs, and it's four years before anything he says can affect that. So I think I'll just sit tight, talk reasonably and more or less politely, and take no action until I have to. I'll keep you advised."

"And I, you." Looking anxious, she cut the circuit.

From roughly sixty miles away, *Arrow*'s sensing cameras could bring the macroGate very close indeed. Watching that image at an aux screen in control, the circle full-on from this perspective, Marnie was puzzled: why were a pair of diametrically opposed objects, each maybe thirty feet long and ten high and who could tell from here how wide, racing around the perimeter? Completing the circuit in about—oh, twenty-two seconds, a little more.

But why? The macro ring spanned over eight hundred feet, so these passenger coaches or whatever they might be were clocking about eighty miles an hour. No huge rate. Except that—well, yes! Passengers in either or both of those pods would be feeling just about one gee, centripetal.

The Gate's equivalent of *Arrow*'s exercise belt.

There had to be access stations, airlock couplings and such. And to avoid putting torque to the Gate ring, small traction thrustors would drive the units. Marnie wished she knew more details. What kind of track held the cars? What kept them straight across from each other, in balance? But those people didn't tell everything they knew. Not to superannuated ship deeks, they didn't.

Oh well . . .

Over several weeks she'd almost gotten used to the noise, the crowding, the air of bustle. Reversion to a less hectic pace should have come as a relief, but somehow Marnie couldn't quite relax. Maybe she was too well acclimated to edgy anticipation, to constantly waiting for the other shoe to drop.

Whatever, it shouldn't take her too much longer to readjust.

Right now, Ptiba and Coyote and Trish were taking the DV down, with a load of items specially ordered by the colony from ship's supplies. Marnie wished she could be along; going in from twenty thousand miles, the view would be something to see.

Central to the ring a flash of light caught her attention, like regular Gate flares but much larger, and more diffuse. Its dying revealed a smallish vessel, moving directly away.

Marnie hit the intercom key to her father's digs. "Clancy! Something just outGated from the macro."

She saw the object turn and double back, now passing outside the ring, to aim itself straight for *Arrow*.

"So that's how the Bryan problem looks to me," Clancy said. "The cabal part, that's all blue sky, so far. And I see no point in bothering the others with any of it. Yet."

Before Nicole could answer, Marnie's call came. "I'll be right there." Rising, he headed for the transfer ring.

As he swerved into control, awkward on Velcro because he was trying for too much speed, Marnie already had comm with the newcomer. ". . . no idea," a man's voice was saying. "A test drone went through not twenty seconds before, no action, so I took the short cut and *woops*, here we are!" The speaker, slim and rather lean-faced, looked and sounded quite young. After a pause, pushing reddish brown hair back from his forehead he said, plaintively, "Only where are we? I forget which Gate this is."

"I don't know its number," Marnie said. "You're talking to the starship *Arrow*, about sixty miles back from the macro's *in* side." She checked a list. "The Gate call frequencies are . . ."

"I told you, Rich." The man standing beside the first speaker probably wasn't much older, but his self-image certainly was. This one had both height and bulk on his colleague; contrasting with dark hair, his pale round face carried the responsibilities of the ages. *Be serious*, his expression said.

So did his voice. "Rich, you never listen. Now you're cold mush. I can't cover for you; you know that—hey, where are you taking us? We should dock at the macroGate and report."

Seating himself, Clancy opened his mike. "Captain Clar-

ence Allaird calling the new arrival. Who are you and who's
in charge?''

"I'm senior," said the reproachful one, "and . . ."

"But I'm flying the crate, Peter," Rich cut in. "*Arrow*, is
it? Then we're better than seventy light-years out, aren't we?''

"And missed your ship," said Peter. "How soon was it due
to leave?" Then, "I insist . . ."

"Quiet!" Clancy's tone carried parade ground echoes.
"Identify your vehicle and yourselves."

The younger man spoke again. "This is the class B cargo
shuttle *Delaware*. The design's similar to your DV but with
more thrust and shorter range; a bit over twice the tonnage, I
think. I'm Richard Stasfort, pilot. This grouch with me is Peter
Hinyon, our group dispatcher; he's all right when you get to
know him. Now, sir; may I ask permission to dock with you?''

"You can't do that, Rich! I'm responsible to . . ."

"Sure I can. Captain, I need . . ."

"I don't." Clancy sighed. "But come anyway." Pretending
to ignore Marnie's look of disapproval, Allaird cut the circuit.

Delaware was too big to slide into the Deployment Vehicle's berth, but its stern held three deep, concentric circular
slots. Of these, the smallest nested flexibly over the rim of
Arrow's now-hollow nose, to a depth of over a meter before
magnetic circuitry kicked in to hold the joining firm.

Marnie wondered who was supposed to fill the DV's former
space with air. The answer was *Delaware*, mostly, but the
donation was temporary; from the vessel's stern came a tu-
bular airbag expanding to leave only a two-meter tunnel, lined
with molded handholds, back to the greater ship's cargo hatch.
No doubt it would pump empty again, for retrieval when the
docking period ended. And presumably one size fit all.

All this came clear when she followed Clancy's welcoming
party to open the tunnel's personnel hatch, admitting two
young men to *Arrow*'s central tube.

"Hi." Stasfort, the younger-looking one, with the excess of
shaggy reddish brown hair and the big grin, shook hands all
around. Slim, and not much taller than Marnie herself, he
seemed to carry around more energy than anyone really
needed.

"Marnie Allaird," she said when it was her turn. "You

really cut through a Gate that was due to fire, any second?''

The grin wouldn't quit. ''Well, it got us here.''

''That's just the problem,'' said Peter Hinyon. And, ''I'm sorry about this,'' he kept repeating, with variations. ''We'll have to take *Delaware* back, of course, and it's not *my* fault the company's lost four years' use of her, but—''

''Not necessarily.'' Trust Clancy, Marnie thought, to cut through the horse puckie and make some sense. ''They'll be sending ships like this out soon in any case, and with a two-year Gate lag no matter what. Why don't you simply take yours over to the macroGate, Mr. Hinyon, contract its services out to the Gate's—uh, administrators? And report the deal back to Earth.''

''There you go, Peter.'' Rich clapped the other man on the shoulder. ''You can steer it that far, can't you?''

Which implied that he himself was staying. He'd better ask Clancy first, was Marnie's thought.

Hinyon frowned. ''I'll have to think this over.''

''Reasonable,'' said Nicole Pryce. ''And since your last meal would be something like four hundred trillion miles back, why don't we go outship a few levels and do something about it?''

Behind all the bravado, Clancy decided, Stasfort probably wasn't a bad kid. A bit of a loose cannon, too much tendency to freelance, but the swashbuckling was fairly normal for his age. Still, Allaird was just as glad that Rich wasn't *his* problem.

Other than being a worrywart, Hinyon seemed sensible enough. Over lunch, Allaird drew out the two men's stories. Rich Stasfort had been nearly thirteen when he and his parents, a third officer and drive chief respectively but he didn't mention which was which, Gated aboard *Scout*. ''That was two ships after *Arrow*,'' Clancy ventured, and Rich nodded. Okay; eight years.

The trip took about twenty-eight months, ship's time, '' . . . and the destination turned out to be Slim Pickins.'' Clancy's brows rose; Stasfort added, ''So bad, they *named* it that.'' An iceworld, summer highs only a few degrees above freezing; lichens flourished briefly, then reverted to dormancy. The air was fine, though. ''People could live there, but like living on Antarctica. Nearly everything was going to need Gating in: energy sources, fertilizer, the lot. It wasn't worth doing. But the colony administrators insisted that everybody had to make a go of it."

Clancy leaned forward. "Including your ship's crew?"

"The colony took over the ship."

Clancy's personal alarms went off. The cabal? "Then what?"

"Actually, except for an advance party, everybody lived on the macroGate. Or on the ship. We weren't equipped to settle groundside, because conditions there hadn't been determined until we were pretty close. It was going to be—oh, I'm not sure how long—until the surface was conquered." Stasfort shrugged. "Well, that's the way the Big Wheeze always put it."

At any rate, after a few months *Scout*'s crew got tired of serving as flunkeys for administrative brass who'd commandeered all the better of the ship's quarters. "So one shift we all gathered on the control level and blocked the transfer ring. We outnumbered the colony ants there, so we locked them in a supply room and Gated ourselves and our duffel back to Glen Springs."

"How would they be let out?" Marnie asked, then mock-slapped her head. "The full-gee ring, sure. But too late to stop you."

The boy gave her an appraising look. "That's how Captain Dailey saw it, when I suggested the idea." Was that a fact, or sheer bragging? "Well, anyway . . ." Back at Glen Springs, *Scout*'s people were out of time with Earth. *Like us*, thought Clancy, *with the Gate crew, and downstairs*. So they and other returnees of comparable provenance lobbied for a ship of their own. "And we may have won; it was still up for grabs, decision pending. But I couldn't sit around in training sessions all that time; I took a job uploading cargo, herding *Delaware*. And today . . ." Abruptly the youngster paused, then continued. "Two years ago, I mean, word on my next pickup spot came late, so I took a shortcut. Wrong move." But still he grinned.

Hinyon didn't. His story held less color. When *Eaglet* macroGated to Tetzl's Planet on its way to a more distant system, he oversaw ship's supplies. Clancy wasn't quite sure of *Eaglet*'s place in the program's timetable, but he didn't like to interrupt. At any rate the far destination, when reached, provided a useful world, where Hinyon supervised downloading from ship and macroGate until a political appointee superseded him. When he Gated back, to *Eaglet*'s relay point and then to Earth, he found a niche riding herd on uploading vessels such as *Delaware*. He'd been hitching a ride downstairs when the shortcut hijacked him. He was taking that development a little better now.

"I'd simply like to get back to my job," he said. "Though what they'll say, four years AWOL and no real excuse . . ."

"I'll write you one," said Rich Stasfort. "Please excuse Peter Hinyon, he didn't mean to play hookey but the macroGate wouldn't take no for an answer. And . . ."

"That's enough," Clancy said. "I'll send a report back with Mr. Hinyon; you needn't bother." Leaning forward he tried on his official frown, just for size. "Now, Mr. Stasfort. You did mention some kind of necessity. What is it that you need?"

"Right!" The grin vanished, as Stasfort said, "I want to sign on here. Join your crew."

In the back of his mind, Clancy had been afraid of that.

Marnie thought it was a great idea; Rich Stasfort struck her as someone who *did* things. Not too disciplined, sure, but Clancy could sort him out. Her father, though, cocked a skeptical eyebrow. "There might be a few problems. What's your program status? On the record, I mean."

Stasfort cleared his throat. "Most of our *Scout* bunch were in the old-timers' group trying to get *Paragon*. That's a century-class ship, a hundred in the crew. First of its kind." He paused. "Your ship here was the first to use foldout fins to make up its macroGate. With *Paragon* the entire hull unfolds that way." Trying to picture how it might work, Marnie kept losing track of the ways things would have to fit.

"So we'd already have our operating and exploration crews," Rich went on. "Instead of your DV there are four cargo loaders, something like *Delaware*. The mission plan was still in the argument stage. One option was Gating to *Falcon*'s macro, but we hadn't heard for sure yet."

When Allaird didn't comment, Rich said, "A ship's a ship;

if I do my job, what difference can it make to the brass?''

"And what might that job be?" Clancy asked. "Aside from small craft pilot. Which would put you working for the macro people anyway; our DV needs are well staffed."

"Let's see . . . I'm weakest on drive, haven't studied it much. Nor Gates, except operating procedures. But besides loader jockey I'm good with instruments, taking and evaluating navigation readings, control systems upkeep. I can even cook!"

"Cook?" said Peter. "That's his story." He didn't look as serious as usual. Stasfort grinned again but made no protest.

"You, Hinyon," Allaird said. "If you're going back, would you like to see a little of the place first? You can Gate from this ship to Glen Springs, or strictly between macroGates."

"I'll have to see to *Delaware*. . . ."

"Leave it to me. If you'd care to, that is." Marnie's eyes narrowed; Clancy wanted something out of this. But what?

Hinyon nodded. "All right; I'll Gate from here. Groundside may be a bit less hectic to report to. And right now's as good as any; get it over with."

So the man had a sense of humor, after all. Earlier Marnie hadn't liked him much; now as he stood to leave with Clancy, saying thanks for the lunch, she was rather sorry to see him go.

Others began drifting away also; Rich Stasfort, apparently in no hurry to be anywhere, poured himself more iced tea. Marnie did the same. And after a moment asked, "How old are you, bio?"

"Sixteen. And, umm—a half, call it. You?"

"Fifteen, in a couple of months."

"Do they let you do much yet? Real work, I mean?"

"I've been standing regular watches . . ." How long was it, now, since Paula Trent left? "Nearly two years. We lost some people—not dead, just had to leave, one way and another. And with Gate lag you can't wait on replacements."

"Full watches; no kidding? How'd you like to ride *Delaware*? I might let you try the controls."

This lad needed straightening out. "Could be interesting, to land it." She paused. "See if it handles much different from the DV, when I took it down its first trip."

Before he found an answer, she left.

* * *

Resting, Nicole sat up when Clancy entered quarters. "One thing after another, isn't it? First Bryan and maybe the bogey man back home, and now this. Did you see young Peter off?" He nodded. "How about the other one? Rich. You didn't exactly welcome him with open arms."

"Would you? Oh, I like him well enough; I just don't want to be stuck with housebreaking him."

Laughter escaped her. "Do you think he's in real trouble?"

"You're making my point, Nicole. He's not my problem and I won't let him be. If I think of any good advice I'll pass it along and welcome. But he's not my responsibility."

A snicker slurred her answer; at Clancy's request she repeated it. "You hope!"

He scowled. "Well, there *could* be some complications."

"Let's save them for later," she said. "I'm on duty in another hour."

She didn't have to tell him twice.

After Nicole left, Allaird dozed. Her voice on the intercom brought him awake. "Clancy, it's the Villereal woman. Says she has to talk with you. You're supposed to call her back, using level three scramble. Whatever that is."

"There's a switch setting for it. I'll be along in a minute."

On the way he tried to think of the channel number she'd given him; as he entered control he remembered. At the comm panel he called groundside and asked for CV-One, then threw the scramble switch.

The woman who came onscreen was not Carmela Villereal. This one was younger, and seemed agitated. "Captain Allaird you've got to help us! They took the chief—they say she's sick but she really isn't—it's house arrest, that's what it is. And . . ."

"Hold it. Who did this?"

"Bryan. And his people. It's some kind of takeover, I'm pretty sure of that; he's been talking privately with a group up on the macroGate, but he kept saying it was merely a matter of improving coordination. We . . ."

There was a pause; the woman looked back over her shoulder. "Somebody's coming. I'll get back to you when I can."

And the screen went black.

Turning to Nicole, Clancy wondered if he looked as blank as she did. She said, "Is this Villereal's conspiracy? Don't forget; Stasfort mentioned some kind of takeover shenanigans at Slim Pickins. Do we have reports of anything, ourselves?"

He thought. "Not at Tetzl's Planet or the Triad Worlds; of course those are the only two we Gate with, directly. Regarding later ships there's been no such word. Not here, at least."

Pryce nodded. "Politics back home could be getting rough. It wouldn't be the first time in history."

A cabal within the agency as Villereal claimed—growing over the years, infiltrating administrative cadres and macro-Gate crews? If so, what the hell could Clancy Allaird do about it?

Or was it none of his business? Shrugging, he said, "Our move is, we keep our own council and see what happens next."

He stood. "First thing, I'm going to see that *Delaware*'s fuel tanks are topped off."

That chore took longer than he expected.

Trish Pembrook didn't know what to do. After letting her land the Vehicle, Ptiba had taken Coyote along and gone outside. Twenty minutes later the man Roland Bryan came onscreen and invited Trish to debark also. Her orders said otherwise; she declined. Bryan showed her Ptiba and Coyote, under guard. "If you have any concern for your comrades' safety, do as I ask."

Concern? Of course she had. But three hostages were no improvement over two, let alone giving up the DV. The trouble was, Trish wasn't *used* to this sort of thing.

She tried to call *Arrow* but her receivers blared hash; these scabheads were jamming her! By the time she found a usable frequency outside the blocked band, Bryan had made good use of her distraction; the landing leg's Station LL camera showed her friends, now handcuffed, positioned directly below the Vehicle. "You see?" said Bryan, standing safely off to one side. "Lift, and they're dead."

The jamming had ceased. "Now I'm ready to talk to your captain. Go ahead and call him. And patch me through on a conference basis. I want to hear every word you both say."

There wasn't much Trish could do, except comply.

* * *

How could he have known to guard against something this blatant? Clancy shook his head: *damn*, he'd completely forgotten the DV was scheduled to go down today, let alone that it *had* gone. Stalling, staring at the split screen images on his control panel as he tried to think of something he could use, he recited Bryan's demands. "With or without us, you want the ship. And the Deployment Vehicle, and now this cargo shuttle. Seems to me you're trying to operate way out of your jurisdiction."

"I've made it mine. I doubt you can argue with that."

Seeing Ptiba and Coyote helpless, Allaird really couldn't. He countered with, "Back on Earth there'll be arguments raised." Or maybe not, but it was the best line he could think of.

"Two years before they hear anything, even if you've already started tattling. And another two before the first possible response here, of any sort. I think we'll have matters pretty well nailed down by that time."

So Bryan wasn't sure of the Earth end. It didn't help. "Fait accompli? Accepted because that's the easy way out?"

"You understand well. Now tell your co-pilot to come out of the Vehicle, please."

"Plain barefaced hostage blackmail, is that it?"

"That's a harsh way to look at it, captain. I'm merely ensuring that you negotiate in good faith."

For a time Allaird said nothing. This was hard lines and no simple solution. He must have muttered that much aloud; Nicole said, "There's only one answer, isn't there?"

"You mean, we don't accept the hostage principle?" She nodded. "But I have to ask myself, could I decide that way if it were Marnie down there?"

"She isn't. But yes, you do have to ask that."

"All right." He turned back to the console. "Trish? Ptiba? Coyote? Can you all hear me okay?"

When he was assured that they could, Clancy took a deep breath. Then he told them what the choices were.

Delaware massed over forty thousand tons and carried better than three gees of thrust. Straight down from twenty thousand miles, add on the planet's own gravitational pull, and

". . . well over thirty miles a second, at impact." Much too fast, going in vertically, for atmospheric friction to ablate much of it away.

The colony would be gone without trace. Lake Dimple, assuming it still existed as such, would expand into a second, adjoining crater. "Once launched, there's absolutely no way to deflect the vessel. Twenty minutes later, that's all she wrote."

Bryan shouted that he'd never get away with it, exclamation point. Clancy forced a laugh. "If I say it was an accident, who's left to argue?"

Then, seriously, back to the captives. "But I won't do this unilaterally. The decision must be unanimous."

"Let me get this straight," said Coyote Benjamin. "Napoleon here demands you give him the ship, the DV, the works; let him be total boss. Or else he kills Ptiba and me. You say he lets us go, DV and all, or you scrag the place. And yeah I know, you can't get us out." He shrugged. "What do *you* say, Ptiba?"

She looked miserably uncomfortable, sweat running down her forehead and no hands free to wipe it off. "I say, I'd rather be somewhere else. But don't give this coprocephalic our ship!"

"Copa–*what*?" Bryan sounded more puzzled than offended.

"Try shithead," Trish explained. Her face showed scared, but her voice didn't.

"Well, there you have it," said Coyote. "Play your hand, skipper."

Trish couldn't believe this was happening. "Ptiba! Coyote! You're asking to get us *killed*?"

The man looked up toward the LL camera. "Not you, Trish. Ptiba and I are all the handle Bryan has on you. If Clancy lowers the boom you have plenty of leeway; just lift off."

"I *couldn't*."

"Sure you can," said Ptiba Mbente. "At that point we're dead anyway and you're not. So get your young butt up and out."

"No." Trish struggled to understand her conflict and found an answer. "I could leave you, maybe. If I had to, under orders. But I can't kill you myself, with my own drive blast.''

"I'm afraid it's not convenient to move them," said Roland Bryan. "It does seem the matter is up to you, Allaird."

Frustrated to fury, Trish felt her teeth grind. Movement caught her eye: a guard, looking up at the DV and shifting uneasily. Almost without thinking, she yelled. "You there! With the big gun and the twitchy feet. Are you deaf or just stupid? Do you want to bet your own ass, this sonofabitch can make his bluff stick?"

"Well, you saw," Ptiba said, nursing the second half of her bourbon after she'd gulped the first. Coyote was taking his gently from the start, while Trish seemed satisfied with coffee. Just in case, though, Allaird left the bottle open on the galley table. For one thing, he was still hung up on the question he hadn't needed, after all, to answer: *would he have done it?*

Mbente wasn't finished. "When Bryan wouldn't give it up the guards turned on him: cuffed him and turned us loose. They wanted us to wait until they dickered with Bryan's loyalists to free Ms. Villereal, and talk with her, but Coyote said we'd rather come up and watch from the balcony. So here we are."

"We were lucky," Coyote said now. "Those guards were only foot troops, not hard-cores with a stake in the action. Otherwise . . ."

Sitting at the outskirts of the group, Rich Stasfort spoke. "I know it's not important in the big problem, but I'm sure glad you didn't have to waste *Delaware*. I'm in deep enough without having my ship used to wipe out a colony." As Allaird turned a curious gaze on the youth, Rich added, "Can I take it over to the big Gate now, and get contracted to do some work? Just to keep busy until you sign me on here."

"Not just yet," Clancy told him. "There's some question, you see, of where those people's loyalties lie. So for now, Rich, *Delaware* is off limits. Except on my orders."

Crestfallen, the boy nodded.

From control, the intercom came on. "Pilar Velez here. Captain, downstairs wants to talk again."

One cheek bruised, hair down loose and tousled, dress torn at one shoulder, Carmela Villereal looked like the wrong end of a mugging but game to go another round. "Captain! I'm glad you got your people away unharmed." Clancy decided she hadn't heard about the proposed alternative. "But I must warn you. A coded message arrived for Roland Bryan, who you will be pleased to know is confined, pending charges. I had his tame crypto expert bounced around a bit until he agreed to decipher it for me."

Oh-oh! She was looking serious again, as she said, "It was a notification that according to plan, two *armed* spacecraft will outGate here soon. Mission, to establish security control over this star system and all ships within or near its reaches."

"Control for whose benefit? The cabal's?" Armed ships? What sort of crap was this, anyway? "And what kind of armament?"

"I'm not certain. On either count. But I'd assume the Howitzer's group, yes. The message came from something called Special Colony Coordination. It was *not* routed through top headquarters for endorsement."

"Have you heard anything else new, that might relate?"

Villereal shook her head. "Nothing. Captain, if I were you, the thought of armed bullies emerging into nearby space would disturb me."

"Don't think it doesn't. But more important, right now, is your end. Can you round up enough muscle to arrest as many as possible of Bryan's gang and Gate them home under guard? With a comprehensive bill of charges signed by you? I mean, widespread conspiracy or not, cleaning out your own lodge hall is a good place to start. Spreading a stink back at Earth isn't a bad move, either. And it wouldn't hurt to lean on Bryan first, see if he knows just how far this thing really goes. If you have to bounce him a little, too, for effect, it's in a good cause."

Another thought. "If you see you're losing, though, round up all you can of the good folks and Gate the hell home. There has to be *someone* you can trust there, go to for sanctuary."

"That is my last resort, of course. But what will you do?"

There were several possibilities. "I don't know yet. Call me if anything more needs talking about."

The screen went dark. Clancy thought, how did everything get so screwed up so fast?

*   *   *

Scanning through the backlog of routine bulletins no one ever had time to read, Nicole found some answers; in quarters she summarized them for Clancy. "Those ships Villereal mentioned won't be armed in the usual sense. What they are is prospecting vessels, to probe asteroids and small moons. They're not built to land anywhere, by the way; just to dock at macroGates for refueling and such. What they carry is lasers to vaporize surface rock for gas spectography and torpedoes with various kinds of warheads: thermite, explosives, and so forth. These things *can* be used as weapons, but that's not the intent."

"It's Bryan's intent, all right, him and his group." Allaird stood. At her questioning look he said, "I'm going to find Coyote; then he and I will go prowl Phil Henning's personal terminal. He just may have filed something we can use."

After a moment, Nicole thought she understood.

What Marnie liked about Rich Stasfort wasn't just that he was roughly her own age but also that he came from her *time*. What she didn't like was his unspoken assumption that he always belonged first in line. Trish, it turned out, had much the same impression. "After all, though, he was the only kid on *Scout*."

"And I was the only one on here. So?"

"I'd say his parents, the officer and the drive chief, let the crew make a pet of him." Pembrook laughed. "I can't imagine Clancy doing that, or Nicole. Or my own folks, back on macroGate Two. What you and I got, Marnie, were the limits that go with being a kid and then growing into responsibilities. Rich must have got it from the other side: first privileges, then rights."

"We've had some of that, too, haven't we?"

"Sure. The balance was different, is all." Trish's smile had mischief in it. "Has he asked you any favors yet?"

"Like what?"

"Never mind. He will, I bet."

So a little later when Rich tagged after Marnie to the exercise ring, just the two of them working out, she kept notice of him. On the *outside* he wasn't grinning. . . .

About halfway through the hour they'd scheduled, a little out of breath from the exercycle he asked, "Would you like to make sex with me? I haven't since we came through."

He wasn't creepy like Alton, let alone Carl; just brash. Still, he *was* out of line. "And how long before that?"

He laughed. "All right; quite a while. But I did on *Scout*. Told her my father said to find someone to show me, but keep it quiet because my mother didn't approve. So I know a lot of good ways to do. What do you say? Would you like to?"

Marnie shook her head. "I don't think so." He wouldn't have an implant, any more than she had. But even if he did . . .

"Any day you change your mind, the offer's still open."

"I suppose I might, someday." So much for the carrot; now the stick. "Maybe when you grow up."

Surprising her, he smiled. "Then let's give it another twenty minutes hard sweat, here, and go get something to eat."

Whatever else, she told Trish later, you couldn't call him a bad loser.

"You can't work the field phases from control," said Coyote. "Even if we had time to hook up the circuits, we can't clear enough spare switch locations there. Anyway, Clancy, you'll have plenty to do as it is, getting position and knowing when to say when. And keep in mind: I'll have all three node controls multipled, but only number one is certain to be dead on the money; the other two may vary a bit."

"They should be tuned close enough. Anything else?"

"How long a hit?"

Allaird thought. "Full power, only a few seconds. Three, call it. We don't want . . ."

"I know. Okay, that's how long you'll get."

Matters settled, both men left the drive monitor room and went outship for coffee. First, though, Clancy left word in control: if anything came outGating, hit the panic button. A little later he went back and gently eased *Arrow* up even with the macroGate, to lie only a few hundred yards from its outer rim. "We don't want them having a lot of time to evaluate the situation, once they pop out."

That night and the next he didn't sleep very well.

When the alert sounded, Marnie ignored the "strap in" warning and headed hotfoot for control; she was sure she could make it in time and she didn't want to miss anything.

As she left the transfer ring the ship began to swing, but the handlines were still in place so she got to control all right.

Under Clancy's glare she strapped in and watched as the screens showed two midsize craft, larger than *Delaware* but dwarfed by any real starship, cutting a turn in tight formation from beyond the macroGate to bear on *Arrow*.

About a quarter mile short, both vessels began slowing; soon they neared standstill. Tense-faced, Clancy hit comm. "Ahoy there! New arrivals! Identify yourselves."

An aux screen, split, showed two men and a woman at their own control positions. One said to another, "He's not one of ours." Then, "To the ship *Arrow*: cast loose the cargo dinghy at your bow and prepare to be boarded. Resist, and we'll fire on you. This is the only warning you'll get."

"And a hearty welcome to *you*," Clancy muttered. *Arrow*'s turn was nearly completed; as the interlopers drifted closer, its stern swung to face them. "They're well within range, Coyote," Clancy said. "In, in, in—*now!*" The rear view screens showed rainbow spectra blooming, out from the drive nodes to envelop the newcomers. Whose own drives, already dim, faded to nothing.

". . . two, three, off!" came Coyote's voice. "Drive normal."

"Right." Allaird opened offship comm again. "You out there! Cut your drives and keep your hands off your weapons! Unless you want some more freezeframe."

The drives, briefly revived, died again. "*Arrow!* What the hell did you do? We've been sitting here six days. Going no place, the stars gone, fuel and life support feeds dead, we . . ."

"Shut up and listen. Ten minutes of the Portaris Effect, up close, aged the Liij Environ twenty thousand years. I gave you just three seconds, low power, and at a distance. *And my hand's on that switch.*" Well, Coyote's was.

From the ships, several talked at once; then a woman's voice overrode. "All right, we surrender. What is it you want?"

Ego betrayed the woman. When she demanded her rights on authority of the Howitzer, Clancy ordered Earlyne Ragin to suit up and take a walk, leaving the airlock accessible from the outside and using her reaction gun to get clear of the two ships. "I'll send the DV to pick you up." She tried to haggle her way out of it, but her foot was stuck too deeply in her mouth.

From there it was simple: "Everybody else Gate to Earth." If they lacked Earthgates they'd say so, but if he asked about it they might get bright enough to try stalling, so he didn't. And now, "You have thirty minutes to gather your belongings; then I give both ships about six months' freeze. Your air won't last."

There'd be ways to sabotage those ships, but Allaird was betting he had their crews too rattled to try. Even if he'd left them any time for it. From one ship and then the other came word that the last person aboard was now leaving. Waiting another thirty seconds just in case, he had Coyote give both ships their promised shot of energy-draining freezeframe.

"Okay." Shaking tension out of his shoulders, Clancy thought. There was a whole lot that needed doing. First, before he forgot, "Coyote? Let's us get another switch panel installed here. I can see where controlling the whole phase thing from this one place could make a lot of difference."

But right now, "Ptiba and Marnie. Take the DV out. I need to get that woman in here and question her."

"Excuse me, captain."

Clancy hadn't noticed Rich Stasfort entering control, quite against the orders to stay strapped in. "Yes?"

"Mightn't it work better, sir, the other way around?"

XXII

Earlyne Ragin told a lot; Allaird hoped some of it was true. While Ptiba let the woman grab a stanchion on the DV's hull and towed her to one of *Arrow*'s peripheral airlocks where a fin used to be, Clancy began making vidcap copies of her testimony so far, his recent bout with the two new ships, and the showdown with Roland Bryan. He'd already Gated that bit home but only in two copies; now he made enough to saturate the market. Glen Springs, agency HQ, the House and Senate committees, White House, several levels of UN oversight, and major international news services.

"Anybody tries to sweep *this* under the rug . . ."

Brought to control, Ragin refused to unsuit. A current of air told Clancy why, so he let it go; spacewalking wasn't for everybody. "All right; let's run over this again. Then you can go clean up and we'll Gate you home."

"No!" Space wasn't all that scared her. "They'll kill me."

"For talking? I see. Well, if you want asylum you'll have to earn it. Let's hear you fill in some gaps."

Scared, sweatsoaked, bedraggled and stinking, she wasn't at her best and she knew it. Obviously grateful for the cup of coffee Nicole handed her, Ragin began again.

Switzer's organization wasn't so much large as widespread, and well entrenched in positions of authority. Repetition brought out names and connections she'd missed, earlier. To date only four colonies were involved: the coup at *Scout*'s had apparently succeeded, *Falcon*'s had failed, *Nomad* was still to be heard from. "And it looks like you gave us a setback here."

While Ragin didn't have complete listings of agents at this colony site, either groundside or on the macroGate, she could access Roland Bryan's files using the cabal's system of data security codes. "Because I'm here to take over from him."

A hint of defiance came. "You may not find him so easy to deal with. Roland's more dangerous than he seems."

Clancy smiled. "We sent him home in handcuffs. But maybe not all the fleas left with the dog. Let's have those codes."

He passed them to Carmela Villereal via channel CV-One. First she told him of rounding up Bryan's troops. "It went well at first; we caught quite a few of them unarmed. But others became suspicious. We had fighting, casualties; more than a few of our suspects escaped. Now let me check this list of yours."

Minutes later she reported back that her own screening had

missed a number of plotters—including the head of a section that was becoming notable for equipment breakdowns. "And several, including some we already knew of, are out in the field," she said. "So we still have our work cut out for us; I'll keep you advised. My thanks to you, Captain Allaird."

"And welcome. Incidentally, there's also some stuff about passwords, you may need to utilize later on. I'll pass that down when I know more about it."

Break time was over; back to Ragin. Clancy said, "Now tell us what else you have, on the macroGate troops." She knew more than he'd expected, but the picture still had blank spots.

Nearly an hour later Chauncey Ng took Earlyne Ragin away, bound for the room where Irina Tetzl had once been held. He was careful, Clancy noticed, to stay out of smelling range.

After some argument Allaird persuaded Tyran Galer to meet him on a closed circuit: scrambled, no listeners. In the macroGate chief's expression, suspicion lay evident. "Let you probe our files here? Why in Hades should I do any such thing?"

"Because there's a power conspiracy." How big, Clancy hesitated to say. "And if you won't let me try to root the agents out for you, I have to assume you're one of them."

"I'll call you back."

But he didn't, and when Allaird tried again, someone he hadn't seen before said that Galer was down with the flu. "So we're posting quarantine." Translation: stay the hell out. . . .

The two mining ships weren't going anywhere; their drift moved them out and back from the macroGate, but slowly. Not long after Allaird's rebuff, two suited figures emerged from the macro; trailing a lifeline they used reaction pistols to move toward the ships. At less than halfway the line ran out; a bit farther, in free flight, so did the hand jets. One of the suits, though, was on course for the nearer ship.

"Can't have that," said Coyote Benjamin. "He gets in, picks up his buddy, they can potshoot us from beyond our range."

"You're right." Allaird gave some orders.

* * *

"You have the most suit experience," Nicole told Trish, so now the young woman rode outside the DV, relying on stirrups and safety harness as she wielded the long cutters tethered to her tool belt. Ptiba maneuvered the Vehicle near the macro's open airlock, a protective shield for Trish as she cut the slack, trailing lifeline. After securing its length to a hull fitting at her feet, again she grasped handholds for extra purchase.

"Got it," she reported, breaking comm silence for the first time. "Let's go after them." For her next step, she already had instructions. "You two out there! Throw away everything you're carrying outside your suits." *Protest.* "Because I can't tell from here what's a weapon and what isn't." No compliance. "I can wait." One of them was closing on a ship, but Ptiba could simply nudge him away if she had to.

Suddenly both suits began shedding minor objects, tossing them free. And a shout came. "We have to give up; we can't help ourselves." Why did the man sound so desperate? "We did the best we could but we're not armed, our jet guns ran out . . ."

Then another voice: "They could turn their drive on us, or run us down and ram; maybe they've got weapons, too. We can't help it, we'd run out of air soon; we just have to!"

Quickly, it seemed, yet so smoothly that Trish felt no sudden jerk or tug, the DV overtook and passed the floating men, then slowed and yawed, to let the towed line's inertia belly it forward and give it a sidewise flip. One man caught it cleanly; for the other, Ptiba had to give the DV a further twitch.

Then both were climbing hand over hand toward Trish. And near as she could tell, neither had any weapon. She herself unsheathed a ten-inch blade with razor edges and a needle point. The nearest man gestured no fight; she saw his lips move, and heard, "They're demanding we cut comm. She has this knife; these suits won't stand up. I'm sorry; Lavelle out." One and then the other, the subliminal hiss of their carrier waves died.

The man spread his hands, then beckoned; when she nodded he pulled himself closer, touched his faceplate and pointed to hers, held a forefinger up to the plate in the "shhh!" sign. So she cut her own voice transmission and touched faceplates with him. The contact would conduct sound, but no one could overhear.

"Look; they sent us to get inside a ship and bring it back. There's only nine of those bastards but they have guns and took over. We have to do what they say; my wife's on there, and my buddy's freemate. Hostages, like." Trish knew about hostages; even so, she decided it was safe to put the knife away.

The second man made faceplate contact. "You know something? You really put us in a shit fix, barring us from that ship. Our people could get killed because we didn't make it." Trish heard him take a deep breath. "So are you going to help us?"

"The captain decides that. Right now you'd better hang on."

The lifeline provided an easy route for Trish to bring the two men into *Arrow* through a fin airlock where Chauncey Ng took them in charge, and that's how she escorted Marnie and Rich back to the Vehicle before loosing the tie. So for the first time, Marnie experienced open space. Not long enough to get much feel of it; she entered the DV's rear lock as Ptiba emerged to join Trish and Rich outside. All according to Clancy's orders, and so far, so good.

Handhauling herself along the tunnel Marnie reached the control deck. The pilot seat was empty so she strapped into it and turned to Nicole, sitting alongside with faceplate opened. Right; they had comm with those outside by way of the consoles. Marnie opened her own suit; no point in taxing its air supply. "Okay. What first?" And Nicole told her.

So she eased out to the nearer ship and achieved a state of near rest with respect to it while Trish and Ptiba swung out on the line and reached the open airlock. Alongside it Marnie saw a namepatch: their prize, it seemed, was called *Overlode*. Ptiba went inside; Trish pulled herself back to the Vehicle. There was a wait until Ptiba called. "Air's good in here; fuel and water supplies look all right. After you've moved clear I'll play with the thrustors a bit; when I have the feel of them I can bring this can home."

"It's all yours," said Nicole. And to Marnie, "Now the other one."

A little more jockeying this time; the airlock was on the far side and needed some finding. Its patch read *Cold Rush*. Both Trish and Rich went in; he knew more about intermediate-sized ships and could give advice if need be. But Nicole made it clear she wanted Trish at the controls.

It was a long wait, while the two mining ships were brought in. Not until Coyote at one of *Arrow*'s fin airlocks and Clancy at another had each craft secured by mooring lines, riding a bit outward and behind the larger ship to maintain light tension on those leashes, did Marnie dock the DV. By now it was easy.

Clancy looked at the timepiece. He'd juked the speed of its hands several times, all the way from rapid spin using one button to near stoppage with the other; now, back to normal, it seemed to run okay. "All right," he told Coyote. "Our limits are about twenty to one, either way, at six feet. Question is, which mode gets us the best results, in the clutch."

He hefted his jury-rigged device, the stripped-down guts of a DV trim thrustor unit with a crude stock welded on. "It's like toting a jackhammer," he complained. "Plus, there's the backpack power supply." Wearing a suit, this wasn't going to be an easy weapon to handle. But within any distance you'd find indoors, even on a macroGate, he could jigger anybody's time rate pretty much. Still, though, "Fast or slow; to flummox the opposition, make 'em ineffective, which *is* best?"

For the past twenty minutes Chauncey Ng had been observing; now he spoke. "Why not a little of both? As an option, I mean. Put a chopper circuit on a third firing button: say, one second stretch, ten seconds speedup. The guy will feel it just the other way." He chuckled. "Drive him crazy."

Allaird looked to Coyote; Coyote nodded. "Let's do it."

The battle of the macroGate, Clancy thought later, had to be unlike any in all of history. It began in standard enough fashion. Ahoy, open up! See you in hell first! I'll huff and I'll puff and I'll blow your air out with my laser here. Something like that. First Clancy from *Overlode*, and when those inside presumably gathered to defend that point, Nicole in *Cold Rush* at the ring's opposite side. Just to keep the situation fluid. And the threat to breach the hull itself short-circuited any move to fill the airlocks with hostages. "We *can't* let them hold the

Gate,'' Allaird said, "and they may as well know from the start. It should give them pause, a little."

Even if only nine aboard the macroGate were active cabalists, *Arrow* didn't have the troops to match them. Going in suited with Clancy was Coyote Benjamin, leaving Ptiba at *Overlode*'s control. Nicole was to stay on *Cold Rush* with Trish; Chauncey Ng and Pete Larue made up her boarding team. Others, notably Gina Todisco and Pilar Velez, had protested being left out. The operating criteria, though, were as Clancy said: "We've only got four time jukers and they're too damn heavy." It wasn't as though *Arrow* carried anything like conventional handguns.

While the Gaters scrambled to save their hull by unsealing the two threatened airlocks, both suited teams unreeled lifelines, triggered their reaction pistols, and moved in. At the entrance hatch, feeling several kinds of brand-new phobias but keeping his breathing steady, Clancy secured the line's end. He and Coyote entered the lock.

"Now we'll let 'em wait, some," Clancy said, and brought his device near the hull alongside the hatch. He didn't put it in contact; when Anne Portaris did that, she affected an entire structure, and he didn't figure his gadget for enough power to manage that trick. Holding it steady, he gave any nearby defenders an estimated hour's delay. They wouldn't be able to communicate with anyone elsewhere in the Gate; the time rates were too far out of whack. If anyone tried to leave the area he'd get a few yards away and apparently, in the view of those remaining, slow down and almost freeze in place. Allaird doubted that anyone would, though; from within the area of timespeed, all lights outside it would appear to fade and possibly die.

"They should be softened up by now." Clancy turned his juker off and opened the inner hatch—to face a bigger crowd than he really needed. He lunged to one side, clearing Coyote's field of fire, and fumbled for his second firing button.

Many facing him weren't armed. A number of those dropped to the floor; taking themselves out of play, he decided. A few did have weapons; that quintet looked every bit as spooked as the rest, but guns came swinging up to point at him. But then he found the slowdown button and it gave him time to duck.

When the guns were empty he went to mode three. After a minute or so of their personal time rates jumping and stalling wholly out of control, the five remaining actives were still disoriented when he and Coyote cut the fields; awkward and bruising though the brawl became, it wasn't long before five wrists were taped, sloppily but effectively, to their respective owners' opposite ankles. Behind them, of course. "Easiest hog-tie there is," Ky had said, and he was right.

"You okay, Coyote?" As his ally nodded, Allaird ignored the hesitant-seeming neutrals. "Right. Take cover there and keep a watch on the approaches while I check in."

Back in the airlock, inner hatch sealed and outer one open, he called Ptiba and reported. "How's the far side?"

"No word yet. I'll ask Nicole again." Clancy waited, and eventually Ptiba said, "Pete and Chauncey had a little trouble, armed goons hiding behind conscripts."

"Same here, sort of. Not much a problem, though."

"No. They got that part under control. The thing now is, the boss pirate got away. It's that Kyle Ferris, the foxy, snooty one. He's holed up in the power center and calling all points inside, says he'll blow the whole place unless *we* give up. You didn't hear him making demands?"

"Must have missed our segment here. What's Nicole's idea?"

"What to do? Not much, yet. Chauncey's on the box to Ferris, stalling, saying nobody's been able to contact *you.*"

"Tell him they still haven't."

"What are you going to do?"

What, indeed? But maybe . . . "Where is that power setup from here? Do you know?"

"Trish would. Let me patch you through."

Done talking, he recycled in to brief Coyote. ". . . from compartment C-7 you'll have to go through the bulkhead, so find yourself a torch. Don't start cutting until I say; I'll route through Ptiba to Nicole to whoever's on the intercom at the far airlock. And when you get in there, just jump hard and hang on."

He looked around. "You having any trouble with these?" Then he recognized Bet Carou, now holding a gun, and grinned. "I guess not. Hi, Bet."

Back outside he called Ptiba, then freed the slackened lifeline and took a couple of turns around one arm. "Okay, see
if you can ease me *real* slowly along here. It's about sixty
degrees; four hundred feet, call it." And added, in case she
was curious, "I want to save the kick pistol for fine-tune maneuver."

After longer than he liked, though he realized it did give
Benjamin more time to get into position, Allaird reached the
hull section Trish had cited. Cinching the line around a bitt,
he called for some slack and pistoled across the width of a
hull plate, where he took another bight. Between those points,
just inside the hull, lay the main power board and the con-
troller's console. And where else was Kyle Ferris likely to be?

Holding the face of the time juker a careful inch away from
contact with the hull, Clancy hit the freeze button. "Allaird
to Benjamin, all relay points. Go get the sonofabitch!"

Considering all the assumptions they'd had to make, Clancy
said, the attempt succeeded beautifully. "But what *happened*," Marnie wanted to know, "when Coyote went in
there?"

She always liked the way Coyote smiled. He said, "Clancy
told me just jump in and grab. Well, when I charged into the
field it didn't *feel* any different. I got to him and held on.
Other people coming in the room seemed very fast, but then
Clancy got the word and cut the field, and things went back
to normal." He laughed. "If that's what you call this . . ."
Maybe, she thought, he was referring to having brought back
three of the guns at Clancy's request, with holsters to match.
Up until now, *Arrow* had gotten along just fine without such
things.

Still, the outcome was really great, and Marnie was pleased.
Except, why did *she* have to miss all the interesting parts?

Allaird had not gone back into the macro. Coyote saw to
the release of Tyran Galer from house arrest—and, he reported
later, satisfied himself that if Galer wasn't up to coping with
nine prisoners, Bet Carou was.

Disposition of the nine hadn't yet been determined; that was
one of several things Clancy wanted to talk about. And not
only with Galer but with Carmela Villereal also. Of the three,

only she lived in a true day and night situation, so Allaird got some sleep during the colony's night. Then, after a good breakfast, he and Nicole went to control where he set up a three-way call.

When he had the macro chief and colony administrator splitscreened at his console, Clancy wasted little time on preliminaries. "All right; the Gate's clear of Switzer's agents and so is the colony. Yes, Ms. Villereal, I know there's still a few out in the bush down there and they may be alerted. But I trust you're on watch for them, and your major base is clean."

He paused. "*Now* it is. But new personnel are apt to Gate in at any time. You both need a way to screen them. It happens they have a password system to identify themselves to each other. My thought is, it could work just as well for our side."

Right; the arriving cabal agent would expect to be validated by giving the right countersign to a password. Instead, "*you'll* use it to finger them, put 'em on ice."

It was a bit more complicated; the words changed, with each contingent bringing the shibboleth applying to the next. But from Ragin they had the currently applicable words and phrases. "So what you do is . . ."

Ironically, Allaird himself first had occasion to use the procedures he'd devised. Just to be on the safe side, he had Trish and Pete hook in an alarm circuit to blink and beep at the pilot's console if anything or anyone outGated from Earth. Less than a day later—right after the small impromptu party when Marnie's fifteenth birthday, bio, had been remembered at the last minute—the precaution paid off. Taking Ptiba and Chauncey with him and all three armed, he went hotfoot to Earthgate and found four newcomers looking all the world like scouts for a point squad. Alongside the Tush sat an inordinate amount of luggage.

Assuming the best stupid smile he could manage, Clancy said, "Welcome to *Arrow*," introduced himself, shook hands all around, and turned to the apparent leader. "Well, let's do the routine. You'll check any weapons with my provost here," indicating Chauncey, "until we've had our individual interviews."

Kent Beringer, the man addressed, didn't seem to know the routine, possibly because it was entirely Clancy's own invention. But outflanked by a trio with highly visible armament, he learned fast. In the supply room next to control, with Ptiba for backup, Clancy tried out the password. "Today's task . . ."

". . . brings tomorrow's reward," Beringer responded.

"Good, good." Another handshake. "What's for next time?"

The man cleared his throat. "You say 'The wise.' The other party should answer 'will follow.' If they say 'know who to follow' instead, they're unreliables, sent here for disposal."

"Seems the hard way. My aide here will escort you to quarters; you will stay there until I've cleared all four of you, one way or the other. Place him next door to Ms. Ragin from *Overlode*, Mbente; I'll meet you back at Earthtush."

One down, three to go. Chuck Leroy recognized no passwords; he was put with the two men Trish had brought in: not prisoners, exactly, but stashed out of the way. Ollie Gorman snapped out the countersign, then got belligerent when no one showed interest in returning his gun; Clancy frog-marched him to the room beside Beringer's, using a hammerlock secured by a rather painful split-fingers hold. So it was a relief when Sheila Logan frowned at hearing "Today's task . . ." repeated twice, and said, "How would I know? I just got here; haven't even seen the duty roster yet."

Galer reported relatively similar results with a cadre of seven that outGated to the macro, and asked, "What are you doing with the agents you uncover? Gating them back directly?"

"Not yet. You and Villereal did that with the first batches, but maybe we need to reconsider. She thinks maybe some of them can be straightened out, and Lord knows she could use a few extra grunts. So I'm sending my own catches groundside; if you like, we could take yours along." Well, yes, why not?

So when Carmela called next, and Clancy wasn't sure how they'd gotten to a first name basis, he said, "We have two from here and four from the macro, definitely the Howitzer's ammo. Are you set up to handle the ones who turn out hostiles?"

She was, she said, and by her own count there were no more than ten or twelve hideouts still on the loose. Since by now her colony roster listed over twelve hundred, Allaird's native skepticism discounted her assurances. But considering the odds against serious invasion by so few, he authorized ground-side delivery of all doubtfuls by the next day.

It was time *Delaware* began to earn its keep.

The ride down from twenty thousand was as spectacular as Marnie had hoped. Even though Ptiba in the co-pilot seat told Rich to keep it smooth, he still cowboyed some; maybe he just couldn't help it. Nobody complained; obviously Chauncey and Trish and Coyote, in passenger seats, were enjoying the trip.

For the prisoners, fifteen in all, down in an empty hold, things might be considerably less comfortable. No one topside seemed especially worried about that possibility.

The man Gorman had balked when he saw the hold. "They're gonna lock us up and let our air out, is what."

Kyle Ferris sneered. His rusty red hair, prominent cheek-bones and long lean jaw, with greenish eyes generally kept narrowed, all gave Ferris a foxish air. Marnie remembered him from before, when the Gate crew was on *Arrow*. And hadn't liked his looks then, either. "Don't be stupid," he said now. "If they wanted to space us, why go to all this trouble?" So Gorman shut up and went in with the rest.

Below, surface features expanded rapidly; from where she sat, Marnie couldn't read the drop rate, but it made her own descents look like a stroll in the park. Instead of slowing grad-ually Rich waited longer than Ptiba's expression approved and then hit the drive all at once; gee force went to nearly three standards for long seconds before he eased back and came almost to rest, hovering about fifty feet above the ground.

Empty crates littered the landing area; now the drive's blast began to tumble them. "Let's give it a good sweeping," said Rich, nudging a yaw thrustor. As *Delaware* tilted, it moved slowly across the area and indeed swept it clean. "This is what we call walking your dog," he said, grinning. "Comes in handy if part of your cargo's waiting on the wrong side of the port." Tilting the other way, he brought the vessel back to the clearing's center and landed with hardly a jar.

Then it was time to unload, and go look around some.

*   *   *

Chauncey and Coyote temporarily joined the waiting security team, helping guard the prisoners to wherever they were being taken. Trish stayed aboard to maintain comm—both men carried talksets, as did Ptiba Mbente—while Marnie and Rich went along with Ptiba. The third officer was delivering a prototype lightweight time juker to Carmela Villereal, along with apparatus drawings and a dozen sets of circuit parts, spares from the macroGate. "Show 'em one," Clancy had said. "They can build the rest themselves." Thus saving *Arrow*'s people a lot of work.

The new device was a joint effort. Coyote had first pointed out that since the maladjusted drive unit didn't have to push at space anyway, why all the heavy bracing? Use these circuits, and these, and you'll need that one, too; put them in a new housing, light metal with all excess bulk removed, better shaped for hand-held use. Pete Larue designed and fabricated the new chassis; Trish Pembrook laid in the wiring. At a third the weight of the original model, even with a miniature power pack built in, the Mark Two juker worked fine. It looked something like a shoulder-held, short-barreled flare gun.

Villereal wasn't in her office; a secretary gave directions to the woman's residence and put the boxes of parts and drawings in a storage room; Ptiba retained the prototype. Outside then, the dirt path and heavy, vaguely scented air had for Marnie the feel of an outing, a vacation from daily routine.

The administrator's house lay on the outskirts, near the edge of woods, about three hundred yards from the hodgepodge-built Admin building. Carmela Villereal opened the door. "The office called; I've been expecting you. Please come in."

She led them into a sparsely decorated living room and offered tea. As they drank it, Mbente explained the time juker and told of the parts and drawings left at Admin. "Your people should be able to take it from there."

Before Villereal could answer, bullets shattered the window beside her. As Ptiba Mbente yelped and sprawled to the floor, a voice shouted, "Come out! We've got you surrounded."

Rich Stasfort made a dive for the juker, but without even thinking, Marnie had picked it up. She gave the pounding at the front door a dose of freeze as she crawled to it, then reached up and threw the bolt. "Is there any place safe here?"

No answer; half dazed, Marnie moved back to see about Ptiba.

Gripping her left thigh where blood seeped but at least wasn't spurting, Mbente gasped words into her comm set. "We're under attack, Trish. At Villereal's quarters. I can't raise Coyote; see if you can reach him or Chauncey. Mbente out."

"You didn't tell her you're hurt!"

"I want Coyote fighting mad, not worried sick. Besides, nothing's broken, Marn; it just knocked me over. Hasn't started to hurt, yet. I could walk, I think."

"To where?" Rich griped. Then, "Marnie, don't you want me to take over that thing?"

Their one main weapon, he meant. "I can handle it."

"I don't want you getting hurt!"

"Come on! They're shooting blind, out there. Holding this or not can't make any difference."

"All right. I'll see if I can help Ptiba any."

Good. But Marnie still needed answers. "Ms. Villereal! Is there someplace here, they can't get at us?"

"Upstairs. You could pick off anyone who tried to come up."

Marnie was about to object; people can shoot up through ceilings, easy as not. But another crash interrupted, and a flaming oil-soaked bundle skidded across the floor.

Heedless of burns, Rich grabbed the fiery thing and made a shovel pass through the empty window frame. Outside, someone was shouting orders. Scuttling to the room corner nearest the sound, Marnie held down the juker's third button and heard that voice alternate between chipmunk and blue whale. But other fiery missiles arched toward the house, and one landed in the room alongside; turning the device off again she yelled to Stasfort, "Stop! You can't get 'em all; you'll just hurt yourself."

From somewhere outside, for several seconds the roar of a wideband soundblaster shook the building. Then it faded, not turned off but pointed somewhere else. Across the room more flames erupted; Marnie yelled, "Carmela! Forget upstairs. What else is there?"

On hands and knees now, Villereal looked shaken. "Back along that hall. Bedroom closet, trapdoor. Crawl space."

*   *   *

It was, Marnie decided as she and Rich helped Ptiba down through the opening, more crawl than space. Before carefully repositioning the ceramic-surfaced piece of flooring from below, Villereal laid a few shoes on it, then draped a robe across one end. The random-seeming clutter wouldn't exactly hide the segment, but didn't leave it conspicuously clear, either.

Shining her belt-hung handlamp around the space below, only a foot and a half high at best, Marnie saw it was limited to the house's downhill corner; the rest of the building's floor slab rested on firm soil. From the corner the gap extended only a few feet before soil rose abruptly to meet the slab above.

The place didn't smell too good, either; dank and stale and musty. "We need more air," Marnie said. "Somebody find a vent."

"I'm afraid the foundation walls are solid." Carmela's voice. "We'll have to put up with the discomfort."

Discomfort? Try suffocation! From above, Marnie heard the crackling roar of fire out of control. "Ptiba?"

"I know." Into her comm set Mbente spoke. "Trish, we're underneath the house and they're burning it down. Tell Coyote, get here *fast*. Trapdoor's at the northeast corner."

Fast might not be good enough; already the air was becoming tainted. Marnie quit listening; pointing her light around, she saw her companions were pretty well bunched. "Please! Everybody stay put!" Scrabbling to the far end of the crawl space she laid the juker down facing the group, then braced herself; timing was going to be tricky.

Crouched beside the device she set the freeze button, then thrust with both legs against the dirt bank, to slide herself into its rainbow field alongside the rest.

When Trish finally raised Coyote, he wasn't loaded with good news. "They came busting out of the woods and broke the prisoners free; we dropped a few, before Ketch Garber's soundblaster scattered the attack, but there's nearly two dozen on the loose. And all armed now. I see the fire but we can't get to it; they have us pinned down, out of soundblaster range. Chauncey's going to be okay, though." Which was the first Trish knew that he might not be.

Onscreen Clancy Allaird jittered, obviously wanting to give an answer he didn't have. Several times he'd started to speak and then by main force shut himself up. Now he said, "Just sit tight, Trish. Keep us in touch; that's all you can do. I wish there was something more, but there isn't."

But she'd quit listening; the side screen showed Carmela Villereal's house a blazing torch. *They're under that*, and heat conducts down as well as up. A sudden thought made her reach for the controls. "Anything Rich Stasfort can do . . . !"

As *Delaware* lifted, wobbling, and began to tilt, she had no attention to spare for Clancy's startled protests.

To Marnie it was about two minutes until the trapdoor raised and Coyote Benjamin came bulleting down, then slowed to her time rate. "You're all right?" Topside, peering from the opening, others chittered unintelligibly and moved with lightning jerks.

Below, everybody talked at once; then Marnie pointed. "Crawl over and turn that off, would you? You're closest."

Coyote blinked, then complied, and the people above slowed to normal. Well, vice versa really, Marnie knew. "Thanks."

They climbed out. The house was gone, nothing but truncated wall stubs and charred floor. Several other buildings, on a line toward where they'd landed, looked more or less stomped. A few yards to the far side sat *Delaware*, tilted precariously with one leg on the flattened remains of what had been someone's home. Marnie could guess what happened—but not how, or maybe who. Rich asked, "Did the raiders get away?"

"A few." A local security officer answered. "Some didn't didn't run soon enough; your shuttle's drive blast got them. Most of the rest we've caught. The hunt's still going on."

A medic aide looked up from her work on Ptiba's thigh. "Two patches and a shot, that's all it takes. This is going to be very sore for a while, but no permanent damage." And for now, Mbente seemed content to ride a stretcher. Rich Stasfort had more than a few blisters but only one bad burn, on the underside of his left wrist where a burning fragment had clung. Bandages and burn ointment smoothed tension lines from his face; the usual grin, though, didn't quite make it yet.

Villereal said, "I must go to my headquarters; if I can aid you in any way, please ask. And thank you for your help."

With a security trio in attendance, she walked quickly away.

Well, then. Marnie headed for *Delaware*; if Trish was all alone on that bucket, Marnie purely wanted to hear her story.

Rich Stasfort followed. At the ladder Marnie paused to help him, left hand awkward in its wrappings though thumb and fingers were mostly free. "That was really something, you did there," she said. "Doesn't fire scare you?"

No grin now; Rich looked embarrassed. "Sure it does. Look; any way I say this it's going to sound gootzy—but the truth is, when that stuff came flying in I was scared stiff. For *you.*"

Which left Marnie with no answer at all. She settled for patting his shoulder, and they went on up.

Anyone else took the DV down that way, Allaird would have relieved from duty with extreme prejudice. Once Trish cut comm on him, though, Clancy got to it fast and popped loose faster, then pushed every redline in the total procedure. He still had a lot of time to sweat before he landed, which was no sure bet until the last second when he didn't crash.

He'd known all along that he couldn't get down in time to do any real good, but he had to come anyway. Now in Carmela Villereal's office he tried to put everybody's stories together, to understand what happened.

After a time he thought he had it straight. Trapped in the crawl space, Marnie used juker freeze to stretch their air supply and retard conduction of heat from the fire above. Then Trish walked *Delaware* across the blaze, blowing it away. And incidentally killing several marauders while scattering the rest.

Pembrook hadn't foreseen that possibility and was taking it hard. She maintained surface composure now, but tear stains on her cheeks betrayed her true feelings.

Words couldn't express Clancy's; with Marnie at one side and Trish to the other, he hugged both.

"From there," Coyote said, "the security people took over. And Ketch here. If it hadn't been for that soundblaster of his ... Incidentally, he has an idea how the break was set up."

Garber had been to the wars, all right, but he looked cheerful. "After Carmela nailed most of the gang down here, it looks as if Ferris still had comm with the ones out in the bush. Including, dammit, two in my own crew! Up on the macroGate, when you had him cornered, he must have played it both ways: that if he *didn't* blow the Gate, he and his people just might be brought groundside, so watch for it and be ready.''

He shrugged. "I'm afraid they surely were."

"Where *is* Ferris, by the way?" Clancy asked.

Chauncey Ng, one cheek bandaged and right arm in a sling to protect a broken collarbone, hacked out a brief laugh. "In a cell. I broke his jaw for him. Southpaw." So not even a fracture had stopped this tough little man.

Losses hadn't been totally one-sided; Carmela's forces had suffered fifteen casualties including seven deaths. But of the twenty-nine known enemy—including three previously unsuspected sleepers among the field contingent—twelve had died and thirteen more, some hurt and some not, were captured. "Those other four," she said, "now that they are known and we are in direct pursuit . . . it will not take long. So now—"

Her deskcomm sounded. "Hmmm; a direct channel." She flipped a switch. "It is CV-One, captain. Perhaps . . ."

He came around the desk in time to see the screen light. On it, Nicole appeared, and recognized him also. "I was just going to call you," he said. "We're all pretty much all right, and—"

Her face, if not her words, showed relief. "You need to get up here. Everybody. We can talk on the way." She held up a readout sheet. "This came at Earthtush. We're ordered home."

How there could be such a hurry with double Gatelag involved, Marnie had no idea. But Clancy was doing things fast. He had skeleton crews ferried over from the macro to take charge of *Overlode* and *Cold Rush*, telling Tyran Galer, "Use them to stand guard. If anything hostile outGates, their lasers and torpedoes should command the situation."

Those ships' drives couldn't be altered for time juking; neither could *Delaware*'s. "All the units are hardwired, sealed," Coyote Benjamin reported, catching the Allairds on a lounge break. "Field phase adjustments are automatic and held within tight limits. According to the modification dates on the specs, nothing since *Scout* has our kind of haywiring capability."

Clancy nodded. Feeling glad, Marnie supposed, that *Ar-*

row's own phase-changing capabilities could now be switched at control. "*Delaware*, though," he said. "Groundside and the macro have no other link; we'll have to leave them that ship. Well, there's an extra pilot in the group we brought over for *Overlode*."

At the intercom he paged Rich Stasfort; when the young man arrived, Clancy told him the news. "So if you have any gear aboard there, now's the time to move it."

Rich shook his head. "No. It's what I have on here. I can't go back without that ship, so I guess I'm staying with it."

Watching him leave, Marnie felt betrayed. She'd thought her mind was firmly made up, but that was before he'd taken such risks at Villereal's home, and his words later. She knew guys could say all kinds of things when they wanted something, but if there'd been any calculation in him then, she sure hadn't sensed it. So maybe her decision wasn't as solid as she'd thought. And now he was taking away any chance to change it!

She stood. "Excuse me," and headed for the galley. Chauncey was cooking; as she'd hoped, he was really busy. "Say, could I pick up some pain caps for Rich?"

"In a while. Or does he need them right away?"

"Well . . ." Then, "What's the compartment number? I could get them." So he gave her the med storage key. At her quarters terminal she brought up medical files, found the category and item she wanted, read the directions twice, and noted its compartment location.

In the storage room she remembered the pain caps, too.

Twice she knocked, before he opened the door. "I changed my mind."

"Huh?"

"You said if I did, the offer was still open."

She had to assure him that lacking an implant she did have morning after pills.

She'd thought she was ready, yet at the last moment panic hit: looming memories of Carl, and of Alton Darnell. Then Rich touched her, the bandages not getting in the way much after all, and his unsure smile banished those ghosts as if they'd never been. "Yes," she said, and she was right.

It lasted quite a lot longer than grapevine hints had indicated and was considerably better than she really expected. Not so good as she'd secretly hoped, maybe, but what *could* be? She would have stayed longer, when he asked—she wanted to—but right now she needed to be alone, sort out her feelings.

He'd been nice about everything, though, very nice, and she made no bones about telling him so.

And then, saying good-bye, "I'll leave word with Glen Springs, where we go next. If you ever catch up with us, I'd like that."

"So would I. I'm not staying because I *want* to leave you." Kissing got better with practice, but she did have to go.

And now it's done. Seventy-four years, roughly, since Glen Springs. Most of it at twenty-five to one, but it's still there.

Odds against us *were* like drawing a straight flush, but we hit anyway; how about that? And tore out this end of a nasty weed, to boot.

So now what's back there for us? Besides our paychecks . . .

Pointing *Arrow* toward the macroGate, Allaird gave his drive a nudge and waited to see the colors bloom.

XXIII

The macroGate's color flare taxed the viewscreens; as afterimages faded slowly, Marnie saw the stars had changed.

A sudden rush of voices caught her attention: "That was quick!" "Course it was; wha'd you expect?" "Did we get there all right?" "What's our planet like?"

She looked around; within the local Tush their six missing crewmates stirred, jostling about, as Fleurine Schadel stepped free. There'd been no warning flare here! Suddenly Marnie realized: the decel group's Gate lag must have elapsed *during* the ship's. No one had known whether the two would or would not run concurrently; this Gate-within-a-Gate thing was something no one had ever considered. Whatever, all six had outGated at once, not at intervals, the way you'd expect them to go in.

Overriding an uproar of greetings, Clancy said, "It's a good world, but I'm afraid we're back home now." The newcomers looked puzzled; he said, "I don't have time to tell it, just yet; I need to learn our situation here. Marnie, you're in charge of bringing people up to date. In the lounge, maybe?"

So when the flurry of hugs and handshakes ended, that's where they trooped. Once everyone settled down with refreshments of choice, she said, "There's a lot to it. The macroGate did get set up—well, obviously!—and the colony's getting started okay. But we ran into some kind of takeover plot, don't know how big it is; I think we helped stomp that end of it pretty good. But then we caught orders to Gate back, and no explanation. So here we are." She thought. "The planet's about ninety percent water, but there's one fair-sized continent . . ."

Attentive, the decel group listened as Marnie related the happenings since arrival at Straight Flush. There was no hurry, she decided, in telling about Junior's dim companion and the forty-four-billion-mile mistake it had caused.

From the troublesome sub-continuum issues still another unexpected phenomenon. Extrusion of a type that has become familiar now includes another, one spatial-path device enveloped within a second, the combined dimensional interaction expanding to involve yet another sub-plenal vector bundle.

Among those most afflicted with consequent inconvenience and discomfort, agitation occurs, to the end that total dissociation of the overall affected dimension packet from the greater plenum again returns to earnest consideration.

Except for the macroGate and then the two mining ships, space around Straight Flush had been all *Arrow*'s. Not so in Earth's neighborhood. Clancy had no preconceptions as to where this end's macroGate might be placed; now he saw it lay well out from Earth, certainly nowhere near synch orbit. "Nicole. Can you locate us?"

"We're in lunar Trojan position. Ahead or behind, I can't tell yet." But with Earth and moon on the same wide-angle screen, he'd seen that much for himself. Because each bore the comparative size it would have if viewed from the other's surface. Ergo, they and *Arrow* formed an equilateral triangle.

"Privileged priority," Chauncey Ng commented. "There's only two earth-moon Trojan spots; how did we rate one?"

"Not all that prior," said Nicole. "Check a rear screen."

Seeing that view, Clancy's involuntary laugh was half gasp. Not merely one macroGate rode there, but a cluster, joined rim to rim and forming a sort of faceted, lacy shallow bowl: one central unit, built more heavily than the rest, ringed by six more and then by several of what could grow to be an outer circle of twelve. Two of that group were still in construction.

"Well," said Allaird. "You can't say these folks aren't efficient." Completing just a second ring would provide nineteen Gates. And there was still the other Trojan point . . .

"Anybody spot which one we came out of?" No one could, for sure; some had been too busy explaining, to those wakened by Clancy's call to brace for thrust, just what was happening.

By now *Arrow* had coasted quite a few miles beyond the array; gently Allaird slowed and turned, pointing back toward it and drifting. It made sense that both ends of a Gate link might use the same comm frequencies, so he tried. "*Arrow* calling the Straight Flush macroGate; Clancy Allaird here."

A receiver came to life. "We have no Gate bearing that designation. One moment, please; we'll ring the commandant for you. Go to screen, please."

At first he didn't recognize her. "Amalyn Tabard, commanding the forward Gate array. Set to scramble three." He did. "Clancy, what the hell are you doing here?"

"Orders; how else? And for that matter, what are *you*?" She'd left the ship over sixty years ago and was pushing thirty then. Forty-eight when Marnie saw her on Earth, and that was . . .

He lost track. By her looks, though, she wasn't much past sixty, if that. Her hair, now white, had finally been almost tamed. Not quite, but close enough. "You've been out some,

I take it? Stretching time?'' As Ellery Dawson had not . . .

"Oh yes. Shipped as drive chief, we had some problems, I got stuck with command. Gated home, shipped again, no trouble on that run, came back and wound up in this job. Which satisfies me well enough.'' She paused. ''And I've remarried. My husband's Jamison Walker; he coordinates ship loadings, including Gate inputs, with construction. To meet departure dates.'' If she wanted to impress him she was certainly succeeding.

She stopped talking; it was Clancy's turn. Gatelag being what it was, Tabard had official colony reports up to the time *Arrow* had inGated for home; he told her how some of those same events looked from his side: the arrival of the colonists, their attitudes, the hassle over naming the newly found world . . .

"I'll hit Glen Springs on that,'' she said. ''It's always been the discoverer's prerogative, and by God it still is!''

"Thanks.'' He went on: the escalation of pressure with the hint of a wider conspiracy, the overtly hostile demand for his ship's surrender and how he'd handled it, the storming of the macroGate, and finally the jailbreak and shootout at groundside.

"The Portaris Effect?'' She leaned forward. ''For God's sake! How did you get onto *that* dodge? All this time, the whole thing's been kept deliberately under wraps. That much was decided on macroGate Two, they tell me, at the time of the event. And to make sure nobody rediscovered the effect by accident, none of the later Traction drive units can even be fiddled with.''

"I had help.'' Anne's story, for starters; then Phil Henning's curiosity about it and his carefully filed research notes. Plus the refinements and embellishments suggested and implemented by Coyote and Chauncey. ''Lacking other weapons, that's what we rode with.''

"What about the mining ships? Lasers, and so forth?''

"Oh, them. Well, we didn't want to blast the macroGate open unless we had to.''

"You always did have a knack, Clancy. For going all out with a safety belt.''

Was that a compliment or a slam? He said, ''What's your

latest word from the colony? Who won? Has Glen Springs
said anything?''

"I'm not on that grapevine. But if someone's building a
shadow empire across the colonies, I know who it has to be.''

"So do we," Allaird said. "Senator Switzer, Howie the
Howitzer. We got some answers from one of his people, before we'd bring her and her suit in from the big bad vacuum.
But aside from using foul tactics in a presidential campaign—
for what that's worth—I don't know beans about the man.''

Tabard filled him in. A four-term senator, Switzer had
gained the space committee chairmanship sixteen years ago
and gradually built a wall of secrecy around its operations.

"He doesn't have much of an apparatus in my bailiwick,
or Jamison's. Maybe a few paid leaks, but not much more.
Oh, it's quite illegal to discriminate in hiring because of past
associations or political affiliations, but we have our ways.''

"So you've kept him stalemated?''

"On my own turf, not otherwise. And he's up to something.
He's a lame duck now, lost his Senate seat, but he's using this
last gasp in office for *something*. I just wish . . .''

She looked to one side, then back again. "I'd been rather
hoping you'd return our cargo lifter, but I see you haven't.''
So he knew she'd viewed *Arrow* on screen.

"Well, the colony still needed transport to and from the
macroGate; it was either *Delaware* or our own DV, and you
people have more spares than I do.'' After a moment he added,
"At any rate, I gather that Mr. Hinyon reported adequately.''

"Yes. And wherever young Stasfort may be, the Port Authority's waiting to bill him for more money than he'll ever
earn in his life. Four years' lease on the vehicle already, and
the time still mounting.''

Clancy wasn't going to touch that line. Then, remembering
that Marnie for some reason had a soft spot for the young pup,
he relented. "Two years, maybe. When we left, he expected
to lease it out to the colony. And lease fees include wear and
tear; that can didn't have any, those first two years.'' He didn't
push it; Amalyn would take the point. But, oh hell—at *this*
distance, did he still have to keep wiping the boy's nose for
him?

Sidetracked, he lost hold of the conversation. ". . . docking
sleeves, along the open parts of Gate One's perimeter,'' Tab-

ard was saying; it took a moment to realize she was giving him instructions. "For this move it doesn't matter which side you come in from; I'll spot you a vacant one and start its beacon lights blinking. Just slide in slowly and come to rest. There's clearance, and when you're in place we inflate the collars to center you and maintain air seal. You use the air-locks, where your fins used to be, to enter the Gate proper."

"Best invitation I've had all day," said Clancy. This kind of maneuvering was a slow business, so he got started.

When the ship shuddered a little, Marnie figured Clancy had it docked someplace; a few minutes later he and Nicole came in. "Welcome home, everybody. Sorry I was too busy to greet you properly, before." He went on to say that the macroGate array commandant would offer greetings right here on the ship, and maybe it wouldn't hurt to tidy up the lounge a little more.

Wearing that I-know-something look he could never hold for long, he said, "You all know the commandant. But she's shipped out some since you saw her, won't be as old as you might expect."

Still, Marnie thought when Amalyn Tabard finally appeared, there was quite a difference since they'd last met. And the tall man accompanying her certainly wasn't Ellery Dawson.

Greeting Marnie, Amalyn made a face. "Leaving the ship cost me the fountain of youth, didn't it? You're still not old enough to vote!" Then, "Oh well; it's been definitely worth it."

After some brief socializing, Clancy and Tabard and her man left with most of the ship's command personnel. Marnie didn't try to follow; the departing group looked all business.

Jamison Walker didn't waste time. Barely giving Clancy time to offer the hospitality of his and Nicole's quarters, the tall, lean man began on his agenda. "You heard about the *Paragon* experiment? From young Stasfort?" Allaird nodded. "Well, it didn't pan out. Good idea, staffing a big ship with old-timers, experienced people more or less cut off from Earth by sheer passage of time. But it failed politically; the ship went out crewed by trainees of today's vintage. Well, of four years ago."

He looked around. "But maybe that's good. As other ships and crews return, our gang of pioneers has grown. And kept busy, doing odd jobs around the System and catching up on technical advances, including some that may surprise you. So they're available now, and preparing for a different mission. One for which they're particularly suited. Operation Seed: a ship that heads out and just keeps going, dropping lesser ships off en route to scout colony sites. Are you interested?"

"I could be." Seeing nods and receptive expressions from most of those here assembled, Clancy added, "You might tell us a little more about it."

"Like where do we fit in?" said Fleurine Schadel.

In trailing Trojan position, back past the moon, the rear macroGate array orbited. Near it, by Clancy's best guess something over four hundred thousand miles from *Arrow*'s current docking sleeve, floated the ship *Beyond*. "It's big," Walker said, and his face showed his enthusiasm. "Almost as large, in fact, as our present macroGate fields can encompass."

"Excuse me," said Phil Henning. "Doesn't interstellar gas resistance go up rather drastically as frontal cross-section increases?"

Surprising Clancy, Walker beamed. "I do like it when people know the physical ground rules. But *Beyond*'s more than a traction ship. Gas resistance isn't one of our problems."

"I'm not sure I follow that." Nicole Pryce looked puzzled.

Phil did, though; Clancy saw his expression light up. "You've solved the Liij plasma foursphere!"

"*And* the devices its power capacity makes possible. Space-time converters—ingestor and re-creator—and then the final hurdle: the ingestor energy field, that lets it handle objects larger than the physical orifice. Plus inertial translation, which is the fancy term for controllable artificial gravity. Actually we had all that three years ago; the difference now is, we've got it built. *Beyond*, my friends, is a pint-sized version of the Liij Environ. And when your ship eats space-time and then spits it out behind, there's no resistance to worry about."

To look at Walker, Clancy mused, you'd think he did it all himself. Well, why not? "So that's your old-timers' ship?"

"With a sufficient number of those people thoroughly

trained on the Liij-derived equipment. Do you folks want to sign on?''

Personally, Allaird did. But, ''We'll have to have a meeting, the full crew, see what everybody thinks. Some may have personal reasons. . . .'' He paused. ''Might be a good idea to see your roster, find out what kind of slots are open.'' Because if all the chiefs' spots were taken, the crew of *Arrow* might not care to settle for grunt work. Environ or no Environ.

''Don't worry about that part. Coming in late to the mission doesn't affect overall seniority status. And even now, the group isn't all that large.''

A little history: after *Scout*, several ships were sent not directly to their destinations but through established colonial macroGates and on to stars relatively near those relay points, from which they could then Gate home in one jump. So there were more than the first three *Arrow*-class ships to draw from, now. And later ships had carried larger crews.

Still, vessels launched to date didn't account for all the macroGates riding fore and aft in lunar Trojan. ''Some are more local. To Niflheim, for instance, and two in the Oort Cloud.'' Standing, now, Walker said, ''I can give you a fuller briefing on paper. Expect a printout over Amalyn's comm link. And we can talk again tomorrow.''

But before that could happen, and in fact only a few minutes after the two left, Clancy received a summons from Glen Springs.

To scoot downside ASAP and testify. It wasn't mentioned that if the hearing went wrong, he could wind up facing charges.

Not only did Senator Switzer sound off like a howitzer, he was also built like one: short, stubby, and solid. His ruddy bulldog face, punctuated by the stub of an intermittently smoldering cigar, didn't stop at the forehead; only a fringe of red stubble decorated that bullet head.

The cigar, a flagrant offense against law and custom in places like this hearing room, was the only thing Allaird liked about the man. It reminded him of summers at his grandfather's lake cottage, and maybe the smoke *had* repelled mosquitoes.

The hearing's auspices were less than clear; Clancy had no

idea who was in charge—or for that matter, under the gun. At times the Howitzer jumped up to cross-examine witnesses, while judge and attorneys alike seemed powerless to control procedure.

When he himself was called to the stand, the entire scene went nightmare. Switzer charged down the aisle to wave papers at him and began shouting. Accusations, mostly.

Alongside Nicole in the gallery, Marnie wasn't always sure just what was going on. Enoch Dailey, *Scout*'s captain, told how at Slim Pickins a clique of administrators backed by armed goons took control of his ship and treated its personnel as flunkeys; except for greater detail it sounded much the way Rich Stasfort had told it. A serious-faced, balding man of medium build, Dailey gave an impression of total sincerity. In his turn, however, Howard Switzer bulldozed the captain, catching him in minor contradictions and forcing him to admit he had no direct evidence tying the senator to any of the crew's grievances.

A striking, somewhat harsh-featured woman spoke for *Falcon*. Cassandra Monlux's bright red hair probably wasn't natural, but it fit her overall bearing—or so Marnie felt. Monlux spoke briskly. "Captain Pennington thought we should keep on being polite, even when the carpetbaggers were pushing us around the worst. But when Penny came down with something and had to Gate home sick, Chuck Bolton moved up from first officer, and he had other ideas. He and I and some muscle took to blindsiding his staff people, one or two at a time, and icing them down in our local Gate. Feeding the boss remora—Clyde Norris—fake memos, saying that his straw bosses had gone away for a few days. Upcountry maybe, or out to the islands. By the time he caught on, he still had his army but his chain of command was gone. So with the help of the decent element groundside, we took the colony back and set up a more representative administration."

"You cast an interesting if hardly credible light on those events as reported to our offices." One of Switzer's aides said it. "And another matter: the rest of your crew returned here some years ago. But not you. Where have you been?"

A crooked grin. "Oh, I came back. But not with the ship. I Gated in to Glen Springs and left again immediately, to visit

Tetzl's Planet. It was interesting to see Governor Tetzl again; I'd met her once, before she ever rode a starship.''

"*How old are you?*"

"None of your business. But I've actually experienced only six years, a little over, since *Starfinder* set out.''

She cut off the man's protest. "You're off the point. Which is, that Norris bleated on your boss; I have datacaps implicating the senator up to his flapping ears.'' As the caps were played, for entry into the hearing record, Monlux went to sit beside a stocky man wearing captain's insignia, who had come in a few minutes back; he put an arm around her shoulders. So he, Marnie surmised, would be the enterprising Chuck Bolton.

Senator Switzer's scowls, after his protests were rejected, would have brought down thunderbolts.

Going up to testify, Clancy looked as if his shoes were too tight. He'd just begun to answer a question when Howard Switzer rushed forward, yelling, "Your record stinks! You began by smuggling a minor child aboard *Arrow*; then you flimflammed a Federal marshal ...'' Charges, complaints, rumors, speculations: the Howitzer scattered them like birdseed. Or maybe birdshot, if Marnie had the second vowel right. And it didn't take a genius to figure out that even if Switzer's accusations had validity, any applicable statute of limitations would have elapsed decades ago.

"... by threat of illegal force, compelled the crews of two ships to Gate back to Earth!'' "... coerced my representative Roland Bryan ... willfully ordered the slaughter of colony functionaries in the pursuit of their sworn duties ...'' That would be Trish walking *Delaware* across the murderous arsonists. "... unlawfully captured and detained my provost Kyle Ferris ...''

Clancy Allaird stood. "*Enough!*" He looked flustered and confused but he wasn't done yet. "I ask the chair's forgiveness but this man piles lies on *damned* lies until there's no sorting them out. I beg leave to run datacaps bearing directly on some of these accusations before the *senator* proceeds further.''

"Leave granted.'' And over the Howitzer's protests the board of inquiry viewed Bryan's own coercive behavior, the threats by the mining ships' spokesman, and Earlyne Ragin's rather frantic revelations which pinned the tail on Howard Switzer in no uncertain terms.

"The woman was obviously intimidated!"

"You have a patent on that tactic?"

"I'll see you hounded out of space, Allaird!"

The gavel. "In light of need to evaluate today's testimony at greater length, this hearing adjourns until Monday morning, when you are all charged to appear."

At the DV a time later, Clancy still looked shaky. "Take us up easy, Marnie. I need the breather."

But what with making slow and confused work of the traffic protocol and then waiting for clearance, she barely had the can out of atmosphere when Ptiba on *Arrow* patched through the call from Jamison Walker. Accordingly, she changed course.

Docking on *Beyond* was different. Following instructions, Marnie eased the DV toward an opened cradle. As she neared it a force pulled the Vehicle to a snug nesting, and the doors closed. Well, Clancy had reported that this ship had gravity control!

Sensors showed the bay had air, so the three clambered their way through the tunnel and through the airlock. Beside a hatch directly behind the DV a sign read "Caution: Gravity Change," and when Clancy led the way it became obvious that the sign meant business; with a startled grunt he went lurching to one side. When he reappeared, only head and shoulders visible in the opening, he seemed to be horizontal. "Watch out for that first step; it's a killer."

So, entering in turn, Marnie wasn't surprised when gravity turned her sideways. After all, this was Liij technology.

Beyond's corridors, and there seemed to be miles of them, were wide and well lighted; unlike *Arrow*'s, plane surfaces rather than curves formed floors and ceilings. The place wasn't empty; quite a few people moved purposefully along the halls. Some nodded or smiled in generic greeting and some didn't. Like anywhere else, Marnie decided, until from a side passage came a group of at least a hundred, following a woman who directed them by means of a miniature bullhorn. Clancy only shrugged, waiting until they all passed by. It wasn't a short wait.

There was never any need to ask the way; at each major intersection a screen displayed a directory map, and Jamison had specified conference room B. At point-six gee, or so the directory indicators stated, walking was easy enough. The only major point of confusion came when it turned out they needed to go up four levels and the nearest elevators were back quite a distance, the way they'd already come. Clancy hailed a woman, explaining his problem and asking, "Aren't there any stairs?"

She had an attractive laugh. "First time aboard? They never tell us enough ahead of time, do they?" She pointed. "See that door?" It had a sign like the one in the docking bay, warning of a gravity change. "Just go in there and walk up." And not, Marnie was certain, on stairs.

"Thanks." Again Clancy led, and here, with more space available, the maneuver was simple: the floor curved and the gravity stayed perpendicular to it. They "walked up," but on a surface which to them seemed quite horizontal. Egress to the upper corridor was equally facile, and almost immediately they found the designated room. A meeting was already in progress.

"Sorry if we're late," Clancy said. "This place is a little confusing. And what was that big bunch of people we ran into?"

"A departing tour group," said Amalyn Tabard. "It's a political thing of some sort; I haven't paid attention. They're brought up here in converted cargo uploaders, like *Delaware*. It's been going on since Monday, several runs per day. The tour fares raise funds for something or other, I'm not sure what."

She paused. "And now perhaps we should get to business."

"The question of command here," Jamison Walker began, "seems to turn on the dates each of you first assumed that status. As near as I can tell, it's pretty much even. Allowing for t/t_0 rates changing with vee, I believe you first took that responsibility on *Arrow*, Clancy, just about the same time Enoch Dailey here accepted command of *Scout*, prior to Gating."

This, Clancy hadn't expected. He'd hoped for an officer slot and preferably first or second; the captaincy hadn't been in his thinking. He said, "I don't know beans about this ship."

"What you both know about navigation and command is all that's really needed," said Amalyn Tabard. "*Beyond* can't be captained like ordinary traction ships; your technical staff is there to fill in the blanks."

Well, maybe. But, "Command was to be yours, was it, Dailey, until I showed up?"

"Yes, it was." The man sounded defiant, somehow. "And now I gather you're asserting a prior claim?"

"Hell, I don't know. When I first took over for Ellery it was *de facto* because he was in our local Gate. It didn't become official until—actually, I'm not sure just when that happened. So I'm not claiming anything. I'll go with however the record reads, and either way's okay with me."

For the first time, Allaird saw Dailey smile. "In that case, it's yours. I wouldn't serve under a power jock; I'd resign first. But with you, it's different. Shake on it?"

Walker sighed. "I'll admit I'm very much relieved at this outcome. You probably haven't thought about it, Allaird, but you're somewhat of a symbol. First to take a ship the whole way, and on the longest trip to date, at that. Plus, you were on the first traction ship ever: *Jovian-Two*, before even *Starfinder*. Having you in charge of *Beyond* is—well, fitting."

"The Howitzer won't think so."

"After Monday," said Walker, "it may not matter what he thinks. Carmen Villereal arrived at Glen Springs today."

He cleared his throat. "A little briefing, here. *Beyond* starts with a crew of a hundred and something; there'll be a complete set of command and drive officers for each watch, with a staggered rotation system so that all the individual expertise gets passed around." Captain and drive chief, Clancy gathered, would not stand watches as such. He could cope with that. . . .

Walker had only begun. "But the ship can hold over a thousand; in other words it's a colony in itself, not only living but also breeding and expanding. That's optional, of course: an individual matter."

"Actually," Nicole whispered, "it takes two to tango."

Bombshell. He looked at her; she wasn't kidding. On the other hand, though, "Once the trip shakes down, there's worse places to raise a kid,"

With a wink she nodded, as Walter continued, "So to start with, you build vee by traction drive until the Liij space-time converter becomes efficient, fueling by ingestion of matter and energy. Because of inertial translation, your acceleration affects nothing *within* the ship; artificial gravity in any section can be set as desired. So there is no need to use your local Gates to protect the crew.''

"But it has a pair anyway?" Nicole asked. "What for?"

"Not one, but several," Tabard said. "And all activated. *Beyond* carries three full-sized ships, modified *Arrow* class, for Operation Seed. In cradles similar to the one you used, though larger, of course. One of these, however, is also a Tush; thus the supply of ships is renewable. And *Beyond* also stocks landing pods, which can be dropped off near promising-looking worlds. Each of these would take along a Mouth from one Gate pair and a Tush from another. Making the planet permanently accessible to Earth." She smiled. "You like it?"

Pryce did. Something else, though, she brought up; by obviating all resistance, not only frictional but that of space-time itself, the Liij Environ had exceeded the speed of light. "Does this ship?"

"Undoubtedly it can. Whether it does so will be up to the captain, on consultation with his tech staff, according to how the situation looks on the instruments when c is reached. We have no data on what happens—time ratios and all. It will be your job to gather some." The utility of hyper-c, Clancy thought, would be limited. Certainly no normal non-Liij vessel could be dropped free in that situation . . .

At any rate, so ended Jamison Walker's agenda for today. On the way back to the docking bay, the trio's progress was impeded by a new, incoming tour group. This one seemed larger.

Beyond popped the DV out of the opened cradle with an apparent surge of light reverse gravity. Gently the Vehicle drifted outside; fascinated, Marnie paused, long enough to see that the doors were now left open, before orienting on the beacon from the forward array and heading for it.

She found the long ride home, mostly coasting, more restful than not. And docking with *Arrow* had become a matter of habit. Reentering the ship, all three headed for the lounge.

What Marnie didn't expect was to see Rich Stasfort there, concluding preparation of a fresh batch of coffee.

* * *

"Rich!" She rushed to him, at the last second restricting her greeting to a fierce hug. "How come you're here?"

"I got bumped off my pilot job. Seniority. So instead of sending the leasing credit voucher home by Gate I brought it back personally and turned it in to the agency." He'd wangled a good rate, better than the ship could earn here at home, so crediting the lack of wear-and-tear costs for the two years in Gate, his debt had been mostly cleared and the remainder assigned as payroll deductions. "Gated directly between macros, and the tech at this end told me where you were and how to get here."

He turned to Clancy. "So, can I sign on now?"

Allaird frowned. "Hadn't you better look up your folks?" And explained that the veteran crews' group hadn't won *Paragon* after all. "Likely they're in *Beyond*'s crew, which we'll be joining. I'm afraid I didn't think to ask." He shook his head. "Marnie, why don't you tell him about *Beyond*? I need to see if I have any messages in control."

So, sitting down with coffee, she began.

At first Rich seemed interested, but after a time he broke in, saying, "Look; can't we go someplace?"

"Go? What for?"

He gestured toward the others enjoying the place. "So we can be by ourselves. It's been a long time; I've missed you."

Not that long, really; still, "Well, I missed you too. But now here we are."

Leaning closer, he whispered, "We can't do it *here*."

"We're not going to." In a rush he was asking why not, hadn't she liked it, was there some other fellow, what was wrong, he'd thought they . . . "That was different," she cut in. "You were the first person I ever met, I even *might* want to, with. And what you did, when they tried to kill us, and then said why, after . . ."

"I didn't do it just for that. Not any of it."

"I know. And then, maybe I'd never see you again, how long before I meet anybody else right? So I thought yes, and I did like it and I'm glad we did. But not to keep on with, yet; it's too soon for me, I'm just not ready."

She looked at him. "You see how it is?"

He blinked. "I . . . guess so." His grin came. "Like I said before, any day you change your mind, the offer's still there."

"Sure. And if we go on *Beyond* there's a lot of days."

He really was going to be the right one, she thought. And it was nice to have her choices open again.

Clancy called council, the full crew. "Here's the setup," and he and Nicole explained the possibilities of shipping on *Beyond*. When he thought the picture was clear as could be made, he put the question. "So. How do you all feel about it?"

"I don't think I want to," said Ptiba Mbente. "Coyote and I, we'd like to go home. To our own people. Both."

"But they're not *there* now!" Marnie protested.

"Yours, maybe not," Coyote said. "Lots of change; I know. Ptiba and I, we've been down, looked around. Found a few of my downtime kinfolk; living differently now, but they think pretty much the same as always. And Ptiba's folks, descendants of relatives she knew—it'll take time to get to know them, but I want to."

"We'll miss you." Nicole got in the first hug; then Ptiba assured everyone that she and Coyote weren't leaving for some time yet, probably when everyone else moved to the new ship.

For the most part, to Allaird's relief, the rest of the crew seemed inclined to do just that. When the time came, of course.

Answering her door chime, Marnie greeted Trish Pembrook. "Come on in. Get you something?"

"Juice, maybe." Then, with both seated, Trish said, "I hate to tell you this, but I'm leaving, too."

"But why? I thought . . ."

"So did I. But you see . . ." Scouting around in her spare time, Trish had visited one of the new, half-built Gates and talked a crew chief into letting her suit up for outside work. "I hadn't realized how much I've missed it. Well, retrieving the mining ships I enjoyed that part a lot, being out there. And this gang's not like those gootzes at Straight Flush; they're more like *us*. Barr—that's the crew chief, Barr Jencik—he's my age plus a couple, and he's second generation born at

Niflheim macro. He asked me if I'd like to join his section.''
Her cheeks had gone pink. "I think I will.''

So it was personal, too, not just the work. Trish said, "I've really loved it on here, and I'll miss you fierce. All of you, but you specially. Don't forget me, Marnie.''

When nothing else suits, hug. "We'll have to have a party; stick around for that. You and Ptiba and Coyote . . .''

Getting back to Earth really wasn't much fun at all.

Monday morning when the hearings reconvened, Clancy and his family arrived early and waited for the fireworks. The first witness, Carmela Villereal, spoke briefly and then showed the datacapped testimony of Kyle Ferris. "The operation began a long time ago. I don't know who ran it before Switzer took over, or how many colonies are targeted, but so far only three of the ships have reached destination: *Falcon, Scout*, and *Arrow*.''

Clancy scowled. What about *Nomad*? Then he relaxed; Kyle Ferris didn't necessarily have all the latest news. . . .

Switzer, it seemed, maneuvered to infiltrate the upper echelons of colony administrations and macroGate staffs with cabal members. Looking harassed or possibly scared, Ferris reeled off lists of names, dates, and places. "Eventually he'll have a colony network that can treat with Earth on an equal basis. Or even better. And then you'll see some tails twisted!''

That revelation stirred some alarmed side comment; Clancy could see why. Big frog, little puddle was one thing, but this looked like a real threat to existing human order.

Ferris was still on screen. Ship crews, he said, were beyond the Howitzer's reach; since the "Alton Darnell" scandal their selection was firmly in the hands of veterans who now controlled Glen Springs; others might propose, but they disposed. And on that note, Ferris wound down.

When Villereal's testimony concluded, Howard Switzer was called, but did not respond. Several reported seeing him leave during the Ferris screenings. Accordingly, the hearing adjourned until further notice.

As Clancy put it, you can't have much of a fox hunt without the fox. So Marnie again punched the DV up to dock with *Arrow*. Clancy was glad to be home.

Well into the next day he got the worried call from Amalyn Tabard, to bring a few good thinkers over to *Beyond*.

"What the hell?" he said. "Let's take everybody." After all, *Arrow* was under macroGate security now.

Met by an escort this time, Allaird and the crew followed the young man to a lounge area and spread out among several tables. Among those at a fairly large one, about half-filled, Clancy saw Cassandra Monlux sitting alongside her captain and expounding to several, including Enoch Dailey. "How about over there?" he said to Marnie and Nicole, and they joined that group.

". . . from the beginning," Monlux was saying. "I knew some of the first crews to ship out. It was different with them: relief cadres lived twelve months on the ship and returned to an Earth fourteen years further along, but they'd followed the news, and twelve years' space pay helped cushion the sharp edges. More importantly, they knew their situation and were mentally prepared for it."

Clancy saw her point. "Whereas going all the way, we had to put Earth out of our minds. When the time came to take heed again, things had simply changed too damned much."

Monlux nodded. "I saw how the rotating crews Gated home and fit back in. Then I went out on *Falcon* and came back expecting to have it that same way." She made a face. "It didn't work. Even Chuck and I together, which we have been since my side trip, can't seem to plug into Earth's culture again."

She slapped the table. "This ship: a sort of spaceborne colony, filled with our own kind; that's the only place I really belong now."

No one around the big table even tried to disagree. And then Walker announced it was time to go convene for business.

Flanked by Walker and Tabard, Glen Springs director Edgar Harmon ran the meeting, attended by many more than Allaird had expected. "We were hoping for liftout in two to three months. Now we may be stuck with a two year delay." He turned to Enoch Dailey. "Would you summarize the situation?"

"About an hour ago someone reported seeing a man inGate

at one of our local pairs. That man has been definitely identified as Senator Howard Switzer.''

A lot of whats and whys interrupted, but Dailey cut back in. "We wondered, too. So we began checking—and we *think* he's only the latest of perhaps two to three hundred who bolted the same way, over the past few days.''

"The tour groups!" said Nicole Pryce. "The one we met coming in was considerably bigger than the bunch we'd seen leaving, earlier. But why . . . ?''

"The intent,'' said Jamison Walker, "would seem rather obvious. Two years from now, well away into space, the Howitzer outGates—and his whole damned army just ahead of him.''

"Groundside,'' Harmon interjected, "is birthing hyenas. I promised to report back as soon as we concluded the initial briefing, so let's take a recess.''

Feeling dry, Allaird asked directions to a rec lounge and found refreshment for himself and Nicole and Marnie. They were barely settled at a corner table when Rich Stasfort brought a man and woman to meet them. Clancy spotted some resemblances.

Introductions: Ian Stasfort had been *Scout*'s drive chief, Elane the third officer. Judging from conversation, neither parent seemed much concerned about their son's Habgate junket. But why should they? After all, Clancy reflected, the departure was four years past and Gating was never fatal. Besides, Rich was back now, wasn't he? Oh, well; both the older Stasforts seemed capable. And overall, Allaird liked them more than not.

A paging call came over the intercom. Back to session.

The equation, Nicole thought, was simple enough. Switzer's men would be armed—how, she didn't know, but they'd have to be. It was *not* feasible for the ship to carry a similarly armed counterforce for those two years. And assembling and Gating such a force now, to retake the ship after the fact, would only ensure a bloody fight at the far end of Gatelag. Having said as much, she concluded, "So aside from the ship going on a two-year hold, what can be done?''

"Build a cage." Fleurine Schadel speaking up surprised Nicole. "Like on *Arrow* with the bandits." She explained.

"It could work," Harmon agreed, "but it would present the crew with a very nasty situation to handle. At best."

"Look," said Cassandra Monlux. "Why not simply download the suspect Gates to groundside and build the cage there? You could replace—"

"Not feasible." Walker. "There are twelve pairs and we don't know which were used; someone's gimmicked the activation counters so they all show several hundred usages, which is impossible. Simply, we can't replace that many in a reasonable time; we'd be looking at months of delay, and the new units would then require another two years to become operational."

Nicole frowned. There had to be an answer! Wait a minute. . . . "You could plug the Tushes, fill them with supplies. There'd be time right now to Gate a tactical squad in; when they arrive, unplug one Gate at a time and deal with what comes out."

Edgar Harmon shook his head. "You people don't understand the political situation. *Beyond* is the major effort of two decades; construction costs alone are over a dozen times that of a normal ship, and the Liij foursphere project, culminating in *Beyond*'s space-time conversion drive, dwarfs even that amount. Further, we're speaking of a new concept: Operation Seed. This construct will *carry* at least three ships such as those you're used to, as well as dropoff pods for reconnaissance. Exploration of an entire sector hinges on this one thrust."

Waving aside all attempts at comment he said, "We barely had the clout to get *Beyond* for you veterans in the first place; now the opposition's blaming *you* for letting the mess happen, and they refuse to trust you to handle it away from Earth, out of their sight. It was bad enough when we thought Switzer was trying to take over a few colonies. Now it looks like he wants to become a superpower in his own right. That simply can't be allowed to happen; world politics isn't perfect and never has been, but the powers that be will *not* permit the emergence of an adventuring 'strong man,' a space age 'man on horseback.' No—the situation will be resolved *here*."

He shrugged. "So, shipping or Gating troops is out, and so are the cage and the idea of plugging the Tushes. All that's left is replacing the Gates or simply waiting out the lag and letting regular troops do the job, before launching out. And I tell you now, if there is any significant delay you will lose this ship."

Four options distant in space, the other two in time, and none of the six acceptable. Marnie struggled with confusion, with half-formed ideas, as Clancy said, "There's still time to find another answer; departure isn't due for another two months at least. We don't need to panic, here."

"I'm afraid you do," said Harmon. He didn't look happy about it. "During our break I was given an ultimatum to pass along. If we can't provide an acceptable solution by noon tomorrow, you are all dismissed from duty aboard this ship and a new crew will be chosen."

He paused. "Of course you're not dependent on the agency. *Or* on the current state of the general culture. With the accumulated space pay most of you have coming, you could set up your own enclave and . . ."

"That's not what we want," Chuck Bolton said. "We—"

"There's two fuckin' *months* yet!" On her feet, Fleurine Schadel was shouting. "Where do these bastards get off . . . ?"

Harmon's regretful scowl silenced her. "I'm afraid a UN committee can shrink time just as surely as relativistic velocities."

The feeble attempt at humor drew no smiles.

As a sudden thought came to Marnie, beside her Clancy Allaird yelped; startled, she released her unintended viselike grip on his knee.

"Clancy! Has anybody ever tried to juke time on a pair of *Gates*?"

XXIV

Full dimensional analysis of compounded extrusion provides unpredicted result. The specific configuration of this further encroachment now delineates a larger, triplex subplenum which would, given purposeful admixture of a fourth six-vector grouping, comprise a cohesive and easily buffered quadrum. Such supramorphic oddities may by manipulation be partially detached from the overall continuum, the domain of dissociation itself pursuing chronal progression such that protective isolation of the augmented sub-plena remains always congruent to current nowtime. Importantly, however, contiguous wholeness with the greater continuum prevails both before and behind, in duration achieved as well as in that which ever approaches.

Analyses of interchronal relationships indicate that within the sub-plena considered for manipulation the major available alternative chronal-prime vector, with reference to greater expedition of spatial translation for its volitionals, is of a curvature such as to encourage reverse chronal progressions overriding normal damping effects, with disruptive repercussions throughout the all-continuum.

Thus, efforts toward further communication with and greater understanding of such volitionals are deemed to possess negative desirability. Accordingly, dimensional adjustment as stipulated is essayed and completed.

Mounted onto carts and drawing ship's power, the hastily jury-rigged yaw thrustors from the DV's spares looked to Clancy like a bad day at beginners' welding class. Nonetheless their carefully mismatched phasings produced a maximum time-juke ratio of approximately twenty-five hundred. After seven hours of exposure and barely short of the UN committee's deadline, the first Tush disgorged its load of brigands to the custody of a tactical platoon. Not long after, the committee's ultimatum was withdrawn. The rest of the cleanup, said Edgar Harmon, was only a matter of time. If he noticed his own pun, he didn't let on.

Wisdom of decision is affirmed when during process of manipulative dissociation a significant strand of the augmented sub-plenum's chronal-prime vector inexplicably undergoes violent compaction at point of now, recurrent of greater and more alarming phenomenon in duration long achieved. Dissociative process concludes with no further harm resulting. Loss of access to prime subject volitional, however, precluding more intensive observings, elicits isolated expression of dissentive regret.

With plenty of time for farewell parties, downside business, and just plain sightseeing, all of it somehow shoehorned between training sessions, *Beyond* left orbit on sked. Seven months out, under the gentler accel its bulk necessitated, the great ship passed the speed of light. By now its ingestor field was producing beautifully, but at the moment c was reached, its fuel and supplies outGatings quit cold.

Surprise! No data existed on the matter; in those respects the Liij Environ was self-contained. Even so, after it left Earth and again passed lightspeed, persons and materials had continued to Gate freely to and from that construct. Clearly, the Liij vessel embodied parameters unknown to the builders of *Beyond*, not to mention Clancy Allaird.

So, as he reported to Glen Springs after dropping below c, until somebody figured out how the aliens managed that trick, the necessities of supply and communication limited *Beyond* to sublight speeds. Except, now and then, for trial runs.

Much like herself and Richie, Marnie thought. The day *Beyond* hit c, her bio-age reached sixteen; somehow she couldn't resist the idea of their celebrating the coincidence.

Since joining *Beyond*'s crew Rich had changed, and was still changing. Oh, he still enjoyed making bravura gestures, but under Clancy Allaird's impartial eye and thumb he took that enjoyment *after* his responsibilities were taken care of. "I liked you before," she told him; "you know that. But when it came to folks depending on you . . ."

"*You* could always trust me, couldn't you?"

"Yes." That much was true. At Villereal's house, without even thinking, he'd put her safety before his own. "But now the ship can, too."

After a moment, he answered. "I think I see what you mean."

Following that rather joyous incident they continued to meet, on special occasions only, for lovemaking. It wasn't always easy to find a special occasion, but motivation helped.

Early on she told Clancy and Nicole. Well, mostly: somehow she didn't get around to mention that such relations had first occurred, once only, on *Arrow*, before the Gating back to Earth.

Clancy surprised her; after an initial protest he thought it over and decided he approved more than not. "I'll be taking a more personal interest in the young man's training program; you can be sure of that."

So he, too, had come to realize this was permanent. Good. "When he moves in," Marnie said, "that should simplify a lot of things."

"Moves *in*? Not by a long shot."

"Why shouldn't they?" said Nicole. "I don't see . . ."

"When she hits eighteen, bio," Clancy insisted, "and not before." And no matter what Marnie said, keeping voice and words temperate because she and Clancy had never had a real fight and she wasn't going to start now, that's where he stuck.

As if she hadn't been legally adult since forever . . .

He'd come around, though, once he got tired of being stubborn. He always did, when things made sense.

The
LENS OF THE WORLD
Trilogy

Named *New York Times*
Notable Books of the Year — by
R.A. MacAvoy

"One of the most talented writers
we have working in the field"
Charles DeLint, author of *The Little Country*

LENS OF THE WORLD
Book One
71016-1/$3.95 US/$4.95 Can

KING OF THE DEAD
Book Two
71017-X/$4.50 US/$5.50 Can

THE BELLY OF THE WOLF
Book Three
71018-8/$4.99 US/$5.99 Can